The Black Marble Griffon

& Other Disturbing Tales

E.W. Farnsworth

The Black Marble Griffon

Griffon

& Other Disturbing Tales

E. W. Farnsworth

ZIMBELL HOUSE
PUBLISHING, LLC
UNION LAKE, MI
2016

For permission requests, write to the publisher at the address below:
"Attention: Permissions Coordinator"
Zimbell House Publishing, LLC
PO Box 1172
Union Lake, Michigan 48387
mail to: info@zimbellhousepublishing.com

© 2016 E. W. Farnsworth
Book and Cover Design by The Book Planners
http://www.TheBookPlanner.com

Published in the United States by Zimbell House Publishing
http://www.ZimbellHousePublishing.com
All Rights Reserved

Print ISBN: 978-1942818-95-3
Kindle ISBN: 978-1942818-96-0
Digital ISBN: 978-1942818-97-7
Trade Paper ISBN: 978-1-945967-37-5
Library of Congress Control Number: 2016912841

First Edition: October/2016

10 9 8 7 6 5 4

Dedication

Kasia and Wil

Contents

Curse of the Ship Burial

Dr. Ainsworth and his four crew members drove at dawn to their dig site on the plateau of Giza, well outside the extensive area that was reserved for the Great Pyramid. Ainsworth's group was considered to be composed of light-weight archaeologists, because they took no interest in producing yet another boring monograph on the stellar orientation of known passages in the pyramids, or on the curious absence of visual representations of hieroglyphs inside those supposedly 5,000-year-old monuments.

Instead, they were digging in ground that was presumed to hold, at most, odd shards and remnants of the tool work that, over centuries, had created the giant stones that formed the structure and facing of the pyramids. If Sir Flinders Petrie had scoffed at digging there, how could the acknowledged experts of Egyptian antiquities do otherwise?

Ainsworth was not concerned about what others thought about his work. He had been focused on the site ever since a discovery in the wrappings of a mummy found in the Valley of the Kings. The find had been unquestionably verified by laboratory analysis, but because no one could explain its presence in an Egyptian tomb that had been carbon-dated at 2,550 BCE, it had been ignored.

Ainsworth had written speculative papers on the find, but he could not find a reputable publisher for them. Editors' comments included words like rubbish, trashy, shoddy, irresponsible and, the worst phrase of all, "reprehensible from a supposedly responsible member of the Egyptian scholarly community." The idea of tobacco leaves having been found in the wrappings of an Egyptian mummy four thousand years before Columbus's discovery of America held an implication that Ainsworth found ineluctable through the received scholarly tradition. It required a new approach. Only by excavating proofs in the form of artifacts would Ainsworth's theories hold any weight.

He had considered writing fictional works about his theory under a pseudonym, but if he were ever discovered to be the man behind the fictional name, he would be ridiculed out of his profession and never regarded seriously again.

What brought Ainsworth to look at the site along the southern boundary of the plain surrounding the Great Pyramid was a set of images made by airborne ground-penetrating radar, indicating what looked like a giant ship buried under sand and stone tailings. He had worked with imagery analysts of the American Navy to produce from the radar image a scale drawing of the outline of the object buried at the site. Unable to find a sponsor in the United States, Ainsworth went to Europe where he pitched his theory and showed his preliminary evidence to a Dutch princess who liked both him and his idea.

The princess provided seed funding for Ainsworth to prepare a very professional, one-time briefing about his proposed project for other royalty friends and eccentric relatives of hers throughout Europe. She used her own considerable persuasive powers at the briefing to line up funding for a five-person dig with ten-year duration. Then, she personally lobbied the resident antiquities director in Egypt to fast-track the process for approval of the project.

Ironically, approval came because the project was deemed not to be a serious, scholarly expedition, but the whim of a European princess.

Finally, the princess presided over the ribbon-cutting that initiated the actual archaeological work. In the press, the event was considered so insignificant it received only a few lines of mention in the Dutch press. A stock photo of the princess in all her finery was used to accompany the text, because the Dutch royal family did not approve of the photo showing her appearing next to "her explorer" and the Egyptian antiquities director in their expeditionary costumes with dust on their garments and sweat stains from the blast-furnace winds that were caused by the sweltering desert heat. The princess returned to her native land and received Ainsworth's annual reports until her untimely, tragic death by an unaccountable illness. She was only thirty years old when she died.

She was not the only one to die in a mysterious, untimely fashion. Within six months of her death, the antiquities director who had posed in the picture taken at the opening of the dig site, dropped dead in his office in Cairo. Around the same time, two of Ainsworth's four crew members had been stricken with a disease that was still undiagnosed, but they had recovered from their near-fatal illnesses and were now in the field again with their major professor.

Ainsworth himself and his other two workers had some symptoms, but they were never hospitalized. Ainsworth joked with his team that what saved them from certain death of the dreaded disease that had killed the others was their habit of smoking cigarettes. The professor and his crew averaged three packs a day each, and each year, they laid in not cartons but boxes of Marlboro cigarettes that ended up as part of the stash in their tents near the Giza plateau.

It was in the fourth year of their dig that Ainsworth knew his theory held significant weight because he had verified the object shown in the aerial radar imagery was indeed an enormous ship, larger than any Egyptian ship known to have existed from historical and archaeological records. In fact, the ship was larger than any known to have been built until the time of the Spanish Armada in the late Sixteenth Century.

Ainsworth once again enlisted the help of the U.S. Navy to do detailed design drawings from the artifact that his team had unearthed. The two naval engineers, who worked with him at the direct order of the Chief of Naval Operations, had experience doing detailed drawings of Noah's ark from biblical records and the archaeological finds high up on Mount Ararat.

They told Ainsworth they were astounded by the find because the Egyptian vessel would have had the strength and carrying capacity to sustain voyages not just up and down the Nile River and in the Eastern Mediterranean Sea, but all over the world.

It was their judgment that from the time of Noah to the time of the building of this buried ship, shipbuilding had undergone a radical transformation. They thought such a transformation would only have been possible in a prolonged age of enlightenment and stress, much like the period the world had recently witnessed in the Twentieth Century, which against a backdrop of two world wars had birthed supertankers, aircraft carriers, and container cargo ships.

Ainsworth used the design drawings to catalyze funding for the reconstruction of the Egyptian vessel, but the new Egyptian antiquities director took umbrage with the archaeologist's project and tried to shut it down on a pretext. Temporarily, the project was shut down, and Ainsworth and his people were forbidden to return to the site until "certain matters" were deliberated at "appropriate levels." Ainsworth was not faint of heart, so he decided to continue his work clandestinely by poring through scholarly records all over the world.

He targeted the fabled Vatican Library chart, a copy of much earlier documents. It featured an Antarctic Continental chart showing the medial fissure of the continent that had only in the late Twentieth Century been determined by advanced scientific means. That meant to Ainsworth that at some point within the last five thousand years, Antarctica had been ice-free. It also meant some nautical power had the technology to do the charting necessary to produce the artifact that finally was transposed to become the artifact in the Vatican Library in the days of Henry the Navigator in the late Fifteenth Century.

Of course, the Vatican curia buried the manuscript chart because it was entirely too controversial to copy and deliver to the public. Only privileged members of the black Collegium Romanum were permitted to see and analyze the chart. Since the records of the Collegium Romanum were still in the Twentieth Century kept close-hold among the curial office, Ainsworth hit a brick wall in his attempts to discover Catholic analysis of the chart.

Ainsworth went to visit the library archives of the world's greatest tobacco companies to discover any record of tobacco growth outside America throughout antiquity. He found no such record, and he was told by the more intelligent and imaginative archivist, who was a scion of the fabled Duke family in America, that only a few channels by which tobacco seeds and products could have been conveyed to Asia or Europe existed until the arrival of Columbus in America in 1492.

One channel was very early and retraced the migration route of the earliest inhabitants of America, who came from Asia via the Bering Strait land bridge ten thousand years ago. The other channel was Nordic and occurred during the Tenth or Eleventh Century AD. The possibility of an Egyptian channel for transmission of tobacco products was thought remote, but not impossible.

Ainsworth's discovery in Giza intrigued the imaginative archivist enough to incentivize his briefing the wise people of the Duke family about his ideas. It was not luck, but good business sense brought about the Duke family's funding of Ainsworth's project to build a replica of the ship whose remains he had found in Egypt. Funding was generous enough to support not only the building of the ship but its testing and operational trials that led to experimentation to determine its durability at sea.

The result of Ainsworth's project was proof a vessel such as the one he built could have explored waters from the Arctic to the Antarctic and from Egypt to China in the third millennium BC. As Thor Heyerdahl in his Kon-Tiki adventure, Ainsworth and his team actually conducted the voyages that proved the Egyptian vessel's potential.

Even in spite of the acclaim Ainsworth's proofs made in the open press, the Egyptian archaeological stalwarts remained uniformly opposed to Ainsworth's "quirky and unprofessional approach." Where, they asked, were the documentary records proving the Egyptians had a program of navigational exploration encompassing an area beyond the Eastern Mediterranean Sea? Ainsworth, to his credit, agreed that capability did not translate into accomplishment, and he sought further evidence to advance his theory.

While he was probing the earliest discovered Egyptian records for evidence of some secret, prior Egyptian history involving global navigation, Ainsworth suffered the tragic loss by a mysterious disease of his chief researcher, Mabel Davies. The young woman died in agony of a disease that apparently had no diagnosis. When Ainsworth asked his worker's doctors to look for commonalities among the symptoms first presented by both the Dutch princess and the director of Egyptian antiquities in Cairo, they admitted similarities existed, but the medical guilds persons still were clueless as to the nature and cause of the disease that had killed them all.

At first, Ainsworth had been inconsolable about his assistant's demise. They had been friends, as well as close collaborators. He did not eat properly and walked around in a daze, thinking about the girl he was mentoring for great things. Gradually, though, Ainsworth recovered from his grief. He could think of no greater memorial for her than to complete the work they had begun. Having no replacement for Ms. Davies, he took on her workload himself.

Ainsworth shifted his strategy after Ms. Davies's death. He began looking for things that might tangentially prove his theory, such as the incidence of mysterious deaths among ancient peoples. He particularly sought evidence of disease that had no prior counterparts in the medical record.

He discovered in tablets of Mesopotamia the earliest mention of an army's encountering an unknown disease that decimated its ranks and threw the balance in favor of their enemies. Formerly, it was thought among medical historians that the disease had been the earliest record of the black plague, but Ainsworth was not at all sure of that.

The stone tablet recording the ravages of the disease did not have the detail or language that would allow a determination, only the disease's ultimate effect, which was an enemy's victory in battle. Biological warfare in the third millennium BC might have been possible, but Ainsworth thought another cause might have been just as likely. Forensics was impossible because all the combatants had died and their bodies had returned to dust, but the mummy of the pharaoh who had been wrapped in tobacco leaves remained.

Ainsworth arranged with the still-hostile Egyptian director for antiquities to have a sample from the mummy sent for analysis at the United States Army Medical Research Institute for Infectious Diseases, USAMRIID, in Maryland. His successful argument for the analysis was based on the three deaths that had occurred surrounding his investigations. Ainsworth threatened to give a press conference, at which he would allege that ancient Egypt had been so beset with plagues it was dangerous for anyone to do archaeological research until the possible threat of plague could be explicitly eliminated. He further stated he would sue the Egyptian government and the antiquities director personally for the losses they and their families had sustained due to the mysterious illness that had caused their deaths.

Ainsworth's sample went to USAMRIID, but he was informed shortly after the analysis began that the sample and all derivatives had been labeled Biological Warfare Level 5 (BL-5) status. That meant that what the scientists had found in the sample they had been given was so lethal it had to be handled with the highest biological security levels possible.

USAMRIID wanted to seize the mummy and any other samples deriving from it, wherever they might be. A team of four men and three women combed the world for possible derivatives while the U.S. government had consultations directly with the Egyptian government about the disposition of the mummy itself.

Finally, after significant negotiations and many meetings, the USAMRIID scientists were allowed to take custody of the young pharaoh's mummy and his coffin, and all other artifacts discovered in the tomb in the Valley of the Kings where the mummy had been found. They extended their immediate impoundment to the lab that had done the analysis for the initial discovery of tobacco leaf in the wrappings.

In the process of their assessment, USAMRIID scientists found a trail of mysterious deaths, six total at the lab that had found the tobacco and five others at the Egyptian Museum of Antiquities, where the mummy and coffin had been stored.

Ainsworth himself was kept in the loop on what was becoming an urgent epidemiological containment exercise. He was the archaeologist who knew the most about the history and storage of the artifacts, and he had lost a key researcher to the cause, though he and his other colleagues remained alive. Dr. Anne Wayland, the epidemiologist on the USAMRIID team, spent long hours discussing the history of the project with Ainsworth, and in exchange for the information Ainsworth gave the woman, she also gave him periodic reports on the ongoing investigation into the cause of the outbreak.

For example, Wayland informed Ainsworth that an extremely rare virus was the imputed cause of all the recorded deaths. Its only counterparts were viruses found in bodies of fresh water in the Arctic that had only recently become accessible for analysis on account of global warming.

Ainsworth asked the woman, "Was the same virus found in any core samples from Antarctica?"

Wayland seemed shocked he should ask this question since, indeed, one secret group in USAMRIID was working on an analysis of preliminary results suggesting just that.

She said, "The matter is highly classified, so I can't go into details, but the answer to your question is, yes."

"Can you tell me more?"

"You know what USAMRIID does. Research on top secret biological weapons is a specialty. I must caution you to hold close and tell no one what I'm now going to tell you. I'll deny I revealed it to you. Chinese and Russian scientists are involved in secret research programs. Their top-level biological warfare engineers are thought to have been weaponizing the virus illegally, as well as developing a vaccine."

Ainsworth asked, "Have any forensics on early Native American artifacts been done along the lines used on the Egyptian relics?"

She replied, "I know of no such efforts, but I think if the virus was extant in the Americas, unaccountable deaths should have been much in evidence. Any large-scale epidemic or waves of epidemics might have driven the virus out of the Native bloodlines, making the survivors immune to any continuing ravages of the disease. Other factors might have been involved."

"Such as?" Ainsworth pressed her on this because of its urgency.

She said, "One of the lab workers, a heavy smoker of cigarettes and cigars, told his cohorts he probably had the best protection against the virus—his being a heavy smoker. His colleagues had jibed at him for his jocularity in such a serious pursuit, but he told them he was very serious about what he said. He stated that tobacco had a curative value which society had forgotten in the prospect of lung cancer." Dr. Wayland shook her head at the idea.

Ainsworth thought about this theory for a while, and he emailed Wayland, "Among those I know who made contact with the artifacts, only the heavy smokers, myself included, have survived. The Dutch princess and the Egyptian director of antiquities were non-smokers, and my assistant researcher had been trying to stop smoking in the months before she contracted the disease. The USAMRIID team should probably check on the smoker status of all those who presumably died of the mysterious disease."

Wayland meticulously ordered her team to do as he requested. After the findings had been analyzed, she reported to Ainsworth that all who had died were non-smokers. All colleagues of those who died were smokers who consumed two to three packs of cigarettes each day.

Ainsworth brooded over this evidence, and he decided to visit a cultural anthropologist friend from his graduate student days. The man specialized in early American customs. He was a chain smoker who had for many years been fascinated by the use of tobacco among Native Americans before the arrival of Columbus. Ainsworth and Dr. Clyde Forsythe met at an exclusive smokers' bar and enjoyed cigars while they talked in a low key so none of the others in the bar could hear.

Taking a sip of his double martini, Ainsworth asked the critical question: "You're probably going to laugh at what I have to ask, but does your research in pre-Columbian tobacco usage indicate that tobacco was used as a cure for pandemic disease?"

Forsythe looked shocked. He then took a long drag on his cigar and exhaled. He looked at his drink and peered into Ainsworth's eyes as if trying to assess how much the man knew of his research. "Francis, that's what my whole line of research has indicated, but I can't publish what I've found because I have no hard evidence. Besides, as a smoker, my non-smoking colleagues would say I was doing special pleading to use the argument."

"So, Clyde, what if I told you that I know of a virus which could only have been active around five thousand years ago in the Americas and evidence of the virus extends from the North Pole to the South Pole?"

Forsythe squinted and gave Ainsworth a funny look.

"Wait a minute—don't laugh, there's more. What if I told you the only people who have survived contact with the virus in our time are heavy smokers just like us?"

Clyde sat up in his seat and became excited. "You're baiting me, right? What have you been smoking? No kidding though, if what you say is true, it would surely make my day. I'm shocked—actually, I'm bowled over—that you might have stumbled on the very evidence I need to make my case. Why, I could publish my work tomorrow, and no one could laugh at my thesis."

The bar area was silent, dark and smoky. The only light came from the door on the other side of the room, and then only when it opened. The men smoked their cigars, lost in thought. They drank also, but their devotion was to tobacco, which was rapidly becoming taboo in America. No suspicious movements were detected by either of the academicians. Their desire for privacy had the right environment. Ainsworth reflected this was the closest place to a crypt they might have found.

Nervous and excited, but still speaking softly so no one but Forsythe could hear, he said, "Now that I've let you in on the secret—and for now, this is just between us—I have to ask whether you know of anything that might indicate, from American pre-Columbian history, that tobacco might have been used, say, to protect a dead body from the pandemic in the afterlife. I would expect remains in tombs, for example, and in stone representations or manuscripts." He spoke in a steady, serious voice. His eyes fixed on Forsythe's eyes with determination.

"I see you're serious about this. Instead of firing from the hip, I'll stop what I am researching right now and dig through the artifacts and records to see what fits your vision."

"Look, everyone knows about Native Americans smoking peace pipes and using tobacco in ceremonies. I'm going to give you, in confidence, another piece of this puzzle. You must promise not to tell anyone about it."

Forsythe leaned forward conspiratorially and nodded with a serious expression for him to continue.

"My project in Egypt has focused on the remains of tobacco in the wrappings of the mummy of a pharaoh that was interred in the Valley of the Kings around twenty-five hundred years BC. I found in debris around the plateau of Giza, the remains of a ship." Ainsworth was visibly trembling with nervous energy, and his eyes glittered with infectious excitement as he divulged this secret information.

"Yes, I've been following the voyages you and your team have taken to prove how extensively the Egyptians possibly traded and colonized around the world. I've frankly wondered whether those Egyptians managed to make it to America. Now, you link tobacco in the mix with scientific evidence. I have to go back to square one to examine whether any but the most obvious connections can be drawn between Native Americans and Egyptians."

"So what do you mean by 'obvious connections'?" He was upset about the word "obvious," which implied a wealth of unstated information. His tone was almost accusatory as he relentlessly probed for more information.

Forsythe spoke defensively after looking to be sure no one else could hear. "Pyramids, for one. Writing in hieroglyphics for another. Some burial customs. Architecture. Many things in Native culture could not have come from Asia. Most scholarship puts Western contact too late to have had influence before the Vikings." Ainsworth heard Forsythe's tone modulate from matter-of-fact rendition, to actively delving deeper into their conversation. Both men were now on the edges of their seats, huddling together like a two-man cabal.

Ainsworth excitedly pursued Forsythe's logic further. "If the Egyptians sailed all over the world in ships that could have reached America not just once but many times over the period, let's say, of a few centuries, could those contacts have left the influences you cannot otherwise explain?" He took another long drag on his cigar and blew smoke over his shoulder, as he craned his neck to be sure no one had come up behind him to listen to their conversation.

Clyde confided, "Carl Jung 'explained' the connections as belonging to the archetypes in all humans, but I've never bought into that. It's absurd. If it were true, why didn't Native Americans invent the wheel? It's just like tobacco. You have to transport the plant or the seeds; otherwise, you cannot have tobacco in two widely divergent places any more than you can have a rhinoceroses' herd without a mating pair to start breeding."

Ainsworth nodded as he reflected on Forsythe's deduction. He decided to plunge deeper into the matter and took another sip of his martini to punctuate his observations.

"I have two points of connection: the tobacco and the virus, and I believe those two are themselves connected, the one being the cure for the other. I am struggling to put everything together, but I have some evidence that somehow Egyptians carried both the virus and the tobacco back to their own country after they obtained them here in America. They did not realize at first how the two connected, but whole armies died of the virus—I think I have a contemporary record of that."

Now Forsythe could hardly sit still. His eyes were wide in anticipation, waiting for the rest of the astonishing revelation.

Seeing this keen interest, Ainsworth pressed forward, "In Egypt, some magician put two and two together and realized tobacco was the cure, but all the Egyptian traders brought home were the leaves of the plant, not the seeds. So the precious leaves could be used to protect the pharaoh from the virus in the afterlife, but it could not protect the people from dying in a great pandemic. From the Egyptian point of view, the cause of the dreaded disease was the transoceanic contact with distant foreigners."

Forsythe nodded and took another draft on his cigar before he embarked on an exploratory sequence of ideas that demonstrated he could think through the data, as well as his associate. He put his conjectures together, tying them together with the facts that had just been revealed.

"So—let me guess—the priests inveigh against the whole enterprise of worldwide commerce because all it was bringing home was death and destruction in invisible agents no one understood. The priests convinced the panicking hierarchies that unless overseas transport stopped forthwith, civilization would become extinct."

"Precisely, so they ordered the great ships to be buried and all records and other evidence of their use to be destroyed. The only evidence they could not destroy were the ships themselves and the tobacco used in the pharaoh's mummy wrappings."

"I can see why the mummy survived. The Valley of the Kings was thought to be super secret, booby-trapped and such with all the grave preparers killed. Why not burn the ships instead of interring them?"

Ainsworth said, "Hold your thought for a moment while I visit the restroom."

"That's a good idea. All this excitement requires a break. I'll join you. Go ahead. I'll order another good cigar and a double martini for each of us. By the way, I'm buying. This is the best academic conversation I've had in years."

When they returned to their seats to break out and light their fresh cigars, they saw only a few other customers remained in the bar area. There were loners at tables near the back, where their smoke drifted slowly to the ceiling. There would be no danger of their overhearing. Even so, Ainsworth and Forsythe continued to speak in low tones, Ainsworth picking up where the conversation had left off before their break.

"Evidently, the Egyptian priests did not see the ships as being the problem, only their use in foreign trade. There might have been a thousand reasons for discontinuing the building of those ships. Perhaps their designers and builders died of the pandemic. Perhaps there was a problem with financing such ships when the Egyptians began conquering other land powers and used their captives as slaves to build the pyramids. Perhaps the genius sailors piloting those ships died without successors. Who knows why the ships could no longer be used?"

He let the question hang in the air while he smoked and drank his martini. He then put the capstone on his conjectures. "The critical thing from the priests' point of view was that the ships should not be used for long-haul transit any longer. What did the Egyptians do with things whose use had died? They interred them." While excited by delivering his penultimate conclusion, he was speaking even more softly than he had before.

"So you've found no Book of the Dead for ships? As I recall, E. A. Wallace Budge's translation mentions a number of boats used in funeral rites."

"Yes, Nilotic crafts were extremely small vessels by comparison with those used for transoceanic travel. Think of the difference between a hearse in a funeral cortege and a supertanker on the high seas. I've thought through every reference to water travel in the Book of the Dead and in all the pictures in Egyptian tombs, but only one fits the pattern I am looking for."

"Then your boat must be the one rowed by the Grateful Dead."

If he weren't so well informed, he might have laughed. Instead, he nodded and said, "You've got a point. Only the Grateful Dead row a celestial vessel through the heavens for eternity. The rock group of the same name took their name from the passage in Budge, and it has haunted me throughout this project. How could the Egyptians have possibly come to their conception except by having, at some time, sailed and rowed around the known world? For the minute, forget the circumnavigation aspect and think of long-haul voyages. Perhaps with colonization. And, of course, transport of exotica back from foreign climes for the pharaoh's personal use."

"Yet, besides the tobacco, you have no artifact to bring to the fight?" This was not academic pedantry speaking. He was merely stating a fact and asking for clarification.

"None with the compelling argument behind it that tobacco has."

"I'll do some research on this line because it can help both of us, and if I find anything you might find useful, I'll let you know."

The men finished their cigars, lost in their separate thoughts. They had shared critical insights and facts with profound implications. Now, they had to dwell on what they had learned from each other. When he was ready to leave, Ainsworth drank the last of his martini. He took one last look around the smoky bar before he plunged into the sunshine as if into another world. He left Forsythe in the bar contemplating the tab he had volunteered to pay.

• • •

Something in the conversation he had with Clyde struck Ainsworth as being significant, but he could not put his finger on what it was right away. Some weeks had passed before he discovered what made him uncomfortable: it was Clyde's statement about the Grateful Dead. If he thought the ancient Egyptians had been so struck with long-haul voyaging that they had made a fundamental reference to it in the Book of the Dead, their most ancient and sacred record for the afterlife, then perhaps the referent for the boat the Grateful Dead had rowed might be the one he had uncovered near Giza. Boats suggesting the heavenly voyage appeared in tomb paintings, but nothing explicitly linking the heavenly voyage to an earthly one.

Could it be the reason the boat had been interred was that it could then continue in its service after its own lifespan just as for human mummification served the purpose? All this was pure speculation, but Ainsworth wanted to stretch the limits of his imagination in case such brainstorming led to an insight he could use in his archaeological work.

When the Egyptian director of antiquities decided that earning money was preferable to holding a grudge, Dr. Ainsworth returned with his crew to the Giza site where the ship he had found now lay under an enormous canopy. To either side of the excavation area lay enormous earthworks of sand and rocks that had been removed to uncover the ship. To support the hull of the ancient ship, wooden struts and supports had been introduced. Within the artificial underground area around the ship, was a perimeter path of three meters in width. Ainsworth walked the path with his crew, examining the walls carefully for signs of a hidden chamber or entry to a chamber.

Nothing looked promising along the walls, but on the floor that had been uncovered and swept clear in the excavation process, three areas seemed to be covered with large, apparently flat stones that had been cut to measure. On impulse, Ainsworth directed his crew to clear the edges around one of those stones and fit a pry bar in the space they created in doing so.

Using the pry bar with much effort, they lifted the stone and saw that an empty volume lay under it. Having removed the stone entirely, they saw an incline leading downwards. Never shy about pursuing a new avenue, Ainsworth grabbed a torch, jumped into the opening and proceeded down the incline with his crew following close behind him with their torches. Typically, they all kept smoking their cigarettes as they went down the thirty feet to a level floor that opened into a gigantic underground room cut out of the native rock under the plateau.

What they found there astounded them because nothing quite like it existed in any of the scholarly literature about ancient Egypt. On all four vertical walls were painted pictures of Egyptians landing in a ship like the one they had uncovered on apparently foreign shores. They recognized the tobacco plant growing among other American foliage to the left, which was the western wall. They recognized figures that looked Chinese coming to greet the voyagers on the east wall. On the north wall, were figures whose bodies were painted blue and red.

Ainsworth guessed those would have been ancestors of the Picts in what today was Scotland. He recognized nothing in the mural on the south wall, except for what looked like a stylized penguin. Perhaps that was supposed to be Antarctica. Looking up at the ceiling of the room, the crew made out constellations oriented in such a way that the cardinal directions indicated by the walls could be verified against celestial signs.

"A little world made cunningly," Ainsworth said to his crew. Then he told them to fetch the camera gear.

They had only three hours to take their photographs and then close up the area where they had entered this room because it was clearly beyond the boundaries established for their dig. Under Egyptian law, they could be prosecuted for trespassing and grave robbing if they should be discovered here.

While his people made the photographs, Ainsworth used a sketch pad to make notes about the dimensions of the room and the approximate sizes of the major images there. Here was all the proof he would need to make his transformative case to the scholarly world and change the course of Egyptology irrevocably.

The crew knew the enormity of the find as well as their leader. They were recording, they were convinced, the counterpart of Tutankhamen's tomb. The years of their lives they had devoted to working with the professor had finally paid off, and they would be featured in the history books. So, when they retreated from the room back up the incline to the area where the ship lay on its supports, they were both exhausted and exhilarated.

They chain lit their cigarettes and began to talk excitedly now, where in the depths of their new find, they had worked in tense silence. They carefully placed the flat stone back over the hole that led to the incline and the room. At Ainsworth's direction, they then swept sand into the cracks around the edges of the stone so the entry would be difficult for anyone else to discover. Ainsworth said they should meet at his tent for a brief discussion before they did anything else.

At their meeting in his tent, the first thing Ainsworth told his crew was that they had made history. He congratulated them and thanked them for their hard work and their faith in their common vision. He then admonished them that what they had found could not be made public until they had gained permission to extend their dig to include the volume of the room. For many reasons, he explained, early disclosure would jeopardize not only their future access and permission to publish but also their ability to enter and leave the nation of Egypt as they saw fit. Early discovery would essentially make them outlaws: they would be pilloried as desecrators of Egypt's sacred heritage.

It did not matter, he said, how important their find was or how crucial it was for them to be the ones to announce and interpret it. They would have to be patient and stage the revelation of the room they had found carefully. He swore each person individually to silence, and he collected all their cameras so he could have the films developed by a special expert he had often used. She had the ability to keep a secret indefinitely.

He said he would be departing with the evidence on the first flight out of Cairo the next afternoon. He ordered the others to break their tents and depart in a leisurely fashion not later than four days after he had left. He asked them all to rendezvous at his university campus office in one week.

Ainsworth felt light-headed from his discovery because it confirmed everything he surmised and more. He was exceptionally watchful just in case someone became suspicious and sent a watchdog after him to find out why he had departed earlier than the Egyptian authorities expected. In fact, his early departure was noticed by the USAMRIID team, who met him at the airport and accompanied him back to the U.S. When they were back in America, the team leader told Ainsworth he should accompany him to visit the USAMRIID facility in Maryland to discuss the latest developments with the viral research that was being conducted.

Ainsworth did not feel constrained by USAMRIID's request. In fact, he was interested in getting an update, and he felt he needed a change of pace to calm down and gain perspective on his latest find.

When he arrived at USAMRIID, he was greeted cordially by the director and technical director, both of whom thanked him for coming on short notice. They then led him into an underground conference center where they offered him coffee and doughnuts, and told him they had three hours of briefings for him if he had the time to experience them.

Ainsworth told them he was agreeable, and the show began. The evidence at first appalled Ainsworth and then alarmed him. The number of unaccountable deaths surrounding his dig and the artifacts associated with it had gone asymptotic. Over three hundred people had died, and another thousand were identified as affected. Of those who were known to have contracted the illness, the death rate was 90 percent. The incubation period for the illness was between two and four years, so the virus had the longest incubation and highest lethality of any previously known predator on the human species.

USAMRIID's epidemiologist reported the predictive analytic data, indicating within the next five years, over five million persons would have contracted the new plague, and four and a half-million of those would perish. She explained that the USAMRIID scientists were scrambling to produce a vaccine, but the virus seemed to mutate as fast as their research, so when they developed a potential vaccine, the virus had segued to a new strain that was invulnerable when confronted with the vaccine that had been produced.

USAMRIID had never recorded a faster rate of structural change in another virus. Even flu could not compare. The problem, she said, was that no one would believe the virus was natural. All the major nations would think the virus had escaped from a biological warfare development program gone amok. This put the U.S. in a difficult position. What they needed was a strategy to let the world know the source of the virus was not a biowar lab, but an archaeological expedition with momentous implications not only for the past but for the future.

Ainsworth listened carefully to what the epidemiologist said, and he saw the director and technical director nod their heads in agreement with her judgment. The director thanked the epidemiologist for her presentation and asked her to leave the room while he talked with Ainsworth with his technical director.

When she had departed, the director turned to Ainsworth and said he had become a party to information that, if divulged outside the room they were in, would render grave damage to the United States. He, therefore, insisted that Ainsworth sign national security papers indoctrinating him into a named caveat and granting him a top secret clearance. The papers he signed pledged him not to divulge anything about the virus's origin or its spread to anyone unless the information was approved in advance by USAMRIID in writing.

Ainsworth realized he did not have a choice but to comply, so he did so. With the stroke of a pen, his academic freedom disappeared. His chance to publish what he had found went to zero. When he had left Egypt, he had felt he was on the brink of announcing the discovery of the millennium. Now he felt he had been forced to betray his mission and his crew because of national security.

When he signed the papers, Dr. Ainsworth was informed he was now working for USAMRIID full time, and his university would be informed to grant him a sabbatical of indefinite scope and duration while he performed duties necessary for the security of the United States. He was told his dean had already agreed to the terms. He was also told his colleagues and crew would be informed by the government that he was on special assignment. In this way, the archaeologist became part of the USAMRIID's epidemiological team to fight against the spread of the dreaded disease that unintentionally he had been instrumental in releasing upon the world.

Now it was Ainsworth's turn to brief the USAMRIID team on his findings, including his latest discoveries. He was told he should omit nothing because of the critical importance of what he had done. He was also told his latest discovery was the most important part of his briefing since it may have opened an entirely new dimension of the emerging threat. So, Ainsworth was permitted to collect his thoughts for seventy-two hours and to compile a brief that gave first the history of his dig, then the sequence of his discoveries, and finally, the thoughts he had about how what he found came together into a coherent vision of how the virus had affected its environment historically up to the present moment.

Ainsworth realized that classified as the brief would be, it was the closest he would ever come to publishing his findings. It no longer seemed to matter that publication would be to a very small audience of listeners. What mattered most, was how USAMRIID could mobilize the world's medical community to combat the disease which was killing people quietly in ways no other epidemic had ever done.

Ainsworth's brief, which is still highly classified, was a tour de force. In the opening three slides, he focused his audience on his grand theory about the presence of the large ship burial at Giza. In the subsequent five slides, he showed how his team had accomplished their excavation and what they found at each stage of their work. The final slide in this part of his three-part sequence included a montage of the photographs his team had taken within the subterranean room under the Giza plateau.

The photographs had been developed by a special USAMRIID team devoted to the purpose of assisting the professor in compiling his brief. Ainsworth concluded his brief with statistics on the use of tobacco as an antidote to the virus, showing that heavy smokers survived while non-smokers perished. His final slide showed his conclusion: the plague induced by the virus ended overnight a centuries-old global nautical exploration enterprise by the ancient Egyptians. Vestiges of this ancient maritime trade could be found in certain documents, but ultimate proofs could only be found in the subterranean room he and his team had discovered, but not yet disclosed or published, because of complications of the means of discovery.

The director of USAMRIID requested a copy of the brief, and when he received it, he flew to Washington, D.C., where he briefed the slides to the Director of National Security and the National Security Council. His presentation was a resounding success, and he was invited to deliver the same brief to the Director of National Intelligence, who took the USAMRIID director directly to the President of the United States.

Meanwhile, at USAMRIID HQ, Ainsworth refined and amplified his brief, and worked with the epidemiological team on a strategy for combating the virus using tobacco in a wide variety of ways. Because of his conviction that tobacco could cure the root cause of the disease, he became a guinea pig for the agency. Increasingly concentrated samples of the virus were injected into his veins and his blood was withdrawn every six hours to determine how his antibodies attacked the virus.

At the same time, he was encouraged to chain smoke throughout his waking hours. He was also subjected to compresses and poultices of ground tobacco, which were applied to various parts of his body to test their maximum effectiveness by location. Ainsworth lived through this experimentation, and he asked whether USAMRIID had used a control in parallel with him. He was informed that the female epidemiologist had heroically volunteered to be the control, but she had contracted the virus after the second week and was now in critical condition in the USAMRIID medical facility. She was not expected to survive.

Ainsworth was outraged, and he demanded that the woman be given tobacco instantly to thwart the virus. He was told she refused to use any tobacco products because they were harmful to a person's health. So, Ainsworth realized a Catch-22 situation had arisen, and there was no way to break the deadlock as long as the woman's free-will was still in the equation. The woman died of the virus within seventy-two hours and received a posthumous commendation for her self-sacrifice.

Ainsworth, however, was defiant and denounced USAMRIID's methods and purpose. The director of USAMRIID told Ainsworth to prepare a scholarly article about his discoveries so the government could explain through it to the people just how the virus had entered the present world from the ancient one. Ainsworth did as he was ordered to do, and then he gave his paper to USAMRIID rewrite experts, who tailored his paper to their needs. They explained there would be no need to have his paper refereed in the usual manner for scholarly papers because USAMRIID had its own ways to deliver information to the public.

Ainsworth's paper was published in a top epidemiological journal. In the revised version that was published, Ainsworth was made to appear like a rabid archaeologist who would do anything for his own fame. His hubris had led him to a seemingly impossible thesis that turned out to be true but backfired on him and others when a virus hidden in an artifact escaped and began multiplying among the innocent populace.

Ainsworth was distraught with the substance of the article, but the public outcry against him and his team was savage and indignant. Overnight, he became a villain both in the U.S. and abroad. USAMRIID put out the word that it had contained Dr. Ainsworth to get to the bottom of how exactly he had orchestrated the escape of the virus. The agency made it sound as if he had been made a prisoner, who would be punished by the government behind a cloak of secrecy.

Meanwhile, Egypt flew into a diplomatic rage over the allegation that its ancient forebears had ever ventured on water beyond the Blue and White Nile, the Nile Delta and the eastern Mediterranean Sea. The Egyptian authorities demanded a brief from USAMRIID on their secret findings so an appropriate public rebuttal could be formulated. They also rescinded the dig permit that had been granted to Ainsworth and his team and closed off his dig site from public access.

Ainsworth's university expelled him from the faculty and initiated legal action against him for using his affiliation with the university in his infamous article. His crew was summarily dismissed from the university as accomplices.

When Ainsworth protested that he had been treated unfairly by his host agency, he was informed by the director that any formal protest by an employee of USAMRIID must be registered with him first, and he would block it going forward on the grounds of national security. When he objected to what had been published in his name, he was informed the difference between what had been published and what he had briefed was due to redactions in the name of national security and, as such, offered no grounds for a formal objection.

Essentially, Ainsworth became a scapegoat and a tool of USAMRIID. When he tried to make people understand the importance of tobacco in the solution, he was informed it was impossible to use tobacco in any form, because of U.S. health policy. How could the public be told that smoking would help them survive the plague when they had been brainwashed to think that any use of tobacco was tantamount to taking a poisoned pill? So, Ainsworth realized the tobacco connection was a non-starter. Fortunately, he was allowed to continue to smoke. In fact, the endless supply of tobacco products was the one blessing in the whole mess that USAMRIID created around him.

Every two weeks, Ainsworth was briefed on the progress of the plague, and after the briefing, he was tasked to brief his minders about what he had discovered in the interval since his last brief. Ainsworth realized that what he said would not be regarded seriously, so he extrapolated on his findings in wildly imaginative ways.

He used the imagery he had seen in the room which, he presumed, no longer existed. He explored the connections his friend Clyde had suggested to draw the ancient world of Egypt together with pre-Columbian America. He drew parallels between the virulent reactions of the ancient Egyptians to international navigation and the virulent reactions of USAMRIID to the global extent of the plague. No one listened to him. Instead, in their briefings, they reported that all of Ainsworth's crew had died under mysterious circumstances which may or may not have been related to the plague.

Ainsworth's friend Clyde had also succumbed, even though he was an inveterate smoker and, in the good doctor's opinion, should never have perished. In the briefings, the numbers of victims of the plague were reported to have reached over one hundred million, because the plague had reached China and Japan.

Each nation accused the other of deploying a biological weapon to destroy its people. The Vatican, meanwhile, denounced the kind of archaeological forensics that would bring a plague upon humankind. So, once again, the Collegium Romanum went to work to bury all evidence that Ainsworth had adduced.

An international group composed of altruists and billionaires demanded that new archaeological investigations around the Giza plateau should be vetted through the United Nations prior to their authorization. This guaranteed no new digs would be authorized until the measures were relaxed. When archaeologists asked about opportunities for them to examine Dr. Ainsworth's site, they were told the site had been condemned and dismantled, and the artifacts, including the mummy, the coffin, the ship, and the murals were destroyed because of the threat of the plague.

An outcry went up from the entire archaeological community at the sacrilege of willful destruction of historical artifacts, but the public, in a frenzy whipped up by the international media, insisted that the people involved in the studies that had released the virus be prosecuted to the fullest extent of the law.

Jurists speculated on instituting the death penalty for just such offenses. The health industry, noting that tobacco had been invoked as a possible cure for the virus, assailed the very idea that tobacco could be an effective weapon in the war on the plague. The American Medical Association threatened to sue Ainsworth for practicing medicine without a license and to sue USAMRIID for publicizing Ainsworth's nefarious views on tobacco, which everyone knew caused cancer and was no cure for anything.

The plague raged on while the international health community did everything but find an effective vaccine for the virus. Nature found a cure when the institutions of humankind failed to do so. Analysis showed the virus mutated so fast that before a year had passed, it no longer had any of the characteristics with which it started. Its virulence dropped to twenty-five percent lethality, then ten percent, then one percent. Finally, the virus was not killing victims but only incapacitating them for, at maximum, a week. By the time it was in its last stages, the symptoms reduced to a mild headache and nausea.

The plague had burned itself out, and only two hundred million people had perished. USAMRIID took the credit for conquering the dread disease, and Ainsworth was dismissed from service with USAMRIID because he was no longer needed now that the pandemic was over. Panic in the press was transformed into retrospection. Now, the even-handed analysts began sifting through all the evidence looking for lessons that could be learned so humanity would not have to go through the kind of torture the virus had represented ever again.

• • •

An investigative reporter found Ainsworth working at a Walmart store in Cincinnati and asked him whether he would do what he did again knowing what he now knew. Ainsworth screwed up his mouth and said he might, but he would not want to give up smoking in any case.

The article the reporter wrote was spiked by his editor on account of the remark quoted about smoking. It was the newspaper's policy not to promote statements that encouraged smoking even obliquely. The reporter was a fighter, so he sold his article as a freelancer to a North Carolina newspaper that was tobacco friendly.

The same investigative reporter traveled to Egypt to see what had happened to Ainsworth's dig site. He discovered there had never been such a site. The director of antiquities drove him to the area where the site was supposed to be, and it was an enormous new parking lot for fleets of tourist buses. The reporter could see flocks of people were arriving to visit the Great Pyramid now that the threat of plague had been lifted.

The reporter was savvy, and he asked the director of antiquities what had happened to the ship burial discovered near the Giza plateau. At this idea, the director shook his head. Egypt, he explained with a sigh, had never been known to bury ships. In the Valley of the Kings, they had buried many mummies, yes, and many of those could be seen in the local museums.

Of course, he said, boats sailed up and down the Nile just as they did today. He said ancient Egyptians wrote about the sun as if it were a great ship that the dead rowed through the sky. This was recorded in the Book of the Dead. As for the rumors of ship burials, the rumors themselves were a curse.

The reporter rejoined that the plague was real, and many millions of people died. The director looked sad and said he regretted very much that people died, but what can humans do against a new virus?

"And now," the director continued, "the threat has gone away. Do you want to see the Great Pyramid before you leave? I think maybe you have seen enough of the great parking lot."

With that observation, the investigative reporter could not agree more.

The Zombie Tontine

Hans Grover was getting hot, and it was only in small part due to the weather.

"Leticia Fontaine is a bokor, make no mistake about it, and her claims about finding the manuscript of the monk who followed Columbus is pure bunkum. Besides, even it was true—which I sincerely doubt, a Fifteenth-Century manuscript is not admissible in a court of law."

Grover paused in his fulmination. Then he continued in a more rational vein. "Haitian law is straightforward on the matter. If a human is in a coma because someone attempted to kill him, we have attempted murder until that human has died. If, on the other hand, a human is buried, regardless what happens afterward, we have plain-vanilla murder. So the real question is whether Cyril Blacker was buried. If we can prove that definitively, we can prosecute Leticia Fontaine for murder. Can I prove it yet? I'm not sure, but I have a method. Witnesses to the burial keep disappearing, and we don't know what is happening either."

"Look, I'm just a policeman doing his job. My police work continues, and we'll get to the bottom of this matter. It'll take a little time." Officer Oboku shook his enormous bald head as he leaned back on his six-foot-seven frame and considered the enormity of his task. He rubbed two fingers together indicating perhaps money could speed up the investigation process, but Hans wasn't having any part of bribery, and he ignored the gesture.

Grover's eyes narrowed and locked onto the officer's eyes menacingly. He knew how hard it was to budge the Haitian authorities. In order to compromise, he ventured, "We've got precious little time. Would you object if I continue my work in parallel with yours and share whatever I find with you as I go? I'll take your silence as a YES. So thank you. If you need to be in touch with me, here is my card. Call me on my cellphone number at any time. Cheerio, then. I'll check back tomorrow to see what progress you've made."

Insurance investigator Grover then drove down to the old cemetery on the cliff above the wide, blue Caribbean. Diggers were working on many of the existing graves. Here and there, backhoes were craning their necks as they drew scoopfuls of rich, black earth. They were forming graves for the newly dead. Port-au-Prince gravediggers were having a difficult time keeping supply in balance with demand. Things were bad enough without their having to deal with zombies always climbing in and out of graves and leaving a mess behind them.

By day, Grover saw what lay before him now—a green paradise-like complex overlooking the sea. By night, it was the inverse—a zombie's paradise. Even with the sea breeze, the noxious, pungent stench of decaying human carrion and excrement was unmistakable. No wonder the zombies were drawn here for their feasting. No matter how many times Grover came to this particular graveyard, he shuddered at the thought of the unholy feasting that happened here.

As he walked the immaculately mowed grounds, Grover took out his cellphone and worked his thumbs rapidly to make some notes. From the headstones, he took down names from desecrated graves. He'd check those against his database when he got back to his hotel, but one name was an unmistakable correlation—one who was murdered, or rather buried and presumed to have been murdered.

Was that a distinction without a difference? Haitians thought so, but Grover was not so sure. When he finished his survey, Grover returned to his air-conditioned hotel, waved at Rene, the maître' d` as he went up the stairs to his room. When he reached his room, he fired up his laptop computer and checked his email. Finding nothing new from his company, he updated his database. Yes, he was right, Abel Arnette was a witness who had been murdered and buried, but his grave had been desecrated overnight.

The cause of the man's death did not matter, given the nature of the insurance policy on his life. The company only required verification of death to pay the face amount of the policy to his beneficiary. So, he would have to authorize the payment of $500,000 to the company that had insured Arnette. The problem, by Grover's lights, was the fact that this was the twentieth such policy paid in a similar fashion in the last six months. That made the current total paid a cool $10 million.

In each case, the policy had been in force for over two years so presumptive suicide would pay if suicide were the cause of death. In the case of murder, the policy would also be honored. Grover thought that the same company insuring twenty murdered men was beyond all expectations and belief.

He could, of course, just forget about the coincidence, but he was an ethical man, and he felt personally affronted that a scam was being perpetrated on his company. He wanted to get to the bottom of the business, and he had only another three days to do so because he had a vast caseload, and this was only one case in many needing resolutions.

The insurance investigator's work routine included conducting research and interviews by day, and prowling the country by night as much as he dared. Grover had interviewed Leticia Fontaine early during his visit since she was eagerly awaiting payment of the proceeds of the policy. She had provided the evidence Grover needed, and she demanded immediate payment. She said she appreciated the fact that the insurance company had rules, but the case of this policy was cut and dry.

Grover had temporized, and he used the time he had bought to snoop around the island and ask questions. In the process, he discovered Fontaine was a bokor who controlled many zombies on the island. Many of her zombies' names were among the list of her company's current and former employees.

This female CEO had taken out policies on her employees as a condition of their employment because they were key persons without whom, her company could not operate. So her employees' deaths, she claimed, had a financial impact on her operations, and the insurance proceeds from them helped her adjust after their untimely deaths.

The insurance agent who sold Fontaine's firm the policies through Grover's company was richly rewarded with high premiums for writing the work, but Grover thought the man might as well be one of Fontaine's zombies the way he looked and acted. A stench about him physically repulsed Grover, and he had a ghastly grin with those hideous, carious and decaying gums that pulled back from his sharpened teeth.

At the right time, Grover would give this man the check, made out to Fontaine's company, and authorize him to deliver the check to the CEO. The agent, having his own interests in delivering the check as soon as possible, told Grover the woman was a bokor. What Grover wanted to know was how that mattered with respect to the sequence of twenty murders.

Grover's investigations into the finances of Fontaine's company brought out the fact that her gross revenues corresponded precisely to the amount of proceeds she had received from Grover's insurance company. So, in a real sense, her business was collecting insurance money.

A student of the insurance business for as long as he had been a top investigator, Grover knew a tontine when he saw one, and this was clearly a tontine. The fact that he could not find a policy written on Fontaine's own life didn't matter, because her corporation was the entity that would be the last to survive if all her employees died. If he could somehow prove she was running a tontine, he could have her prosecuted and have his company terminate all the insurance policies that were written on her employees. He hoped Arnette might be the key to unlocking the tontine.

While Grover contemplated his next move, he heard a noise at his hotel room door and saw that a ghastly purple envelope had been thrust under it and now lay on the floor like a poisonous snake. Grover opened the envelope and discovered a formal invitation to a corporate party at the graveyard he had just visited. The time for the party was midnight that night.

A handwritten note appeared under the formal notice, and it was signed with Ms. Fontaine's initials: *"Bring the check with you, and check out of your hotel before you come. Tonight all your questions will be answered. I promise. L.F."*

This sent a chill down Grover's spine. Immediately after this, the insurance agent knocked on the hotel room door asking Grover to accept his invitation of a ride to the cemetery because he also had been invited and he wanted to be sure the check arrived safely. Grover accepted the agent's offer of a ride and told him to pick him up at eleven-thirty p.m.

During the long afternoon, Grover wrote up all his findings and recommendations, and then he e-signed the documents and emailed them as encrypted attachments to his life insurance company's home office. He then took a short nap. At 10:00 p.m., he awakened, dressed in business casual and packed his computer and other things. He called down to the front desk to have his bill tallied and told Rene he would be checking out at 11:30.

The agent picked him up as planned, and Grover checked out of the hotel. He and the agent put his belongings in the trunk of the agent's Mercedes. By midnight, they had arrived at the graveyard, but no one else seemed to be there.

The agent was not at all surprised to have to wait for the party to begin, and he suggested that Grover consider with him his own insurance needs. Grover had experienced on many occasions, the solicitation of business from his own company's agents, but this agent was importunate in the extreme. As his rhetoric rose, the stench from his mouth and body became oppressive, so Grover suggested they get out of the car with a flashlight and walk around. It seemed to the agent to be a good suggestion.

The two strolled among the open and closed graves by the light of the flashlight, and as they walked, the agent drew very close to Grover. He seemed to be trying to breathe on Grover's neck, and Grover either slipped, or the agent accidently jostled him into an open grave. The agent offered a hand to help Grover out of the grave when drumbeats sounded, and the area around Grover and the agent was lighted by torches held by tall figures that swayed from side to side.

The stench was now overpowering because all wind had stopped. Through the crowd of figures, walked a man who looked a lot like Officer Oboku, only instead of a police uniform, he was dressed in formal wear and sported a top hat on his head and a long cane or staff in his left hand. Behind him came a woman dressed in formal wear the color of Oshun blue. It was Leticia Fontaine, and she gestured for the tall man, her escort, to lift Grover out of his grave. The drums continued in a frenzied rhythm, and the assemblage moaned and waved their torches. Then the CEO's escort waved his staff, and the drums stopped beating.

The CEO stepped forward, being careful not to fall into an open grave, and she bade everyone welcome to her annual corporate party where the living and the undead could celebrate the company's having another successful year. She uttered a special welcome to Mr. Hans Grover, who had come all the way from Cleveland, Ohio, in the United States, to attend the ceremony. She paused here for effect. Then she called the roll, and each name evoked a response from one of the figures surrounding her. Among the names read were all of the twenty that Grover knew had died and triggered the payment of the insurance policies on their lives.

"You see, Mr. Grover, all your questions have been answered. Every one of your customers can attest that he or she has died. Each one, therefore, contributed greatly to the success of our company both by living and by dying. By Haitian law, those who are buried are dead, so no laws were broken by collecting the policy benefits. How good it is that Baron Samedi here, Officer Oboku to you, is present to witness what I'm saying." She smiled as she said this, making the investigator bristle indignantly with rage.

Grover, wanting to cut through her façade, bluntly asked, "Ms. Fontaine, did you murder the twenty employees whose undead forms surround us now?"

"Mr. Grover, don't be impertinent. Why should I murder employees who love me and give me their all? I didn't murder any of them. They gave their lives for the good of our firm, willingly. In a very literal sense, the body of the corporation is the sum of the bodies of its employees. When anyone dies, he dies for the good of everyone. Sometimes, of course, the undead help with our processes. Not everything can be entrusted to Human Resources these days. And your agent, here, is one such helpmeet." She spoke with authority, but her eyes were mocking him, and her lips were pursed in annoyance.

At this, my agent smiled and let his pointed teeth shine in the torchlight. Grover made out Rene coming up beside Ms. Fontaine, dressed in a flaming red suit, which seemed to be more fire than fabric.

Interpreting what she said as an admission, he asked in a measured tone, "So you're saying this man, my agent, murdered his own clients on your behalf?"

"No. He's no murderer, just look at him. As a man, your agent has been your faithful employee, doing everything his company asked him. Let me put a simple question to you, Mr. Grover. If one of the undead kills, is that murder? I find no such injunction in any law in any land." The figures around her gazed at the man with eyes full of animated hatred.

Grover's eyes never left hers. He pursued his logic relentlessly. "But if, Ms. Fontaine, the agency by which the murder is committed is not in the undead but in the bokor who directs it, then what?"

She shrugged and sighed. Exasperated with his questions, she said, "I see we're splitting hairs and spoiling our corporate gala." Then she turned to her associate and asked, "Rene, what have you devised for our entertainment this night?"

"Mr. Hans Grover is the evening's entertainment. He has filed all his reports and checked out of the hotel. His belongings are in the trunk of this agent's car. He has two choices, but he may choose only one of them, and he must do so right now."

"So, Rene, tell him his choices." She said this looking Grover directly in the eyes in defiance, as if she were totally in charge of the situation.

"Mr. Grover, you may join us in our feast, or you must become our feast. In one other matter, you have no choice. If you choose to join our feast, you must take out an insurance policy on your own life, with Ms. Fontaine's company as the sole beneficiary. Choose wisely. So he has the proper ambiance, let the drums begin! And when the drums cease, you will give your answer. Any hesitation will signify that you have chosen to be our feast."

So the drumbeat began, and as the tempo increased, the assemblage pressed into a smaller and smaller circle around Grover. Finally, when Baron Samedi raised his staff and began to laugh, the drums stopped.

"I choose to live and sign," Grover said calmly, as his eyes passed over the crowd of hostile retainers, some of whom licked their lips in anticipation of a feast. He was afraid, but he was not going to show his fear.

"Mr. Grover," Rene rejoined, "let's rather say you choose to live, feast and sign because feasting with us is part of your bargain."

Grover had run out of choices, so he nodded his acquiescence.

"Let the feasting begin," said Leticia Fontaine, "while I discuss private matters with Mr. Grover." The zombies began to dig in the graveyard and exhume bodies for their feast. As the bodies emerged, the zombies ripped and tore into them and devoured their flesh noisily. The exhumations having ceased, the feasting became general. Sometimes arguments would break out, and zombies tore into each other's flesh, but largely the feast was civilized and subdued.

"Mr. Grover, I think we now have the basis for a close, working relationship. Your agent has your insurance papers ready for your signature, so please sign them now."

Grover did not bother to read what he was signing, but he signed using the pen that his company's agent offered him. The agent was very pleased with the thought of the commission he would receive for writing this work for his company.

"Mr. Grover, I'm sure you're familiar with the insurance laws about suicide. So you'll know why we want to make every effort to keep you alive and hale for the next twenty-four months, at least. But, now let's drink to our higher purpose. Rene, bring the goblet. You see, Mr. Grover, what I was telling you about Rene, the monk who accompanied Columbus when he first came to this island was the truth and not a fairy tale. Behold, this is the same Rene whom you waved at every time you entered your hotel. He checked you out. He will now administer your first real communion. When he hands you the goblet, don't drink it all, since all of us must have a sip after you have taken yours."

Rene, like a good living priest, raised the goblet and muttered some Latin about what the goblet contained. He took a sip himself and looked positively seraphic, and then he passed the goblet to Grover, who ignored the noxious, pungent smell of the contents and took a draught and swallowed it.

A cheer went up among the assemblage, and the goblet made the rounds, first to Ms. Fontaine, then the agent and Baron Samedi, and then all the others. When the goblet had been emptied, Rene retrieved it and wiped it with a cloth that hung from his belt. He looked very pleased and might have raised his hand in a blessing, except he was no longer a priest of the Catholic Church, but an undead minister to the dark forces of voodoo.

The drums began to beat again, and the zombies continued to feast. Some dropped by to hail their CEO and offer her a gobbet of flesh or a putrefying eyeball. One offered her a handful of human brain that had turned dark gray, but what did that matter since its owner had lain for over a decade in the fetid Haitian ground?

The revelry went on all night, and the zombies danced and jostled each other as the principals retired into the darkness one by one. The first to go was Ms. Fontaine, who vanished in the night as if she had been an apparition. The second to go was Baron Samedi, who before he departed, grasped Grover's shoulder in his large hand and congratulated him for having made the right choice.

Rene was next, and he confided to Grover that he greatly appreciated Grover's being pleasant about his stay. He said he hoped to see Grover again soon. That left the agent and Grover, and the zombies and what was left of their feast. Grover concluded that with the bokor gone, anything might happen, so he urged the agent to make haste in getting him to the airport before the sunrise.

In the agent's Mercedes, Grover rode to the airport with all the windows of the automobile down, because Grover was uncomfortable breathing air that contained the smell of rotting teeth and gums of his company's agent.

On the way, the agent confessed he was comfortable with what the zombies did, only he preferred living flesh to dead flesh. Smiling with his sharpened teeth showing along his lips, the man told Grover his people had all been cannibals. He was the only person at the party who genuinely regretted Grover's decision. He said he had looked forward to feasting on

Grover's cheeks particularly, but now perhaps he'd have the opportunity another time when Grover returned to Haiti. Grover's frisson at this parting thought was a break in the intense heat of the island at sunrise.

The agent gave Grover his copy of the signed binder for his new insurance policy. Only when he looked closely, did the insurance investigator see that the agent's signature was in blood. He thought he heard the stewardess welcome him aboard with the greeting, "Have a nice fright."

As he settled into his business-class seat, Hans Grover detected a distinctly evil smell. He looked around and finally concluded the pungent smell was coming from his own clothing, and when he raced to the bath compartment to wash his hands to mitigate the smell, he looked into the mirror, and when he bared his teeth, he thought he saw that his gums had started rotting already. He looked again but saw nothing unusual, so he settled down and rinsed his mouth out thoroughly with water.

As his plane took off, Grover vowed he would never again set foot on Haitian soil. His consolation was short-lived, because when the steward came by to ask him what he'd like for breakfast, Grover looked into the steward's eyes and saw Rene, who winked at Grover, recommended that he try the red wine, and told him that he could continue feasting throughout the flight home. Rene said he would bring Grover anything he liked—anything at all.

The Cold Ghost Tentacles

Inspector Ian MacFarland was not surprised by receiving another missing persons report. In early October, statistics spiked in the vicinity of the Loch for no good reason. Anywhere from five to ten persons went missing every year. Anywhere from one to three people of those who went missing were found alive and well.

The inspector got involved when cases had elements of mischief or malice associated with them. The present case of Mrs. Leslie Holbrook was certainly one of those. According to the woman's husband, Hemlock Holbrook, she had gone out in the late afternoon to fetch some tea leaves as was her habit on Wednesdays. Mrs. Holbrook had not appeared at the tea confectioner, and she had not returned home. She had simply vanished.

The inspector investigated her disappearance, examining her husband and the grocer, and retracing the route the woman was supposed to have taken after she left her home. The inspector did not rule in or rule out any suspects in what might have been murder most foul. For example, he contemplated that the woman's husband had a motive for murder because of a life insurance policy for which he was the beneficiary. That seemed a remote possibility because of habeas corpus: the husband would have to wait the statutory seven years before collecting the money.

The inspector expanded his search. He stopped at five houses along the woman's intended route and talked with each of the owners about any suspicious activity. All the owners knew Mrs. Holbrook and her eccentricities. She kept to herself and always seemed preoccupied with some dark secret. She never spoke even when greeted. She kept her head down and pressed forward, preoccupied and mumbling quietly to herself. None of her neighbors had recollected seeing the woman on that particular Wednesday.

The fifth of the homeowners, a Mrs. Julianne Shelby, told the inspector over tea that the afternoon in question had been chilly and very foggy. She had been out walking her two Shelties and saw nothing, but she had heard what she thought was the sound of a woman shrieking with uncontrollable laughter. The episode lasted for a few minutes and was followed by silence. Mrs. Shelby could not account for what happened. She had never heard Mrs. Holbrook laugh so she could not say that the laughter was hers.

Mrs. Shelby recalled her dogs had barked at the sound, and the dogs continued to bark for some time afterward. Mrs. Shelby conjectured the route might be haunted. She had sensed danger along the path from time to time for the last forty years. The pattern was always the same. A gust of icy wind sliced through the landscape like a knife. It raised goose bumps on her arms and caused her dogs to bark. Twice before she had heard the sound of uncontrollable laughter, and on both occasions, neighbors had disappeared. The disappeared had never returned.

The inspector feared he had now uncovered a possible serial killer, so he took careful notes on his conversation with Mrs. Shelby. She kindly consulted her diaries to get the dates right, for she recorded all such anomalies with meticulous attention to details.

When the inspector had access to police records, he checked the lists of missing persons for the last forty years. He discovered that the pattern Mrs. Shelby had recognized in three events could be compounded tenfold by correlating October disappearances in the vicinity. Those who disappeared were a mixed lot, including ten men, twelve women including Mrs. Holbrook, and eight children. All had disappeared between the first and fifteenth day of October.

Checking weather statistics, the inspector verified that climactic conditions were the same for all thirty incidents: chilly with dense fog and unaccountable occasional cold streaks. The inspector saw no possible human motive which could cover such a variegated mass of the local population. No bodies had ever been found. The way the land heaved in springtime after the unbinding of the ground, at least one body was likely to have become disinterred in that time.

The inspector had a friend who claimed to be clairvoyant, so for completeness, he consulted the elderly crone in her cottage. She poured him three fingers of a peaty single malt. While he sat by her peat fire and the two smoked their briar pipes, Mrs. Poundworth told the inspector aspects of his case he might not have found in the records.

The clairvoyant said, "Mrs. Shelby has hit on the clue you need, but it is buried in what was said. The critical clue is in the knife-like draught that cut through the chilly, foggy atmosphere on the occasion of each disappearance. If normal winds had been blowing, the fog could not have settled as thickly, or the fog would have blown away."

Nodding her gray head, she continued, "I've been told stories about those slicing winds before. In each case, ghosts were thought to be involved. In one particular case, I myself had been walking early in October, in the late afternoon fog. I felt the chill increase suddenly, and something like a ghostly tentacle swept right past me. I remember the date precisely because on that day, my nephew disappeared."

The inspector consulted his notepad and verified that, indeed, the crone's nephew was one of the children on his list of disappeared persons. The inspector asked her whether she had a theory about what had happened to her nephew. She maintained she had more than a theory. Because Cuhulan was her favorite nephew, she summoned her clairvoyant powers and saw mystic patterns indicating that the white tentacle that she had seen emanated from the Loch.

Every October, some force within the Loch was sweeping over the landscape looking for prey. Mrs. Poundworth felt lucky the tentacle she saw did not grasp her. It might have done so, she thought, except that she had stepped off the path to pick some mushrooms. She only saw the tentacle passing as she looked sideways, with averted vision.

She believed the tentacle had found her nephew instead. He had been staying with her, and she thought her nephew had followed her down the path for some reason. When she returned to her home, he was gone. She had reported the disappearance to the police the next morning. Exhaustive searching yielded no evidence of her nephew. She had repeatedly been interrogated as if she had murdered her own favorite nephew. Since there was no motive, no body, and no weapon, the case was finally closed.

The inspector was out of his depth. He found the crone's report of her missing nephew among the police records. He also found the then inspectors investigative reports. Everything validated the crone's account. Her suspicions about supernatural causes were duly recorded, verbatim. She had even written out a sworn statement and signed it.

The inspector, on a hunch, began reading through all such reports about the other persons who had disappeared.

Among those, he discovered interviews with one Dr. Liam MacDugal of Stirling University. Dr. MacDugal was a historian who specialized in phenomena related to the Loch. The inspector rang the professor up and arranged to interview him about strange Loch phenomena between seminars at the staff club of the university the next afternoon.

Professor MacDugal was excited to be consulted by the inspector in an active case of disappearance. Over a glass of aged port wine, he was ebullient about Loch lore. In fact, he was full of stories from folklore he had traced to factual data. That is, he and his students had adduced scholarly evidence to back up every one of the fanciful stories of Scotland.

The professor's eyes brightened and sparkled when he learned about the crone's having had a close encounter with what he called "the cold ghost tentacles." He made a careful record of the details, and the inspector gave the professor contact information for his friend the crone.

The professor told the inspector a tale that grew with every layer of evidence.

"First," the professor said, "Persons were not the only beings who had disappeared in modern times. Animals also suddenly disappeared all around the Loch. Dogs, cats, deer, and cattle, especially the latter, had disappeared. Because these animal disappearances were not often recorded by police, my students interviewed hundreds of farmers and householders to gather data on where and when the disappearances had taken place. I assembled the data in graphic form, and the known regions for disappearances extended twenty-five miles around 360 degrees of the Loch."

"Second, historical evidence demonstrates the Scots' belief that a blood-eating monster inhabited the Loch from time immemorial to the present. At times, people who lived near the Loch offered sacrifices to the creature. In early

October each year, they tethered sacrificial cattle, goats, pigs, dogs and cats all along the Loch to propitiate the beast lest it should prey on humans. Whenever the sacrifices failed to be offered, persons disappeared for no reason in increasing numbers until the sacrifices once again were offered on the shore of the Loch."

The professor paused to let this thought sink in. Then he went on.

"Third, I collected a catalog of images from ancient inscriptions and accounts of monsters, particularly monsters associated with the Loch. Among those were indications that a long, tentacle-shaped monster slithered across the surface of the Loch or extended itself beyond the Loch shores. Like the tentacles of a gargantuan octopus or giant squid, these tentacles were shown either extended at length, curled like springs, or grasping living beings, both animal and human, and dragging them to the Loch.

"In one ancient Scottish volume, I found a charm that purported to offer asylum from the tentacle, but the poem's provenance is uncertain. I have enough evidence to convince a reasonable man like you that there is a tentacled creature in the Loch, that the creature craved the blood of warm-blooded animals, that the creature extended its tentacles' reach over the land as far as it could to take the blood it required, and that the tentacles' extension occurred in early October every year."

The professor said he had consulted with colleagues from many disciplines, both in Scotland and abroad. Scientific expeditions to find the creature had found no evidence of a physical creature. Everything pointed to a paranormal phenomenon, like a ghost. Presumably, Dr. MacDugal said, in prehistoric times, a flesh and blood monster had inhabited the

Loch. Its ghost survived its demise. The ghost continued to need blood for whatever reason.

The inspector's head was reeling with ideas that strained his rational mind. His investigation had led him to speculation about a monstrous ghost whose only restraint was the length of its tentacles.

He asked the professor for documentation of the beast, and the professor immediately escorted the inspector to his office, where he inscribed a copy of his monograph, which he gave as a gift. The title of Dr. MacDugal's scholarly monograph was, "Investigations into the Perennial Appearance of Cold Ghost Tentacles in the Lochs of Scotland: Winnowing Fact from Fiction." The monograph was illustrated and included photographs purporting to show the tentacles themselves extending over the land.

In parting, the professor stated that the monster had managed to devour what it needed while not overly exciting the population it fed upon. When the creature could no longer be satisfied by a measured annual feast, the people would learn about the monster's wrath.

In early historical records, the case was clear: the monster would ravage until its blood-lust was fulfilled.

"One thing more," the professor said with a grim smile, "My wife and protégé both disappeared while conducting experiments on the shores of the Loch."

To prove this, the professor gave the inspector copies of the newspaper clippings reporting their strange disappearances.

Returning to tell the crone what he had learned from the professor, the inspector encountered thick fog. An icy tentacle flew effortlessly through the hair and grabbed the professor by his ribs. He laughed uncontrollably because of the way the tentacle tickled him.

The crone, who was out gathering mushrooms farther off the path, looked up from the side of the path and shook her head. She thought she had heard that chuckling sound. This time, it sounded like the inspector. She was once again relieved that the tentacle had not come for her.

The Wasps

The Halperins, Ross, and Greta, bought their new home in Phoenix, Ariz., right at the bottom of the market. They paid an unbelievably low price for a modest two-story house that exactly suited their needs. Since their purchase two weeks ago, their house had increased $100,000 in value based on comparables.

The house had easy access to grocery stores, gas stations, emergency health clinics and pharmacies that they would frequent for their daily needs. The Halperins had no children, but the house was large enough for a sizeable family, and nearby schools were some of the best in Phoenix.

The front yard was tastefully done in crushed rock, with a sculpted fig tree that required very little water even at the height of summer. The backyard was well landscaped with a green sward and mesquite and citrus trees, but it required a lot of watering and gardening that the Halperins felt were well worth the money.

Featured at the center of the backyard, was the Halperins' dream swimming pool, surrounded by dense foliage and fed with water constantly through a stepped waterfall into the back side of the pool. Their backyard attracted birds of all kinds and some insects.

In their side yard, was an ornamental orange tree that always held fifty to one hundred apparently ripe oranges hanging from its boughs. In short, the house and grounds were a kind of desert garden paradise, a classical hortus conclusus, in all seasons—or so their realtor had assured them they would be.

In March, the Halperins had moved all their belongings from icy, snowy New England, and they had arranged everything to suit their new style of living in a land of nearly perpetual Arizona sunshine. Every day, they sunned themselves cautiously, and then in the late afternoon and sometimes in the evening, they dipped in their pool.

In early April, they noticed a visitor to the pool, a large golden wasp, which they tried to lift from the water with their long-handled pool net. The wasp was not, as they had thought, dead. It was not only alive but wary. As the net approached, the wasp rose from the surface of the water, hovered for a moment to get its bearings, and then flew away.

The Halperins mused that the wasp had been using the surface tension of the water to support itself and that the wasp was apparently cooling itself and then possibly taking some of the moisture back to its nest just as mud daubers out East did from standing pools of muddy water.

The next afternoon, the wasp—or a wasp very much like the first one the Halperins had seen—came to dip in the pool. It did not seem to mind that the Halperins were swimming there. It assiduously avoided the area of the waterfall and the shaded area under where the squat, tri-partite palm tree bent down over the water lending shade.

The wasp clearly liked to take the water in the sunshine. It avoided shade. The wasp would bathe for perhaps three minutes, then rise from the surface, hover and fly away. It seemed to want to avoid the Halperins and any objects that happened to be floating in the pool. Even when the wasp was wafted by a gentle breeze across the pool, it seemed to enjoy the surfing effect, up to the point where it entered the shaded area under the side of the pool. Then the wasp would take off, hover and fly away.

Until the middle of April, one wasp was the daily limit. The Halperins reasoned the wasp had needs for which it had adapted, and the Halperins' pool was perhaps the nearest such pool to the wasp's nest, wherever that was. Since no activity by the humans seemed to perturb the wasp and since the wasp did not in any way threaten the humans, the Halperins stuck to their policy of "live and let live." Why not?

The one day that Mr. Halperin had experimented with the net to see whether he could drown a wasp by taking it underwater with the pool net, he discovered that holding the wasp underwater for three minutes had no effect on the wasp. After the wasp had been brought to the surface after submersion, it revived immediately, hovered and flew away. The wasp had not attempted to swim while underwater, and it had not been stimulated by the threat of drowning to attack Mr. Halperin, or even countenance his presence.

At the end of April, Mrs. Halperin detected that there was a second wasp. She had noticed a very large wasp was floating on the surface at the usual time in the afternoon, and as it rose from the surface to hover, a second wasp had hovered and landed on the water.

A day or two later, she noticed the pattern changed slightly so two wasps swam at about the same or nearly the same time. The wasps kept a half-length of the pool between them, and they did not seem to communicate with each other in any discernible way while they were on the water.

A few days later, Mrs. Halperin was a little unsettled when she realized the two floating wasps were relieved on station by two additional wasps, who took the places of the first pair of floaters after they had flown away.

Ross's research on the Internet did little to discover the species or habits of the visiting wasps, but the Halperins began to scan the surrounding houses from their elevated porch on the second level of their house in an attempt to spot from which adjacent yard the wasps originated. This attempt proved unsuccessful, but the Halperins thought that a house over their back cinder-block wall might be the source.

They decided to walk around to the front of the neighboring house to see what they could. The house was under renovation. On the sidewalk in front of the empty house, they found a swarm of black honeybees had nested in the city water feeder unit set in the ground by the walk in front of the property.

The Halperins decided to call the city about those bees because the city's meter readers would be mightily surprised to find the bees, possibly at the risk of having the bee swarm sting them badly. Even if the bees were dangerous Africanized bees, they were not wasps, so the Halperins were still perplexed about the source for the wasps that visited their pool each afternoon.

On the next day after they found the black honeybees, a very small version of a golden wasp floated on the surface of their pool at the usual time. The small golden wasp seemed to have no trouble discovering how to land, maneuver, hover and fly off after its bath. Mrs. Halperin marveled at the power of nature to force adaptation across generations of creatures, enabling each successive generation to accomplish what its predecessors had done without explicit training or apparent example.

Now, six wasps took turns in the pool, only two floating at any time, and one wasp gently landed on Mrs. Halperin's arm while she rested in the water by the sunny side of the pool. Mrs. Halperin did not panic, and the wasp arose from her arm and flew away. She was becoming increasingly alarmed, not because one wasp had landed on her arm, but because of the increasing number of wasps.

It was Mr. Halperin who first noticed that one of the wasps flew off, not over their back wall as the rest had done, but right into the palm tree at the back of the pool—the palm with the overhanging fronds and the thick, oozing fruit tucked under its boughs.

Now, the Halperins thought their exterminator might help, so they called IOS Exterminators. Ramon Gonzales, their IOS field representative, drove right out to investigate, but he found nothing in the palm to indicate the presence of wasp nests. He opined that the wasps were probably not from the Halperins' yard.

Ramon was the exterminator who, on an earlier call, had swept away the messy black cobwebs that Mrs. Halperin thought had been caused by black widow spiders. He had said, at the time, that the webs were definitely not characteristic of black widows.

Now, on the subject of wasps, he assured his clients that they need not worry. Ramon thought that wasps were normal, like the large black beetles, big as hummingbirds, that flew around the palm in the early evening.

"Those beetles do bite, so be careful," he warned, and then he departed.

Ramon did not mention at the time that the Halperins' call had been the fifth wasp-related call he had answered that very day. He had learned when he returned to the office that calls from all over Phoenix were pouring into IOS with complaints about golden wasps.

No one knew the source of the wasps, but they all knew golden wasps were common in the Phoenix area. This year's crop of wasps seemed larger than normal. That was all. No one had reported being stung, but it was getting hot now in unprecedented ways.

Ramon recalled that wasps generally did not like excessive heat. In the heat, wasps became almost crazy and stung anything around them out of frustration and rage at what they could not control.

Two weeks later, Arizona began to experience what were called three-digit days, when the temperature every day rose above one hundred degrees Fahrenheit in the late afternoon and stayed at that level until darkness, before lowering to the mid-to-high seventies in the early morning hours.

Some people swam in the late afternoon after work on those days, but most swam well after dark when their yard lights went on low, and their pools were like exotic aquariums under the starry desert sky. Skinny dipping was said to be popular among young and old alike. Wasps did not come after dusk, so no one gave their swimming habits any thought.

The temperatures rose in late May to 108 degrees Fahrenheit, and Phoenicians shod their dogs' paws in special Velcro-attaching doggie shoes to protect them from the heat of the pavement during their walks. By June, it was clear that temperatures would break all prior records, regularly rising above 110 degrees.

The population kept within their air conditioned houses or made haste between one air conditioned building and another all day long. Siesta time was not spent poolside, and pool activity was limited to the night.

The Halperins, being retired, did continue to use their pool during the daytime, and they noticed that the wasps began their floating in the early morning in increasing numbers, and they continued until the hour before sunset. Now not in ones or twos, the wasps came in dozens, and they covered the surface of the pool like a skein of miniature golden oblong globes. They came and went with such insistent regularity that they were a marvel to behold.

The first incidence of a wasp sting occurred in the middle of June when the temperature had hit 118 degrees Fahrenheit. A wasp had reportedly stung a small child. The wasps seemed to be everywhere in Phoenix now, and IOS was becoming frantic with the level of their activity. They had avoided public panic by waiting for a truly alarming development.

Ramon knew that a wasp stinging a small child was probably not going to be the catalyst for newspaper coverage. What would stimulate the press to begin their feeding frenzy would be a swarm of wasps stinging someone nearly to death. Unavoidable coverage of that event would lead to public outcry, and that, inexorably, would catalyze actions by the mayor and the governor.

Ramon's guess was close, but only IOS management knew the true scope of the matter, and they had already stimulated a press campaign alleging that Global Warming was to blame for unprecedented temperatures and for infestations well beyond anyone's ability to predict the consequences. Likewise, the medical community put out radio warnings for citizens to stay inside, to avoid swimming during daylight hours, and to call exterminators immediately upon finding infestations, particularly of golden wasps.

In fact, quiet phone calls had been made by the mayor to the governor and from the governor to the head of FEMA. Teams were frantically gaming alternatives against loss of vital communications, electricity, and water as an emergency grew into a catastrophe.

Evacuation routes were reviewed. Police and National Guard leadership personnel were informed. Readiness was priority one, but still no hint or warning went to the public. In fact, the authorities put out classified notices to all their people that they should not inform the citizens of what was happening since the public would panic and worsen the situation. Public servants and national guard persons made preparations for evacuating their own families. Their children disappeared from schools.

The prime catalyst came on an extremely hot day when the Halperins were taking their afternoon dip in their pool. Ross and Greta had become so accustomed to their visitors that they had no sense of panic when literally hundreds of wasps sat on the surface of their pool while others hovered over the whole yard and took turns relieving the floaters.

Greta, now totally unafraid of the wasps, felt them land on her hair and even on her eyelashes, then rise and drop to the water's surface. Ross marveled when he scooped a handful of pool water and twenty wasps landed in his hand and along his hairy arm.

The couple shared a proprietary look as if to say, "Look at our golden wasps! Who would believe this?" They would descend under the surface, and the wasps would rise and hover, waiting for them to resurface. Some of the wasps would ride on the human bodies when they descended, and then fly off when the human bodies broke the surface again.

It was on such a day that Ramon called on his daily rounds, sweating from the sweltering heat and impatient to be done with his monthly sprayings and inspections. Entering their backyard, he saw the Halperins in the pool and the clouds of wasps hovering over them, and he thought he was witnessing the apocalyptic moment just before the world would end. Quietly he raised the pressure on his sprayer and was about to begin hosing the air with his deadly spray.

At that moment, Mrs. Halperin called out, "Cheerio!" She told Ramon, "Go right on to your next appointment."

Mr. Halperin said, "Ramon did not know what he was seeing. He shouldn't spray the wasps because they're really friendly."

Ramon was on the verge of panic now. Had the Halperins been so badly stung that they no longer had reason?

Seeing Ramon's hesitation, Mr. Halperin told him, "Just go back outside the gate, lock it, and go away. Everything will be all right."

Ramon knew an order when he heard it. He stood down on the sprayer, backed through the gate, locked it and returned to his white IOS truck. He was about to climb inside the truck when a swarm of wasps flew over the gate as if in pursuit of him. He must have thought that because he instinctively turned on his sprayer and raised it.

He then let loose the spray with its full effect, spraying all around himself and the truck, and then dived inside the truck. But his efforts were both futile and much too late. The wasps enveloped him and the truck, excited by the heat and the threat of the spray. They covered and stung Ramon with total fury.

Strangely, Ramon felt no pain. He felt the presence of wasps on his eyelids and his neck, indeed on his entire body. Perhaps, he thought, he was feeling the effects of adrenaline. Then, he sat up and got out of the truck, marveling at the swarms of wasps that surrounded him and flew in all directions as far and as high as he looked.

Slowly the golden wasps dispersed. All of them disappeared. Ramon was left feeling euphoric. He knew he should probably race for the emergency medical facility, but he reasoned that he was probably too late for that. He called IOS headquarters to give a status.

He could not get through because of communication problems. He figured that the state of emergency had begun.

Communication was going to be impossible as long as the emergency lasted. Steeling himself, he decided to be a good citizen. He would not flee. Rather, he would try to help as he could. So he went back through the Halperins' gate fully expecting the couple to be dead.

He was very surprised to find the Halperins exactly as he had left them. They were surrounded by wasps, but entirely at ease. They were playing together and with the wasps. Ramon shook his head.

Mr. Halperin waved to Ramon and said, "As you see, everything is just fine. Why have you returned?"

To this Ramon threw up his hands, turned and walked away. Sitting in his truck for a long while to digest what had occurred, Ramon finally put the key in the ignition, started the engine and drove to his next appointment. He turned on his radio and found the emergency frequency, but nothing was on the station but static. As he hit one of the major grid roads, he noticed that swarms of wasps were visible in every direction.

By everything Ramon had ever known, he was facing an enigma. Clearly, the wasps had proliferated beyond all prior experience. They were swarming all over Phoenix. The heat was such that their excitement should be pressuring them to sting everything and everyone in their sight. Yet that was not happening.

The Halperins and he himself were proof that the wasps were not dangerous. If the wasps had been dangerous, the couple and he would surely have been stung to death.

Ramon drove not to his next appointment, but instead to the IOS headquarters. There, police and emergency vehicles were rushing in and out. Inside the office was pandemonium. He rushed up to the dispatcher to report what he found at the Halperins', but he was told to write up his report right away and submit it to his supervisor. Then, he was ordered to stand by for dispatching.

People were calling from all over the city about gigantic swarms of wasps. An evacuation was on the brink of execution. The National Guard had been called up. The governor and the President of the U.S. had declared Phoenix a disaster area. Troops and money were on the way. Command centers were being set up across the city and the state. All the news networks were feasting on the story.

On the way to his office to write his report, he met a reporter who had sneaked into the facility. The reporter was Ramon's friend. He looked shocked, then very relieved. He said that he thought Ramon was dead, stung by a swarm of wasps while servicing a client. Ramon's body had been positively identified. What a miracle it seemed that he was here alive!

The newspaper man veered off suddenly saying that he had a lot of news to get on the wire, including the news that Ramon was alive after all. Ramon shook his head in disbelief.

Then, he had one of those sudden epiphanies. He pinched himself or thought he did so. He yelled out loud his own name—Ramon Gonzalez! No one seemed to hear him. He went back to the dispatch desk, and this time, no one was present. He went outside and there were no automobiles, police cars or emergency vehicles.

He looked up into the sky and saw that the wasps had totally eclipsed the sky from horizon to horizon, and the cloud of wasps was thickening, subsuming everything, including the trees, the cactuses, the street signs and the streets. The wasps seemed to him to be enveloping his own body, swarming over every one of his limbs and his face, head, back, and shoulders.

In early September, the remains of Ramon Gonzales's body were found in the driveway of Ross and Greta Halperins' home. According to IOS records, he had been dispatched to investigate the presence of golden wasps in the backyard of that home at the time just before the general emergency had been sounded.

His sprayer was found beside his body, and it was empty. An autopsy showed that he had probably not died immediately from wasp stings. His was a slow and agonizing death, the coroner thought, but he told Ramon's mother that the death had been instantaneous.

In any case, the cause of Ramon's death was ruled as cardiac arrest resulting from massive numbers of simultaneous stings. Five hundred thousand people of Phoenix had suffered the same fate within the same two weeks. In a panic, the remainder of the population had fled the area by any means available. It was said to be the largest unplanned evacuation of citizens America had ever witnessed.

Of course, like many others, Ramon did not know that he was dying of wasp stings. In his final hallucinations, he thought he was still alive when he went back to his office.

Chain failures left a land devastated because it was stripped of every vestige of civilization. When the power failed, all air conditioning in greater Phoenix failed, and the water and sewer systems failed, too. Communications failed early and stayed down the entire time. The much-touted FirstNet had become mired in politics and funding crises, so it had never fully come online.

The golden wasps literally took over the greater Phoenix area. When they had completely engulfed the area, from mountain to mountain and desert edge to desert edge, the peak daytime temperatures ranged for twelve consecutive days over 124 degrees Fahrenheit. One day the temperature spiked to 140 degrees.

At this point, which in hindsight was the apex of the emergency, all the golden wasps were in the desperate grip of madness. On that day, at precisely four o'clock in the afternoon, the temperature spiked, and then the wasps, as if they were one single organism, suddenly collapsed from the many days' accumulation of heat. They died in flight and fell to the ground all over Phoenix, like volcanic ash five to seven inches deep everywhere.

Some wasps were believed to have escaped by flying to the North, but scientists had no proof of that, only theories with which they garnered grant money. The scientists did opine that not one wasp in Phoenix proper could have survived the infernal heat.

Local authorities, relieved that the panic phase of the emergency might be over, began to comb the Phoenix area, building by building, and yard by yard. It took them two months to execute the beginning phase of the clean up. Wasp bodies were harvested, compacted and stored in a mound for possible use as a fuel. Human bodies were buried in mass graves or burned in huge funeral piles. Disease was a major fear, but no plague occurred. This was nothing short of miraculous.

The stench of death and decay set in and hovered over Phoenix like an evil spirit for over a year. The religious among the people of the city thought of the incident as similar to the biblical plagues, only worse. Some fanatics proclaimed that the End of the World was near. Flagellants whipped themselves through the streets. Jeremiads were uttered on several major street corners. Hair shirts were sold and worn with muted pride.

It would be nice to think that all these events never occurred. The authorities certainly tried to make events seem like distant memories of the global pandemics of yore, or like more recent tsunamis that struck in distant oceans and killed many hundreds of thousands. All people like to put the worst behind them. After they suffer through a genuine disaster, they like to get back to normal as quickly as possible. They revert to the mean as best they can.

Therefore, it should not be surprising that, after a very expensive reconstruction with many hundreds of thousands of properties sold as fix-up investments, in the same neighborhood, in the same house as was formerly occupied by the Halperins, a sign went up in early March of the year selling "the next best thing to paradise" with a swimming pool and beautiful landscaping at a relative song of a price.

The realtor introduced the property to a newly retired couple, who loved it at first sight. The couple wasted no time before moving in. As soon as they could, they plunged right in the pool. Finding a small golden wasp on the surface of the water did not bother them in the least. After all, everyone said that the disaster was over, and everything was back to normal in paradise. The sunshine and all that blue sky, all those brilliant green palms proved that they were safe and secure here in Phoenix, Arizona.

The Black Marble Griffon

Grandfather's garden, leaf-strewn and haggard in the autumn cold, sports many odd sculpture figures, none so engaging as this writhing griffon sculpted from black marble as if from life.

At dusk, this particular macabre sculpture seems to come alive. Its eyes shine. Its smooth skin undulates in the chilly moonlight. Sometimes, like now, I feel its goose bumps form as if they are my own.

This evening, I am resting from a day's work cleaning up the garden and the adjacent family cemetery with its iron rectangular enclosure over there behind the gate. I have worked hard all day since dawn. I am sweaty and dirty. I ache all over from raking, delving, weeding, walking, bending and rising, crouching, carrying, and blistering and scratching both my hands. Do you see the pile of brambles by the wall? That is the midden of this year's haul, laid on the decaying compost of past hauls going back ages.

I owe this annual ritual of manual labor to my forebears who have been interred here for five generations, every root and branch of the family tree. The gravestones in the cemetery are askew because of the watery ground and many winters' groundswells and heaving.

In New England, every garden has its crop of rocks, and that goes double for cemeteries. Nature is always trying to reclaim her own. She lays her hand on your soul and does her best to pull you down beside her.

In this rich black earth, life will grow in green profusion, then crisp up and finally return to somewhere like this darkening place. Eastern worm snakes will coil around the buried bones or dart up from sunken tombs, then wiggle down again like pink ropes whipping back and forth through cracks in the stone. Who knows the dead as intimately as silent feeding worms and microscopic all-engulfing bacteria?

Grandfather brought me here each year when I was little. He taught me how to tend this garden and cemetery, which became his final resting place. He told me stories that made my hair stand on end. He told of the family's hardships, betrayals, even murders. He laughed when I said I was afraid.

At least once each year, he would silently sneak up behind me when I was in reverie. He would take his glove off his rough hand and hold it to a cold pipe. Then he would grab me by the nape of my neck just to see me jump with fright. I did not disappoint him. He said that was good training for the time when Death himself would come to take me home.

I was there when Grandfather passed. I saw him tremble right at the end as if a cold, resolute hand had grabbed him by the neck. Whenever I am in this place, I feel so close to Grandfather, I could almost cry. But I do not cry because grown-up women do not cry. I hear Grandfather's voice say that so clearly this evening. He is listening to us now. He knows why I conjured you. Can you hear him? No?

Just there, inside the gate, you can see the grave of my Aunt Matilda, the in-law who, according to Grandfather, poisoned my Uncle Clem to get his money. From her epitaph, you would hardly believe she was a witch. Her stone reads, "Here Lies Patience, Patiently Waiting for the Lord."

I watched her here by moonlight gather the fatal berries that ended my uncle's life. I saw her mash the black, deadly nightshade in the kitchen and mix the berries' juice with Uncle Clem's drink night after night until he died. I never saw her ride on a broom or gather newts' eyes, but I know what she was.

Now, she lies there beside my uncle, grave by grave, prim and proper. She was laid out like a bride for the coming of the Lord. Grandfather figured it was a good thing she was buried in an asphalt coffin to protect her from the flames of Hell. He said the longer Apocalypse waited, the better for a great many of my ancestors, himself included.

Back by the wall, you can find Great-Great-Great Grandfather, who, Grandfather claimed, took the life of the farmer whose land lay adjacent to ours. After he had done the violent deed one foggy, ill-starred night, he married that farmer's daughter although she knew the truth. Grandfather told me the farmer's daughter, his Great-Great Grandmother, finally got her revenge. She waited until her husband was too weak from age and drink to rise. She then smothered him with a laced pillow. She lies there by his side as if nothing amiss had ever happened.

That entire farmer's land is now in the family's estate. Just now, if you listen, you can hear the lowing of the herd coming to the barn to spend the night. I hear the lowing of herds that stretch back generations. I see the white from their breathing in the cold. Do you see them breathing in their long file? No?

Do you see the stone mausoleum in the center of the cemetery? That's the place of Grandfather and Grandmother's tombs. I took special care to clear the overgrowth from the little house without furniture. I could not do much with the thick moss and lichen. There is no way to mask the unmistakable smells of dank, rotting earth and the peculiarly human stench of graves.

I cried when my brothers brought Grandfather here that final time. When they interred him, I thought I heard him tell me to come to visit, often. Grandmother and I never had the bond that I had with my Grandfather, and she deeply resented it. There was nothing she could do, and it rankled her right up to her own death.

Grandmother's internment did not affect me at all, except I felt relieved. Grandmother had been an unhappy woman all her life. She had made life miserable for Grandfather, though he did everything he could to make her happy. When I get near their mausoleum, I can feel the shades of those two tugging at me on both sides of my mind. I shiver to think of their invisible hands on either beating half of my pounding heart.

Come with me now and let us light the torch. It is time. Watch your step as the very ground will take you down, or a stone, a stray branch, or a gnarled root. See how the statue's eyes watch and flicker in the firelight. Walk around it with me. See how its scales ripple and how its body undulates. Look at the way its sharp eyes follow us. We're not alone. Don't laugh at me! You are always smiling.

Now look toward the mausoleum. See how the firelight throws the shadow of the griffon against the mausoleum's wall? It darts and rises with the flickering. The wild, flickering fire lends the marble life. I have often dreamed that one night, like tonight, Grandfather would come to me, as he always did, and grab me on the nape of the neck with his cold, rough hand.

I fancy that I would then turn, like so. He'd then laugh and shake his finger, so. No, your hand is warm, not cold like his. Your lips are warm. I like the feel of your arms around me. I like the feel of your breath on my ear. You're nothing like Grandfather. You're nothing like Grandfather's descriptions of you. I thrill in your embrace. We are meant for each other.

Yes, the griffon is pointing to the mausoleum. So are you. Yes, I will go with you to visit the little house. Will you help me with the heavy door? Will you go inside with me? Will you hold the torch so we can see the tombs? Will you lie with me on the cold, crypt floor? Will we mock the scourge of life with all our might and vigor? Yes, I know we will. Yes, I know you well enough.

The ground is uneven. Watch your step. The gate is heavy, but today I oiled the hinges. We will not make such squealing noises as will wake the dead. I also prepared the mausoleum door as best I could without you. Yes, I will take your hand, which now is cold and rough. You have to promise not to smile so when we are inside. I do not intend for us a comical interlude.

I waited for you this long. Be patient with me now as I prepare. How sad I am to be caught so rough and bleeding from my chores. How ready, even so, am I for your embrace? Now we are inside. How narrow and cramped is this little house? See Grandfather's tomb there, and Grandmother's tomb there beside him on the floor? There is space enough for us. I shall lie here above Grandfather. You shall lie there above Grandmother. The torch has extinguished. Not to worry. I have your hand. Now descend and lie with me. Now fold me in your arms, so. Yes. Though I cannot see you, I can feel you all around me.

I know you are smiling. I do not mind. I do not mind at all. Your perpetual smile reminds me of what I am. I will now begin to laugh a little with you in this cold, damp place. I feel your arms and your cold hand all along my body. I understand you now. I am yours alone. I will sleep in your arms until we awaken. I have found peace at last. Grandfather, is it really you? Please say something. Ah, your cold hand startled me. Yes.

Helen Screaming

My name is Sister Helen, and I would not have had these memories if I had not picked blackberries on that bright summer's day when I had just turned sixteen years old.

The berries were so very beautiful—as big as your thumb, warm, black, and shiny. I felt that those berries were beyond my deserving, so I asked my brother Kevin how I might use those berries to make someone else happy. He suggested that I take them to the cloister, put them on the ground outside the gate, and ring the bell for the Mother Superior to come and fetch them for the sisters to eat in their refectory. I had never before given that nunnery a thought, but I did believe Kevin had a good idea.

That very afternoon, I left those berries outside the chained fence with the locked peek-a-boo and the chain with the little silver bell. When I pulled the chain, I heard the tinkle of the bell, and then only silence. Behind me, I sensed movement. I felt breath on my neck and turned to see a toothless man of middle age very close to me, nodding to himself. He looked at me as if appraising my intentions. He did not speak, but instead, he stepped aside to make a way for me to get around him and depart. I ran home.

I never had an inkling of what had happened to those berries for many years. I had done what I was told to do. The rest was not my concern, or so I thought at the time. After depositing the blackberries, I took a great interest in the cloister. I planned my walks so I could get near enough to hear what went on behind the walls.

Some of my friends had considered entering orders. One took the veil, and I never heard from her again. She went into orders then moved far away. She took the name Veronica. Sister Veronica looked so sad when she said goodbye. She had told me she was going to the great beyond. Veronica said she was grateful to be able to live a life that was dead to the world, and devoted to God and the Blessed Virgin. She was happy to be moving past sodality.

I never seriously considered becoming a nun. It was always an option, yes, but I knew myself. I was too much flesh and blood and interior fire to isolate myself, even when it was for the greater glory of God. The nuns I had known through the years were soft on the outside, but steel on the inside. They wanted to control themselves and other women. What they wanted most was to be controlled.

From the Ancrene Wisse onwards, well, you know, the penchant for control has been very strong in the Church. So, on All Hallows Eve, when I heard the first cries from the lonely, hallowed place, from deep within its walled enclosure, my spine tingled the same way it had when that man had appeared behind me at the gate of the cloister. My heart flew out to the prisoners inside. I wanted to leap over the wall and free the spirits that were constrained there.

As things turned out, I did take the veil after all when I had just turned eighteen. Father Greeley, my confessor, had introduced me to the Mother Superior, who was very devout and, I thought, holy. I had never met a woman so like an older version of myself. The first thing she told me was how much she and the sisters had enjoyed the blackberries I had left at the cloister door. Did I know that for the Church Fathers "going blackberrying" meant sinning against the wisdom of the Lord? Of course not.

Under her patient instruction, I found the true path in the light of the Lord. When I arrived at the cloister, she introduced me to the toothless old man who had frightened me on my first visit there. He was the cloister's groundskeeper for whom all the sisters prayed when they weren't pointing out his foibles and making fun of him behind his back.

When I got to know him, he seemed the type of man who was very shy and private, especially around women, but he looked physically very strong. The Mother Superior knew exactly how to deal with her groundskeeper. She gave him explicit tasking, and she followed up to be sure he did things exactly as she directed. I heard rumors that the groundskeeper, who usually worked alone, had a special assistant on one day of the year for special purposes. I did not believe the descriptions the sisters gave of him with his glowing red eyes.

I did not realize how close the Mother Superior and the groundskeeper were until I listened carefully to the other novices talking about them in the weeks just before All Hallows Eve. They said the groundskeeper was much stronger than he seemed to be, and when he grabbed you, you could not get away. When a sister became unruly, they said, she would be visited late at night, and the groundskeeper would hold her while the Mother Superior beat her soundly with a whip. The nun would be sworn to secrecy, and no one would ever complain because of the shame it would bring on the sister and her family.

The more I listened, the more I learned that nearly all the nuns had, at one time or another, been held firm by the groundskeeper and felt more than one taste of Mother Superior's whip, usually on her bare behind.

Some of the novices had heard the Mother Superior counted up each nun's sins for the year and on All Hallows Eve, visited those whose infractions had become too onerous. The nuns were never told that they had reached the magic number of sins, so they all trembled on that frightful day until the stroke of midnight when the punishments were over for the year. Each nun prayed fervently in her cell from the time of the last meal in the refectory until the final stroke of the midnight bell.

On my first All Hallows Eve in the cloister, I thought I heard a cry on the other side of the cloister. I snuck out of my cell to see what was happening. I passed near enough the area where the noise was loudest to hear the shouting and a struggle inside a young novice's cell. The air was so clear and cold that the sound carried a long way off, and I was super sensitive to nuance and suggestion.

I distinctly heard the sound of someone being beaten, very hard. I heard voices of protestation, anger, frustration, and rage. I heard the stern sounds of commanding voices. I felt empathy for the nun who was being punished. I could very well have been the woman who was being disciplined. What sins could she or I have committed to deserve such torture and abuse?

I ran to the door that led from the cloister, pushed it open, and went outside into the night. I could still hear the sounds of beating and the cries of pain. The sounds finally stopped and the silence of the black night became profound. I decided to go back inside the cloister and return to my cell.

When I turned to re-enter the cloister, I found the door had locked from the inside. Terrified of having infracted, I went up to the gate and pulled on the little chain and heard the familiar tinkle of the silver bell. I stood there in the moonlight waiting fearfully. I listened hard, but all was silence now.

Then I felt a cold breeze on my neck and shoulders. I shuddered. Then I felt a cold hand grab me by the back of the neck. I struggled, but I could not free myself. My heart was racing fast, and I felt faint. Yet, a shot of adrenaline made my strength greater than I have ever known it. I forced myself backward, then down and around.

No one was there. I turned again to look at the gate, and now on the other side of the bars were two glowing red eyes. I heard a growl—an animal's growl, from maybe a dog or wolf. The gate creaked open, slowly, on iron hinges that needed oil. The figure with the fiery eyes motioned that I should enter. I took a step backward and into a male figure who was standing right behind me.

It was the groundskeeper. He took my arms from the back and spoke rapidly in a language I took to be Latin. I was too terrified to concentrate on translating what he said. I wanted to flee, but I was caught between the groundskeeper behind me, and the wolfish figure coming at me through the gate. At that moment, I began to hear more screaming. Then, I must have fainted.

When I came to, I was lying on a small cot in a narrow cell with no other furniture or decorations. It was very dark. I felt very bare and cold all over. The only light was coming from the quarter moon through a red stained-glass window set high on the wall.

The door suddenly flew open. The Mother Superior and two huge nuns stood outside with lanterns and what looked like whips. They were clearly looking for me. Behind the nuns were two figures: the gatekeeper whom I had seen by the gate so long ago, and a werewolf-like man with red hot eyes just like the sisters had described as the gatekeeper's assistant. The male figures came past the Mother Superior and reached for me.

All I can remember beyond that is the sound of screaming. As I mentioned, I am Sister Helen, and I think I should know when I hear Helen screaming.

Body Wagon

The desert asphalt road was so molten that I fancied I could see the tracks of my old body wagon in my rear view mirror. With the air conditioner cranked to high, I figured my car was making three or four miles per gallon, max. Without the A/C, the black beast would be guzzling only seven miles per gallon.

Normally, it would just barely make the six-mile run to the cemetery and back to the funeral home at a stately pace of twenty-five miles per hour at the head of the funeral cortege. Today, however, I had to do a relo on a major artery leading into the heart of the city where the receiving convent was. The convent, from which I had picked up the coffin, was thirty miles to the south, and the late afternoon sun, always the hottest, signaled that soon the desert night would come like the shutters of a shade.

While I was on the road, I did not want the air conditioner or the engine to blow, or the tires to burst in the 120-degree heat because then, while I was waiting for help, the body in the coffin would decompose even more than I thought it had already done. Even now, the body exuded a horrible smell that gave me goose bumps.

I envisioned the kind of rapid microbial decay that would make the abdomen swell and burst with a bang, or the slow, silent oozing of putrid fluids flowing out through every orifice. Pardon me if you think I am graphic with my description, but I do not like to mince words about the serious matters of bodies. It had been a long night for me with another coming just after sundown, and I wanted to deliver my body and get to the nearest gas station before they all closed for the night.

The body in the coffin in the back was not making its first trip in this wagon. Three weeks ago, I drove the same coffin to the convent from which I just picked it up at three o'clock. My former friend Joseph, also in the body moving trade, got me the job, and I was thankful for it in these days of healthful living and supercentenarian aging.

He told me that if I asked no questions, I would have a steady thing with no risk. All I had to do was pick up a coffin when they called me and drop it off where I was told to take it.

"It's a piece of cake," Joseph said smoothly, with an unctuous smile.

If I did not think about it, he was right. Money was paid in cash on delivery, and I was always on time or early, so sometimes I got bonuses. Before I knew it, my body wagon was hauling coffins all over the region between all the religious houses.

The wages of my steady job with the funeral parlor could not compete with what the Church was prepared to pay, and the Church paid for gas, repairs and general wear and tear as well. When I received my LLC papers, I finally quit working for the funeral parlor and became a consultant body driver for the Church.

I say I worked for the Church, but that is not precisely correct. What I meant to say is that I worked for Father Corpus, a fat and jolly old mendicant priest with a cellphone and a thousand irreverent stories. At our first meeting, he told me that he would be my dispatcher and paymaster. He had a full-belly laugh and a twinkle in his eyes. His hand shook mine like a gigantic bear's paw. He gave me the cellphone that I used to do his jobs, and he always paid cash for my hire and expenses.

Where he got his orders and his money, I do not know or care. I was not particularly religious then, and Father Corpus confessed to me that he practiced religion more in the breach than in the observance, whatever that might mean. We had a partnership for hire, pure and simple, but he kept insinuating we formed a cabal. We were, he said, communing in an ancient, mysterious enterprise.

In my work, I see a lot of religious people because they traffic with the dead as a way of life. They are not the technicians that funeral directors are because, they say, they are interested in the souls and not the bodies of the people in their care. Funeral directors, on the other hand, are careerists whose concern is respectful preparation and handling of the corpse. They also are attentive to the feelings of the bereft if only for their future business's sake.

When I began my trade, I was instructed on how to dress and deport myself with serious regard at every stage of a funeral. I was drilled in all the protocols of funeral driving under stress. What impressed me was the masterful integration of the offices of all those many people who made it their business to process the dead.

In my reflective moments, I thought of writing a Book of the Dead for our culture that might rival the ancient Egyptian work by the same name. All those thoughts vanished when I began working for Father Corpus because I learned that not all the dead are processed in the same fashion.

The coffins I now drove never went to a cemetery or mausoleum. Instead, I drove them from religious house to religious house. I know this because I am a connoisseur of coffins, and I recognize a coffin that I have transported as you might recognize a fine wine by its label. I know for a fact that the dead who lay in my coffins never went to an undertaker, a funeral parlor, a crypt or a grave.

Imagine, please, bodies cycling among religious venues with no ultimate resting place and, strangely I thought at first, no prayers or religious formalities.

Today's delivery was an example of what I mean. The sister who showed me down a ramp to the cellar room where the coffin lay on an old oak table told me the time had come to make the transfer. She made no sign of the cross over the coffin. When she passed in front of the cross on the wall, she paid it no heed.

With her long, pure white hand she gently caressed the lid of the coffin as if the wooden form itself were alive and in need of comfort.

Then, as if she were coming out of a trance, she stepped back and told me curtly, "Get on with your job because you're late and have to get moving. You must make your delivery before nightfall!"

I was dumbstruck. I was not late by my reckoning, but I did not argue with the woman. The dead do not know time as humans do, or so I thought.

I pulled my trolley alongside the oak table and slid the coffin from the table to the trolley. Then I wheeled the trolley with the coffin up the ramp and out of the convent to my body wagon. I lock-loaded the trolley into position with the vehicle so it could automatically retract with the coffin.

As I had walked pushing the trolley, I thought the nun was right behind me, but when the coffin locked in place inside the body wagon, I turned and discovered that the nun had disappeared. I found it odd I was not asked to sign a receipt for the coffin, but I figured the Church trusted me to do my job. After all, I would not be paid unless I delivered the coffin to its proper destination. Besides, what would I do with a coffin anyway?

I shrugged, climbed into my vehicle and drove away from the convent slowly. It seemed to me that no human witnessed my departure because I saw no living thing except for a pair of huge, black boat-tailed starlings with their beaks pointed upwards toward the sky.

When I first started driving coffins with bodies in them, I got a frisson up my spine as when, by chance, I encountered the fresh carrion of some now unrecognizable animal that had been killed alongside a path in the woods. Some kinds of road kill had the same effect on me, and once when I saw a motorcyclist killed right before my eyes, I felt the chill and vomited violently when the rider slammed into a car that cut across its path. The rider was wearing no helmet at the time. When his skull hit the road, his brain instantly became a mass of blood, bone and a gummy fluid that glistened under the street lights.

Now, with what I chauffeured today, I felt only a slight nausea from the noxious smell that escaped from the black box in the back. I had no sense that the coffin held anything that might ever have been human. Its presence was repellent and abhorrent to me, but it was not challenging in the mortal sense. That's it precisely: the coffin was not a memento mori for me at the time, even though I thought it should have been. I felt vaguely guilty for my insouciance.

My mind wandered with thoughts about the dead and about the physical denotations of death. I must have been crawling along the road because the shadows lengthened quickly, the temperature dropped like a stone and night fell like a cerement over Phoenix. There was no moon that night, and the stars winked on in the blackness as if some great power had thrown a switch.

The nun had been correct: I was running late. I thought I would arrive at the convent within the hour, but then I heard a stirring and a thump in the rear of the wagon. I shook my head and became fully alert because I thought the coffin had come loose from its moorings in the back. I decided to pull over to the side of the road to check that the coffin was secure.

As I did so, the thumping continued and grew louder. It was the sound of knuckles knocking on a wooden door. My hair rose on my head and arms, and goose bumps formed. While I pulled to a stop at the side of the road, I resolved to be sure the coffin was in place and locked down. I got out of the wagon, and the knocking became rhythmical. At first, I thought it was the tapping of Morse code, but it was just regular repetitions of knock, knock, knock, and so forth. The only message I could derive was that something inside the coffin was knocking to get out.

I had eased far enough off the road that the nighttime traffic would have no trouble getting by me, even with the door opened wide. I stepped out of the wagon and went to the back hatch and opened it. I checked to be sure that the coffin was firmly in place, and the trolley was also locked down in its rails.

The knocking continued, so I placed my hand on top of the coffin and felt the knocking through the wood into my hand. I raised my hand, made a fist and knocked back in the same rhythm as I heard. The knocking from inside stopped for a moment. When I stopped knocking, the knocking from inside began again. I deduced that whatever was knocking must have some form of primitive intelligence.

I wondered whether someone was playing a joke on me. Could a nun have crept into the coffin to escape her cloister?

Could the nun who escorted me to the basement room have somehow gotten into the coffin while I was attending to the transfer? In any case, I reasoned that whoever was inside the coffin would not have much air to breathe. I had to let the person out to save its life.

I decided to remove the trolley with the coffin on it from the body wagon right there on the side of the road. The roadside supported the trolley well enough, so I looked for a way to lift the top off the coffin. Finding that the coffin lid was well battened down, I found my crowbar among the tools under the trolley assembly in the rear of the wagon and used it to pry off the coffin's lid. As I did this, the lid flew off, and I heard a great whoosh.

Then, I heard great leathery wings beating and then silence. I looked inside the coffin and rubbed my hands along the perforated silk where the body should have lain. The coffin was empty. I lifted the heavy coffin lid from the ground where it had fallen. I restored it to its place on top of the coffin and used my padded hammer to knock the lid back in place. Then, I engaged the trolley and slid it with the coffin into the body wagon.

I was in a quandary about what to do, so I drew a breath and thought about my mission. I had been tasked to convey one coffin from point A to point B. I decided I could still accomplish my mission. I decided to make my delivery as planned.

Around nine o'clock that night, I drove into the U-shaped driveway of the convent that was to receive the coffin that rode in the back of my body wagon. I found a small bell on a string by the door to the main building and pulled the string. After waiting for a few minutes, I pulled the string again. The night was still, and I could hear what seemed to be insects or frogs. In the dim light afforded by a bulb above the door, I made out a scorpion edging across the steps. I crushed the scorpion with the toe of my boot.

A voice from inside the grate that was next to the bell asked, "Have you brought the coffin?"

I answered, "Yes. Where should I put it?"

The voice did not answer, but the door swung open, and a short nun in her habit gestured for me to bring the coffin inside. I went to my wagon and extracted the coffin on its trolley and wheeled it into the convent.

The little nun preceded me down a long hallway, at the end of which lay a double door with a great lock. The nun selected a large key from a ring of keys she carried by her side, and she opened the lock with it. She swung the doors open and continued walking down a decline into an underground cavern with small enclosures set into the circular wall around the floor of the cavern.

The nun pointed to an empty enclosure and told me to put the coffin on the table that I found there. I transferred the coffin to the table and pulled the trolley out of the enclosure. The nun nodded and gestured for me to follow her back out of the cavern up the incline and down the hall to the front door. Instead of opening the door to let me out, she gestured for me to enter a waiting room and have a seat. She then retreated and left me alone with my thoughts.

As I sat waiting, I noticed the room in which I had been situated was furnished in Spartan fashion, with the seat on which I sat and a small table in front of the seat with nothing on it but a framed picture of His Holiness the Pope, a handsome male figure in his Cardinal dress. On the wall behind me, I saw the inside of the grate through which the nun had spoken to me when I stood on the porch ringing the bell. Aside from the grate, the room was windowless. It was also tidy without a speck of dust. The wooden floor was bare. One dim light bulb burned high above me.

When she came, the mother superior made no noise whatsoever. She was not there one moment, and then she materialized before me. She asked me whether I had brought what I had been instructed to bring, and I said I had brought the coffin that I had picked up at the other convent and conveyed it to the enclosure in the basement of this building.

She asked me, "Did you experience any difficulty in transit?"

I hesitated before I said, "The coffin was the same one I picked up. It remained on its trolley until I transferred it to the table in the enclosure in the basement."

She nodded. Then she turned and, over her shoulder, ordered, "Follow me and bring your trolley."

I did follow her back through the door at the end of the hallway and down the incline into the underground cavern. There she instructed me to use my trolley to rearrange several coffins from one enclosure to another. As I recall, I moved eight coffins in this way, but I could not see any essential change since the same twenty-five enclosures now had the same number of coffins. Only the locations of eight coffins had been changed.

When I had completed this work, the mother superior nodded with satisfaction and gestured for me to accompany her back up the incline through the door, down the hallway to the main entrance, which she now opened. When I looked back down the hallway, I saw that the doorway to the cavern remained open.

A flock of bats flew in through the doorway over and around my head, and they continued down the hall and into the cavern. I was startled, but the mother superior was unfazed. She handed me an envelope of cash as per my agreement with the good Father Corpus. She thanked me for taking the extra trouble and bid me adieu.

I worked my trolley into my body wagon and heard its latch connect. I closed the rear door and went to the driver's side, opened the door and swung inside. When I closed the door, I realized with a shiver of fright that I was not alone.

In the passenger seat was a male figure in a brown cassock. He wore a tonsure. He held up his bony left-hand index finger and gestured for me to drive.

He said, "I've been waiting for a very long time to meet you. I've heard many good things about you from my friend, Joseph. Have you seen Joseph lately?"

I told him, "I haven't seen him for a long while."

The monk nodded sagely and said, "I thought you might have seen him this very night on your way to drop off the coffin."

I assured him, "I would know if I saw Joseph or not, and I've definitely not seen him."

The monk said, "If you've not seen Joseph, perhaps you have heard him."

I shook my head and told the man, "I've neither seen nor heard Joseph this night. I know Joseph's voice very well, and I haven't heard that voice in a long while."

Then, I thought I heard the sound of a leathery wing, but it may just have been the sound of the monk opening his passenger window for a whiff of cool night air.

He said, "I've always marveled at the desert climate where temperatures can drop thirty degrees in a matter of a few hours."

We continued silent for a while, and then I asked the monk, "Where would you like me to drop you off?"

He said, "I'll go wherever you are heading."

I smiled and said, "I'm going home to sleep."

He said, "That's fine. We'll be working together now for a while, so we should get to know one another well."

This alarmed me. I told him brusquely, "I don't care whether we're working together or not, but I don't like close relationships."

The monk seemed to understand me. He said, "I don't like close relationships either."

When I arrived at my apartment, I parked the body wagon in the garage I had rented to store it. The monk got out and said he was going to walk around the neighborhood a little, but he never returned to pick up our conversation.

I went to sleep thinking about what had happened during that day, and I was confused and bewildered rather than enlightened by my cogitations. When I fell asleep, I dreamed of an enormous cave with bats hanging from the ceiling. I was a figure on the putrid floor of the cave, and I felt the warm droppings of bats like a rain of red blood in the night.

The next day, Father Corpus called early, and he asked me whether I had met his friend the monk.

I told him, "I drove him from the convent where I dropped off the coffin, to my apartment, but he disappeared upon our arrival."

Father Corpus laughed and said. "That's just like the monk: he'll appear suddenly and disappear the same way. The monk is always full of surprises." He paused to reflect on what he had just said. Then he changed the subject.

"The mother superior is grateful to have had your help rearranging the coffins in her basement. She was reluctant to ask the nuns to help her because she didn't have the machinery like your trolley to do the heavy part of the work. You'll now be working hard to fill the unfilled enclaves in the mother superior's basement." This was the first I had heard of this task.

"We'll be working on a tight schedule, and coffins have to be moved at the rate of one each day to be ready in time."

When I asked him what he meant, he became evasive and told me to focus on the hard work ahead.

As an afterthought, he asked, "Did the mother superior pay what you were owed?

"Yes, she did."

Father Corpus seemed to be satisfied. Anyway, he gave me my next assignment.

For the next three weeks, I had my hands full hauling coffins from every conceivable religious institution of the Church to the mother superior's convent in the center of the city. Typically, I would pick up a coffin late in the morning or early afternoon and arrive at the destination convent early in the afternoon or just before evening.

The little nun would meet me at the door after I had rung the bell, and I would follow her with my trolley and coffin. I would transfer each coffin to its designated table, and then I would be escorted back out of the convent with my empty trolley. The little nun gave me an envelope of cash each time upon my departure. I was happy making easy money.

I did not see the mother superior again for almost two weeks. I did not see the monk either. I got my instructions from Father Corpus, and I followed them to the letter. I always got paid in cash, so I asked no questions and had no concerns.

It was on the thirteenth successive day of my special coffin deliveries, that an agent I had never seen paid me a visit early in the morning before I departed for my job. He was a hard man, and he demanded rather than requested that I allow him to share the ride to the convent where I would pick up my latest coffin. He said he did not intend to harm me unless I did not take him along for the ride.

He said his name was Al Capito, and he showed me certain marks on his neck as if they were supposed to tell me something. I asked him to climb in the passenger side, but I told him I would have to drop him off before I picked up my coffin and that I could not see him again until my day's work was finished. He agreed to my terms, and we set off.

Al Capito said, "I'm a hunter, and my prey is vampires."

I told him, "I know the bats live in this area, but the real bounty is south of the border in Sonora, Mexico, where they inhabit large caves."

He shook his head and smiled. "Actually, they range widely in this area all the way to the four corners region, but I'm not hunting ordinary vampires."

When I asked him what kind he hunted, he gave me a look of surprise as if I should know full well what he was talking about.

Seeing by my expression I was clueless, he said, "I hunt human-like creatures that have been turned into beasts that thrive on human blood all over Sun Valley. It's a mystery where they dwell during the day, but at night they spread out over the land and find their prey.

"Repellant as it seems," he continued, "The more they feed on their prey, the more their prey became as they are." Now, he explained, the Greater Phoenix area was suffering from an outbreak of vampire transformations. Estimates of the numbers for the vampire population ranged from twenty-five to five hundred. He said that if the vampires were not stopped, they would take over Sun Valley. "Humans who are their food will become vampires at a geometric rate."

I was intrigued, and I asked him, "How do you expect to deal with any vampires you find?"

At this point, Al Capito brought out from under his shirt a pair of stakes that were needle sharp on one end.

He said, "I plan to drive a stake into the heart of each of the vampires until they all perish. The stakes I have are the only antidote anyone knows for the plague. My only hope is to find the sleeping quarters of the vampires during the day so I can ram his stakes through all their hearts before sunset."

We were approaching the convent where I had my daily pickup, so I dropped the man off on the side of the road and continued to do my job. I did not get the chance to ask Al Capito why he was telling me about his quest. I knew nothing about vampires, and I did not know how I could help him find what he was looking for.

That afternoon, I thought coincidentally, the monk appeared again in the passenger seat of my body wagon after I had made my delivery to the mother superior's convent.

He seemed to be very well informed because the first words out of his mouth were, "Al Capito has been to see you." I nodded, and the monk told me a story as I drove home.

The monk said I was lucky that I was still alive because Al Capito was actually a vampire. You could tell he was because of the marks on his neck. Those marks were unmistakable feed marks made by vampire's teeth that had made his blood flow so a vampire could lap it up.

The monk said, "Al Capito's strategy is to pretend to hunt vampires so he can protect them, not kill them. Anyone who knows where the vampires stay by day would be a mortal threat to vampires. By testing those he thinks might have the secret, Al Capito can eliminate anyone who might be a danger."

I felt very lucky indeed to have been judged an innocent, and I told the monk exactly what we had said to each other during our ride. The monk smiled and nodded.

He advised me, "Be very careful because your friend Joseph has not been careful, and he has become a vampire himself. That happened shortly after he recommended you for the job you now hold."

I shuddered to think of Joseph becoming a diabolical vampire, and I wondered how I could avoid sharing his fate.

It occurred to me only after the monk had vanished that he might have provided counsel about how I could avoid becoming a vampire. That night I had nightmare visions of a vampire feeding at my neck, and in the morning, I ran to my bathroom mirror to examine my neck for the telltale signs— but found none.

Al Captio was hanging around my garage in the morning. He wanted to ride with me again, but I said that we should talk right there rather than sharing a ride because someone had told about our riding together the previous day. I said it might not be good for either of us if we showed a pattern in our encounters.

Al Capito agreed and asked me whether the person who mentioned our meeting was a monk. I said the monk was exactly who told me about the meeting, and he seemed most knowledgeable about the quest and the motives for it. Al Capito smiled an evil smile and asked me whether I knew who the monk really was. I told him I only recently met him, and I did not know his name.

He said the monk was a famous vampire who was reputed to be over two hundred years old. The monk had come from Eastern Europe in the mid-1800s and feasted on humans throughout America, always moving from place to place using the Church as his cover. Al Capito said the monk was the vampire who put the teeth marks on his neck, but he had foiled the monk's attempt to make him a vampire by producing a token of his faith.

At this, Al Capito pulled out a silver cross that hung around his neck. He held it in the palm of his hand and said that no vampire could do that because of the vampires' fears of the power of the holy cross. He asked me whether I had ever heard the monk say a prayer or make the sign of the cross. I admitted that he had done neither, but then I had not seen the mother superior do either of those things or the little nun or Father Corpus.

He nodded sagely and gave me a silver cross on a chain to wear around my neck. He said it might save my soul one day. I am not superstitious, but Al Capito was so convincing I hung the cross around my neck anyway and pressed forward to complete my day's work.

I did not see the monk that day, but when I took my envelope of cash from the little nun after I had completed my delivery, I let my cross fumble out of my shirt to gauge her reaction to it. She might have averted her eyes, but perhaps she only nodded at the sight of the cross and then she retraced her steps. I thought she mumbled something about getting back to her duties and needing to talk with the mother superior about something important.

The next morning, I heard nothing from Father Corpus, though I was sure that our schedule had not changed. Al Capito knocked on my door at around ten o'clock and asked to come in for coffee. I suggested that instead of coming to my apartment, we should go to a local Starbucks. That was all right by him, so we went.

Over coffee, Al Capito asked me whether everything was going well with my business. I told him that everything was going fine until he came along. He seemed to be alarmed by this news, and he pressed me for details. I saw no harm in letting him know what I had seen.

I told him about the little nun's reaction to my cross. I told him that Father Corpus had not called this morning as he had planned to do to give me my next assignment.

Al Capito then asked me, "Where do you drive your vehicle all day within Sun Valley?"

I told him the truth: "I drive it moving coffins all over from one religious house to another. I work as a freelance consultant, but I formerly worked for one of the best funeral homes in Sun Valley. A close friend recommended me for special work that's become my entire focus now."

Al Capito seemed to be very interested in my personal history, and he asked who had recommended me for my present job. I told him the man's name was Joseph, but the monk told me that Joseph had subsequently become a vampire. I laughed to think about the coincidence, and I pulled out the cross that Al Capito had given me and dangled it before his eyes.

The man was suddenly very interested in a woman who was sitting at a nearby table tucked in the shadows. He grabbed his own cross from his neck and went over to say hello to the woman. He showed her his cross, and she recoiled like a snake. She actually hissed at Al Capito and bared her teeth.

Before she could avoid him, he pulled down the green kerchief she wore around her neck to find the telltale marks of the vampire's teeth. He then drew one of his stakes and drove it through the woman's heart right there in Starbucks. The woman reeled and then became a puff of smoke.

Al Capito returned to our table as if nothing had happened. No one else in the Starbucks seemed to notice what had just happened. I wondered whether I had been the victim of hallucination. After I calmed down, I asked Al Capito whether I could have one of the stakes he carried, and he gave me three of them.

He said, "There will be more if you need them. All you have to do is ask for them."

That evening, I spent a lot of time surfing online, studying vampire lore. I must have spent four hours gorging on the lore, and also the hard evidence of vampire activity in the American southwest. I learned that there never was a time in the southwest when vampires had not been a threat to humans. Until recently, the number of vampires had been fairly constant because vigilantes had used sharpened stakes to strike back when their population reached a critical mass.

I thought that Al Capito might be an equalizer of the kind that always seemed to emerge when the vampires became too numerous and when the balance was about to tip out of control. The more I read, the more I became convinced of the righteousness of Al Capito's cause. At the same time, my bills had to be paid, and I wondered how long it would be before Father Corpus called me again with work.

The next day, when it was time for Father Corpus's call, I received a call from my friend Joseph, who wanted to meet on an urgent matter that he could not discuss over the phone. I asked him to meet me at the Starbucks where I had met Al Capito, and Joseph agreed. He said he would be sitting at a table in the back of the place where we could talk without being conspicuous. So we met at the same table where the woman vampire had been slain by the stake of Al Capito.

That was so coincidental that when I reached out my hand to shake Joseph's, I held my cross in my hand. When Joseph gripped my hand and felt the cross, he might have been given a 50,000-volt charge. He bucked and dropped into his seat holding his right arm as if I had shocked it. I thought his palm smoked.

He looked up at me with such malice, I could not restrain myself. I drew one of my stakes from my belt and thrust it deep into Joseph's chest. He worked his jaws, and I saw his fangs. He writhed against the stake, but then, like the woman the day before, he disappeared in a cloud of smoke.

The monk had been correct: Joseph had been turned into a vampire. He was sent to try to convert me. He had failed. I was sorry to have had to eliminate my old friend, but he was no longer the man he was when I knew him. As a vampire, he had become a menace to society, and to even his closest friend.

I backed away from the table in the shadows and held my cross aloft, showing it to everyone in the Starbucks. The patrons thought I was some crazy born-again Christian to flaunt the cross like that, but I saw no reaction that seemed the least suspicious. I went out into the street and put the cross around my neck so it lay outside my shirt now.

When I arrived at home, I carefully cleaned the stake that I had driven through Joseph the vampire's heart and put it back with the other stakes in my belt. Father Corpus called me an hour later with a late delivery order. He apologized for being out of touch, but it had been unavoidable. He said we would have to make up for lost time if I was willing. I said I was most willing and eager to do the job.

When I arrived at the garage to get my wagon, Al Capito was there.

He said, "I don't have much time, but I want to know whether you are with me or against me. I know what you did to Joseph. You hold the key to my quest, and if you do exactly what I require, we can together take care of the vampire problem in Sun Valley tonight."

I told him I was definitely with him. He examined my neck carefully to see whether I had been contaminated, and he touched my cross and asked me to clasp it in my hand. Satisfied that I was still myself, Al Capito outlined his plan for us.

He rode shotgun in my wagon to the convent where I had a scheduled pickup. He got out of the wagon before I entered the convent grounds, and he re-entered the wagon after I left the grounds with my coffin. On the side of the highway that led to my destination, he and I rolled the coffin on the trolley out of the body wagon.

I opened the lid of the coffin and there lay a corpse that sent a chill through my body. It was the monk, who appeared to sleep peacefully, only I could see the humps where his fangs lay beneath his sallow upper lip. Al Capito wasted no time but took out one of his stakes and drove it through the monk's heart. The monk seemed to come to life for a moment with a look of total surprise on his face.

He grabbed the stake with both his hands and tried to push it out, but Al Capito pushed his hand down hard. The monk vampire perished with a whistle and became smoke. Al Capito wrapped himself in the monk's now empty garment and climbed into the coffin. I laid the crowbar in the coffin with him so he could do what he planned to do at the convent. I then restored the lid of the coffin but did not hammer it closed.

Al Capito could push the lid off easily when it was time to do so. Then, I reloaded the trolley and the coffin in the body wagon and drove to the mother superior's convent. There, I went through the same process that I did with all the other coffins. Once I had situated the coffin on the table in the last enclosure in the cavernous subterranean location, I followed the little nun back to the entrance, received my envelope of cash and departed.

I returned to my apartment apprehensive about what was going to happen next. I had left Al Capito in what he thought was the central repository of vampires in Sun Valley. I had no idea what risks he was running into or what would happen to me if things went awry.

At midnight, I was dreaming of vampires taking over Greater Phoenix when I received a call on my cellphone. It was Father Corpus asking whether he could drop by in a few minutes to talk. He said he knew it was extraordinary to see me, but he thought there was something I needed to know before the morning light.

I could not refuse him, so he came, and we had coffee at my kitchen table. When I had made and poured the coffee, I asked Father Corpus why it was so urgent for him to see me. He had an uncharacteristically wild look in his eye when he said that tonight would determine whether good or evil ruled in the world. I remarked that it was perhaps extreme to place the primacy of good or evil on a single night or a single action. He said that everything depended on what happened at the convent where I had delivered all the coffins.

I asked Father Corpus what he meant. He was quite open with me.

He said, "I know you've been placed between two great forces for good and evil. On the one hand, is the figure you know as the monk. On the other hand, is the figure you know as Al Capito. For the moment, it appears Al Capito has the supremacy because he thinks the monk perished under the stake he drove into the vampire monk's heart.

"Yet the ways of evil are devious and profound." He said this with such conviction that I could not help but draw out my cross and dangle it in front of the priest.

He and I drew from our belts the same stakes at the same time, but I was faster than he, and he perished right at the table.

His smoke smelled like brimstone. I picked up his stake, which had fallen to the ground, and I discovered that it was identical in every respect to my own. I washed them both and stuck them in my belt. I now knew what I needed to do with the rest of this night because I had finally discovered both the riddle and the answer to it.

I was glad to have gassed up my body wagon because I did not know how far I would have to drive once my job had been completed. For the first time, I drove not to some remote religious house and then to the mother superior's convent; instead, I drove directly to my destination. There, I rang the bell and waited—and waited. Finally, the little nun sleepily spoke through the grate.

She asked, "Who's calling at this ungodly hour?"

I told her, "I need a receipt for the coffins that I delivered earlier. I can't wait an instant longer to receive it."

The little nun admitted me into the little room where I had waited before. She said she would have to awaken the mother superior. She turned to depart, but I grabbed her shoulder and forced her around to look at my cross while I pulled aside her vestment to see the vampire teeth marks. She shrieked and I stabbed her in the heart with my stake. She fell to the ground writhing and disappeared in a sulfurous plume of smoke.

I picked out the key ring from the vestment that lay on the floor, and I hurried down the hallway toward the door to the basement cavern. Suddenly, the mother superior appeared before me with her vampire's teeth bared. She seemed ready to spring at me, but I rushed her and plunged my stake into her heart.

She writhed against the stake and tried to drop to the floor to dislodge it. I held on and pushed the stake home again and then held it fast until she gave up the struggle and became smoke.

Now I unlocked the door and raced down the decline. There, I saw that Al Capito had pushed the lid of his coffin open, and he had pried open the other coffins and thrust a stake into the hearts of all the vampires that had been sleeping there. Twenty-five vampires, less one, had been killed in that cavern tonight.

Crouched on the floor at the center of the cavern was Al Capito, exhausted from his herculean effort and hyperventilating as if for another effort. I knew that the hero had only one final act to accomplish to make his night complete.

I stepped in front of him and dangled my cross in front of his face. He threw up his hands as if he had seen a horror, and I thrust the stake into his heart just as he was about to thrust his stake into mine. It was a very close thing, and Al Capito struggled with greater strength than I had expected. He perished and vanished like all the rest.

I picked up all the sharpened stakes that he had used to wreak havoc here tonight, and I carefully locked the door to the cavern as I left and finally pulled the outside door closed after I had locked it from the inside. I placed all the stakes in the passenger seat of my body wagon, and I climbed into the driver's seat.

Glad to be alive, yet now without a job or any prospect of a livelihood, I drove back to my garage and parked my vehicle. Then, I went back to my apartment, showered and went to bed.

As I fell asleep, I heard the thump and thump of small creatures hitting my window screen. It was probably bats, I thought. They could detect insects flying outside the screen in the dark, but they were so intent on feeding they did not realize their momentum would hurl them into the screen after they caught their prey.

As with those bats, so it was, I thought, with vampires. The last face I reviewed before I fell asleep was the pale white visage of the little nun. She knew that my stake was going to be the death of her, but she looked at my neck as if it was the most delectable thing in the world. If only, she must have thought, she could use her razor-sharp vampire teeth on that neck and feed, she would have died in ecstasy.

Pandemic from the Grave

By the time I received word of the flu outbreak at Brevik Mission, Alaska, in 1918, it was far too late to do anything but gather a mining crew with the right tools, proceed to the mission area, dig an open pit grave and get the seventy-two dead Eskimo bodies into the ground as soon as possible.

My crew had to do this without themselves becoming infected with one of the fastest-acting, most lethal viruses ever to hit the global population. Once the virus hit anywhere, ninety percent of victims died within forty-eight hours after raging fevers, uncontrolled vomiting, convulsions, hot-and-cold flashes, and spreading contagion. We were being paid very well to do this in-and-out job, but what good is all that money when you are coughing and sweating with a high fever, and perhaps have only two days left to live?

We arrived at the Brevik Mission to find only eight survivors of the original eighty Eskimos. Why they had survived is anyone's guess. The survivors were in a daze of disbelief, guilt, and remorse for having withstood the ravages of a sickness like none they had ever seen. They could not account for their having been deselected by death. They had lost all their friends and relatives to the unseen infectious disease. This was no ordinary bereavement. It was post-apocalyptic.

The survivors could help us identify where the bodies lay, but they were reluctant to remain within the dwellings for fear of the contagion. The way I saw it, Inuits were survivors of a landscape so savage that it took all they had just to get through a single winter. Thousands of years of adaptation had produced a resourceful and frugal people who knew how to live with scant food for long periods. Removed from the general population, they were vulnerable only to disease. Because they had no regular contact with outsiders, they had developed no immunities. And because they lived close together, when disease struck, it took ninety percent of their population.

The Lutheran missionary at Brevik Mission was nonplussed; he had no explanation for the devastation. He kept saying something about the mysterious ways of the Lord, but this was little consolation to his decimated flock. In spite of his bewilderment, he was businesslike and efficient with us.

He and the other survivors had marked out the area where we were to excavate the mass grave. He showed us the area, and he said the grave area should be dug seventy-two inches deep. It was a large area of permafrost, not unlike some of the terrain that we had excavated while looking for ore. We pitched our tents, marshaled our gear, and spent that first night making our plan. The next morning after coffee and tack, we began to dig.

If you have no experience of permafrost, you do not know that it is an amalgam of frozen earth, snow, ice, and rocks. It is not hard like granite, but it in winter, it comes close to being that hard. You have to use your picks, and sometimes you have to blast. In spring, the permafrost is like a semi-solid lake that moves and swells. Houses rooted in permafrost can be heaved around. What is buried in permafrost can work its way back to the surface.

Our job was to clear that permafrost to the depth of six feet. After the bodies had been arranged in the grave, we were to cover those bodies, and then fill in the grave with the permafrost we had just dug out. The process was complicated by the configuration of the bodies since some were in an advanced stage of rigor mortis and others had been placed outside in the elements. Handling of the bodies themselves was not something we looked forward to, but we were assured by the minister that he and the survivors would be helping with that part of the task.

We worked rapidly on the excavation while the minister and survivors staged the bodies in a defined area, each one covered with a simple white sheet. The plan was to mark the mass grave with a cross at each end. The minister would take care of those markers. He continually emphasized that we were doing holy work, that the ground was holy ground, and that the bodies must be given every sign of respect. My team of mining engineers just wanted to know the rules for what we were doing. We did not care about the names of each former person whose remains we were interring, or about the offices of the dead that the minister intended to perform to consecrate the site.

It was soon evident that our labor doing the excavation might take more time than the few days that the plague had taken to kill the seventy-two Inuits. This was a sobering thought—memento mori. The plague seemed almost biblical to us. Without effort, and in less than a week—five days, to be precise, the invisible scourge had leveled ninety percent of the town's population.

Only with a great deal of effort, and significant time, would my team and I be able to complete our job. Meanwhile, news of the continuing plague came to us with staggering numbers of losses around the world. No lonely island, no desert area, no walled city was immune to the onslaught of the pestilence. Medicine had no answers. Clergy had no answers. Whenever contact was made, the plague infiltrated and began to kill. When the killing was done, people had to bury their dead in mass graves as best they could.

We completed our first day of digging, and we finally understood the scope of the task before us. It seemed to us that we had only scratched the ground. We had all worked hard, so sleep should have come to us easily. Yet, being near all the dead and the pestilence that had invaded everything in that town, we were all afraid that the disease would strike us too.

I personally had continuing nightmares. I had worked above "the Circle" since the turn of the century in every sort of mining work, but this was the first task that brought to me the sense of vastness and isolation of this frigid landscape. I had seen the images that were made by the Eskimos. They were fierce and demonic. This plague seemed aptly represented by their fearfulness and rage. I feared the invisibility of the flu. I feared what I could not know or see. I feared for myself and for my team. Had we miscalculated when we agreed to do this work?

That first night in Brevik Mission, I heard the wailing of one of the survivors. It was a lost and outraged soul pouring itself out over the Seward Peninsula. I saw the minister go out into the night to find and console his parishioner. I understood why we should make every effort to complete our mission as quickly as possible. Our mission was as much to complete the action begun by the flu, as it was to do justice to the people whose carrion had begun to decompose.

We shared the food that we had brought with the minister and survivors. They were grateful for the food and for our company. Having been through their five days of hell on earth while death chose the many, the remaining citizens of Brevik Mission had acquired a dark, cadaverous look of despair. The flu had taken the young, the adult and the aged among them, without apparent discrimination. Looking into the faces of the minister and his flock, I tried to find some sign whereby I could understand why these few remained. They were like spectral figures that witnessed but did not signify.

The minister blessed the food and our work, and when we began, I stressed the importance of our working swiftly by my own efforts, by gestures, and by looks. I saw that my men understood as much as I did. We worked in silence, steadily, not to find a bonanza, but to achieve a certain emptiness or void into which we could pour some meaning.

We labored without stopping, except to relieve ourselves, to drink water, and to change tools. The small piles of permafrost and rubble grew by the hour. Our work took on a rhythm. No one slacked. No one complained. Even the two or three men, who usually grouched about anything, remained silent. No one cursed. Small pains from the digging, the lifting, and the hauling were forgotten in the motions that we shared to get the job done.

At the end of that second day, I thought I could smell the putrefaction of the dead. I thought in that smell lay the disease. By the time we retired to our canvass cots, I was convinced that the entire town had become redolent of the plague. I was beset with visions of those sheet-covered corpses, rising in the night to help the dread disease complete its mission by eliminating us.

The youngest of the surviving Inuits came into my tent for something. When I asked him what he wanted, he ducked his head and backed out of the enclosure, pulling the flaps back together. The Arctic winds blew fiercely all night long. My tent pulled against the tent poles. I feared that the wind would sweep the tent away as it had done on many occasions in the past. I had survived the bone-chilling cold—so cold that my teeth chattered uncontrollably. My bed pan, laden with hot coals from the evening's fire, had gone stone cold. The fires had been extinguished long ago.

Here on the top of the world, in a place where the dead outnumbered the living three to one, I dreamed of one human in four being called by death for the final accounting all over the world below. It was a damnable lottery, emblematic of what? The cutting, wailing wind was like the passing of a frigid spirit, or of the plague.

When I was a young miner in Alaska, I was once caught in a storm with such violent winds that my tent was blown away. I was with three other men at the time, and we realized that having no shelter, we would surely freeze to death that night. The oldest among us, the leader of our group, said that we should heap together and take heat from one another, using our coats and provisions as our covering. By daybreak, he said, the wind would subside, and we could take stock.

I was at the bottom of the heap of humanity we formed that night. I could barely breathe under the load, and my every breath seemed to etch my lungs. My feet were entirely senseless. I feared that my feet had frozen beyond frostbite. I thought my legs and arms would freeze, too. I still do not know how I managed to make it through the night. I kept awake the whole time. I kept silent. What was there to say?

At daybreak, the wind did subside. Of us four, I was the only one left alive. My fellow miners had frozen in the night. It was all I could do to disentangle myself from their corpses. Tonight, in Brevik Mission, the details of that experience came back in full color. Like the survivors among the Brevik Mission Inuits, I had once been subjected to the kind of experience that they had just endured. The difference was that I, being young, rejoiced that I was still alive.

The Inuit survivors, young and old, had no such sense of relief and enjoyment. It was as if they had died along with their tribe. I still remember the ice blue eyes of the frozen leader of my mining expedition, the man who told me that the winds would subside by daybreak. The eyes of the dead Eskimos were brown to black.

The days of digging continued and the routine had a calming, if not numbing, effect on all of us. Each of my team kept his thoughts to himself. No one picked a fight. No one complained that this or that team member was not pulling his share of the load. No one went on strike for additional wages in the middle of the mission. I did not have to threaten anyone. I did not have to touch my weapon to instill fear.

The missionary talked too much for my taste, but I figured that he felt guilt. Consider his conundrum: his faith and prayer could do nothing for his flock in the face of the plague. Even if he had used the Bible's book of Revelation to justify the pestilence as a judgment on humanity, the pillars of the world still stood fast. His prayers availed nothing from his parishioners' point of view. The first of the horsemen of the Apocalypse had not come. Many people had died. His God had failed. Lord help him, I thought, and Lord help me.

We raised that pile of frozen earth and ice, and our grave became well defined. We did not need to achieve rectilinear perfection, only the objective depth. We were soon ready for the interments.

I saw at once that the insertion of the bodies would take some careful engineering. The excavation left a wall of permafrost six feet high along the sides of the tomb. The residue pile was imposing on one side. We would have to lower the bodies, one by one, on a gurney with a pulley system. Two men would be positioned at the top of where the pulley was, and two at the bottom. Two additional men with guy lines would stand fore and aft of the bodies to keep them level while they descended into the mass grave. After I had worked the engineering on this, I drew up a plan and went over it with the minister. He agreed with my plan.

So one by one, we delivered each body to the mass grave. Once the gurney had been lowered and received by the men deep in the grave, the body was transferred to a position alongside the enclosing wall, or alongside another body until all the bodies lined up, all heads facing in the same direction and all feet facing in the opposite direction. We took utmost care to treat each body as if it were still alive. The minister was pleased with the process and our results. Even the enormously obese woman's body was engineered into position, her mound rising well above the others in their sheets—ominously.

The minister then said his words of benediction, and he led us in the Lord's Prayer. He went through the burial service by the good book. My team stood by, waiting patiently. The surviving Inuits stood impassive, intent on witnessing silently. The minister read out the names of each of the seventy-two victims, one by one. He could pronounce the Eskimo names—I never could have done that.

He then asked each of the survivors to say a few words. Each said something, but I could not hear them because they seemed to whisper in their native tongue. Finally, the minister took a spade full of the permafrost and shoveled it into the mass grave. The debris scattered randomly over several bodies. He nodded to me, and I gave my team the order to cover the grave.

We had discussed how we would do that, and we worked steadily until all the bodies had been covered with a thin layer of permafrost debris. Then we worked steadily to fill layer upon layer of the permafrost in the excavation from which it had come. We did not stop until we had completely filled the mass grave. We had more residue than was required to fill the grave, so we piled the rest on top in a mound.

As night fell, I asked the minister if he wanted to do anything further. He nodded, and without a word, he planted the two crosses at each end of the mound. Alone, he raised his hands and prayed as darkness enveloped the site.

We did not gather our things until the next morning. Since we had completed our work, I went to have the minister sign off our work order to signify that we had done what we had been sent to do. He did sign the order, and he thanked me for all the team. He seemed most grateful.

My team had broken camp and almost finished packing our tools when the young Inuit who had come to my tent in the middle of the second night ran up to me. He said that he had a gift for me. He pressed something into my hand. He then looked me right in the eye. Afterward, he fell back and walked away, not looking backward. When I looked in my hand, I found a figure of a walrus carved in bone. I still have that bone figure on my desk as I write this account, but I have no idea what it means.

● ● ●

"Jack, this is madness. You have no proof. Wild speculation will get you fired and could get you committed to an institution." Ernie was serious: Jack Horner could be dismissed and disgraced for making his discovery public.

"Ernie, what would you do if you were in my shoes?"

"First, I'd chill out. Then I'd ask for two weeks' leave, and take a much-needed vacation to relax and forget everything. Then I'd come back to focus on my research. Period."

Ernie never speculated and did everything strictly by the book. Because he never "went off the reservation," he was the perfectly trusted United States Army Medical Research Institute for Infectious Diseases, or USAMRIID, employee. He had been Jack's friend from his first foray into disease control. In fact, he was the Lab Director who had urged Jack to read the first-hand accounts of the Brevik Mission to get a feel for what happened during the Great Pandemic. Ernie's grandfather had bequeathed his grandson a bone walrus that was his memento of that grisly excavation and mass grave.

The horrific flu outbreak had sped around the world three times in 1918 and 1919 to kill more people than any other epidemic in history. At Brevik, an index case from outside the Inuit community brought a flu that everyone caught. High fever, splitting headaches, vomiting then dry heaves, chills alternating with hot flashes, parched throats, uncontrollable shakes—and death within forty-eight hours.

The flu seemed to spread not like a disease, but like an evil spirit. Ninety percent of the Inuit population of eighty had died within two weeks: men, women, children, infants, everyone—without discrimination. The accounts were so graphic that Jack had obtained permission to survey Brevik and interview any remaining relatives.

None of the eight survivors of the flu were still living when Jack arrived. The current pastor showed Jack the mass grave in which the victims had been buried by a special team of construction engineers. The mass grave had been opened.

The pastor explained, "They exhumed two bodies and flew them off in plastic bags two weeks ago in an Antonov. I thought your people were involved, because of all the protective gear they wore. It took them two weeks of hard digging through permafrost to get there, but they knew what they were looking for: a body that was still preserved enough to harbor the flu virus. Now, why would they want that? Heaven knows, we don't need another pandemic. My people are still superstitious about the last one."

When he called his office, Jack's alarm resonated among his colleagues at the USAMRIID. He asked the Director for funding to mount a special team to harvest what they could at Brevik, and also to discover the purpose and extent of a Russian germ hunt that evidently included the pandemic flu virus.

Jack phoned his wife Jill to say, "I'm sorry but I'll be out of the area for a few weeks longer than I anticipated. I'll let you know where I'll be. No, I don't know when this will end. It's important." That was all Jill could know because Jack's quest was now classified.

Jack's team of four arrived in Brevik to exhume samples from one corpulent Eskimo female corpse. Two of the team, Sandy and Alex Rhodee, both virologists, bagged and flew the samples to USAMRIID for analysis.

Jack and his other two team members, Mark and Ellen Filament, both bacteriologists specializing in epidemiology, flew to Norfolk, Virginia, where an unmarked mass grave had been opened six weeks prior by a Russian team. Again the flu pandemic was the target, and again Jack's people took samples and flew them to their lab in Maryland.

While the Rhodees coordinated viral analysis in a Level 5 Bio Lab, Jack, Mark and Ellen flew to Siberia, where they heard that a third mass grave had been opened, and finally they flew to Vanuatu, where the Russian team was finishing its work exhuming corpses from a cordoned cemetery. There Jack tried to interview the leader of the Russian team, Yuri Bogdanovich, but the man said only that his work was humanitarian, and that he was not privileged to speak about it to persons outside his team.

Jack, the Rhodees, and the Filaments returned to USAMRIID and met in a secure room to discuss their findings. Jack opened with, "Clearly the Russians are scouring the world for samples of the 1918-19 flu. But why?"

Alex Rhodee answered, "Two reasons, both bad, I'm afraid. They could be preparing to manufacture a biological weapon. They could also be preparing to manufacture a vaccine against the possible resurgence of the pandemic flu or against the use of a biological weapon that amounts to the same thing. It makes sense that they would develop both simultaneously, anyway." His wife nodded her agreement since they worked closely together on everything, particularly epidemic analysis.

Jack starts by asking his team questions to get their brains working. "So their 'humanitarian' effort might be partly true, but insufficient to explain the situation. How are we doing in our efforts to isolate the virus?"

Sandy answered, "As I emailed you, we have successfully isolated the virus from the specimens we gathered, and we are successfully doing our DNA analysis now. I estimate that we could have a vaccine within two years."

"Alex, how long would it take the Russians to manufacture a flu pandemic weapon?"

Alex said, "Anywhere from a year to eighteen months, unless they decide to do a down and dirty."

"And that would mean?"

"Two weeks? Perhaps even one day. All you would have to do is accidentally contract the disease while doing research and not observe strict quarantine."

"Give me a scenario."

Ellen Filament opened her laptop and connected it to the large screen display. Then she projected her visualization of her analysis of the spread of the pandemic flu if the virus escaped from USAMRIID as a notional example.

"All of the continental U.S. would be infected within three weeks, and with air traffic left open, the world would be infected within a month. It would make the recent ebola outbreak in West Africa look like an isolated case of sniffles. If the virus escaped from anywhere in Russia, its effects would be far less contagious, simply because that country doesn't have as porous borders as we do."

Jack said, "My wife, Jill, said she was getting a bug yesterday. What do you think?"

With a gasp, the team shouted the single word, "Quarantine!"

Jill was transported immediately from her home to a special hospital unit at USAMRIID for treatment and observation. Jack told her, "This is just a precaution. Don't worry. You always wanted to know where I worked, now you'll see it from the inside."

Blood samples indicated that Jill had contracted the pandemic flu, so Jack and his team were quarantined. Jill's condition worsened, and she became a textbook case of how fast this flu acted. She died within forty-eight hours under circumstances that Jack now understood in all dimensions, particularly emotionally.

Jill, in the process, became a human guinea pig for pandemic research. All this time, Jack and his team exhibited no symptoms, and their blood work showed that the flu virus was not present. Jack wanted from the first to make Jill's condition known and to alert the people via the media, but the Director refused on the grounds of creating unnecessary panic. Five cases of possible flu in persons Jill knew well were quarantined at USAMRIID, but none contracted the pandemic flu.

Jack mourned for Jill, but he had little time to do more than bury her because he and his team were now in the thick of research to develop a vaccine. Meanwhile, Jack learned that the Russian Yuri Bogdanovich was no longer with the biological warfare lab of what was formerly the USSR, but a commercial bio researcher.

A friend in the CIA told him that the noted virologist and bio-weaponeer was still up to his old tricks. The Agency was watching him closely, because he was fiddling with a number of historically nasty microbes, such as the original version of the Black Plague, whose samples he culled from catacombs in southern Europe.

The Director quietly called Jack into his office, and he commiserated with him about his wife. He said that dwindling funding no longer permitted continuation of the pandemic flu virus research. He directed that all research be brought to a conclusion and made a matter of record, with all samples maintained in the archives. He further directed Jack's team to revert to their duties prior to the Brevik visit. Jack was about to object when the Director said that his orders came from the President of the United States. There was no further discussion.

Jack was burning with rage, but he called his friend and mentor, Ernest, and received the counsel that might have saved his career. Jack did ask for two weeks' leave and left the area—and disappeared. One rumor had it that Jack went to Russia, but no record of his having flown there exists. Another rumor was that Jack, despondent about losing Jill, took his own life in some private place.

The Rhodees and Filaments reverted to their former duties sadly, and they have always regretted not being able to continue their work on the pandemic flu virus.

Alex Rhodee put it well when he said, "Today we have a glimpse of a solution to a pandemic that could sweep the world. Once we box up our research, it will take a year or more to resurrect our project, and then it will be too late to avert a catastrophe. The gleaners have an advantage only when their findings are followed up with action."

In the event, Alex was correct to a point. When it came, the pandemic was far more impacting than the Filaments predicted.

The Creature from the Black Stone Reservoir

Arizona's Professor Michael Fortier was the world's expert in groundwater issues, so it was natural that the city elders of Phoenix would pay for his consultation about maintaining the city's water supply indefinitely.

Competition for water was accelerating faster than the growth of means to capture or recover and store precious water. Canals had been constructed to catch and direct the torrential rains that occurred during the annual monsoon periods, and sedimentation in the riparian preserve allowed the city's sewage to be recycled safely. Diverted Colorado River water was available, but in limited quantity, and the so-called prehistoric water deep under the city was being pumped to capacity.

The city had been forced to ration water usage during heat waves some had attributed to Global Warming, and to a degree, the price of water affected utilization. Still, farmers inside and outside the city limits needed water for their crops and livestock, and citizen needed to keep their lawns and gardens green. Although the agrarian-industrial shift was continuing, the city was known as a garden paradise, and the quality of life of its citizenry depended on the kind of foliage that only abundant water could nurture. No one wanted Phoenix to revert to the parched desert scrub from which this green paradise had risen.

The tradeoffs involving water issues were complex, but Dr. Fortier had worked with cities in China and Eastern Europe with situations much more dire than the situation in Phoenix. His specialty was to do "the impossible," and he did that in record time for the city of Phoenix. His innovative recommendation was to excavate what he called the Black Stone Reservoir to catch the significant rainwater runoff during monsoons, while at the same time to suck up the deep prehistoric water through gigantic pumps powered by incineration of the city's plentiful garbage supply and by solar power.

Essentially, the doctor proposed expanding the current riparian preserve by twenty-seven miles, but the reservoir extension would not be situated on the surface. Instead, the Black Stone Reservoir would be created by enlarging an existing and quite massive underground cavern system that would be filled from above with monsoon floodwater runoff, and below by tapping aquifers that lay deep underground. The design was the man's final effort, and it became his legacy.

By the time his design was funded as a city program one decade after it was conceived and approved, Dr. Fortier had died of old age. By the time the excavation had been completed and the symbolic ribbon had been cut by the city's mayor, three decades had passed. Within that span of thirty years, the original riparian preserve had become one of the biological wonders of the southwest, featuring more species of birds and fish than any comparable acreage in America.

The situation with the city's water supply had been impinged on many fronts. Water from the Colorado River was being rationed now for all users. Phoenix had grown from being the seventh largest city in America to the fourth largest, and it would soon be the third behind only New York and Chicago. From the air, an airborne passenger could see greenery and swimming pools stretching well out into what was once a sandy desert. The two pockets of contaminated ground water known when Dr. Fortier began his analysis now were fifty in number, and leaching from the upper ground layers to the deep aquifers was progressing at an alarming rate.

It would be difficult to justify the assertion that the Black Stone Reservoir had been completed "just in time to avert catastrophe," but there was no question where the rainwater runoff would settle when back-to-back hurricanes pelted southern Arizona shortly after the program's final delivery and ribbon cutting. Much of that hurricane flood water made its way by gravity into the reservoir, and the city fathers congratulated themselves on their good fortune at having constructed a place where water—that would in the past have just disappeared—could be stored for useful purposes.

One waterworks supervisor of Chinese extraction quoted the passage in Confucius's Analects about the wise finding pleasure in water as the moral justification for what had been accomplished. As a result of their reservoir, the citizens of Phoenix suddenly had no shortage of water even in summer's 117-degree weather. Some considered selling back the rationed share of Colorado River water to California because of the city's current surfeit, but wiser minds looked ahead to a future when prolonged drought might drain the reservoir or when the population reached the tipping point. Besides, all the runoff had not filled the reservoir to more than one-quarter of its potential volume. Although, theoretically, the reservoir was "watertight," no one knew for sure that its water would be retained or bleed off gradually through percolation.

Drains all over Phoenix fed the underground reservoir while, carefully guarded, one single massive entry to the reservoir led downwards via an incline to the water level, and all along the perimeter of the twenty-seven-mile-long underground cavity were leveled areas like terraces, off of which waterworks personnel could land and launch boats to take the samples that were then analyzed to assure the water's quality. Once a month, a crew in a motorboat would make a slow circuit of the underground reservoir to check the feed drains for problems on the inside.

Inevitably, one of the crew, who liked to fish, decided to troll a line with a beef kidney on a hook behind the slow-moving motorboat, and his reward was to catch an enormous river catfish. He released the behemoth and not long afterward caught another, which he decided to keep for dissection and analysis. Wildlife officials were bewildered by the catfish since they had presumed that no fish would survive underground. An article about the catch appeared in the Arizona newspapers.

Consequently, fishermen all over the southwest wanted to know more about the contents of the reservoir since the catfish that was analyzed was record size, and it had been dwarfed, the fisherman solemnly swore, by the catfish that he had caught and released earlier on that same venture.

The wildlife groups of Phoenix decided to open the underground reservoir for fishing. They required a special license and equipment, and they posted a game warden underground just inside the entry. All fish and other animals taken in the reservoir had to be weighed, photographed and then released. Exiting the reservoir, each fisherman had to subject his records and photographs to review by the warden, who kept computer records in a spreadsheet that was visible to members of the game commission and to citizens who paid a special fee to see them online.

The number and variety of fish taken in the reservoir in the first month after it had been opened for public fishing were astounding. Giant catfish topped the list of whoppers, but huge carp and koi were also taken. Snapping turtles with long necks and tremendous beaked mouths surged from the depths. The recorded and photographed animals made the reservoir a must-visit item on every fisherman's itinerary. Whenever fishermen explore a previously unknown body of water, tall tales about the fish that got away become part of the lore of the place. The reservoir was no exception to the rule.

The Black Stone Reservoir warden compiled a long list of the reservoir's fish tales because he had no idea what some of them might mean. For example, a fish finder with side-looking sonar detected numerous swimming objects moving underwater at great rates of speed at all depths. As another example, fishermen trolling with huge lures and high-test line had their entire rigs torn from their hands by fish that must have been larger than any they had encountered in fresh or salt water, short of the larger sharks and, of course, whales. As a third example, one fisherman also reported an enormous head that might have been a super-large snapper or an enormous beaver or otter. Whatever the beast was, it had raised its head beside the man's boat, but ducked under water before he could take its picture.

Where large numbers of fish and fishermen come together, some things happen that are very suspicious from a warden's point of view. One twenty-foot catfish had been bitten in half so all that remained were its head and tail, which were found on a terrace all the way across from the entry. The warden suspected that fishermen had brought the fish alongside and butchered it, but he had no proof that anyone had taken the fish's meat out of the reservoir area.

If a fishing party had decided to roast the fish and eat it on one of the terraces, most of the meat would have gone to waste. The warden, on random patrols, had discovered fishermen building fires and cooking fish that were supposed to be released alive after they had been caught. Citations for such obvious violations kept the number of infractions in check, though certainly they did not stop all fishermen from doing what they did everywhere else in the world. The fish and game people thought about increasing resources for enforcement, but their budget did not support that. Infractions continued with a wink and a nod from the authorities.

Fishermen eating fish was one thing, but fish eating fishermen was another thing entirely. Since the warden kept a time-stamped record of all persons who entered and left the reservoir area, in the fourth month he discovered that two fishermen who entered one month earlier had never exited. Since his records included the fishing license numbers of those men, the warden requested that the police check whether the fishermen had somehow exited the reservoir without being recorded as doing so.

A police check indicated that the men had been reported by their families as missing since one week after they were recorded as having entered the reservoir. Now for two weeks, the police searched the reservoir area for the two missing men, but they found no trace of either man or of the boats that they had separately launched off the entry incline upon their arrival.

When the police broke off their search, they posted pictures of the men and their boats on a bulletin board by the entrance to the reservoir and on the warden's website. A notice in the post requested information from anyone who had seen either man or his boat. From this time forward, the warden informed all fishermen upon entering the reservoir that they had to complete their expeditions within one month from the date of entry, or face a fine that increased every day after their limit had been attained.

When a third solitary fisherman disappeared without a trace, the fish and game authorities decided that no one would be permitted to enter the reservoir area to fish alone. Fishermen scoffed at this new regulation, but it did not decrease the number of fishermen who entered the reservoir. In fact, the mystique of a place that was dangerous brought curious and adventuresome sportspersons to the venue.

Two such men found, at a campsite along one terrace, the remains of the third man horribly mutilated, as if he had been torn apart by vicious animals that ate only part of him and left the remainder of the carcass behind. Police cordoned off the area, and the police forensics people went over the area and the remains of the corpse with a fine tooth comb. Clearly, the fisherman had not been eaten by a giant fish, but what had killed him and partially eaten him on the shore? The forensics team reported that the victim had been killed by a man or a large, predatory animal and then had been partially eaten by an animal with powerful jaws and long, sharp teeth.

Police homicide detectives preferred to opt for the man-eating-predatory-animal scenario rather than a human-murderer scenario because the forensics team had not been able to decisively rule in human agency. Now at the entrance to the reservoir was posted a warning about the possibility of large, man-eating animals on the terraces. This warning had the unintended effect of stimulating sport hunters to visit the reservoir to hunt the predators, but this posed a quandary because the fish and game people did not know how to classify the animal that was lurking along the terraces along the reservoir. Was it a bear? A wolf? A mountain lion? No one knew for sure because no tracks or spoor had been found.

Intrigued by the report of an unknown animal in the reservoir, hunters with weapons and special equipment arrived in droves to search the terraces in the underground reservoir with the initial working assumption that the demonstrably dangerous animal must live on land rather than in the water. The fish and game people were glad to have reinforcements in their search for whatever animal had killed the lone third fisherman.

The police, on the other hand, lobbied to have the reservoir closed off to all visitors until they determined what had done the killing and eating. The mayor decreed that the reservoir would remain open because city police resources were insufficient to search every terrace for the animal and because the hunters would provide the manpower that the police lacked.

Mayor Grimes also felt that the reservoir, like the city, had a large area with increasingly many people in it. Murders and animal attacks, regrettably, were normal occurrences everywhere in mankind's checkered history. He would not shut down the city on that account, and he would not shut down the underground reservoir either.

The mayor's comments, which were published in the local newspapers, could not have been timed worse than they were, because a fourth fisherman was declared missing on the following morning. The mangled, half-eaten corpse of the fisherman was found a week later, on a terrace on the opposite side of the reservoir from the location of the third victim's remains. This time, fishermen who were in the vicinity of the killing about the time it happened, came forward to say that they thought they had heard a man screaming and what sounded like grunting, slurping and cracking of bones around the time that the forensics team estimated that the victim had died. The two fishermen had called out to the victim, but got no response. They then tried to locate the distressed man by using their flashlights all along the perimeter to either side of the position where they heard the man's screams.

Since they were on the opposite side of the reservoir from the entry, they reasoned that trying to fetch the warden or the police would be a futile exercise, because by the time they reached them, nothing useful could be done. So, they spent the next eighteen hours scouring the terraces for signs of the victim, but they found nothing. There was so much area to cover, that they figured a best effort was all they could manage before they set out for the entry.

When they finally reached the entry, they told the warden what they had heard and done, and the warden called the police, who took signed statements from both fishermen. Police units were dispatched to search the perimeter on the far side of the reservoir where the men said they had been fishing. When the police found the remains of the victim, they cordoned off the area around the remains and called in their forensics team.

The results of forensic analysis were much the same as for the third victim. What intrigued the team was the location of the killing of the fourth victim. It would have been impossible, they thought, for a single quadruped to have done both killings, since the terracing did not extend completely around the perimeter. They thought it unlikely that the predator, if a mammal, would swim the long distance across the reservoir.

One extremely intelligent member of the forensics team, a very tall, lanky officer named Bekkah Roundel, was the first to postulate that because no tracks, spoor or hairs had been found at either of the two sites of physical mangling, it was highly unlikely that a quadruped mammal had done the killings. She theorized that whatever had killed the men, it had sharp teeth, sharp claws and no paws.

The animal sounds heard by the two fishermen who had been closest to the event, indicated to her that the killer had large jaws that were strong enough to break bones. She wondered whether the remains of the giant catfish that had been found by the man from the waterworks could be included with the victims of the creature. She also speculated that the first and second missing persons could have been killed in the water instead of on land and that their boats had been sunk by the creature in its process of killing the fishermen.

Continuing with her line of speculation, she told the forensics team leader that the killer probably lived under the water rather than on the terraces, because the majority of its food could be found there. She did not know why it had gone ashore on two separate occasions. She would not speculate whether there might be more than one creature of the same kind, though she did not exclude the possibility.

Officer Roundel felt so strongly about the creature's living in the reservoir water that she wrote a speculative analysis piece defending her view. She tested each part of her thesis against the evidence that had been assembled to date. Because hers was a theoretical exercise, it was not made public. Another public warning sign was added to the others on the bulletin board at the entry so visitors, whether they were fishermen, hunters or curiosity seekers, could not complain that they had not been informed of possible danger.

Over a week after the discovery of the fourth missing person, two fishermen who shared the same boat disappeared along with their boat, tackle, and weapons. According to their families, the two friends had set out together in a single boat on a two-week expedition in the reservoir to catch fish and hunt down the man-eating creature. Both men were experienced fishermen and hunters, accustomed to stringent and demanding wilderness conditions. Both were strong swimmers and dead shots.

Their families could not understand how any animal could have killed them both without becoming injured or killed in the process. One of the missing men had formerly killed a charging rhinoceros; the other had successfully hunted walrus, lions, and bear. Both men had gone diving in waters known to be haunted by great white sharks. For these reasons, their families continued to hope that the men had somehow survived and would eventually come home. The police were not as sanguine as the families were, so the men were classified as possible victims five and six.

As the months rolled on, other fishermen and hunters disappeared in the reservoir without a trace. By the time one year had passed since the record of the first two disappearances, twenty possible victims, and the two known victims had been tallied. The creature seemed to be focusing on killing people in pairs in their boats and destroying and sinking the boats in the process. Since the fifth and sixth victims, no telltale signs of screams or cries for help had been noted. It was as if some people were entering the reservoir area only to vanish.

Arizona had seen its share of prospectors disappear in Superstition Mountain, or expire in the dry heat of the desert and have their bones picked clean by scavenger birds, coyotes, and foxes, but the creature in the reservoir was now taking on the mythic and horrific characteristics of an Indian ghost. The creature of the Black Stone Reservoir was even becoming a tourist attraction, drawing fascinated visitors with highly technical equipment that might catch the creature on film, either on a terrace or underwater.

Two U.S. Navy SEALs were among the fascinated visitors, and they brought special underwater sounding and viewing capabilities. After searching the bottom of the reservoir with their special gear, they announced that they had found the sunken remains of eight boats, and they had taken pictures of something very large swimming through the depths that had characteristics of a frog-like man with webbed feet and hands. They had managed to track the creature on their display for almost five minutes after the first contact, but the creature was very strong and capable of making headway that exceeded the speed of the boat the SEALs were motoring.

In fact, the SEALs said they had never seen an underwater creature swim as fast or remain underwater as long as this one did. They were sure the creature must have some form of gills because no air-breathing animal could have remained beneath the surface as long as the creature did. The imagery the two men gathered was blurry because of the nature of the sensor, and there was no reference to verify the scale of the beast. The SEALs estimated that the creature was fourteen feet long and five feet wide at the shoulders. Its proportions were those of a human, but the head area appeared to be more like a reptile or fish.

With the police identification team and with the recordings taken from their own sensor displays, an image emerged that looked like a fantastical creature in a video game. The composite drawing might not have been very accurate, but it was the best that could be provided to the authorities under the circumstances.

Officer Bekkah Roundel had worked with the SEALs on their image, and her prior theory about the creature was borne out by the composite image. From her perspective, the trouble was that there was no explicit linkage between the creature whose picture had been taken and the killer. Suppose, she told the SEALs, the creature of the picture was not the killer at all but a red herring.

The SEALs advised her that the city of Phoenix should consult animal experts to determine whether any evidence of a creature like the one they had depicted had existed on earth before now.

Officer Roundel volunteered to consult the experts, but they were no help whatsoever. They said they required a specimen or remains of the creature before they could begin to assess what it might be. They asked whether the police could capture and restrain the beast so they could examine it.

One marine biologist, Dr. Ken Stevens, who had initially studied literature before he got his Ph.D. in biology, suggested that the only image he had ever seen that remotely resembled the composite drawing of the creature was a fantastical image of the fictional creature Grendel, the water monster in the old English poem Beowulf.

The archaic superhero Beowulf had killed both Grendel and Grendel's dam in an underwater battle. No one had ever seen anything like Grendel in real life, so it was assumed that she was, much like Nessie the Loch Ness Monster, the creation of a poet's fertile imagination. Yet Grendel had fascinated intelligent readers for well over twelve hundred years!

Bekkah Roundel was not entirely satisfied with this new thought, but it gave her an idea that she took to the two SEALs. She asked them whether they thought they could get close enough to the creature underwater to tranquilize it. That way, she said, the beast could be examined by the marine biologists. So if the creature was the killer, it could be put in a place where it could no longer do harm to humans.

The SEALs told her that they needed to confer with their superiors and colleagues to determine the best way to accomplish the mission of getting within range and tranquilizing the creature. They said they would study the problem and get back to her within a month. That probably meant that others would die in the meantime, but the SEALs thought that a too hasty attempt to ambush the creature, could be hazardous to their health without achieving the desired effect.

While she was waiting for the SEALs' answer, Officer Roundel saw to it that the composite drawing of the creature was posted to the now-crowded bulletin board near the entry to the reservoir. From images taken from their own sensor displays, a composite image emerged that looked like a fantastical creature in a video game. The composite drawing may not have been very accurate, but it was the best that could be provided to authorities under the circumstances.

Of course, the newspapers got word of the picture soon after it was posted, and they published it on their front pages. After that, the drawing of the creature went viral on the internet. Before a week had passed, the creature had a thousand names in thirty languages. Thousands of people worldwide claimed to have seen the creature close up while diving all over the world. For a week, the creature was a global sensation.

Then it entered popular culture when a creative computer game developer made an overnight sensation by featuring a 3-D version of the creature in an undersea action game. In the computer game, the single shooter in scuba gear with a spear gun hunts the menacing creature in the depths. The creature attacks and devours men in vessels and on land, and it is aware of its pursuers, which it defeats and eats with apparent relish.

Officer Roundel was not amused that the game rendered her real-world case ridiculous, but she reasoned that "the word" was now out in the public imagination. No one could complain that he or she had not been warned as to the dangerous creature's existence.

A boy and girl, Tim and Alice, both Phoenix high school students, unwisely decided to go camping on the terraces of the reservoir. They motored out on the black water and used a spotlight to find their way along the perimeter to the first terrace just above the water level where they beached their boat. Using torches, they broke out and opened their tent. The boy used matches, kindling, and wood they had brought to start a fire.

They sat in front of the fire, absorbing the eerie feeling of being exactly where they were—in a vast underground cavern with the reservoir's lake at its center. Sitting before the fire, they roasted a few jumbo marshmallows that Alice had brought along. Then they cooked some hot dogs on metal skewers with long handles. They fed each other as lovers will.

The boy decided to tell a horror story that focused on a creature that came out of the black water of the reservoir to see what two visitors were doing by a fire at the water's edge. Tim had reached the point where he intended to touch Alice as if he were laying a webbed hand on her shoulder. He thought it might be fun to scare his girlfriend.

Just as Tim was about to touch Alice's shoulder, he felt a giant webbed hand rest on his own shoulder, and he screamed when the savage strength of the creature crushed his shoulder as the animal then tore the boy's head off and bit the boy's torso through from front to back.

The girl, to her credit, had the presence of mind to scramble rapidly behind the pitched tent. She edged her way quickly back to the black wall. There, she hid in the shadows and watched in horror. She watched as, by the firelight, the creature slurped her boyfriend's entrails, and blood and bit one leg off entirely with a one-bite crunch and swallowed it whole.

She realized in fascination that the creature was enormous; in fact, it was twice the size of a very large man. It exhibited graceful movements that seemed human, except for their phenomenal speed and strength, which astonished her. The creature's head was as large as a steamer trunk, and it had enormous teeth that ground her boyfriend's bones.

When Officer Roundel interviewed Alice at the hospital where she was sedated, and under observation, the girl said, "The beast walked on webbed feet that I heard slap the ground."

Shivering and speaking in a whispering voice, Alice said, "I can't say what color the creature was, but in the firelight, it looked dark, perhaps green. The creature's skin was smooth like a frog's skin that was stretched over pure muscle."

Terrified by her memories, Alice told Officer Roundel, "I was so afraid the creature would come for me after it ate my boyfriend, Tim. It didn't do so, though it sniffed all around the camp site. When the creature finished eating, it strode to the water's edge, ignoring the boat, and dove like a human Olympic swimmer into the black water of the reservoir. The creature disappeared below the surface without a ripple and was gone."

Officer Roundel spent two hours with Alice going over every detail of her experience, and then she let the girl rest and called her SEAL Team contact on his cellphone. For an hour they discussed the latest developments and their implications for the plan to tranquilize the creature.

The SEAL said, "It's strange the creature didn't kill the girl as well as the boy because persons have been disappearing in pairs in boats. Alice is the first survivor and witness to an encounter with the creature. Is there any record of a female's disappearance in the reservoir, or of the creature's having ever attacked a female?"

Officer Roundel thought about this for a full minute; then she said, "The creature apparently didn't attack females."

The SEAL let this thought sink in. He then asked Officer Roundel, "Have you ever taken diving lessons?"

She gulped at the implication of this question. She replied, "In fact, I was a champion swimmer. I often take snorkeling vacations at exotic locations. I have current qualifications as a deep-sea diver."

The SEAL said, "Good. Then you are on the execution team."

In this way, the police forensics officer ended up becoming what the SEALs called their "mascot" on the unit that was tasked to tranquilize the creature. She did not know at the time that this meant her role was as the unit's Judas goat or sacrificial lamb. In other words, the SEALs intended to use the woman's apparent invulnerability to the creature as a tool in their plan.

They had no scientific evidence to back their hunch that the creature would not attack a woman, but they needed an edge in this unequal battle. Their plan was coming together rapidly, and it was based on the case of Tim and Alice.

They decided to provide a target for the creature that fit the profile of two isolated lovers by a fire on a terrace where they had pitched a tent. Lance Curlow, the captain of the SEAL team, would sit with Officer Bekkah Roundel by a fire.

Four other SEALs would take positions well back of the tent and lie in wait ready to use tranquilizer guns and, if those failed, to use lethal weapons to take the creature down before it killed again.

Officer Roundel told the men that killing the creature should be the last resort, but these steely-eyed killers and veterans of the Afghan War knew what kind of lethal opponent they were going to be up against. In their minds, the creature was a man-eater and a mass murderer. If the creature had been a pit bull, it would have been put down at the earliest convenience.

At the appointed time, the SEALs deployed in three separate small watercrafts. Bekkah Roundel and Lance Curlow gave the four others a head start of three hours in their black rafts with silenced motors. They were prepared to set up as overwatch at the back boundary of the terrace that had been selected for the operation.

Then, the couple set out in the same workaday motorboat that Tim and Alice had used. Lance and Bekkah followed the script that Alice had dictated to Bekkah in the hospital. They erected their tent by torchlight, built a fire from materials they had carried in their boat, roasted and ate marshmallows, and then cooked hot dogs on long-handled forks.

Lance even told a scary story about the creature in the reservoir and waited afterward for the feel of a webbed hand on his shoulder. The couple waited and watched the fire die, and they decided the creature would not be coming, though Bekkah informed Lance that he told a good story because he had frightened her.

Lance rose from the fire and went to the area in back of the tent to tell his companions that they would have to pack their gear and try another time. By the light of his flashlight, he saw along the black wall a scene of bloody carnage. His four teammates' remains were unrecognizable because they had been reduced to a jumble of bones and entrails.

Among the bloody mass, were scattered the SEALs' tranquilizer guns and weapons that had not been fired. Lance moved quickly to retrieve one of each item. Then he switched off his torch and let his eyes become accustomed to the darkness, and his ears become accustomed to the silence. He heard a rustling sound and then the snapping of tent poles as the tent collapsed. The SEAL made his way in the direction of the sound.

When he saw Bekkah's flashlight wink on and off, Lance caught a glimpse of the enormous creature hovering over the back of the female police officer, who seemed unaware of its presence behind her. Acting on reflex, the SEAL aimed the tranquilizer gun at what he guessed was the middle of the creature's back and pulled the trigger.

By the light of the gun's explosion, Lance saw that his aim was true, but just afterward he heard the slapping of webbed feet coming toward him in the dark. Then the slapping stopped. Lance heard a loud gurgling sound. Then that sound ceased. Lance snapped on his torch and saw that four feet in front of him was the creature, facing in his direction. He held the flashlight steady and brought his weapon to bear.

He was about to fire when the creature collapsed in a heap. Bekkah snapped on her flashlight and ran up to check on the creature. She ran her hands over the slimy beast's body and found a heartbeat. She announced that it had been tranquilized successfully.

Lance told her that the rest of their team had been killed back by the wall. He asked Bekkah's help getting the creature back to the water so they could tow it to the entrance. All the time he spoke, he kept his flashlight and his weapon trained on the creature in case it came out of its drugs-induced trance.

It took all their combined strength to slide and roll the creature along the terrace and into the water. Once it was in the water, Lance secured the beast to the motorboat with a line. He told Bekkah to get in the boat, and when they had both settled in the boat, he motored with the creature tied alongside to the entry. There, they called for police assistance to take care of the mess on the terrace where the four SEALs had been ripped apart. They also called for a flatbed truck to transport the creature as soon as possible to a designated area of the city's riparian preserve.

Lance stayed close to the creature, ready to shoot it in case it came to, and he had an argument with the police veterinarian who wanted to keep the animal alive no matter what. Having lost four of his men, Lance was not in a mood to let the creature live another second, but Bekkah's importuning prevailed. The rest of the police forensics team arrived to help Officer Roundel obtain measurements and vital statistics. They took photographs of the tranquilized animal when it was lifted out of the water by ten strong men and secured to the flatbed with steel cables.

When the creature had been bound to the flatbed and covered with canvas, Officer Roundel made a call on her cellphone to Dr. Ken Stevens, the marine biologist. She then forwarded cellphone pictures of the creature for his immediate analysis. Dr. Stevens received the pictures and immediately texted back one word, "Grendel!" Then, he texted that the creature should not be kept for very long out of the water. He wrote that he would be on the next available plane to Phoenix to examine the beast.

Official processes are slow, so transport of the creature took almost an hour. It was supposed to be lowered into a large, six-sided iron cage that had been placed in six feet of water in advance of the operation to house the creature in the event that it could be caught alive. The area around the cage had been cordoned off, but the press had stationed their telephoto lenses outside the cordon. Pictures of the transfer of the captured creature were broadcast worldwide in real time with stories the reporters made up out of whole cloth.

The mayor and police chief seized the opportunity to correct what was being said by conducting a press briefing about the capture and disposition of the creature. After Mayor Grimes had said his introductory platitudes, the police chief, and SEAL Team captain together gave the operational details, including short statements about the four SEAL casualties that had been sustained in the operation, and the crucial role that had been played by a plainclothes female forensics officer.

While they were answering reporters' questions in the foreground, in the background the creature was being unbound and lifted into the watery area of the iron holding pen. A continuous picture of the unloading process was broadcast as an inset to the main picture of the live press briefing.

The priorities of the news crews changed when the creature suddenly came out of its trance, broke free from the people who were guiding it into the six-sided cage, and dived into the murky waters of the preserve, apparently wriggling its way into the muddy bottom stirring up debris and mud that clouded the waters making detection of the creature impossible.

Emphasis in the live news coverage shifted from the sanitized official account of the capture of the creature to the live footage of the creature's dramatic escape. Now the entire broadcast picture frame was occupied by the slow-motion version of the escape of the creature. The creature's handlers had been flung to all sides as the giant beast shook violently, waved its arms and legs, and plunged into the water, which was its natural home.

A camera close-up showed the empty iron cage with its open door. Then, a forest of mics all trained on the mayor for his initial reaction to the escape. In the foreground, the mayor uneasily said a few words about the unpredictability of animals, while the police chief and SEAL Team captain rushed to the transfer site in a vain attempt to contain the incident.

The creature had been a comatose captive for a little over five hours before it escaped. It was now somewhere in the riparian preserve of Phoenix. Citizens were warned to stay well clear of the riparian preserve, and to report any sightings of the creature immediately by dialing 911. Police helicopters hovered overhead with riflemen posted in the openings. Police had orders to shoot the beast on sight. The National Guard had been called up, and the governor and mayor had requested federal assistance to hunt down and eliminate the creature.

When the marine biologist finally arrived to see the creature in the early afternoon, he had no more to analyze than the pictures that the whole world was privy to from the international broadcasts. He did take the opportunity to talk extensively with Officer Roundel, a keen observer who had actually handled the creature and knew all the details about its tranquilization and transport. The most important detail for him was that the creature had hovered over Officer Roundel for five minutes, while the SEAL Team captain was discovering the slaughter of his men.

The creature had not summarily attacked the woman; in fact, it exhibited no hostile intentions toward her at all. Of course, it had finally been distracted by the flashlight and tranquilizer shot by the SEAL. The creature would surely have killed the SEAL if the tranquilizer's effects had not kicked in, but the drugs' effects had not lasted as long as they should have done. Now that the creature was in the riparian preserve, it was no longer constrained by the reservoir with its single access. In a flash, all the citizens of Greater Phoenix were at the mercy of the creature of the Black Stone Reservoir.

While the National Guard and police surrounded the riparian preserve, Officer Roundel and Commander Lance Curlow had coffee and a pastry together in Starbucks.

Curlow said, "I should have seen it coming. I should have killed that creature when I had the chance."

"We are where we are. So what do we do now?" Roundel was dejected. Her mind was racing as she frantically thought through alternative courses of action.

The SEAL read her face. He said, "This whole thing has become such a circus, I'm not sure we can do much of anything. We have the media in a frenzy. We have every law enforcement resource surrounding the preserve, with the military coming from all possible directions. Adding two more to the mix would not do much to affect the balance." He scowled in frustration.

"I think we may have an advantage, but it's slim and risky." She was looking at her hands still working out the details of a plan that was forming in her mind. She drank some of her latte and looked him in the eyes.

"What do you have in mind?" He ate his oatmeal cookie trying to hide his anxiety as he was fresh out of ideas.

Roundel swallowed and pulled together her thoughts on the fly. "We don't know for sure, but the creature will not attack women. It had the chance but did not attack me. Ditto for that girl Alice. We also know that the creature can be tranquilized—at least temporarily."

Lance did not get her vision yet, so he became sarcastic. "So you're suggesting that we line the preserve with maidens with tranquilizer guns?" He drank his latte and sat back in his seat. He looked around at the people in the Starbucks. They were talking animatedly about what was happening in the street. Some looked at the SEAL with daggers in their eyes. SEALs were expected to be heroes, after all. Why hadn't he taken out the fearsome creature and saved the day? Lance felt humiliated and helpless. He'd lost his entire team with nothing to show for it. He wanted to kill something. His fingers balled into fists. He looked at her pleadingly.

Roundel, with a weak smile, sat up straight and spoke confidently. "I'm going to suggest something close to that. Look, I know you're upset that those four brave, young men died today. For a minute let's put that behind us. There's no way we can bring them back to life. Getting revenge against an animal is just not rational. It's all very sad, but it's over. Okay?"

He breathed in and out to relax. He shook his fingers and folded his hands together. "So what's your idea?"

"A great many military and police are women. So let's see whether we can get the authorities to put the women forward with torches and tranquilizer guns and the men in the rear with the role of overwatch with heavy weapons. I think that we should concentrate the majority of the forces in the direction of the entry to the reservoir. Whether or not you can get the brass to authorize this, I also think that we should have some more marshmallows and hot dogs before a fire built along that axis. It couldn't hurt matters much, and it's better than doing nothing. At least I think so." Roundel finished her broad outline of a plan and shrugged as if to say, "What do you think?"

He nodded and stood with all eyes in the Starbucks following his every move. He gestured for Roundel to follow him. They went to find the authorities to set her plan in motion. She vectored along the way to buy some groceries.

So the SEAL Team captain talked with the chief of police and the commander of the National Guard, and the officers and troops were redeployed exactly as Officer Roundel suggested. Meanwhile, she had bought some jumbo marshmallows, hot dogs, and firewood.

Coordinating via cellphone, the couple met where they had planned to build the fire just after sunset. They broke a city ordinance by building the fire in a public place, but the roasted marshmallows and hot dogs were very tasty. They broke another city ordinance by bearing arms in public. She had a tranquilizer gun, and he had an M-16 rifle. As a sign of their developing relationship, they used their first names instead of their last names to address each other. Lance did not tell a scary story this time; instead, he talked with Bekkah about the heroism of the four men who had died for nothing in this exercise.

"Well, Bakkah, if the creature comes to eat me tonight, let me say that it's been a genuine pleasure knowing you. You're the first woman I have had the pleasure of seeing things eye-to-eye with."

"Lance, I'd thank you, but you know that I'm not wearing heels tonight, and you're wearing those military hi-guys. So there's a reason we're seeing eye-to-eye." She gave him a crooked smile. He liked her spirit and wit, but a sobering thought crossed his mind.

"I'm afraid we'll never see eye-to-eye with the creature. Imagine being fourteen feet, three inches tall!" He took a bite out of his hot dog and contemplated the power of his adversary.

"In its soaking webbed feet, too. Did I mention that the creature has sweet breath, even after devouring the most of four SEALs? I mean it. The creature breathed over me, and its breath was sweet."

He had a creepy thought. "Don't tell me you're falling for this creature?" He gazed into the fire and watched the flickering flames.

"Well, it crashed our party on the terrace of the reservoir, and it was the tallest that arrived. I've never had a date that towered over me as it did." She was clearly impressed by the size and power of the creature.

"Seriously, do you think the creature is male or female?" Lance asked.

She thought for a moment and looked around in the darkness. "I'd guess it's male because it goes all macho man when it gets near men and it goes all gooey when it is around women. I got its goo all over me when I rubbed it down looking for a pulse. Of course, I could be wrong. I don't know women who get along when men are around. If the creature is female, she has a strange way of getting to a man's heart. I don't think a female creature would exclude female humans as victims. I'll ask the marine biologist about this when I see him tomorrow. He speaks of the creature consistently as if it were male. Of course, it could be bisexual."

"Bekkah, I'm glad you survived our close encounter. I'm afraid we all took too great a risk. I'm sorry."

"Don't be sorry, Lance. I was glad to be along for the ride as your mascot."

Looking behind her in the darkness, suddenly Lance's eyes widened, and his body stiffened. She was alarmed and almost swung around to see what he was looking at, but he raised his hand to caution her. He whispered quickly with an urgency and authority that made her hang on his every word.

"Bekkah, don't move. Don't ask me why. Just look at me and when I say drop, hit the ground. Okay. Now DROP!"

With that, Bekkah hit the ground and rolled over to see the creature coming up out of the water right at them. Lance fired his weapon again and again. Bekka fired her tranquilizer gun as well. Nothing seemed to faze the creature until it was two feet away. Then it stopped in its tracks. It stood at full height and raised its left arm as if preparing to strike. Lance aimed carefully for one last shot and put his bullet right between the creature's eyes. The creature collapsed on the ground.

Police and military came from all directions to see what was happening on account of the shooting. Lance yelled for everyone to stand back in a circle and wait until the creature could be examined for signs of life. Bekkah ran her hands over the monster, trying to find a pulse, but she found none. Her hands were gooey and bloodied by the time she stood up with a look of resignation rather than relief on her face. She told Lance that she thought the creature was dead.

Lance identified himself and Officer Bekkah Roundel to the scene area commander when he arrived, and he gave a preliminary oral report about what had happened. The Scene Area Commander immediately picked up his radio speaker and announced to the troops that the creature had been killed. He ordered the creature's carcass to be removed to a place that had been set aside for a thorough examination by experts. Finally, after he had received his orders from the Governor of Arizona, he ordered his troops and the Phoenix police to stand down because the emergency they had been called for had ended.

To escape the chaos in the aftermath of the death of the creature, Officer Roundel walked all the way to her apartment in a daze. When she arrived at her home, she washed thoroughly. As she did so, she watched the creature's blood and slime on her hands and forearms stream down her sink's drain. She took a hot shower and let the soothing water calm her troubled soul about what she had been through and witnessed. Only when she had dried off and dressed in her nightgown did she begin to work out what had happened that momentous day.

She received two calls on her cellphone. The first was from Dr. Ken Stevens, the marine biologist. He wanted to know the location where the creature had been taken. The second was from Cmdr. Lance Curlow.

"I just wanted to know if you're all right. I'm departing right away, but I want you to know I'll be back one day. I want to see you again, outside of business, just to talk."

"I'd like that, Lance," she said. Then she terminated the call because she had work to do.

The next morning, the media were in a frenzy to cover the events of the previous evening. Since Cmdr. Curlow had departed the area, the chief of police gave his version of events, and the police naturally figured prominently in his portrayal of events leading to the demise of the creature.

The carcass of the creature was interesting to the press, only insofar as the commentary on it by one Dr. Kenneth Stevens, a marine biologist who cautioned against speculating before a complete scientific analysis had been conducted after the autopsy that was now underway. All he could say definitively at present was that the creature was dead and that its remains were different from any other remains he had ever seen. He likened the creature's appearance to that of the coelacanth, the fish whose first appearance in sixty-five million years had occurred on October 18, 1974, after which date other live specimens were found, proving that nature had mysterious ways of hiding things from the scientific community.

Not immediately reported in the media because they were exhausted from covering the death of the creature, was the mysterious disappearance of a pair of fishermen in the Black Stone Reservoir two weeks after the death of the creature. Neither their bodies nor their boat was ever found.

Only Officer Bekkah Roundel took notice of this unnerving coincidence, and she posted another notice about it on the bulletin board just inside the entry to the Black Stone Reservoir. It might be the beginning of a new pattern, she thought, and then again it might not be. At any event, she would discuss the matter soon with Comander Lance Curlow, who was going to route his air travel from Dam Neck to San Diego through Phoenix and have dinner with her at Ruth's Chris Steak House next week.

She was determined not to wear her heels to dinner that evening because she did like looking that man in the eye. He had mentioned something about possibly staying over in Phoenix for the night if he could find lodging, but she would see about that. Their last date lingered in her memory, and she wanted to discover whether she could stand intimacy with the man who had helped her stop a monster. In her mind, men and monsters had a lot in common.

The Sand Man's Henchman

The henchman thought that the doctor hovered over his experiment like a spider over a fly, too intent on the chemistry apparatus to pay any attention to his latest live specimen, who was just coming to on the metal gurney in the center of the room. He watched as the distillate beaded around the edges of the retort, then slid down to find the pool at the bottom.

The doctor turned a cock and watched as the distillate made its way through the tubing to a mixing vat, whose contents were blood red in color. As the distillate hit the contents, the color changed to orange and the liquid bubbled. A broad smile came over the doctor's usually severe face. The liquid was ready for the injections to begin.

The beautiful woman on the gurney thought she was in the middle of a nightmare from which she would surely awaken very soon. She saw the doctor insert a large syringe into a vessel containing an orange liquid and draw a large portion of it by pulling on a plunger. She was fascinated at the ugliness of the man. He had the kind of blind intensity that marked the genius, but his movements were mechanical as if he were a machine.

She looked from side to side to determine where she was, but she was not reassured to find herself in a large laboratory with a high roof, odd chemistry equipment, and manikins and contraptions for which she could see no purpose. Her eyes focused on a figure standing in the shadows, watching everything the doctor was doing. It was the man or monster she saw just before she passed out. If the doctor was evil personified and ugly as the sins he perpetrated, this monster was the devil himself.

The monster was taller than the tallest man Sharon, the woman on the gurney, had ever seen. He must have been eight or nine feet tall and as wide as a doorway. She recalled that she saw the monster duck and turn sideways to get into the elevator she was taking from the twelfth floor to the ground. She did not step outside the elevator car, but stayed in the corner alone, hoping that the creature would exit at another floor during the elevator's descent.

Instead, it turned and slowly took out a bottle of chloroform, sprinkled it liberally over a handkerchief. It then grabbed her left shoulder with his enormous left hand while it placed the cold, wet handkerchief over her mouth and nose and held it there with a strength she could not resist. She had passed out, and now she was in this hellish laboratory.

Perhaps there had been a mistake, she thought. But as the doctor turned to her with his syringe, she knew there had been no mistake at all. She was intended to be used in some repellent way, but her restraints allowed her no movements. She struggled and writhed as tears streamed down her face. She felt the doctor's hands on her arm. Swabbing her arm with a cotton swab, he was clearly looking for a vein.

She felt the prick of the needle and a burning sensation as the substance entered her bloodstream. She tried to pull her arm back before the entire syringe had been emptied into her system, but she discovered she could not move a millimeter. Enormous hands held her arm steady, and the two brown, soulless eyes of her captor bore down into her eyes as if to say, "Be still, or it will be the worse for you!"

Before she passed out again, she screamed at the top of her lungs. She shrieked and cursed until her head suddenly dropped lifeless on the gurney. Her body twitched. Then, the body lay still and lifeless.

The doctor nodded because he had more data. He turned to the monster that still held the woman's arm, and he said, "Find me another. We are very close. I must have another soon. You must bring her here to me. Now, take the restraints from this specimen, strip her of all her clothing and jewelry, and deliver her remains to our old friend in the anatomical lab. Quickly now, move. You have done well. Do as I say and you will be richly rewarded."

The monster took off the restraining straps of the lifeless woman, effortlessly lifted the dead weight, and carried it out of the laboratory, while the doctor made notes in his ledger about his experiment. The doctor resolved to add one additional chemical to the mix and to begin the next phase of his experiment in the morning after he taught his graduate students about biochemical innovation for physiological improvement. He mused that the experiments he was doing would revolutionize the field of medicine, but the results would probably not be ready for presentation at an exposition at the 1930 World's Fair as he had originally intended.

Perhaps his results would be ready for the 1934 World's Fair, but that would mean stepping up his schedule. His experiments could not be published in the standard journals that had published all his basic work on his experiments with lower primates before he began his work with human subjects. He had generated interest among eccentrics and geriatrics who would naturally be interested in formulae for increasing human longevity.

No one so far had suspected where his research had been heading, and that was by the doctor's intention. The university was certainly not going to support his studies — the very idea would be repugnant to the university's regents. So the distinguished doctor had done what any genius entrepreneur would do — improvise!

He had used his substances on fifteen human subjects thus far, all with the same result: death. Edison had said that he only discovered the light bulb after a thousand failures. That left the doctor 985 more experiments, at least. Maybe he would be luckier than Edison. Only time would tell.

The doctor's henchman, carrying his nude specimen over his shoulder, stopped at a closet where the body sacks were ranged. He selected a sack that would contain the body he held. Then, he carefully inserted the woman's nude body into the sack, pulled the drawstring and hefted the sack with the woman inside it. He walked with the sack hung over his back. His right hand held the neck of the sack. He thought he still might have time to meet his friend at the anatomy lab before daylight. In fact, the old former mortuary employee was ready and waiting for him to deliver the specimen.

"I'm glad you were able to deliver a specimen. The anatomy professor needed a fresh corpse for the anatomical lab this afternoon. Here is the payment in gold coins, as usual. Tell your employer we could use one more specimen a week until next November, at least. The same rates will apply. If you would be so good as to place the specimen on the anatomical table so I can roll it straight into the theater, I would appreciate it. The professor will be absolutely delighted."

The doctor's henchman lifted the dead woman from the sack and placed her face-up on the anatomical table, as he had for so many other specimens. He would have liked to comb her hair and clean up where she had soiled herself in dying, but her beauty and decorum was of no concern to the anatomy professor's lab assistant.

As the henchman departed from the anatomy theater, he heard at his back the snap and crunch of shears cutting open the woman's sternum and chest cavity. He knew that the anatomist's assistant would lay open the chest cavity so the anatomy professor could begin where he planned to begin. The henchman did not care about what would happen after his successful delivery of the fresh body. He left looking for another victim, because his master wanted it, and because he never failed his master in anything.

The doctor's henchman was not a normal procurer. Other procurers might have wanted to haunt morgues for the Jane Does that popped up and to bribe mortuary officials to relieve them of the necessity of burial expenses for the bodies.

The henchman knew the dangers of involving others in this phase of his work. He preferred, anyway, to make his own selections because he knew what his doctor wanted, and he knew that what he delivered would be accepted by his master, who was a connoisseur of human bodies. This the doctor had proved on many occasions. Had he not personally sampled the sexual wares of some of his female specimens before they had revived from their anesthetic and pronounced them superb?

So the henchman went on the hunt again during the next day, and he had no problem locating his next victim because the city was full of beautiful, single women who would serve the purpose. Chicago thrived on secretaries whose lives were patterns that could be used by observant procurers like him.

On his short list, was a woman named Dalia, who worked as a legal secretary at a major law firm. She was in her mid-twenties, beautiful and for some reason unattached. Those were the criteria demanded by the doctor because he was always careful not to disrupt a happy family. He focused instead on women who had somehow been rejected or ignored in the natural selection process. His taking them out of the breeding chain was therefore not an intrusion on natural selection, but the perfection of it.

The henchman understood the basics of what his doctor was saying, but he reasoned that he had a place in the selection chain too. His penchant was for beautiful women who would have been repulsed to breed with him. Those, he thought, deserved whatever was coming to them. If they died and ended up in the anatomical theater, so much the better for them and their otherwise worthless lives. He was doing them a favor to give them the opportunity to advance science or to advance the budding young physicians that would surgically operate on the general populace.

The next prospective specimen, like her predecessor, left her office late that day, because she was the last one to lock up the office before she went home for the evening to an otherwise empty apartment and an empty life—except for what she experienced through the radio, which was her way of imagining the world.

She was exhausted when she came into the Otis elevator, and she did not think twice about turning her back to the enormous figure that occupied the car already. When she felt the cold, wet cloth over her nose and mouth, she also felt the enclosure of the enormous hands of the henchman. If she had wanted to cry out or try to defend herself, she would have been no match for her assailant. She was unconscious when the elevator was diverted from its course to the first floor and ended at the sub-basement level, where the henchman carried her to his waiting car.

The henchman arranged the new specimen's body on the awaiting gurney so the doctor could perform his experiment on her. The henchman wheeled the gurney into the lab and stood beside it, while the doctor completed his chemical preparations. The doctor paused in his work to examine the specimen, and he apparently liked what he saw because he ordered his henchman to disrobe the specimen so he could observe her in intimate detail.

The henchman knew what his master liked, so he did this rapidly so the woman did not come out of her chloroform trance until she had been restrained as she was before she had been disrobed. The doctor took his time examining the specimen, and he asked the henchman to stand outside the room while he continued his examination. When the henchman returned, he was asked to rebind the woman and stand back while the doctor did his injection.

This time, in distinction from the last experiment, the liquid in the syringe was bluish red, and when it streamed into the specimen's bloodstream, the specimen did not expire at once. Instead, she seemed to look more youthful and become animated. She twisted in her bindings, but she writhed like a woman in heat. The doctor seemed aroused by what he saw and kept his eyes fixed on the woman's face for signs of her recovery from the chloroform. In fact, the woman came to and looked appetitive, gazing yearningly into the doctor's eyes.

The doctor asked the henchman to stand outside the lab once more, and after a long while, the doctor called the henchman back into the room. There on the gurney lay the nude specimen looking at the henchman with a longing that meant only one thing. The doctor gestured for his henchman to do what was necessary. So the henchman took off his clothes, apparently was ready in every respect to join with the specimen and was about to climb onto the gurney when the doctor decided to apply a second dose of his injection to the specimen beforehand.

When the fluid had been administrated, the specimen writhed and arched her body. Her face turned appealing to the henchman to do what he could to appease her appetite. So the henchman did what he could, and he remained above the woman on the gurney for a very long time. She finally arched and lifted the enormous body above her. She wailed and moaned and accepted him within her, and then she collapsed and died with a smile on her face.

The doctor was an objective observer of all that had happened. He used a stethoscope to determine that the specimen had expired. Then, without an extraneous comment, he washed and dressed slowly, and then ordered his henchman to dispose of the corpse in the usual way. The henchman washed and dressed, and then he threw the lifeless woman's body over his shoulder and bagged her before he took the bag to the anatomical assistant, who was eagerly awaiting his arrival.

This time, the assistant remarked on the beautiful color of the specimen, who seemed in the prime of life except that she was clearly dead. He also remarked on her expression, which to him, seemed ecstatic. The henchman simply shrugged, accepted his remuneration and departed. As he left, he heard the signature crunching that meant that the anatomical assistant was opening the chest cavity of the specimen for the afternoon's anatomy theater lesson.

The henchman smiled when he thought how much more enjoyable his own sampling of the specimen had been than the dull third-party dissection that the medical students would have that afternoon. This gave the man an idea that he had not previously entertained, but he did not immediately think through its implications. To satisfy his patron, he did not need to think at all.

In fact, his benefactor had importuned him not to think. The doctor only wanted his specimens. He was, in many respects, like the anatomical assistant who also only wanted his specimens. The henchman was the connecting link, but for them, he was a cipher. He was only their delivery boy working for gold coins.

The doctor's henchman gradually began to see a way that he could improve his own life while doing what he had always done to satisfy the doctor and the anatomist's assistant. He had never been successful with women because he was huge, hairy, ugly and repulsive. Some women had told him that he stank. Others had told him that his face was abhorrent. Now he saw that the way to get what he wanted from women lay in chloroform and subterfuge. So his plans changed, and his manner of delivery accommodated his new vision of himself. He began to take advantage of the time while his specimens were under the influence of chloroform. He was therefore still able to deliver his specimens to the doctor and after he was done with them, to the anatomist's assistant. His next specimen was a case in point.

The doctor's henchman was wary of using elevators after having repeatedly done that kind of thing. Instead, he stalked his specimens to their apartments where he approached them from their backs as they opened their doors. This broke the pattern he had established, but it opened many other issues.

For example, it opened the possibility that the specimen had roommates or temporary lovers. In this case, the lonely woman specimen lived alone and was a recluse. When the henchman applied the chloroform, he smelled her Chanel No. 5 perfume, and he remembered a girl he had once known long ago. He almost left his specimen on her doorstep asleep, but instead he stiffened his resolve and carried the specimen to the basement parking lot where his car was parked. He bundled her into his car and drove her to a motel he had reserved under a false name in advance. There he had his will with the drugged woman, and after he had slaked his lust, he used the chloroform again before he carried her to the doctor, who was only happy to have the delivery, and asked no questions about what had happened along the route.

The doctor was making progress because this specimen not only responded and became a vehicle for propagation beyond any man's dreams, but she also gave both the doctor and his henchman such ecstasy that they believed they had achieved Nirvana. The woman was insatiable, and the two males alternately tried to satisfy her all through the night. They did not achieve their end or hers.

In this way, the doctor created a creature that had the features of a perpetual propagation machine. No matter how either of them tried to satisfy her needs, she had needs beyond their comprehension. The doctor applied many syringes of his new formula, but the specimen only yearned for more satisfaction from her two unlikely lovers. They alternated, not only through the night but also throughout the next week without giving the specimen all that she evidently required.

The doctor applied his elixir every six hours, and the result was precisely the same. He could not account for what was happening, but he recorded the results in his ledger. The specimen was unique in his experience, he told his henchman. The specimen was both insatiable and indiscriminate. She would mate with any male of her species as many times as was necessary—for what? For this, he had no immediate answer.

Ultimately, the doctor concluded that the specimen had no end in sight. She merely wanted to procreate indefinitely.

She was the male's dream confection. The doctor had an insight, and his henchman had understood it before it was articulated: women could be chemically induced to satisfy any male desires without the normal constituent impediments of marriage and family.

The doctor's problem now was the disposition of the evidence, but the specimen refused to be extinguished. This was both the doctor's nightmare and the henchman's dream. So, the doctor told his henchman to dispose of the body, but his henchman did not dispose of the specimen's body in the usual way. Instead, he took the specimen to the motel where he had enjoyed her, and he continued to enjoy her until she expired trying to achieve her personal Nirvana.

Only after she had expired, did the henchman deliver the specimen to the anatomist's assistant. He was glad to receive the corpse, as always, and he paid what was owed, but he wondered about the vivacity of the corpse and the smile that graced the corpse's dead face. What, he thought, might have caused such ecstasy before death, and why would a woman experiencing such ecstasy die?

The henchman did not know what the anatomical assistant was thinking, and his only goal was satisfying his master's needs. So, he moved on to seize his next specimen, and he paid no attention to the thoughts or feelings of either the doctor or the lab assistant for whom he was the procurer and go-between.

The henchman's next specimen was different from her predecessors for two reasons. First, she was a witch, associated with a coven. Second, she was living with another woman in a relationship that was outside the then-current laws. The henchman took her outside her apartment, as he had before, and he took her to a motel to have his way with her before he took her to his doctor. Even though she was under chloroform, she was sexually active and receptive to the henchman's overtures. She was so receptive that the henchman had misgivings about delivering her to the doctor for his ministrations, but finally, he gave in and after drugging the woman again, delivered her.

The doctor's experience with this new specimen was unlike any the henchman had ever seen. Not only did the doctor spend an inordinate time with the specimen alone, but when he was summoned to gratify the apparently insatiable specimen, he tried in vain to accommodate her desires.

So, for over a week, the doctor and his henchman tried to gratify the specimen's sexual desires. The doctor decided they would continue their attempts until they found the specimen's limitations. Days turned into weeks and weeks into months. After three months, the doctor and his henchman knew that they had discovered the dream the doctor had been searching for, but it was not what he expected.

Instead of discovering what would make humans live longer, the doctor had discovered what would make humans attempt to reproduce indefinitely and indiscriminately. The natural insatiability of women was enhanced by the chemical inducement that the doctor had developed. In his ledger, the henchman saw that the doctor had written the results conclusively: "Women can be induced by chemical means to overcome the inhibitions and constraints of society to strive to reproduce indefinitely with males of the worst possible composition. Their reproductive behaviors can become disassociated entirely with natural selection criteria and seek any mate that satisfies the basic need to reproduce."

This finding was revolutionary, the doctor told his henchman, and he said he would suppress it by not publishing it right away. When the doctor excitedly discussed the matter with his henchman, he only said that he needed women of prime breeding age with features that would satisfy any human male's desire for reproduction.

Once he had euthanized their latest specimen, he ordered his henchman to take her corpse to the anatomical theater as always. There, the anatomist's assistant told the henchman that the authorities had begun to investigate the sources for their specimens. The henchman said that he hoped that the assistant had not mentioned his name in this connection, but the assistant did not immediately confirm this.

So, the anatomy assistant was declared missing the following day. His body parts were later found in the city's sewer system, but the police did not investigate because the man was a known homosexual with unsavory contacts in the underworld. As to the specimen that the henchman had delivered, it was an outstanding exhibit for the young medical practitioners who viewed the autopsy at first hand. The only disadvantage from the henchman's point of view was his need to find another outlet for fresh corpses. He need not have worried because in a large modern city corpses have many functions.

The henchman discovered that the university's medical school was not the only buyer for fresh corpses. The other buyer was the Mafia, which did a thriving business in servicing necrophiliacs. The henchman linked to the Mob connection for this trade, and he discovered that the remuneration was triple what he had been receiving from the medical school. The condition was that the specimens must be delivered within four hours of death. They also must be flawless, meaning that they could not be victims of mutilation, patients in a hospital catering to infectious diseases or flagrant tattoo applications. The henchman decided he could live under those conditions, so he shifted his trade to deliver to the Mafia instead of the medical theater.

The doctor told his henchman that he had perfected his potion for injection after a dozen other specimens. He said he was delighted by the consistency of the results. All the specimens had performed beyond his wildest expectations. They had a lave ratio of 500 per encounter, and a duration of indefinite encounters.

Once chemical injection had occurred, they would perform without regard to the identity of their male counterpart. Both he and his henchman were proof that the specimens responded to any males that happened to be present. Instead of having produced a longevity product for humans, the doctor said he had produced a sexual inducement product that provided males with compliant females who would never outlast the human male's procreative desires.

The doctor exclaimed that he had caused a revolution. His injections would break through all inhibitions of beautiful female humans, he told his henchman. In his ledger, the henchman saw that the doctor had written, "A clinical application of this series of injections will eliminate their problems of mating with abhorrent or repulsive males. If the females could be restrained to mate with their intended spouses, all would be well, and the status quo would be maintained. If not, the women might pose a problem for society, because the specimen's insatiability would break the social contracts and open possibilities of universal female promiscuity that would destroy the marital social contract between all men and women."

The doctor continued his experiments, and the injections he gave became pills that could be administered with coconut milk, which would help the patient swallow the pills and keep them down. His female human specimens showed the same reactions to the pills as they had to the injections, but their reaction times were slower than with the injections.

The doctor took part in all of his experiments now, and he encouraged his henchman to take turns with him in trying to satisfy the apparently insatiable specimens that successively adorned the laboratory's gurney.

Once equilibrium had been achieved—meaning that the specimens uniformly performed as the doctor's hypothesis had predicted—the need for numbers became the key quest for the doctor. His hypothesis having been proven, the question of how many subjects was a matter of judgment only. As long as the specimens conformed to expectations, each successive specimen added further proof, but no divergence, from the doctor's newly established norm.

The doctor's henchman had enjoyed his job of procurer throughout this phase of the experiment sequence. His enjoyment of the specimens at the motel before he delivered them to the doctor had been hugely gratifying for a man so hideously deformed as he was, and it was compounded by the doctor's invitation for him to partake of his specimens' pleasure after they had been strapped down on the gurney.

Further, his remuneration for delivering the corpses of the experiments to the Mafia was reaching epic dimensions. The Mob was extremely satisfied with his deliveries, and his contacts told him that the female specimens were shipped over the world to customers who wanted more from where they came from. The henchman thought that there might be a pony for him to ride in this seamless web of transactions. At this point, he could not see his advantage, but he kept alert for the possibilities.

The doctor and his henchman were careful students of media reports that might jeopardize their work. They saw imaginative news investigations that suggested the enterprise for fresh corpses the doctor and his henchman had spawned had become of interest to law enforcement officials.

One particularly astute investigator saw a correlation between a spike in the disappearances of young, single women and the spike in interest in the black sex market for necrophilia. This correlation could not, she wrote, be entirely accidental. Because of the public outcry that resulted from the female investigator's reportage, the authorities began a serious police investigation into what could be the origin of this new pattern.

The interest of the organized crime division of the Federal Bureau of Investigation in the United States was not visible to the doctor and his henchman until the doctor was served a writ that authorized the search of his laboratories on the grounds that he was somehow complicit in supplying corpses to the Mafia for their notorious necrophilia operations.

The FBI sent a team of ten agents into the doctor's lab, but they discovered no incriminating evidence. The doctor offered no resistance during their search, but he recorded what the agents did and told them that he would publish everything so the world would know what happened to scientists who were on the cutting edge of developments.

In the end, the doctor published no such data, but both he and his henchman were delighted that no questions about the henchman were raised in discussions the doctor had with the FBI agents. It remained a mystery to the FBI why the doctor had been implicated in an investigation with the Mafia when no known explicit contact between him and the Mob bosses existed.

What the FBI investigation did was the opposite of what it intended: it cleared the doctor of any involvement and blinded the agency from any further investigation into his possible role in providing specimens to the Mob.

The doctor was not pleased with the federal investigation he had been subjected to, and he resolved to look into the reasons why his henchman's connections to the Mob might have brought the doctor into the limelight. Finally, he concluded that his henchman had no motive to turn him in to the FBI, and the Mob had no interest in terminating a most lucrative deal for specimens.

In the end, the doctor took the whole incident as a perfect cover for his continuing operations, and he told his henchman that the law enforcement community would remain at bay as long as they had no further reason to suspect him. He kept alert for possible informants in the loop, including his own henchman, but he kept on his course to prove the efficacy of his pills.

The henchman noticed that the doctor did moderate his use of specimens somewhat, but the henchman continued to supply the Mob with his usual products, even though many had never passed through the doctor's lab. In fact, the henchman's operation became almost entirely disjoined from the doctor's experimentation.

What did the henchman need the doctor for when he could provide what the Mob needed with chloroform and an unremarkable way of dispatching the victims? The henchman reasoned that as long as the specimens died without blemishes, they would be marketable. He had chemical means to kill, and he used them whenever his specimens outnumbered his doctor's requirements.

In fact, the specimens he delivered to the Mafia were examined carefully, and his Mob contacts were more satisfied by the specimens he had dispatched personally, than by the specimens that had passed through the doctor's lab. On the basis of the feedback he received from his Mob contact, the henchman began to plan for the eventuality that the doctor might at some point no longer require his personal services. The henchman was not stupid about where his interests lay, and he had a penchant for survival.

The Mob saw the growing possibilities of using the henchmen to their own advantage, and his contact was ordered to assure that he was kept happy with their arrangement. Specifically, the boss of all bosses wanted to increase the volume of corpses for his special clients, particularly in Asia, and no other source could provide the quality of product that the henchman did without jeopardizing the whole Mob operation.

To assure that the doctor's henchman remained under the strictest surveillance, the Mob devoted three of their made men to watch the henchman 24/7 as insurance against their sunk investment. That way, if the henchman decided to renege on the deal or turn state's evidence against the Mob, he could be dealt with efficiently with minimal backlash against the organization.

The doctor's henchman did not know the specifics of the Mob's surveillance, but he did know that he had been put under a microscope and that every move he made was being reported to someone who might do him harm. When the henchman told the doctor that he was being shadowed by professionals who were definitely not federal enforcement officers, the doctor told him that the surveillance should not concern him.

Only federal surveillance made any difference to the operation they had invented, he said. The doctor, who was not the fool he considered his henchman to be, made contingency plans to sever all relations with his henchman if the need should arise. Meanwhile, he conducted business as usual, unaware that his henchman had cut a side deal with the Mob for specimens that were superfluous to the doctor's experiments.

As long as the henchman's supply of fresh corpses satisfied both the doctor and the Mob, everything went swimmingly for everyone. Eventually, though, the doctor had a need for an additional corpse to check out his latest adjustment to the dosage of his pills at the same time that his henchman needed to deliver the same corpse to satisfy an emergent need by a key customer in the Mafia stable.

That meant that the henchman had to choose which master to satisfy while looking for a substitute specimen to serve up to the other. The henchman chose to deliver his fresh corpse to the Mob, and he scurried to find a replacement corpse for the doctor without taking his usual precautions. So, it was that the henchman broke his own protocol and selected a common street prostitute as his offering to his formerly primary patron.

The woman the henchman selected had been in "the life" for over twelve years, and that was considered to be an eternity in the sex trade. Her absence from the street was hardly noticed, but there was no guarantee of her purity. That meant that her having active sexually transmitted diseases could not be discounted. The henchman did not mention this matter to the doctor, but he avoided having sexual congress with the woman when she was under the effects of chloroform.

He did participate in the doctor's experiment in the lab, and both the doctor and his henchman, therefore, became infected with whatever sexually transmitted diseases the prostitute had encountered in her professional contacts. Two weeks after their mutual contact with this specimen, both the doctor and the henchman had symptoms of venereal disease.

It hurt them to urinate, and they knew other symptoms would follow.

The doctor questioned his henchman about how this aberration had happened when every precaution had been taken in every prior case. The henchman told his sponsor that he had been overly hasty in his latest selection, but you could never really tell whether a woman had a disease or not before she had intercourse and the symptoms presented in the man.

The doctor had to agree, so he applied the usual remedies to both himself and his henchman. The two men suffered the effects of their diseases and hoped for the best. The henchman, of course, realized that his personal problem was not the disease, but the effects of the disease on the Mob's special customers who had used the prostitute's corpse after the henchman had delivered it to them subsequent to the experimentation.

It took another two weeks for the Mob to start asking questions about why a special primary customer had contracted a sexually transmitted disease after receiving the fresh corpse that had been delivered via the henchman. Two Mob goons visited the henchman to discuss the matter, but the two huge men never returned to report what they had found.

The henchman had understood the reason for their visit, and he had summarily killed both men with two quick punches to their faces. His strength caused massive damage to both their skulls, and when the henchman weighted down their bodies so they could be immersed in the local bay, they were unrecognizable.

The henchman knew then that his days servicing the Mob was over. He, therefore, removed all traces of his former contact, including his phone number, the meeting locations and the means of communicating with him for special orders. It was now as if he no longer existed. If the Mob found him, he would take care of business, but they would no longer have their supply of fresh corpses.

The henchman tried to connect to the replacement for his contact at the anatomy theater, and he was lucky that the man needed his help. So, the henchman resumed supplying the specimens for the medical students' classes. He lost his previous source of income from the Mob, but he had relative immunity from the long reach of the arms of the Mafia, or so he thought at the time. Meanwhile, he took the medicines that the doctor prescribed to rid himself of the scourge of venereal disease. The medications were not working, and his discomfort increased by the week.

The doctor announced to his henchman that he had finally perfected his chemical formulas. He said he would no longer need the supply of bodies that he had been used to, and he advised his henchman to refocus his procurement to satisfy the medical cadavers to the university medical school. Since the henchman was already doing that, the doctor's advice was useless.

What the henchman suspected was that the doctor would want him eliminated as a witness to the long sequence of experiments had been conducted to prove the efficacy of the wonder cure. An added dimension to the doctor's eliminating the henchman would be his revenge for having contracted the venereal disease that had plagued them both.

The henchman had hoped to shift his procurement from the doctor to the Mob, but now that was impossible. He knew the capacity limits of the medical community for the corpses he might offer, so he planned to scale back his lifestyle accordingly. This was difficult since his medical needs were increasing weekly. Experimental drugs were the only option available to him, and they were extremely expensive items, available only on the black market.

The henchman's last meeting with the doctor occurred in the doctor's laboratory.

"I have served you well, and through my devices, you have had the specimens that allowed you to perform the experiments that proved your hypotheses and allowed the discovery and refinement of the drugs you have refined into pill form. I never asked for more than you offered, and I am glad for what you have given me, but now I am in dire straits and need your help. Is there any way you can help me now that I need it?"

"You have done well, and I thank you from the bottom of my heart for your faithful service. I've never had much money, as you know. I've had to scrape together what I paid you, and I've nothing from my inventions yet because I've no way to advertise what I've done. So, I have nothing further for you except for my letter of recommendation. I wish you well. If only we hadn't both been affected by the disease, we'd both be much better off than we are. It's best that we don't meet anymore and that we forget we ever knew each other. Our connection could bring the authorities down upon us and lead us to the Electric Chair. So goodbye." With that, the doctor lapsed and allowed his henchman to embrace him in a fond farewell gesture.

To his horror, the doctor found that his henchman held him so close that he could not escape or breathe. The more the doctor struggled to get free from the embrace, the more his henchman crushed him. His bones snapped, and organs collapsed from the enormous pressure.

The henchman finally released the doctor's lifeless body, which dropped onto the floor of his lab. The doctor's henchman then rifled the lab for anything of value, but the only things he took away were the doctor's personal supply of medicine to treat venereal diseases, the ledger of the doctor's activities, and the precious pills that had been the result of his long illicit labors in the lab.

The henchman wiped down the lab and removed all traces of his having been in the lab before he closed and locked the place, leaving the start of a fire to destroy all other evidence of the doctor's illicit activities.

The henchman now had no master, and perforce he had to steer clear of the Mob. He did have a steady customer in the assistant who required bodies for anatomical dissection in the medical theater at the university. He focused on satisfying that customer's needs, and he did not have to worry about his sexually transmitted disease having an effect on his trade because his specimens would not be encountering sex after he delivered them to his customer.

So, for a while, the henchman continued to do what he had always done. Once a month, or when asked, he delivered a fresh female corpse to the university, and he was paid in the usual gold coins for his services. That would have been a lifetime satisfaction, except that the Mob, desperate to find specimens for their worldwide clients, approached the assistant anatomist with their request for extraneous bodies.

The assistant, without divulging his source, promised the Mob representatives that they could have whatever overflow of corpses he received for an agreed price per corpse. The assistant did not mention to the henchman who his buyers were, but he offered to pay the henchman double the usual amount for additional fresh corpses beyond the needs of the anatomical theater.

The henchman was ecstatic about having a way to earn additional income again. He did not inquire who the buyer of the additional corpses was, although he guessed that his old friends in the Mob might be involved.

The Mob was satisfied, and they took delivery of one fresh corpse a month from the assistant. Each corpse, of course, was marked by the venereal disease that the henchman carried into the game. The Mob's elite customers became infected, and they complained bitterly and demanded their money back.

This direct threat to the Mob's stream of income incensed the boss of bosses, and he demanded answers. The Mob reasoned that the connection through which they obtained the new supply of fresh corpses also involved their old friend the henchman. So, they paid the assistant anatomist a special visit during which, before he died under torture, he confessed the source of his corpses and the time he expected the next delivery.

When the henchman arrived with his next delivery, five hard Mafia men were waiting for him. The henchman delivered the corpse as he had intended to do, and then he slaughtered the five Mob men with no difficulty. They were armed, "made" men, but they were no match for a huge monster for whom bullets provided no apparent effects whatsoever.

The operating theater where he left their corpses had plenty of bodies for the medical students' inspection, but the police had other ideas, and the scale of the slaughter got the mayor and district attorney involved. The university medical school was closed down for a month while the police investigation continued.

In the end, the police report concluded that two warring Mafia families had fought, and five Mafia men with long criminal records had died in the fighting. Since the fight had been contained to the Mob and one lowly assistant anatomical specialist, no further police action was recommended.

The female investigative reporter detailed to cover the case found many unanswered questions, but she saw no way to further the investigation once the police had retreated, so she was redistributed to cover other stories.

The henchman was glad when the whole police incident blew by without affecting him, except by the loss of his primary customer, the assistant anatomist. The henchman had laid away a significant amount of gold coins that he had scrupulously saved from his many procurements, so he figured he had bought some time to discover another angle with which to make enough money to support his expensive habits, including his increasingly expensive medicines.

Thinking of nothing better and wanting to put the Mob's vengeance behind him, he went to the Italian restaurant where he knew the Mob boss of bosses hung out during the daytime hours, and he asked for a one-on-one meeting with the boss.

Rather than being met by a hail of gunfire, the henchman found himself having spaghetti with meatballs and a glass of house red wine across the table from the Mob boss of bosses, who liked to jab his index finger violently to make his points.

"So let me get this straight. You provided fresh stiffs so we could sell them to our customers. You also infected the corpses with diseases so our customers caught the diseases and complained and wanted refunds or refused to pay us. You are now out of luck, because your sugar daddy died—by your own hand, I figure. Now, you want me to cut a deal with you to let you resupply us with fresh corpses again? Have I got all that straight so far?"

"It's a good summary. Yes, you have it right."

"So what if I say everything that is past is past? What if we agree on a price for new, fresh corpses? You would deliver two fresh corpses a month for one year as your probation. If I discover that any of the corpses is diseased, I kill you. If you don't deliver on your promise, I kill you. If you disappear again, I track you down and kill you. What do you say to those terms?"

"What did you say you were going to pay for each fresh corpse?"

So, the henchman negotiated and forged a deal with his new master, who was the Mob boss. The boss had nothing to lose and everything to gain from the deal. He did not care how the henchman accomplished what he promised. He did not care, really, whether the corpses turned up diseased or not.

In any scenario that developed from the deal, the Mob boss was a winner. As for the henchman, he was also a winner from the deal, because he no longer had to worry about the threat of the Mob. He did not have to worry about an income either, as long as he delivered as he promised to do. He knew the way to avoid contaminating his fresh corpses with his venereal disease—abstinence. He knew as well as the Mob boss that the disease that ate him away would finally kill him.

Their diabolical deal converged on death from all sides. The Mob boss told the henchman that he was now working for him and for no one else. The boss of bosses said that the henchman was the Sand Man, but the henchman knew better. The henchman knew that death was the real Sand Man and that the Sand Man would be the final arbiter for everything he did from now on.

The Mob boss and the Sand Man's henchman shook hands and drank to each other to seal their deal. It was a devil's bargain, but both men understood it. It was not only a matter of gold coins, after all. It was also a matter of honor on the one hand, and efficient execution on the other. As for the specimens who were to be the basis for their transactions, neither man cared anything about them, except for their assured delivery without the dread diseases.

The deal lasted for almost ten years, and the henchman provided the boss of bosses with one fresh female corpse a month for all that time. His own condition worsened weekly. The cartilage in his nose eroded so his facial disfigurement was worsened by his flat, flabby nose flesh. His joints ached, and urination caused needle-like pains. He sweated a lot more than he used to, and his feet and lower legs became covered with oozing sores.

He witnessed the same effects in the boss of bosses in their quarterly meetings for accounting and payments. The Mob boss did not die in a hail of gunfire as his Mob rivals did. He died in agony of the ravaging effects of venereal disease. The Sand Man's henchman outlived his boss by two weeks when he was found in a heap on the floor of an elevator by a beautiful, single woman who might have become his next victim. She said that his enormous body stank of chloroform and that he had a chloroform-laden handkerchief in his enormous right hand.

A routine autopsy indicated that every bodily system of the corpse had been so affected by venereal disease that the body was transferred to the anatomical theater of the medical school for the medical students' edification. His dissected organs and brain were preserved in the medical lab, and the rest of his remains were buried in an unmarked grave.

The female investigative reporter who had followed the cases of disappearances of single females for almost two decades noticed a marked drop in the numbers of such disappearances in the city. She traced the timing of the drop to the death of two men, both of whom had died of venereal diseases.

She wrote an investigative piece, tying together the supplying of fresh corpses for necrophilia, and the murder of innocent women in Chicago. She tied this traffic to the Mafia. Her editor spiked her story as being purely conjectural and lacking in substantial proofs. She then wanted to have the mob boss of bosses' body exhumed so the remains could be compared with those of an unnamed corpse that was used in the dissecting theater at the medical school two weeks after the boss had died.

Since she could not provide any convincing evidence of a connection between the decedent's condition and the unnamed corpse that had been dissected, and because the Catholic Church objected strenuously to the exhumation, her request was denied, and she was summarily fired from her job at the newspaper.

The investigative reporter suddenly vanished shortly after her firing. When the woman's best friend, a fellow investigative reporter, tried to locate her, her whereabouts could not be determined.

The friend later wrote in an article her editor spiked, that the investigative reporter's untimely disappearance ironically marked the beginning of a new rash of female disappearances in Chicago, and a restart of the supply of fresh necrophilia specimens from America to Asia.

Clearly, the new Mob boss of bosses knew how to run a lucrative business, and the Sand Man had found a new henchman in Chicago.

Hornpipes for Mariah

Mariah, a single woman, had a dream that she never whispered to anyone except her friend Lily. She was introspective and sad, and she sat evenings looking out her bedroom window.

She occasionally drew the figure of a heart on the window pane and pressed her nose into the middle of the heart. She was in love, but only she knew that her love was impossible, for she loved a centaur that she had never met personally, but only dreamed about—a magnificent combination of a human and a horse.

She dreamed that the centaur would come to visit her and take her away from her drab, ordinary life into the dream world, where the two could be together forever. Her dream was recurrent, and she dreamed in such detail that her dream was more real than anything in her normal life.

Lily, her friend, felt the same way, but Lily's love was a unicorn. Mariah's parents did not know what to do to help her, and Mariah did not know how to express her needs or fears to them. Mariah stood looking out her window, wishing for a miracle and waiting for each night's slumber to bring her beloved centaur to her.

One such night while she was dreaming, the centaur came for Mariah through her first-floor double-doored bedroom entrance, late on Midsummer Night's Eve. The centaur said his name was Amoricon, and he was answering her dream for a centaur who would love her and take her away from her boring, hopeless life and make her feel appreciated and loved. A centaur with flaxen flanks and a mane of pure gold hair, the half-human creature's musculature rippled with power that sent chills up and down Mariah's spine.

Mariah rose from her bed and put out her hand to touch the creature because she wanted to know for certain that it was real and not a figment of her wild imagination. The flat of her hand ran over the beast's flanks, then quickly her hands flew all over Amoricon's body, feeling the rich tail, each fetlock, and the smooth hair that ran down his sides. She sniffed the centaur all over, and she smelled the sweet scent of centaurs. Amoricon paid her the compliment of sniffing her as well, and he snuffled his approval. Then, Mariah knew that the creature was genuine: her dream centaur had become real.

Amoricon told the woman that once she departed with him, she could never return to her former life. That was his only condition for her possessing him completely. Aside from that, she could ask for whatever she liked and the centaur would provide it. Mariah wept uncontrollably with delight just thinking about what she had gained, and without a second thought, she readily agreed to Amoricon's condition.

Then, the centaur lifted the woman with his powerful arms, and placed her on his broad back, and Mariah experienced déjà vu. In dreams as a little girl, she had mounted the centaur many times and ridden it through the sky. And now her long, smooth legs gripped the broad back of Amoricon. It seemed as if the mythical animal were an extension of herself, and the two were one being.

The centaur backed out her door, careful not to hurt their heads, and, leaping, surmounted the high back fence of

Mariah's yard and galloped down the road and out of town. Mariah grasped Amoricon by his flowing mane with both her hands and held on tight as she rode with the wind running through her streaming hair. She found the centaur's pace was gentle, and she rolled with its motions, her strong rider's legs gripped firmly around the beast's sides as she was used to riding horses.

Amoricon galloped for a long time and finally halted at a small thatch-roofed cottage in the country, lifted Mariah from her place on its back, and told her that the woman she would henceforth become, would live in the cottage and that he would return to visit her every night.

If she decided she needed anything at all during the day, she needed only to think of it, and the centaur promised her she would receive it. Then, Amoricon leaned back and told Mariah she should make herself right at home. It said she might be interested in what was in the corral at the back of the property on which the cottage sat, but looking there was up to her. Amoricon expressed delight that Mariah had called him out of her dream. The beast lifted her and kissed her lightly on the cheek, set her down again gently on the ground, reared up and galloped away.

That first day, Mariah enjoyed exploring the cottage and the grounds. She found everything she needed, including a curious bed with a rabbit-skin coverlet and a large kitchen with everything she would need to prepare food. In a cabinet, she found a box of Krinkles cereal and a bowl and spoon to eat the cereal with.

She wished she could have cream to pour over it, and suddenly she heard a knock at her front door. There, she found a little bearded man dressed as a garden gnome with two bottles of fresh, warm milk with cream on top. The creature gave her the two bottles, tipped his hat and left.

Mariah was both surprised and overjoyed. She skimmed the cream off the milk and poured it over her cereal. Life with a centaur was most pleasing—so far.

After breakfast, Mariah went to the corral that Amoricon had mentioned, and there sported two centaur foals, a male, and a female. The male looked just like a younger version of Amoricon, and the female looked just like a younger version of her. Mariah shook her head because she had never dreamed of these. She fed, bathed and curried the young centaurs before she walked them around the grounds with rope leashes she had found on the back of the kitchen door.

Mariah cleaned the corral area while the two foals tripped around, and she went back to clean the cottage before it was time for Amoricon to return. She wished the cottage was dusted and cleaned, and a troop of a half-dozen elves and half-dozen fairies appeared at her front door to make it so. They laughed while they worked and made jokes that made themselves and Mariah laugh. When they had cleaned everything, the elves and fairies bade Mariah goodbye and told her just to make a wish, and they would return again.

Amoricon arrived to spend the night with Mariah, who told the centaur about finding the foals in the corral. She remarked on the foals' resemblance to Amoricon and her. The centaur nodded sagely and told the woman that it was no wonder because he had sired them and they appeared just as he envisioned them both beforehand. Mariah was astonished by this news, and she wondered out loud how the centaur had known about her before the last evening.

Amoricon said, "We came to each other for the same reasons. I came to you from your dreams because you wanted me to, and in a similar fashion, you came to me from my dreams because I wanted you to do so. I envisioned you as a centaur, and so you became one. Now it is time for rest, and you and I will meet in our dreams as centaurs again."

So when Mariah fell asleep, she dreamed she was a centaur named Amorica who loved Amoricon, and the two danced together behind the cottage sweetly. Amorica pawed the ground with her hooves. Amoricon answered by rearing up and trotting around. They pranced together in back of the cottage for a long while, and then they galloped through the night together happily, just as Mariah had dreamed before the night her centaur came to her.

When Mariah awakened in the morning, sweaty and refreshed, yet exhausted too, in the enormous feather bed, Amoricon had departed. In the backyard, she found hoof prints that two adult centaurs had left in the night. In the corral, she discovered the male and the female foals were ready for their breakfasts. She bathed the child centaurs, and they ate heartily when Mariah fed them the rest of the milk that the gnome had left the day before.

Mariah wished she could meet Amorica, the female centaur of the dream she had shared with Amoricon, and she immediately heard the clop of hooves behind her. She turned around and still heard the sound of hooves, but she could not see where the sounds came from.

She shrugged and went back to the cottage, but she could not get through the door for some reason. She looked down and saw that her legs were now those of a horse. Aghast, she looked back and saw that her back stretched out like a horse's broad back. She flicked her tail and shook it from side to side. She made a wild surmise and decided to trot around the grounds.

The experience felt new, but she was comfortable as a centaur, and so she decided to gallop. Now strangely, she had become the thing she wished for: she was Amorica the female centaur. She wished she could become Mariah again, but nothing happened—Amorica remained a centaur. She walked to the corral, and the foals cavorted around her happily, recognizing their mother.

That evening, Amoricon returned to find Amorica and the two foals playing together in the corral. He smiled at his centaur family and embraced Amorica, who was happy in his arms for a few minutes. Then Amorica backed away and told Amoricon that he had broken his promise to grant Mariah's every wish.

Amoricon was insistent that, to the contrary, he had granted Mariah's wish to become the centaur Amorica. She had wished for that, hadn't she? Now she was part of the centaur family on the centaur's side of the dreams, which were not covered by his promise. Once Mariah made the transition to becoming the female centaur Amorica, Mariah the human woman no longer existed.

Amorica considered this for a long while, but as the evening went on, the female centaur played with Amoricon behind the cottage, and then they galloped together very fast through the night, just as they had done the night before. When they returned, Amorica went to the corral and nuzzled the young centaurs while Amoricon looked on proudly. Then Amoricon departed, and Amorica spent the day playing with the foals, giving them milk, teaching them how to flick their tails to keep off flies and to prance, walk and trot.

The centaur mother and foals formed a small herd, and went for a walk through the village together, but none of the villagers paid them any attention. As creatures from Amoricon's dream world, they seemed to be invisible to humans. For example, Amorica's parents passed by without knowing that the centaur Amorica was present, though Mariah's mother wrinkled her nose at a peculiar, unfamiliar smell—of centaur—though she did not know where the smell came from or what it meant.

Mariah's parents were dressed in black and walked to the cemetery where a burial was evidently in progress. A closed coffin lay beside a freshly opened grave, and the preacher was eulogizing a grown woman who loved to talk and dream about fairies and elves and centaurs.

He said it was very sad that Mariah had departed from the human world, but she was in a better place now, and she would never have to look through a glass darkly at a world she did not understand, longing for a centaur who could never live in the world as humans knew it. He said that he hoped that God had granted the young girl's wish to live among the centaurs for eternity.

The gathering wept at the preacher's words, and Amorica and her foals were about to leave when the name "Mariah" was spoken, and she turned to see her best friend Lily weeping inconsolably and clutching her unicorn doll. Amorica wished that Lily would find the unicorn of her dreams, just as Mariah found the centaur of her own dreams. Then she led her foals back to the cottage and into their corral.

That evening, Amoricon returned to visit the cottage, and Amorica joined the centaur in their nightly ritual of dancing and riding through the night. Instead of playing with the foals in the early morning, Amorica talked quietly with Amoricon about Mariah's human friend Lily and the unicorn.

Amoricon listened carefully to Amorica, and said that Lily's wish had come true that night, but Amoricon feared granting the wish would have dreadful consequences for Lily. Amorica was startled by his misgivings, but she felt that Lily should partake of the joys that centaurs experienced if she could do so. Amorica did not consider that the rules for unicorns might be very different from the rules for centaurs.

During the next morning, while she was walking in the back of the cottage, Amorica wished to see Mariah's friend Lily and immediately, around from the front of the cottage, trotted a magnificent unicorn. The animal was milk white, a mare with a flowing white mane and a long, single golden horn on its forehead. The unicorn pawed the ground and rubbed up against Amorica.

Recognizing this creature as Mariah's friend Lily, Amorica decided to gallop with the unicorn in the countryside during the afternoon. They crossed many greenswards and passed through meadows until they reached a silver stream, where the unicorn knelt on one knee and touched the stream with her golden horn.

The unicorn pawed the ground downstream of where the horn touched, indicating that Amorica should drink there. The female centaur drank and felt fully refreshed—so much so that she decided to bring Amoricon and the foals to drink here at the soonest opportunity. At that moment hunters appeared, and the unicorn vanished. Since the hunters did not see the centaur, Amorica listened to what the hunters had to say.

The hunters complained that they could not find their prey, a unicorn of such beauty as to have no equal among quadrupeds of any kind. They talked about the magical golden horn of the beast, which could transform ordinary water into the elixir of Paradise that gave everyone who drank it health and some everlasting life.

One of the hunters said with awe that he had met an old woman who had seen the unicorn touch a pool of water with its horn. Afterward, the pool was considered holy, and people traveled great distances to drink its water and bathe their wounds in it because the water healed all injuries inside and outside.

The hunters said they wanted to harvest the horn of the unicorn because they thought they could sell the horn for money as a healing wand. They did not consider that the horn only worked if it remained attached to a living unicorn. Amorica did not like the hunters or what they said, and that night she told Amoricon about them.

"Amorica, those hunters will never find what they hunt, for only humans who have pure hearts can see the unicorn, and they would never harm it. Do not worry, for the unicorn is a special creature and immortal. As for Mariah's friend Lily, the human girl crossed over to the unicorn as I said, and the unicorn's revealing herself to you was an expression of thanks for deliverance by Lily. But Lily is no longer in the world of humans. Go tomorrow to the village cemetery to see what the humans are doing about Lily's departure."

The next day, Amorica went to the village cemetery just as Amoricon advised and saw a gathering for Lily around a fresh grave, just like the gathering that was held for Mariah's interment.

The same preacher who had spoken the eulogy over Mariah's grave now told the assemblage that Lily had always been enamored of unicorns, and the girl's toy unicorn had been placed in her hands in her coffin so she would have its presence next to her for eternity. The preacher told the story of the unicorn being a beast chosen by God, and he hoped that Lily was with that sacred beast for today and forevermore, since she was always a good girl with a pure heart.

Amorica knew Lily was with the unicorn, but the humans would never know that as a fact because she could not tell them. Amorica would have liked to tell Lily's grieving parents that their daughter would ride the forests of the night as the most beautiful unicorn in the world, but that was impossible. Perhaps, Amorica thought, Amoricon could help in some way.

That night, when Amoricon returned to visit, America was pensive and distant. When the centaur coaxed the whole story out of his friend, Amoricon said that the message of Lily's transition out of the humans' world had been delivered eloquently by the preacher and that all the believers who heard him would know the truth of what he said as if for a fact.

America asked whether her having drunk from the silver stream downstream from where the unicorn dipped its horn would be efficacious, and whether Amoricon and the foals shouldn't drink there also. Amoricon said that they all should go to that place right away and drink as much as possible.

That night, the centaur family went to the place where the unicorn had dipped its golden horn in the silver stream, and they drank, galloped around and drank again. The moon was full, and no clouds were in the sky, and the family watched as the unicorn returned to the spot to kneel and touch its horn to the stream again. Then the unicorn galloped away and vanished.

The centaur family returned to the cottage and their corral, just as dawn was breaking, and as always, Amoricon galloped away. America encouraged the foals to drink milk and rest all day long. At her wish, the elves and fairies came to clean inside the cottage, and outside it around the grounds, including the corral.

Outside among the grasses near a vegetable garden, they found a little garden gnome that America recognized as the same gnome that had brought the milk with cream to Mariah on her first day with the centaurs. Then, America had been Mariah, a mortal human with a dream. Now Mariah had left the earth, but her dreams had become realities. It is true, those magical realities were in the fashion of other dreams. They were centaur dreams that few humans can share, and then only when they have made the difficult, irrevocable choice that brave Mariah made.

Lily, Mariah's friend, had also been a mortal human with a dream. Now Lily had departed from the humans' world. Through her passing, her dream had become a reality. Hers was a reality so miraculous that it was in the fashion of a dream. Humans could only know the truth, as the preacher had said, by grace and faith. Or, perhaps, it could be known by drinking from water in which the unicorn had dipped its magical, golden horn and made an elixir of health and life.

When the centaur came again to her in the night, Amorica asked Amoricon what he did between the times when he departed at dawn and returned in the evening. He said, "All day, from dawn to dusk, I gallop all over the world and visit humans who have forgotten kindness and consideration for others, to teach them the paths of goodness. This is an ancient centaur tradition, like the ancient mentor, the wounded centaur Chiron. The centaur's work is sometimes dangerous," Amoricon said, showing Amorica the wound on his hind left limb caused by a poisoned arrow shot by a malicious human hunter.

He told her that the old wound constantly festered, and would probably never heal completely. It reminded the centaur of mortality. Drinking the water that the unicorn had touched helped ease the pain and lessen the festering of the wound, but the wound wouldn't ever go away.

All that night long the two adult centaurs nuzzled, stamped and snuffled back of the cottage, and in the morning Amoricon departed. Amorica remained in the corral with the foals and taught them what Amoricon had taught her through the night before.

The message was so eloquent and compelling that the elves, the fairies, and the garden gnome gathered around

Amorica and the foals to hear the stories. There they heard of the old centaur Chiron, the young centaur Amoricon, and the milk-white unicorn again and again.

After story time, they danced for joy and played hornpipes until the early evening light, when Amoricon again returned.

The Brass Gong

Symbol of wisdom and hieroglyph for all Egyptian prepositions, the owl sign, permeates ancient cartouches, documents, and glyphs. Uninitiated priests casually pronounced the glyph as if it were not magical. In fact, though, with each proper utterance the owl sign brought either good fortune or, more usually, misfortune to the priest and to all who heard him.

Amenhotshepsibu, who might have become Pharaoh, died of plague after pronouncing the owl glyph correctly. His consort, Amenhotshepsa, also died of plague, which became general, killing over one-fourth of all Egyptians. From then forward, priests purposely mispronounced the owl glyph to avoid invoking its curse.

All tokens of Amenhotshepsibu's existence were purged from all public records. The only remaining records were buried with him in his minor pyramid, which was recently discovered in the Valley of the Kings. The correct pronunciation of the owl glyph and the tale of its terrible consequences remained buried for three millennia.

Recently a team of young, talented Egyptologists recreated the correct pronunciation of the owl glyph though forensic linguistics. Unaware of the curse that they were about to invoke, the precocious Egyptologists uttered the owl sign with the correct pronunciation at an international symposium in Cairo.

The results of their demonstration caused a sensation. Not one attendee of that symposium survived; instead, all died of plague. The curse of Amenhotshepsibu was alive in the world again. Because the symposium was re-broadcast worldwide, plague raged globally in the name of the owl.

Of all the Egyptologists who were subjected to her colleague's pronunciation of the owl sign, only Professor Nancy Higgenbotham, of the University of New Hampshire, remained alive. Analysts opined that her nerve-center deafness was what saved her. Because she could speak, and because she was aware of the latest forensic techniques, the "deaf professor" was able to reconstruct and pronounce the owl sign correctly, though her pronunciation had a slightly different linguistic intonation than had been offered by her colleagues at the symposium. Miraculously, her pronunciation's effects negated the effects of her colleagues' reconstruction. Her pronunciation not only stopped plague, but it also provided immunity to all diseases.

Making use of this discovery to save lives, disease control operatives destroyed all media that contained the original pronunciation of the owl sign, and then they substituted Professor Higgenbotham's pronunciation of the owl sign. As a result, the global pandemic was arrested in all regions where the Professor's intonation of the sign of the owl could be heard. The recording of her pronunciation was ordered to be administered through the public affairs systems of all clinics and hospitals in the world.

Governments ordered that recordings of the Professor's owl sign be played at large outside events and on street corners. Commercial entrepreneurs created inexpensive recordings of the Professor's voice that could be used in universities, schools, day care centers, and home nurseries. As a result, raging plague burned out and then vanished.

Ironically, the deaf professor never heard her own pronunciation of the owl sign. Nevertheless, she became a global celebrity and an instant authority on ancient curses of all kinds. Forensic intonation was said to be her broader specialty, so adventurers and tomb raiders consulted with her before they launched into the unknown.

Among those brave, lost souls was Hiram Himsley, an Oxford physical anthropologist whose passion was early hominid cave burials in southwestern China. A high mortality rate among his predecessor savants was the caution that brought Himsley to the deaf professor's door in New Hampshire that afternoon in October 2005.

Higgenbotham and Himsley had communicated by encrypted email, so she was ready for their face-to-face meeting. While Higgenbotham made tea, Himsley espied on a library table in her living room a pile of human teeth, a small sack of seeds, four round stones, and a brass gong. She brought the piping hot tea on a tray with two cups and saucers. She found her English colleague entranced by her artifacts.

"Professor, the artifacts on your table are simply remarkable," professor Himsley said, shaking his head in amazement.

"Please, it's Nancy if I may call you Hiram. Why do you find them remarkable?" She asked the question while she poured the tea and handed one cup to her colleague. She invited him to partake of her homemade shortbread as well.

"I've found similar artifacts in each of the three cave tombs I've excavated in southwestern China. How did you come by these specimens?"

"Are you shouting, Hiram? Don't exert yourself. As long as I can see your lips, I can understand what you are saying well enough. The artifacts on the table were given to me by an explorer, like yourself, who was doing excavations somewhere in southwestern China in close proximity to your digs, I believe. I am not privileged to say precisely where because of a confidentiality agreement I have with the man's estate."

"So the explorer is now deceased?"

"I'm not sure. I know that he disappeared and now is presumed to be dead. Our consulting agreement novated to his estate one year after his last known contact, which was a year ago last June. I'm afraid I cannot give you details of that agreement. I brought the artifacts from the accessions room of the university museum so you could see the kinds of things my client brought me in payment for my services. Since they were my payment, I own them. Therefore, the covenants of our agreement do not extend to them. I needed to have you confirm that the artifacts are credible because I could hardly exhibit them if they are bogus."

He frowned. "I see what you mean. Quite frankly, my concern is related, I think, to your other client's concern. I have led three teams into southwestern China over the last fifteen years to do my excavations. All members of each of those three teams have died inexplicably. I am the sole survivor. How long I'm going to survive, I don't know. I want to lead a fourth team to the area next summer, but I don't want to risk their suffering the same fate as their predecessors."

"What do you need from me, Hiram?"

His face took on a look of grave concern. "I need to know what may have caused the deaths of my assistants and associates, and what may prevent further deaths on my next expedition."

She nodded in sympathy. "I've read your publications on your digs. I know you have articles in the mill, so to speak. Tell me a little about your findings so far. I'll keep what you tell me confidential."

"May I have more tea, please? Your shortbread is excellent."

"By all means, pour yourself tea whenever you like. The shortbread is my mother's recipe. She's English. She lives in Nottingham near what's left of Sherwood Forest." Professor Himsley smiled and nodded.

"I've been working on the idea that our ancestor homo migrated from the Great Rift Valley region in Africa to southwest China, much earlier than previously thought. A great many anthropologists' reputations will be shattered when the truth is finally known. The evidence I've amassed is fragmentary. Essentially, the same artifacts that lie on your table form the whole of it. The teeth are physically compelling. Carbon dating puts them at 80,000 years, give or take. The seeds may have been gathered in the hunter-gatherer fashion. The stones are ciphers. The gong is an anomaly because the Bronze Age has never been calculated as being anything like as old as the carbon dating suggests."

"I'd like to ask a question at this point. May I?"

"Of course. Please ask away."

"In all your studies of prehistoric remains, have you come across evidence that tomb hunters like yourself preceded you?"

"Often, I've suspected that tomb raiders had taken priceless artifacts and left the detritus like what you have on your table. In one of the three caves in southwestern China, I found the skeleton of a woman who had harbored in the cave and died there."

"Did you find any relationship between the location of the artifacts and the orientation of the female skeleton?" He seemed to be most curious about this particular detail.

"The skeleton's right hand seemed to be holding the brass gong."

Now he seemed excited. "Did you independently carbon date the gong and the skeletal remains?"

"As a matter of fact, I did. Results indicated 5,000 years plus or minus, what I'd expect for Bronze Age artifacts."

"What do you deduce from the evidence?"

"I'd say at least one and probably a team of adventurers went searching for the same caves that I've found. Only they went searching five thousand years ago."

"And that would account for the brass gongs you've found at every single site?"

"It would be a logical extrapolation."

"What about the four round stones on the table?"

"I found the same kind of stones in a tetrahedron configuration in each cave."

"Will you please arrange the stones on that table in that configuration?"

Professor Himsley looked closely at the four stones on the table. He then arranged three stones like a triangle and placed the fourth stone on top of the others.

"That's the way I found them."

"I'm not sure you are right, Hiram. You can see from the slanting light in this room that the orientation of the stones is not easterly as it should be. Let me realign the stones." She aligned the stones so one base stone pointed to the east and the two adjacent stones faced west. If I'm not mistaken, all your caves so far face east. Do they, or don't they?" She said this like a schoolmistress.

"Yes, they do. In fact, I plan to publish my ideas about these primitive hominids' superstitions about sunrise in my next article, due out this December in Physical Archaeology Review." The professor seemed very proud of his achievement, particularly now that his colleague had independently corroborated his thoughts.

"My client had similar conclusions, but he by no means thought of the hominids as primitive. He thought those early precursors of ourselves were uncannily advanced." She smiled while her hand gently caressed the four stones on the table. "Did you analyze the seeds that you found?"

"I had them analyzed by colleagues at Oxford and Cambridge. The seeds are from early specimens of edible seeds that today are considered high-energy health foods. My Oxbridge colleagues were astounded by the high protein and fat contents of the seeds."

"Did the seeds germinate?"

"It's strange that you ask that. As a matter of fact, they did germinate. The seedlings were transplanted into a special archaeological garden at Balliol College, Oxford. The plants are flourishing in a greenhouse there as I speak." He smiled, and his eyes squinted. "You already knew about this?"

"Come with me into my backyard greenhouse." She stood up and walked to her back door while he followed her. In the backyard was a small greenhouse. They entered and were suddenly in a hot, humid environment. Plants luxuriated inside. An entire table of plants was labeled, "Herbs of Southwest China c. 80,000 BCE."

"I've had 80 percent germination of those seeds. That is most remarkable for seeds as old as the carbon dating implies. The seeds are not the normal seeds we associate with prehistoric hunter-gatherer diets. In fact, they are more advanced than we've discovered among the farming cultures that supposedly followed the hunter-gatherer stage of humanity." The deaf professor was reflective when she said this, as if the implications of what she had imparted were profound.

"Nancy, I've been working with a number of colleagues on the DNA mutation patterns and pattern rates of hominids from 100,000 years ago to present."

"All right, Hiram, what have you found?"

"There is no way to join the DNA from the found remains to our present-day humans in that interval of time."

"What do you deduce from that?"

"Either our algorithms don't work or the carbon dating is incorrect, or both."

"My client came to the same conclusion. Let's go back inside to look at our rocks again." Nancy retraced her steps to her living room with Hiram following in her wake.

She picked up the stones one by one from the configuration and laid them in a line.

"Did you do chemical analysis on the four stones that you found in each cave?"

"I didn't do that yet. Would you advise me to do so?"

"Absolutely yes, I would. Let me give you a few hints, though. Invariably, one of the stones will be iron." She smiled while the shock set in and reflected on her colleague's face.

"Don't look so surprised. Meteorites of nearly pure iron have struck the earth for millennia. Another stone of the four will invariably be a geode. Those are the containers for beautiful hydrated crystals of many kinds. A third stone will invariably be roseate quartz with beads of gold. The fourth stone will be filled with silver, tin and lead salts. Encapsulated, then, these four salts look forward thousands of years toward the history of metallurgy as we know it." What she said so matter-of-factly seemed to be science fiction to the Oxford professor.

"Taken together, you're suggesting that Von Danekin and his ilk are right: aliens roamed the earth?" He was incredulous.

"I'm saying nothing of the kind. I'm rather suggesting that we need more analysis of your finds to discover what they portend for your new assistants and what they mean for you."

"I've worried about my having survived when all my associates and assistants perished." His face was a mask of mourning tinged with worry.

"As well you might worry. From the outside, a case might be built that you or someone else eliminated them to hide your potential findings."

"My findings are in line with other discoveries so far." He was now defensive.

"What we've been discussing have not been part of your published work. The deductions we've made may not be publishable for hundreds of years. People are not ready for the good news. Priests and academics who hold the myths of our culture together will be outraged. They'll fight the conclusions with every means available. Some will want to kill to prevent anyone's knowing what we know. Believe me, from my experience with the Egyptian mysteries, I've found that the forces of the status quo are formidable." She said this fervently with her blue eyes glittering.

"Are you suggesting that I stop my excavations and research?" Himsley was clearly upset that his life's work might be in jeopardy.

"No, I am not. I'm just warning you that what you are about to do is dangerous to yourself and others. In your emails, you asked whether I could help you discover how to protect your assistants. Did you mean what you wrote, or not?"

"I do want to protect my expedition. The last thing I want to do is subject my people to danger and almost certain death."

"Nothing in the world can stop fate. All I can do is give you the facts that I know. I may be deaf, but my mind still works."

"Would it be improper for me to ask the last known location of your client when you lost contact with him?"

"For what it is worth, his last email arrived on Midsummer's Day in 2003. The email's contents were simple: 'You were right!'" His previous email on the prior day gave his location as Yunnan Province, China.

"What were the contents of that earlier email?"

"He emailed that he and his team were converging on a new cave site on a yellow cliff side that locals had told him about. In response to that email, I warned him to be careful. I guess he was not careful enough."

"Be careful of what exactly?"

"I'm not sure, but in Africa hemorrhagic fever was contracted by people who had entered caves. The manner of infection was never proven, but I thought skin invasion of the virus might be caused by people not using gloves while they worked."

"The work can be hot, and gloves can get in the way sometimes."

"You mentioned that all your fellow workers died. Were there common symptoms?"

"Hemorrhagic fever may have been the common prognosis. The deaths came so swiftly that no proper diagnosis was possible. The authorities were quick to bury the corpses and hush up the circumstances."

"Well, hemorrhagic fever could link your population of hominids in China to their origin in the Rift Valley. Of course, it could also have worked in the opposite direction if the carbon dating or the theory of hominid dispersal should be incorrect. Did you follow the same protocols as your people when you went on a dig?"

"I needed to show by example what we were to do. Of course, I always followed my protocols. My people, however, did not. Perhaps that caused their unfortunate deaths?"

"We cannot be sure, but I'd advise that this time, you counsel your people to follow your protocols to the letter. At the first sign of fever, engage a medical evacuation team at once and look for Marburg or some other hemorrhagic as the cause." She could see that her guest was shuddering at the thought of the effects of hemorrhagic fever.

"What you're saying is that the hominids I've found carried the disease with them. Do you think it might have caused their deaths?"

"Clinically, it might have, but then how did so many survive over such a long period? I think they knew the secret of the disease without all our modern medicine. They knew enough about it to make their burial places death traps."

"I understand what you're saying. My hominids buried their dead in caves facing east and protected the sites from intruders with a dread disease."

"Now, I think you are ready to consider the brass gongs."

"What we know is that one brass gong was discovered in each of the grave sites we've found so far. Of those, one includes the skeleton of a female associated with the gong. Clearly, the gong did that female no good, so the gong is not the answer to the cause of the disease."

"But the woman may have thought that the gong was the answer to whatever curse plagued the burial site. Brass was known to be a curative from its earliest manufacture. Today, brass is worn to alleviate symptoms of arthritis, for example."

"I've taken your whole afternoon, Nancy, and now I'll have to go. I want to thank you for a most enlightening discussion."

"What will you do now, Hiram?" Her face showed motherly concern. He sat up straight to show his resolve and answered her directly.

"I'm going to China to excavate my next cave. While I'm there, I'll also try to discover what happened to your client."

"By doing that, you may just find another cave site worth investigating. But I'll warn you right now. Be careful. Follow your protocols. Come back alive. And if you come back, please bring artifacts like the ones we've played with this afternoon. Our museum could use them. More than that, they could be my recompense for having these discussions today." She said this offhand, but she made her point. She had done him invaluable service. She deserved to be paid back in kind. He understood her implicitly. Artifacts were the currency they valued. He decided to repay her with what he found in China.

Nancy showed Hiram to the door. There, they shook hands. Hiram drove off in his rental car to Logan International Airport, where he flew to London Heathrow International Airport. He arrived via transit to London, where he had an enormous breakfast in the Automobile Club Restaurant in Mayfair with the man who wanted to fund his expedition.

"Sir Charles," Hiram said, "I'm now ready to take my new team to China if you're ready to fund the trip." He waited while his potential benefactor devoured the remains of his breakfast.

"Hiram, this is the fourth expedition I've backed, isn't it?"

"You've been most generous, Sir Charles! I could not have published my findings without your support."

"Tell me again why this fourth expedition is necessary. Your prior three expeditions have turned up the same evidence. Is a fourth not redundant?"

"It's true that we have additional work to do with the artifacts we've already found. Recently, I've discovered that we need to do analytical chemistry on four rock samples we found at each site. I've also learned that we may not only have one site to investigate, but also another that may have been discovered by another party."

"So you have a competitor in the field? That would be news to me. You know how I like to be funding exclusive projects. I don't know who is supporting another bloke in this line, but if it's true, I don't like it one bit."

"Think of my so-called competitor as a mere grave robber, Sir Charles. I have reliable word that whoever it is has died with all hands in his last attempt. You're well aware that all my assistants on my last three missions have died suddenly."

"So we have a curse afoot?" He said this with a shocked expression as if a ghost had entered the conversation.

"Yes, sir, I'm afraid we do."

"And you somehow survived through it all?"

"Yes I did, and I'm glad to say it, too."

"So, how much did you say you needed again?"

"Two hundred fifty thousand pounds for the expedition and ten thousand pounds for the additional chemical analysis of those rocks. I'd also like to add twenty-five thousand pounds as a medical contingency fund just in case."

"Nonsense. I'll write the bank draft right now for two hundred sixty thousand pounds: take it or leave it."

"I'm most grateful. Thank you." Hiram watched as his sponsor wrote the check and handed it to him.

"Here is your money. Bring back one of those brass rings for my wife specially. She rather fancied having one after I said it was all the rage in China once upon a time. Trophy wives, you know: you've got to keep them stocked with high fashion items. As for me, I'm off to the races. Maybe there, I'll win back what I just gave you with the right bet. Ta ta, now. And, Himsley, please come back alive with all your crew intact." Sir Charles bolted without paying for the lunch, so the professor asked that the amount be added to the man's account with the usual gratuity. The thought of the huge gratuity brought a smile to the waiter's face.

Getting his three-person team together late that evening at Oxford in his rooms, Professor Himsley led the celebration with a toast, "To the earliest hominids of southwestern China." He then launched into a briefing of what he had learned in America from the deaf professor and emphasized the protocols that, he said, would protect them all from suffering the curse that had plagued his prior expeditions.

"Herb, please run around to the assayer with these twelve samples and this order for chemical analysis of the rocks. All of you, please be ready with all your gear to fly to China the next Thursday for a three-week adventure. Herb will coordinate everything for everyone. As for me, I'll be setting out three days early to scope out an additional site."

The idea of having two sites to work brought broad smiles to everyone.

Alyson said, "Two sites on one trip. That's grand! But will you be sure to meet us in China?" As a graduate intern, she was going on her first-ever expedition, and she was excited.

"I pledge that I'll to meet you at the foot of Xi Tang Mountain in Yunnan Province, where our planned excavation is to take place on the Saturday morning after your arrival near the site. Alyson and George, do you have any questions? No? Well, get some sleep and spend a couple of days relaxing. After we start this expedition, there won't be much sleep for any of us."

Herb Griggsby was an excellent choice as Professor Himsley's second. He made sure that everything was well in hand with their team before his major professor headed for the airport.

"Have you any last moment thoughts, professor?" Herb asked before he left Himsley at his departure gate.

"My only regret is that I couldn't get Sir Charles to agree to spend the money for an emergency medical team in case anyone had to be evacuated while we are in China."

"We'll manage somehow, sir. I've been on three other expeditions with others, as you know from my resume and references. I've seen it all, believe me. Have a great flight. We'll see you in Yunnan."

Professor Himsley had a long, but uneventful flight to China. He staged in Shenzhen and flew into the outback, then rented a Jeep as ground transport to the place where his competitor last communicated with Professor Higgenbotham.

Himsley inquired about him at the most likely hotel. He was informed that Professor Chumley, of Clemson University in the U.S., had last stayed there on the night before Midsummer's Day in 2003. He had checked out and never returned.

Himsley described the yellow cliff with caves, but the concierge was unable to help with that, but he summoned a local guide who would take him wherever he wanted to go.

That was how Professor Himsley made his way to the foot of the yellow cliff that the deaf professor had described during his visit. The guide told Himsley that he had led a team to a cave on the side of the cliff, but the team had not reappeared. He offered to take Himsley up to the same cave for a few thousand Yuan, which seemed a bargain.

So, they went up to the cave to find four skeletons in modern clothing on the cavern's floor. The guide went to inform the authorities while Himsley made a gloves-on survey of the site. First, he used his cellphone to take pictures. He then harvested and placed in his knapsack four stones, a sack of seeds, a little sack full of human teeth, a bundle of threads, and a brass gong.

With some satisfaction, he realized that the configuration of the stones was the same as he had seen in other such sites. With a frisson, he realized that the skeleton figure he found next to the brass gong was in the same location relative to the gong as the ancient skeleton had been at his last site. The bag of teeth was found in the right hand of the man he presumed was his competitor archaeologist. A check of the man's wallet indicated that was the case.

The PRC police and army representatives arrived within two hours. Himsley and his guide were questioned and escorted off the site. The policeman first wanted to know how Himsley knew about the bodies in the cave. Through his guide, the professor explained how he learned about the lost expedition from a colleague in the U.S.

The policeman then wanted to search Himsley's knapsack, but he interdicted the attempt by showing the uniformed man the papers authorizing his participating in a dig in Yunnan. The policeman was confused by the fact that the dig noted in the paperwork was different from the current location, but the guide retorted that one permit fitted all such sites in Yunnan. The policeman did not contradict that idea, though he frowned when he handed the papers back to the professor.

When Himsley and his guide made it down to the Jeep, they both breathed a sigh of relief that they were escaping the scene of a crime without a long detention. Himsley gave his guide a tip of twice what he had offered him when they returned to the hotel. It was, he thought, the least he could do for a man who had rendered such timely service.

Then, Himsley brooded on the grisly sight he had seen in the cave. He took out his cellphone and reviewed the pictures he had taken, carefully. He pulled on his gloves again to examine the artifacts he had gathered. He rationalized that he now had time to reach the hotel nearest his planned excavation site in plenty of time to meet his arriving team. In fact, he arrived so early at his destination that he decided to reconnoiter the cave by himself.

Before he set out for the cave, though, he wrote an email to Professor Higgenbotham. He informed her of the fate of her client and attached photos he had taken as proof. She did not respond right away, but when she did respond, she inquired about artifacts. Himsley emailed that he had in his possession all the items her client's team had harvested from the site. He also wrote that he intended to bring those things to her when he returned to the U.S.

The deaf professor expressed her gratitude for his having found the cave with the remains. That was the proof that the man's estate required. She would share the email with the information that the Chinese authorities could not provide further substantiation of the deaths. She warned Himsley to be careful that his own team did not end up like the team he had photographed.

Professor Himsley proceeded to the cave dig site as planned. He did an initial survey and discovered some of the artifacts that he had expected to find there. The stones were configured as always and oriented toward the rising sun. The pieces of woven material were evident, as was the brass gong. He did not immediately see the human teeth or the bag of seeds, but he reasoned that his team should have the pleasure of making some of the finds themselves.

He took cellphone photographs of the interior of the cave. Then, he went back down to his hotel room to compose an email with attachments to Herb, so he could share the information with his team.

Himsley took a long, luxurious, hot shower and slept until dinner. Just before he went to dinner, he received an email from Herb acknowledging receipt of his earlier email with the pictures of the cave attached. Herb reported that he and the other team members were excited by the photos.

The next day, the team arrived and met their professor. After they had a chance to check into the hotel, rest and stow their gear, everyone met for a long dinner.

"I took the opportunity to visit that other site I mentioned. I found both good news and very bad news. The good news is that the artifacts at that site confirm what I've already found at my other digs. The bad news is that I found the skeletal remains of an entire four-person team on the floor of that cave."

The team froze when they learned about the remains of the other team.

"How did they die?" asked Alyson. She was pale with apprehension and foreboding.

"Their skeletons were intact. There were no signs of shattering. My guess is that they all died of some kind of dread disease. It must have been very fast-acting because the bodies were laid out on the cool cave floor almost as if they had died instantly."

"The cave was cursed," Alyson said, in a tremulous tone. "Maybe we shouldn't be going up to our cave in the morning."

"Come on, Alyson. Don't get weak-kneed now that we're so close," said Herb, trying to show some leadership.

"Professor Himsley, what do you think are the risks?" asked George, always the practical one.

"George, I don't know what to tell you. I went into that other cave and came out alive. I also went up to our cave. In both cases, I wore the gloves that I mandated for the team's use. I picked up the artifacts from the other cave, but I left the artifacts at the Yi Tang site, so you could see them exactly as they are without modern human interference. From the evidence, the odds are one in three that you'll come out alive if you count my guide to the other site."

"The prof has proven we can do this thing."

"Yes, but I used the protocols exactly as I trained you to do. I make no guarantees for anyone not following the guidelines explicitly."

Alyson was the only team member who still had doubts.

The next morning, before the team had a chance to gather for breakfast, Chinese police, and army representatives arrived at the hotel and asked to see Professor Himsley. Through their own interpreter, they informed him that the guide who had shown him the way to the cave had died suddenly. The combined police and army team that was trying to remove the remains of the tomb raiders at the other site had all died as well, of mysterious circumstances. The reason they had come to Himsley was to be sure he was all right. They said they fully expected to find that he had expired. They apologized for having inconvenienced Himsley and went away.

At breakfast, Himsley told his team what had happened. He told them that he had made a command decision: they would use his photography from both caves and the artifacts he had gleaned from the other cave to satisfy the requirements of their expedition. That having been done, he said their expedition was over. He ordered Herb to arrange for transportation back to England as soon as possible. The team members were both upset at having been denied their dig, and relieved that they were not going to be subjected to danger, and possibly even death. Alyson was the only one who really took umbrage with the professor's decision.

"Professor, we've all come a very long way to work with you on this dig. Here we are in Yunnan, within walking distance of our objective. You've already been there and scouted it out. You even took pictures. How tantalizing! Now we're supposed to pack up again and return to Oxford like the King of France and his forty-thousand men marching up the hill and marching down again? I, for one, am not going to cut and run. I came for a reason—and my resume, and I'll not go back until I've accomplished my mission. I'll go up the hill alone if I have to. But first, I'm going to have my breakfast."

"Alyson, I understand your frustration. You saw how serious the Chinese were about what has happened. You'll get your credit, and your name will be included in any articles that stem from what we have done. Will that satisfy you? At least let's talk about this over breakfast."

So the team had breakfast, and the professor had a split decision by the end of the meal. Alyson's arguments had appealed to George, but not to Herb. So it was the professor and his second hand against the others.

The professor offered a compromise to break the tie. He said that he would take Alyson and George to the site and let them take cellphone pictures with their gloves on. His proviso was that neither should take off the gloves or touch anything sharp in the cave. Herb was not to enter the cave but remain outside in case of trouble.

While Alyson still protested that she wanted to get her hands dirty rummaging for teeth on the floor of the cave, she knew that she would be overruled. She backed down and acceded to the professor's final deal.

The group went to the cave. Herb stood guard outside while the professor, Alyson and George went inside with their gloves on and their cellphone cameras out. After fifteen minutes, they reemerged from the cave with their pictures. The professor had gathered the visible artifacts in his knapsack.

They lacked only the teeth, but Himsley decided he must have the teeth. So, he handed his knapsack to Alyson and told her and George to go back down the hill. He told Herb to wait outside the cave until he had gathered the teeth. Then, he went inside the cave again with a handkerchief tied around his nose and mouth and a dibble in his right hand. His intention was to scour the surface of the cave's floor for the missing teeth.

Himsley worked for an hour scraping the floor carefully and using his cellphone torch to view what he had unearthed. He could not find a single tooth. This, he thought odd. In every other cave he had found, including the one where the four bodies had been found, teeth were the prizes. They definitively proved that the sites had been used by hominids.

After another hour of delicately scraping around the edges of the interior of the cave, Himsley decided that he had done enough to prove that the teeth were not inside. He figured that negative information was still information, so he backed out of the cave.

There, he met Herb, who was glad that his professor was still alive. They proceeded back down the hill to their hotel, where Himsley discarded his gloves and kerchief. He asked all his team to take soapy showers to be sure that they had not come in contact with viridian materials.

When everyone had showered and changed clothing, Himsley hosted a triumphant dinner. The team had, he said, done their explorations and had in their possession the only artifacts that were available. On a side table, he ranged the stones, the brass gongs, the sack of teeth and the sacks of seeds. Over wine, he lectured on the deductions that he and Professor Higgenbotham had made during his trip to New Hampshire. He also told his assistants about the chemical analysis he had ordered before he left England.

Alyson was intrigued by the thought that some deadly virus protected each of the cave burial sites. Himsley told her that protecting burial sites with chemical and biological agents was as old as time. In ancient Egypt, for example, the tombs of the pharaohs had been protected by agents that scientists were still trying to decipher today.

"I can understand chemical agents because they serve to kill anyone daring to enter and rob from the tombs. I don't understand the biological agent because it could cause widespread destruction well beyond the tomb."

"Consider, Herb, that this biological agent is a deadly virus that kills almost immediately. Think of the four bodies on the floor of that other cave. It must have worked faster than the most lethal viruses known to contemporary man. It is a virus that acts exactly like a lethal chemical agent."

"Professor, that's frightening."

"That's why I was reluctant to subject you to that virus today. I'm hoping that you will not succumb to it as I have not."

"Can you think of any reason why you did not catch the virus when all your other team members died of it?" asked George.

"No, I cannot. Perhaps I am immune. Perhaps the hominids whose teeth we found were also immune, but I somehow doubt it."

"Professor Himsley, isn't it true that the homo at one point defeated the Neanderthals throughout what is now Europe?"

"That's the prevailing theory, yes."

"So is it possible that this virus caused the deaths of those Neanderthals and let the hominids live?"

"If we are related to the hominids you are talking about, they would have died along with their enemies. Consider the deaths of the many excavators, including those from my prior teams."

"One other thing I'm curious about is the implication of the brass gongs."

"Okay, Herb, what do you make of those?"

"They imply that we are not the first to explore these cave burials. Your finding a Bronze Age female holding a brass gong indicates that. So before the time of the first pyramids in Egypt, teams just like ours were scouring the countryside for burial sites that hark back to the beginnings of mankind."

"Go on."

"Well, for seventy-five thousand years, no one cared. Then, suddenly someone cared enough to manufacture countless brass gongs and put one in every burial cave that was found. In at least one case, that caused the death of the explorer."

"At least they made a positive contribution to the burial site."

"How so?"

"They left the brass gongs."

"I see what you mean. We, in contrast, take everything and leave nothing."

"In the case of the other cave that we will definitely not be visiting as a group, if I had not decided to check out what happened to our competitors, all four bodies and what they were wearing would have remained at the site for as long as it took for the next enterprising generation to go looking for those caves again. In fact, how many expeditions have been undertaken to find those caves will not be known until all the caves are found."

"The way some American Indian burials sites were formed in large earthen shapes, we might be searching for a long time to find all those sites." This was Herb's hopeful announcement.

"Yes. That's why we need archaeologists like you three. If you made it your mission in life to find and map the other sites, we might begin to know the mysteries we have uncovered today."

"Are you ready to go back to Oxford and write up what we've found?" the professor queried his team.

"We have enough information to satisfy our course requirements, I suppose," said Alyson.

"Teamed with the professor, we have a lot more than that," said Herb.

"Wait a minute!" interposed George, "We're forgetting something really important."

"What's that, George?" Alyson asked, bored and ready to move right on.

"This virus is pretty deadly."

"Definitely, it is."

"And it could kill a lot of innocent people as well as a lot of grave robbers."

"Go on. Make your point."

"What is to prohibit the Chinese from discovering what this virus is and weaponizing it?"

"That's nonsense," Alyson quipped.

"No, Alyson, that's genius," the professor exclaimed. "That's another reason we're all going to pack our things tonight and depart the first thing tomorrow morning. Herb, make the arrangements tonight, please." The professor had an alarmed look in his eyes. He was anxious to be on the move. Like an infection, his team members caught his excitement without being able to penetrate the source.

The next morning, the four made their way out of China and flew back to England without incident. When they arrived in Oxford, they settled back into their scholarly routine.

Professor Himsley briefed Sir Charles about their expedition and discussed what needed to happen next for planning purposes. The professor was always selling the next expedition, and he was pleased to report that everyone had returned safely from the last one.

He gave Sir Charles the brass gong he had promised to bring for the great man's trophy wife.

Sir Charles almost jumped out of his seat for joy when he received it. The brass gong, having been polished to a sheen, was gorgeous. Sir Charles said he would build a mount for it as a setting.

He was so happy that the professor decided to ask him right then for another twenty-five thousand pounds for his next dig. The man wrote the bank order immediately, and once again, he left the table without settling the bill for the quail and canard, the fine wine and the liquor. Himsley told the waiter to place the cost of the meal with a large gratuity on the great man's account. Everyone was pleased at the lunch, including the Automobile Association.

At Christmas break, Himsley flew back to New Hampshire to talk with the deaf professor, who was glad to see him again. He turned over the artifacts that he had harvested from the cave where the four bodies had been found. She watched as he laid them on her table, glad that he remembered how to stack the stones.

She was particularly interested in the brass gong. She asked Himsley to see what she had made of the other gong that she had shown him on his previous visit. Like the gong he had presented to Sir Charles, this gong was burnished to a sheen. Professor Higgenbotham had mounted it as a gong should be mounted, and equipped it with a baton so it could be struck. She handed Himsley the baton.

"Hiram, strike the gong, please. Don't be bashful."

So Hiram Himsley struck the gong and heard its resonating tone. Happy with the sound, he struck it again and again.

"Nancy, its tone is spell-bindingly beautiful."

"Yes, it is. You may recall we discussed many possibilities for this gong having been deposited in the caves where the burials had taken place, but we never talked about the meaning of the tones these gongs make when struck." She smiled as it dawned on her friend what she was suggesting.

"Tell me, Nancy, what does the tone do?" He leaned closer to her so he could hear her clearly after his ears had been affected by the gong.

"I believe that the gong is the antidote to the horrible virus that infects the caves you've been exploring. Don't ask me how it happens. I'm no virologist."

"I think I understand you, but let me ask a couple of questions to be sure."

"Fire away, Hiram."

"Are you suggesting that the Bronze Age intruders knew that the curse of the graves had something to do with an invisible death-dealing cause and used the gongs as the antidote?"

"They knew nothing about viruses, but they knew about cause and effect."

"Why would they have been left in the caves?"

"Let's assume that they were left to help any who found them, survive the effects of having entered the caves."

"That means that unaccountable deaths had occurred in such numbers that as with our improvised explosive devices, the authorities found it more cost effective to spend on a known antidote than to find the cause of the deaths and remove it?"

"I'd say that's close enough for this Christmas season, wouldn't you?"

"But one female had a gong, but died anyway."

"Proving nothing but that the poor fool did not know how to use what she had."

"I take it that you mounted this gong as an antidote, then."

"I did, and I've not had a single cold this year. That's a first."

"After our celebration, I must get back to tell my team in England about this. But I also must raise the question that one of my assistants brilliantly posed to me."

"Let me guess: what are we going to do about the possibility of weaponizing the virus for use in war?"

"Precisely. How did you know?"

"I was contacted by the authorities from a place called the United States Army Research Institute for Infectious Diseases. They were most serious gentlemen in uniform. They asked all about my connection to that unfortunate professor and his team whom you found in that cave in Yunnan, China. They wanted to know many more details that I could possibly know as a forensic anthropologist. Anyway, you should stand warned that your Porton Downs folks are likely to be calling on you soon to ask the same questions. So, will you have some of my English Plum Pudding with freshly whipped cream? I'll take that as a yes."

After the friends had spent a quiet weekend together, Himsley returned to Oxford where he immediately arranged to have his gong polished and mounted with a baton. He also had lunch with Sir Charles and told the great man the medicinal benefits of the brass gong. The knight grumbled about how difficult it was to keep a trophy wife happy. It seems they were getting a divorce. He said he would mount the polished gong on his country estate by the stables.

"The damned thoroughbreds are always coming down with something. This might do nicely to help with that. By the bye, the boys from Porton Downs dropped by to talk about some virus rubbish you diddled with in China. They were most importunate, I thought. Anyway, they'll be visiting you in your digs in Oxford sometime soon. I'd make time to see them; I would if I was you. What have you gotten me into this time, Himsley? Well, no matter, I'm off to the hounds this weekend. Just sit here and enjoy your port wine. Leave when you like. And have them put the whole bill on my account."

Professor Hiram Himsley sat back in his plush leather seat at the Automobile Club Restaurant. He enjoyed his seventeen-year-old port to the last drop. He mused about the mystery of the brass gong.

He already had, in his own account, the money for his next expedition. Should he return to China to find yet another hominid cave burial? He thought he might look into the new

Indian finds in Belize. At least, he thought as he waved to the waiter, those ruins had not been overrun by enthusiasts from the Bronze Age. How could they have been when they were only constructed two millennia later?

Camp Fire Stories

On a dark and snowy night, three couples sat huddling around a sodden campfire in the snow and drizzle, rent by the roll of thunder and the sudden jagged forks of lightning regaling each other with scary stories and poems.

This was their scary Halloween tradition, and this year, the snowy weather was cooperating with their plan as if they had scripted it. A prize was awarded to the winner of their annual contest, so their competition had an edge, and all their compositions would be published in their school's literary magazine, by permission of that publication's editorial staff. They had prepared for months for this night, and this year, they vowed that nothing was going to stand between them and sheer terror.

The couples had come in costumes that were in the spirit of the occasion, so to speak. Herbert and Ann came as Mr. and Mrs. Death. Paul and Kathy came as Jack Sprat and the wife who could eat no lean. Charles and Diane dressed as zombies with flesh so realistically putrescent that the others claimed they could smell the decay across the fire's hearth.

They had devised an order to their madness. Each couple would tell a story. All their stories had to begin with the words, "On a dark and snowy night." When all the stories had been told, each would then recite a scary poem from memory. The girls would tell the stories. The boys would recite the poems. They drew lots for their order of precedence. They had decided they would vote on the winners of their contest after all their works had been presented.

Kathy was the first by lot to tell her story, which was titled, "Knife Grinder." Kathy was curvaceous, as befitted the wife of Jack Sprat, so she munched her way through her telling.

"You can tell this is my tale because Paul and I, or rather Jack Sprat and his wife, are characters in it." As Kathy told her tale, she roasted and ate marshmallows. This is the story she told that dark and snowy night:

Knife Grinder

On a dark and snowy night, which happened to be a particularly scary dark and chilly Halloween, the rural trick-or-treating was well underway. By custom, around a half an hour remained before the curfew began. The Johnson Farm was under siege. Children dressed in costumes knocked at the door, and Mrs. Johnson, dressed as a wicked witch, answered.

"Trick or Treat?"

"What are you dressed as, son?"

"Can't you tell? I'm Jack Sprat. My sister there is my wife, who could eat no lean. She's really fat. Hey, Jillian, no hitting!"

Paul stood up all of a sudden and posed with his prop as Jack Sprat. Kathy, dressed as Mrs. Sprat, stopped telling her tale long enough to hit him on the arm while she pulled him back into his place.

Laughing, she gave him a roasted marshmallow and put another over the fire before she recomposed herself and continued. "And who is this other fellow?" She held out her brimming bowl of candy and the two children each took one piece.

"I don't see anyone else. Come on, Jillian! It's getting late. Thank you for the treat, Ma'am." Jack Sprat and his wife ran down the walk to the road and into the night.

"Young man, is it? Come forward. Don't you want a treat? What are you dressed as?"

Charles and Diane stood and stretched, their zombie costumes looking positively ghastly in the firelight. Kathy stopped and glared at them while she waited for them to settle back into their places. Paul took the opportunity to add another log to the fire, which hissed and sputtered when he stoked it. When everyone was ready, Kathy stuck another marshmallow in the fire and picked up her story as if nothing had happened.

"Guess."

"Hmm. Let's see. You're carrying a machine. It looks like an old fashioned metal grinding machine. I haven't seen one of those for many years."

"Not bad. That's exactly what it is—a grinding machine. I grind knives. The grinder really works. It makes a lot of racket. Do you want to hear it grind?"

"No thanks. I believe you. When I went trick-or-treating many years ago, the knife grinder had a very special meaning. You're a knife grinder. So what are you meant to represent?"

"Dad says I'm like the grim reaper. The sound of my grinding is supposed to mean that death is near."

Herbert and Ann now rose and did a macabre dance because they were dressed as Mr. and Mrs. Death. Kathy laughed and corralled them back in their places. She gave each one a roasted marshmallow and continued with her story.

"That's scary."

"It's Halloween! It's supposed to be scary. Speaking of scary, who's that behind you?"

The witch did not turn around. Instead, she smiled wickedly so the boy could see that she had only a few teeth, and she cackled.

"The man behind me with the long scythe is death. He lives with me always. I'm glad I didn't ask you to demonstrate your grinder. Don't you want some candy?" She extended her bowl of candies and watched as he selected the one he wanted.

"Yes, ma'am, I suppose the grinding sound would be very bad luck for someone. Thank you for the treat. Have the three cows been by yet?"

"Yes, they came by around fifteen minutes ago. It was a very moving experience. Why do you ask?"

"I've been trying to catch up to them all evening."

"Are you related?"

"Not really. They're sisters."

"Did you see which way the cows went after they stopped here?"

The witch cackled and pointed east. At the same time, the figure behind her pointed his scythe in the opposite direction. Or was he raising it to take a harvest swing? His rictus gave no indication that he intended to laugh.

Instead a dry coughing sound broke the slicing sound as the witch fell in a heap and the scythe reached forward to catch the knife grinder, who was proceeding down the walk as fast as he could run to catch up with the three cows.

As he walked along, the knife grinder began to grind. The sound was like a low murmur, grating to hear. On the main road, the other trick-or-treaters gave the knife grinder a wide berth. None could see him. What they avoided was the sound he made.

Behind him, came the figure with the scythe, trying to reap what it had not sowed. No one could see death any more than they could see the knife grinder, but they knew death was near in the night.

Ahead, were Jack Sprat and his wife. They had joined the three cows and were turning into the Randolph farm. The knife grinder stopped grinding and tagged along behind. Of course, death followed waiting behind them all. Jack Sprat knocked on the Randolphs' door. Mrs. Randolph answered on the second knock. She was dressed like an old crone, with two milky white eyes. She appeared to be blind and groped at the children with one hand while she extended her tray of candied apples with the other.

"Trick or treat."

"I cannot see you because I'm blind. Tell me who you are, and I'll give you each a nice red candied apple."

"I'm Jack Sprat, and this is my wife."

"The one who could eat no lean?"

"That's the one. She's really fat, so she looks the part. Stop hitting me, Jillian!"

"Okay, each of you take a treat. I know there are others out there. Don't be bashful."

"We are the three cows in the meadow, Bossy, Milly and Hildegard. Moo."

"Moo!"

"Moo?"

"I hear you lowing. Come take a treat, one each. Now run along. And who is left now?"

"I'm the knife grinder."

"I heard you coming. Was the sound a recording?"

Kathy was doing a great job making the sound of a knife grinder. The sound she was making grated on everyone's nerves.

"No. I made the sound with my grinding machine."

"You were sharpening knives?"

"Yes, ma'am."

"I was afraid of that. Do you know if he is following you?"

"Who's that?"

"The man with the scythe."

"I saw him at the Johnsons', but I didn't see him following me here."

"I can't see him, but I know he's out there with you. You've come as a pair. Each of you come forward and take a treat."

The knife grinder took his treat, turned and skipped back down the lane to the road. He did not see the figure with the scythe take his harvest. He only heard a whistling sound like a sudden wind, followed by a low moan.

"Wait, no wait!" the woman cried. The knife grinder did not look back because she was not speaking to him.

Out on the road, heading to the Simpsons' farm, were the whole crew of trick-or-treaters. Minnie and Mickey Mouse, Goofy, Aunt Jemima, Jack Sprat and his wife, the three cows, and the Big Bad Wolf and Little Red Riding Hood, were all there in a throng. As before, Jack Sprat knocked on the door as everyone crowded around expectantly. Mr. Simpson answered the door dressed like an undertaker. Behind him was his wife, dressed all in black for mourning and holding a lighted red candle.

"Trick or treat!"

Mr. Simpson smiled wickedly and said, "So, what if I choose trick?"

"You can't do that. It's not fair."

"Treat, treat. We want a treat!"

"I just received two calls from my neighbors. That's why we're dressed for the dead. The wicked witch and the blind old crone are dead. We're in mourning. Don't be frightened, children. Sooner or later, you all come to me. I'm the undertaker. Do you know what that means?"

"It means we have to trick you, Sir, to get away." This was the knife grinder speaking. The others all parted way so he could approach the undertaker.

"I have a figure following me. I will leave him here with you. If you will prepare him for a funeral, we'd all appreciate it very much."

"And who, pray tell, are you?"

"I am the knife grinder. Do you want to hear me grind my knives?"

"Why, I'd be delighted. It's the kind of music that lifts my heart, because every time I hear it, it reminds me of my wedding day."

Ann and Diane looked at each other in disbelief at what they were hearing. How could anyone like the horrid sound? What did the sound portend, anyway?

The knife grinder began to grind. The others held their ears at the grating sound of metal on metal, except for the funeral director and his wife, who stood enraptured by the sound. As the knife grinder continued, the funeral director bowed to a figure behind the trick-or-treaters. The figure raised its scythe as if to sweep through the children when the knife grinder stopped his grinding and stood back. Death walked straight through the crowd to the door and proceeded past the funeral director and his wife.

"Now that we've played our trick, please give us each a treat."

"Yes, please, Sir, give us all a treat," said Minnie Mouse.

"I'd like cheese!" said Mickey Mouse.

The cows all mooed and bellowed.

The undertaker went back to the coffin that lay in his hallway and drew out a small casket of candies. He took it into the crowd and made sure each trick-or-treater got a treat. They saw that the man was sweating and looked afraid. His wife was smiling at something, but they could not see what it was. None of them could see the figure with the scythe.

As the children meandered back along the path to find the road, the knife grinder heard the sound of a slicing scythe, but he did not look back. Instead, he looked forward at the three cows with keen interest.

Jack Sprat asked Mickey Mouse, "Isn't it time for curfew?"

"We have only just enough time for perhaps one more visit before we have to get home."

The knife grinder knew that his time was almost up, so he played his machine as they walked.

The three cows complained at the racket.

"Have you heard of cattle mutilations? This is the sound that the cows hear just before the mutilator strikes."

"Stop teasing!"

"No fair!"

"We'd better run!"

Just then, flying down the street, came a coven of witches on brooms with a huge black cat leaping and bounding. They waved flashlights in everyone's faces and surrounded the cows. They cut them out from the rest of the trick-or-treaters and herded them home through the darkness.

The hounds began baying at every farm. Across the moon, drifted a lonely cloud. The curfew horns started sounding, one after another. The children raced to get home, all except the knife grinder. He started up his machine again with gusto. The grinder's raucous music filled the cold night air, and other sounds arose like an infernal chorus.

Cattle bellowed. Dogs did bark. Children screamed. The knife grinder's knives shot sparks into the air. Jack-o-lanterns flickered and leered. As the midnight hour approached, the knife grinder thought he saw a figure in a long cape. The figure had a scythe. He was swinging the scythe in the air effortlessly, as if he were slicing through night souls with abandon. The knife grinder saw that the figure was coming straight for him with a vengeance because he had been tricked.

Feeling very small, the knife grinder stopped his grinding as the figure rose up on its tiptoes and raised its scythe.

Here Ann and Diane raised their hands to their mouths in fright, their eyes wide as saucers. The boys were trying not to show they were scared, but their fists were clenched, and their breathing was heavy as witnessed the white coming from their mouths.

"It's time to go home now, son."

All the listeners breathed a collective sigh of relief.

"Oh, Dad, can't we stay out a little longer?"

"We've had a lot of fun this Halloween, but it is now midnight. So our powers have been overtaken. We had our chance and did well. Don't worry because there's always next year."

"Next year I want to wear the cape and swing the scythe."

"We'll see, son."

"That usually means no."

"Hahaha. Did I see the Black Dog passing you in the night?"

"Yes, the Black Dog passed a few minutes ago."

"And what about the Phosphor and the Cold White Tentacle?"

"Them too."

"So we've seen nearly everything tonight."

"And was anyone really afraid?"

"I was afraid."

"Hahaha. You were afraid? Not likely, Dad. Why do you say you were afraid?"

"I was afraid I'd laugh and spoil our game."

"I didn't see you until that last farm. How did you manage to remain invisible?"

"That is a trade secret that my dad taught me."

"So will you tell me the secret?"

"Why don't you tell me how you guessed I was there all the time though you couldn't see me?"

"You remember that Mrs. Johnson and Mrs. Randolph both looked over my shoulder? Well, I guessed you were there somewhere."

"So that's why you knew how to do the trick on Mr. Simpson. That was so spontaneous. Great thinking."

"It was good that you played along, Dad. Thanks."

"But I didn't play along. That must have been someone else."

"Now you've got me scared, Dad!"

Death reached out and grasped the knife grinder.

"This knife grinder was my grandfather's. I used to take it out when I was a trick-or-treater."

"We'd better get home now. Mom'll be worried."

"You're right, son. Lead the way."

Kathy shrugged and screwed up her face in a broad grin. Popping another marshmallow in her mouth, she said, "That's my story!"

"Kathy," said Paul, "that was a truly great, very scary story. I particularly like the allusion to cattle mutilations and the family heritage behind the knife grinder. You were a good sport letting us get up and down during your telling and feeding us marshmallows too. Okay, Diane is next by lot. Are you ready? Yes? Good. Okay, tell your story."

"My story is titled, 'Chainsaw,' and I think you'd all better huddle against each other and watch your backs while I tell it."

Just then, an owl hooted and, as if on cue, the thunder rolled and lightning flashed as the couples moved closer together around the fire. Diane was a dramatic reader and member of the school's theater group. Like Kathy, she could change her voice to suit the characters in the story. She did not overly dramatize her reading. The story was scary enough without her overdoing it. This is the story that she told that snowy night:

Chainsaw

On a dark and snowy night, almost anything can happen. This night, to boot, it was Halloween. More than that, all the power in the Northeast corridor was out, on account of the snowstorm, with no estimate of restoration.

The trick-or-treaters were very disappointed that their night of fun was ruined. Parents consoled themselves by using the candy they had bought for visitors as an assuagement for their children, who huddled together over board games or snuck off into their rooms to play games on their cellphones.

Unfortunately, the seasonal propaganda was accompanied by an actual Freddy-like chainsaw murderer, who had decided to dismember his victims and post the horrific results on the Internet. The sadist who did the postings borrowed from other banned photographs, but the result was what you would expect—pandemonium. The parents were scared. The police were bewildered. The public was on alert because no one was safe. No one knew when or where the chainsaw murderer would strike next.

In a house with a generator, still decked with lights in Nashua, New Hampshire, the general misery of Greater Boston was entirely ignored. Halloween was observed not in the breach, but in the full regalia. Robotic spiders climbed up and down the portal to the entrance. A robotic owl looked this way and that with its red eyes gleaming. The proud owners of the house were ready to receive all comers. The husband dressed as a witch with a tall, pointed hat, and the wife was bustling around the house, touching up the ghastly decorations that were part of the festivities.

The husband and wife had counted all their previous years' visitors on this unhallowed night, and the number averaged seventy, give or take five. They had bought provisions for eighty just in case. Tonight, though, the visitors were few. Yes, they used their cellphones to inform their friends about the benison that would be available at this remarkable house. Probably they would inform them about the robotic snakes that dwelled in the tree wells and the gules of red light that streaked the macabre abode in an irregular display.

At this point in the story Charles tickled Diane, who laughed and made snowballs to throw at the zombie pair. Kathy kept roasting marshmallows and handing the sticks around so others could eat them. Diane calmed down and picked up where she had left off her story.

Pauly and Lisander approached the dwelling with trepidation, but they were determined to have their treats on Halloween night, though the other houses in the neighborhood had offered none. They went right up and knocked, and when the witch answered the door, they shouted in unison, "Trick or treat!"

Silence followed. The witch looked over the two boys and asked each to extend his index finger. When they did so, her gnarled, bent fingers caressed them and checked to see whether they had fattened up to serve her purposes.

They were not found wanting, so she curled her finger with its long, insinuating nail and invited them inside. There, her husband, dressed as Dracula, awaited them. The two boys were not going to be deprived of their treats by a little terror, so they went inside, hoping to be given a treat and allowed to depart straight away. If only things had been that simple.

Dracula asked the boys to be seated on the couch while he fetched them drinks, apparently soft drinks, red in color and bubbling. They drank. Both boys fell into a deep sleep. Dracula lifted each gently and took him into the back room, where he placed them on beds like the others, where his vampires were feeding.

Two began feasting on the new bodies as soon as they were in place. They inserted their sharp fangs to draw blood and then used their tongues to lick the blood as it flowed from the necks. Children had such rich, pure blood, they were natural donors. Dracula and his brood appreciated this in a time when blood stocks were uniformly contaminated by drugs and toxins.

The witch scanned the path and road for other victims, but weather conditions and the power outage were not going to provide the numbers she and her husband required. She remained near the door, keeping watch while Dracula did the best he could to feed their children with the blood of the drugged trick-or-treaters. At midnight, the feasting was done, and that was a good thing because the invulnerability that Halloween had provided was no longer available to them.

It was time to release the children and go back to what passed as normal. Dracula unbound the two boys and the three girls who had been the food while they slept. He revived them with ammonia and gave them warm punch. He loaded their Halloween baskets with candy and cakes. They went away satisfied that they had gotten more than they had bargained for this Halloween.

Only when they were well clear of the gabled, haunted house did they realize how late it was. They scampered home through the snow in the abysmal blackness of the night. Their parents were distraught because they had been out much too long, and they vaguely threatened punishments, except they were so grateful that the children had appeared again, apparently unharmed.

The harm was not apparent, but it was condign. The next morning, the parents of those children realized that the marks on their necks had significance. They did not call the police. Instead, they called on a local necromancer, a warlock of some renown. They marched the five children into his slovenly office for an examination. The warlock did so. He said there was no question: the children had all been fed upon by vampires.

He told them, "They have the characteristic marks on their necks, and they are listless. I advise against informing the authorities because officially vampires have no standing under the current laws."

"So what are we to do?" asked the most energetic male parent.

"The children's blood loss will probably not affect them. Of course, there is a slim chance of the children having become vampire-prone."

The way Diane said, "vampire-prone" gave everyone the shivers. For a moment, Kathy stopped roasting her marshmallow so it burst into flames. Paul grabbed the stick with the flaming torch of a marshmallow and cast it into the fire. Herbert put his arm around Ann and tried to bite her neck like a vampire, but she pushed him away smiling. Charles nodded for Diane to continue, while Kathy picked up another stick and stuck a new marshmallow on it.

"And what, pray, does that mean?"

"Vampires get a taste for a certain person's blood and decide they cannot resist tasting it again. One thing can lead to another, and before you know it, your child has become one of the vampires."

"So what do we do about this?"

The boys and girls held each other's hands and leaned forward while they looked into the fire. Clearly a bad thing could happen. How could the story possibly end happily?

"There is no one-hundred-percent solution. You can try the usual remedies. For example, you can hang a garlic clove and a cross around the children's necks. You can keep the children inside after dark, and be sure that the windows are closed and fastened. You can counsel them to keep away from strangers. That's about all you can do. One thing more, though, statistically, children who've been attacked by vampires and survived are far likelier to achieve healthy lives and advanced age than others. So there's an upside to the encounter."

The parents were not consoled by what the warlock said. They instituted a strict regimen for their children and for a long while, they watched over everything they did, day and night. The children became exasperated by their parents' over-protectiveness and intrusion on their lives. They decided that they would find ways to escape the confines of their perceived imprisonment.

This was particularly true of the two boys, though the three girls were also unused to confinement. It was only a matter of time before the children staged a breakout from the parental envelope that suffocated them. The oldest girl, named Astrid, met Pauly at school to discuss the problem that they faced.

"I have the strongest desire to climb out my bedroom window and run to the nearest woods. There, I'd be free." That was Astrid's confession to the older boy. "I'd feel a lot better about this decision if someone big and strong was there to protect me." Clearly, she implied that Pauly should run away as well and join her.

"I have the same impulse, but I'm not sure I could protect you from the vampires. They are all adults, some probably hundreds of years old. What could I do against them?"

"Have you no courage? Do you want me to be eaten by them and killed, or, worse, turned into a vampire?"

"Astrid, aren't you being a drama queen about this? We have no evidence that the vampires have been watching out for any of us. Maybe they've all gone into hibernation until next Halloween?"

"That's nonsense. Vampires have to feed, and they could never last until next Halloween without attacking someone to feed."

"So let's plan to meet in the woods and see what happens?"

"We'll only have to stay there a little while at first. We can meet at midnight and stay for an hour. If that works okay, we can plan to stay longer, and then perhaps, invite the others."

"Astrid, I'm not at all sure what this will prove."

"It'll prove we don't need all the fuss and bother that our parents are subjecting us to. It'll prove we can stand on our own."

"It'll prove we may be as foolish as our parents. They think we have to be sequestered. We think we have to be totally free. I, for one, am scared of vampires. I can't believe we all became victims."

"You're not scared, are you?"

When she asked this question in her story, Diane tickled Charles. He tickled her back. Everyone started tickling the others until they were in an uproar of tickling and laughing uncontrollably. Herbert and Ann were the first to calm down. They went back to roasting marshmallows. Paul adjusted his seating and gazed into the fire, as Kathy laid her head on his shoulder and looked into the flames. Diane picked up again where she had left off.

"Why shouldn't I be scared? Real vampires are scary. Let me put this another way: if I were to bite your neck and lick your blood, what would you think of that?"

A smack resounded. Ann had smacked Herbert because he tried to bite her neck again. Now Kathy glared at Ann, who held one hand over her mouth and laughed while she pushed Herbert to let him know she was just playing with him.

"You wouldn't do that. I won't allow it. What a disgusting thought anyway. You don't mean it?"

"Of course, I don't mean it. The thought disgusts me too. No offense."

"No offense taken. So it's decided. We'll meet in the woods behind my house at midnight tonight. There's a place just inside the copse of trees, where pine needles make a nice surface under the snow. I'll meet you there. Don't forget. I don't know what I'd do if you didn't show up."

"That would probably be scary. I'll be there, though. Count on me."

The children went to their respective classes and continued their normal routines, until midnight, when they slipped out their back windows, down their roofs, and scampered into the copse of woods in the back of Astrid's folks' property.

"Hello, Astrid, it's dark. Are you there?"

"Yes, Pauly, I'm here. Come on inside. The pine needles are as soft as I said they'd be."

"So, you haven't heard anyone or anything else?"

"I was frightened by the flutter of a large barn owl. It flapped free of the trees and went hunting."

"They grow very large. Some can hunt large rats, small cats, and very small dogs."

"It's chilly, so I brought a blanket we can share."

"I won't need that. So what do we do? Tell ghost tales? It's awfully dark."

"We're here to prove we can be safe outside the confines of our homes for one hour."

"I'm satisfied that we've proved we can be safe for ten minutes. Won't that do?"

"You're afraid, aren't you? Scaredy cat!"

"Shh. Did you hear that?"

"What? What did you hear? Now I'm afraid."

"Over there. See the light?"

"Astrid, are you out there?"

"That's my dad. I'm in trouble now. Look, hide here. I'll go out to meet him. When we've gone inside, you can go home."

"Dad, I'm over here."

"Astrid, your mother and I were worried sick. We thought you'd been abducted. Get yourself inside right now. We are not pleased in the least that you snuck out like that."

"Oh, Dad, I'm all right. It is such a nice night for a walk."

"Get inside right now, young lady. I need to teach you a lesson you'll not forget."

"Ouch. I'm going."

When Astrid and her father had gone inside, Pauly decided to make his way home, but he bumped into a tall figure that grabbed him by both arms.

"How convenient it is for me that you happened along tonight."

"Who are you? What do you want? Let me go!"

Pauly was about to scream when the figure hit him in the jaw. Pauly then heard the unmistakable sound of a chainsaw starting.

"Well, Paul, how do you like the ending?"

"I'm scared. Don't you hear the chainsaw revving now?"

"You're making me shudder just thinking about it."

"Okay, let's move right along. Ann, it's your turn now."

Ann was the intellectual among the friends. She was prim and proper and a rule marm par excellence. She told her tale, titled 'Rictus II,' with a cold objectivity that lent a stark contrast between the words and their grisly meanings. Ann was a deep one, and her listeners were very attentive for hidden meanings in her tale.

Rictus II

On a dark and snowy night, an ancient man is pushing a hugely overloaded shopping cart around the first circular traffic divider once you leave the town. His cart is full of plastic bags, bulging with the necessities of his homeless life, including a sodden sleeping bag.

The man is wearing an old raincoat over a vintage three-piece suit of faded blue. On his feet, are shoes that are much too large for him. As he walks, they squeak and spill water as they crunch through the snow. An old-fashioned fedora hat sits on his head. It is much too small for him, but it manages to stay fixed, though it is covered with snow and beaded with drizzle from the light rain. The man's long stringy hair, tied in a ponytail in the rear, falls in damp strings around his unshaven face.

The man has been around the circle many times. After each circumnavigation, the man recites a consecutive number. He intones the number to no one in particular. It is three a.m., and traffic has long ago dwindled to nothing. The early morning outside is dark and foggy, and an orange pool of halogen light illuminates the snow-covered traffic circle.

The man reaches the number 665 and stops. Another figure approaches from the main street, from the direction of the town. This figure, a male dressed in black, seems amused to find the man with the shopping cart walking in a wide circle. He falls in silently alongside the man with the cart.

Sated from his earlier blood feast, the figure in black listens for any lingering tell-tale sounds of this special night for him and his kind. The night has experienced its storm-inspired hours of snow and icy rain, but now the large portion of the great storm has passed. The empty streets are slippery wet with slush, and still running with snow melt. By the stroke of midnight, the Halloween crowds disappeared. The denizens of darkness retreated as their adversaries advanced to reclaim the land. All Saints Day came at the twelfth church bell's chime, and none too soon for the mortals who remain.

The figure in black decides to engage the man with the shopping cart in conversation.

He asks, "Where are you heading?"

The man answers, "I'm heading for my grave."

Herbert took this occasion to tickle Ann, who giggled in spite of herself. This caused another bout of general tickling that lasted until Ann straightened her costume primly and folded her hands in her lap until the others settled back down. Paul stoked the fire. Kathy balled up the marshmallow container and put it in her pocket. Charles and Diane nodded that they were ready for Ann to continue telling her tale.

"I can understand that, my friend. Do you think you'll find what you're looking for by going in circles in the snow?"

As if the figure in black has said nothing, the old man continues, "I was there at Los Alamos on the day of the first test of the atom bomb. That great fireball in the sky changed my life forever. It reduced me to my current style of life."

Reaching into his cart, brushing off the snow and finding his cereal box, he asks, "Do you want some food?"

The figure in black demurs when he sees what his companion offers.

"Quaker Oats, though nutritious for some, is not in my diet," he explains. 'Thanks, just the same." He watches while the man munches noisily. He has a thought and asks, "Do you always eat healthy food? Have you ever smoked, drank alcohol or used drugs?"

The man with the shopping cart swallows and says, "I've never done any of those things at any time in my life."

"So you're as pure as no other man I've ever met!"

"Not so. I was affected by the radiation from the nuclear blast. My condition is not fatal though I wish it was. Can you understand what I'm saying?" His yellow eyes look crazed as he focuses ahead on his circuitous path.

The figure in black does not answer because he has been distracted by a female figure in a black cape. She clearly has designs to feast on him. He turns toward her and bares his razor-sharp teeth in a ghastly smile. She smiles in return with teeth like his and does something like a curtsy.

She then looks across him at the man with the shopping cart and nods at him as if in recognition. The man with the shopping cart pays her no heed. Then she rushes around the round-a-bout looking for other prey. In her wake, runs a gaunt figure with a long, sharpened stake. He clearly means the female figure mortal harm.

The figure in black sticks out his foot, causing the woman's pursuer to fall in the slush of the street and his stake to fly out of his hand. The man with the shopping cart leans down and picks up the stake. He examines it as best he can in the orange light. He then shrugs and hands it to the figure in black.

The old man mumbles, "The wood is from a rowan tree — it's a vampire killer."

The figure in black continues to walk alongside the man with the shopping cart, keeping the stake close to his side. Frantically and vainly, the fallen man gropes around the street in the slush for his lost weapon. The female returns to find him there. She mounts him and rides upon his back as if he were a beast of burden. She then leans forward, smiles and begins to feast — on him.

The man with the shopping cart continues his round, completely absorbed in his mission.

The figure in black turns to depart, yet he hears a rattling of the shopping cart behind him. A hooded figure raises a scythe as if to harvest the old homeless man. The figure in black hurls the stake into the chest of the scything figure as it slices vainly through the man with the shopping cart.

Ann paused for a moment while everyone absorbed what was happening in her story. She saw her companions were spellbound at the thought of the figure with the scythe. Satisfied that she had made her intended effect, she plunged into her story's conclusion.

"Hahaha, 666!" The man with the shopping cart continues on his way, oblivious to the pageant that unfolds around him.

In the distance, a cock crows.

"I get the reference to 666," said Kathy.

"I get the reference to Los Alamos," Charles chimed in.

"I get the references to the rowan tree and the cock crowing," said Paul.

"But what does the whole story mean?" asked Diane.

"That's for you to puzzle out, Diane," said Ann cryptically.

"Okay, everyone, it's time for the scary poems. Charles, will you begin?"

"I drew the lot, so I'll recite first. The title of my poem is 'Unholy Names.' Here goes." Charles's recited his poem as follows:

Unholy Names

This day no church bells ring, eve before light
Songs begin unsinging, witches turning,
Eeking, gasp and cry soulless prayers of night.
Black fires run along the marrow burning.

Unhallowed graves yawn wide without stirring,
Waiting for fleshy bones red worms to eat
The lad who dallied and his maid's crimped ring
Mocking the time, their wasted game complete.

Across the moon's pocked face hags still fly high,
Dip, rise, gyre, laugh and brave it till the dawn.
Black cats arch their backs then spring and lie
Expectant while the scythe is backward drawn.

This one day names come empty at the call,
Unholy children lost before they fall.

"Charles, that is one spooky poem. It's clearly a Shakespearean sonnet. It even ends in an epitaph couplet. The last line is absolutely spectral."

"Thank you, Ann."

"Okay, Paul, it's now your turn."

"My poem is titled, 'End Time Constriction,' and it goes like this." Paul recited his poem as follows:

End Time Constrictor

Riding her broomstick o'er damned gabled slough
Flash lightning, roar thunder shrieks white-eyed pain
Where bats dwell and crows line bare lime bough
Cawing or cleaning beaks in bloody rain.

She seeks one handy with his scythe to spare
None. Soul mower, Hell's harvester of sins,
Sod slicer riffing frantic flight: despair
Red gules lit by jack-o-lantern grins.

She waves her gnarled hand as moonrise mocks
Blind children's laughter punctuating raves
Birth pangs drawn from death's cool reckoning knocks.
Between marks lies silence of yawning graves.

With soughing sound and broad blade whistling slow

She smiles grim greeting. He swings. It's time to go.

"Wow, Paul, I'm blown away," said Kathy "It's another Shakespearean sonnet. Only you've changed the perspective three times in the last line—brilliantly."

"Okay, one more poem to go—Herb, are you ready?"

"I am ready. My poem is called, 'Moonstruck.' Here I go." Herb recited his poem as follows:

Moonstruck

Tomorrow's lunar aspect portends doom:
The largest moon we'll ever see blood red.
My hair unleaves as silence laves your loom.
Your fangs divide my living from your dead.

Yellow-eyed tribe, we'll howl and ghastly grin.
The creature I become you cannot change.
Wild winds winnow twinned souls adrift in sin.
A rictus rakes us where our glasses range.

Too horror struck for words, I growl. You glare.
Our supine bodies make standings stumblings.
My claws scratch you, our couch, your ochre chair.
My mouth foams red while we share dark mumblings.

We feast on time as time devours this night:
Tomorrow strikes the moon and dies our light.

"I love the penultimate line, Herb! It's definitely the third superb Shakespearean sonnet we've heard tonight," said Ann.

"I like the resonance between time and light, brought together by the moon and the lycanthropy," contributed Charles.

"We certainly have three winning stories and three winning poems this year. Good work, all!" said Kathy. "I like the fact that we had a set of rules, but got entirely different approaches."

"So we're not going to go the next step and judge a winner?" asked Paul.

Diane interposed, "That's right, Paul. Everyone's a winner. All the works will be published in our school literary magazine. That was our goal, and we've done it."

"The snowstorm has blown over now. We're surrounded by a rising snow mist. It's spooky enough to tell some other tales if you're all game. These stories won't have rules. They'll be just for fun. What do you think, Ann?"

"I'm a little tired from listening, but I'll not spoil the fun," said Ann with a cheery smile.

"Who's first, then?" asked Paul.

"I've got a chilling story, but it doesn't start with the catch phrase we used for the others. One thing more—it's very dark in content. Do you think you can stand it?"

"Charles, don't be so dramatic. Just tell your story," Kathy said.

"Okay, I warned you. The story is based on fact. It really happened. It could happen again. It could happen to you. So it is not exactly a Roman a Clef, though each occurrence will naturally have its own key. It shows how fear can be ignored to everyone's peril. My story is titled, 'Waiting for You,' and it goes like this." Charles told the following story:

Waiting for You

Red-haired Sheila was the belle of the ball. Everyone knew that she would marry well and have, as she said, dozens of Celtic children. Nothing was farther from her mind than what lay just ahead.

The first inkling that something was very wrong was a series of postcards that she received in snail mail with words cut out of magazines and newspapers. Invariably, the message was, "Waiting for You." At the same time, she received odd invitations on Facebook from a figure named, "Waiting4U."

Sheila threw the postcards away and avoided friending the creep that seemed to be stalking her. She told her mother about the incidents, and they both laughed at the antics some screwballs will descend to in order to gain a girl's attention. Mrs. Connaught told her daughter to be careful when she went outside but otherwise, ignore the stalker. Sheila's father wanted to inform the police, but Sheila and her mother dissuaded him from taking that step, because of the intrusion that might make on their lives.

The autumn festivities were ratcheting up at Sheila's high school. Sheila was elected Homecoming Queen, and the captain of the football team invited her to the Halloween Ball. What with all her other activities, like orchestra and her clubs, Sheila was working eighteen hours a day just to keep up.

She took shortcuts for efficiency, and one of those was walking from the bus stop through the woods that led to her backyard every weekday evening just after sunset. She was the designer of her club's float for the Halloween Parade, so her days stretched even longer as the deadline for completion drew near. Her walks through the woods were now at eight o'clock and even later.

She had no trouble following the narrow path through the woods with her cellphone spotlight, but the umbra outside the lines of light hid demons and monsters that Sheila tried to ignore. She did not like the dark one bit, and the whispers she heard, or thought she heard, were beginning to get on her nerves.

She thought heard, "Waiting for you," and a shiver ran up her spine. Worse, she thought she sensed a presence right behind her and a cool breeze lifted her hair, but when she dipped and wheeled around to shine her light, all she saw was darkness and the encroaching woods, and nothing menacing at all. She laughed out loud and turned the light back to the path ahead and saw two red eyes glaring at her.

At this point in the story, Kathy audibly gasped. Paul took her hand. Ann edged close to Herbert, who put his arm around her. Diane's eyes widened as she gazed into the fire and poked it with a stick. Pleased with his story's effects, Charles continued while the dark night pressed on them cold, wet and fearsome.

She stumbled but caught herself before she fell. The lights ahead disappeared, and a scuffling sound in the dead leaves of the wood told her that whatever was on the path had gone into the woods. It was no threat. Perhaps it was only Coco the Siamese cat that was always prowling around the neighborhood. She just did not know.

She made it to her back yard and saw that the way was clear for her to enter her back door. She was determined not to become frightened of nothing as she went inside to do her homework and get to bed.

On her Facebook page was a new friend invitation from someone called, "SawU2Nite." She was definitely not playing that game, and in her mail on the kitchen table was another postcard with the annoying message, "Waiting for You."

She tore the postcard into tiny pieces and threw them in the kitchen trashcan. She decided to tell her mother about the latest indignities in the morning over breakfast, but by the time breakfast came, the events of the day sent the family in six different directions. Sheila thought bringing up silly fears was no way to start the day.

Sheila was fitted for her Homecoming Queen gown at a dressmaker's shop that habitually sewed the costumes for the occasion. She laughed to think that she walked into the establishment dressed like Cinderella before the fairies did their magic, and for a moment, did her fitting on a dais like royalty, and then afterward, turned back into Cinderella in her cutoff jeans and vanilla sweatshirt with the big letters, "IN YOUR FACE!"

When she stepped out of her brilliant blue high heels into her Adidas, she felt that she was descending from Olympus back into the humdrum normalcy of existence. Her dreams and her reality were so closely linked, that she wondered what life would be like in the real world after school. Would it be variegated as it was now, or would she be the princess that her father always said she would be?

Walking through the woods that night after a long, sweaty afternoon working on the float, the woods were alive with the sounds of frogs and insects. Surely, she thought, she had not focused on her hearing, or she would have known the sounds were always present there. Still, her hearing was particularly acute this evening. She was aware of the rustling of the leaves and the cracking of a branch.

Above her head, a great rustling indicated an enormous bird was taking flight, perhaps a great horned owl that had been startled by her light, she thought. Now she heard a rhythmic breathing sound as if some enormous pit bull were gasping just off the path to her right.

She turned the light to one side of the path and then the other, to find the origin of the sound. She spun around looking urgently to identify the creature that was so palpably near. In the cold, night air, she heard the distant sounds of teenagers laughing as they romped in the woods. They would be frolicking in the moonlight, she fancied, and they will not be home until very, very late.

Sheila stumbled and fell off the path into a circle of mushrooms that crushed under her weight. She found her cellphone by its light and found the gnarled root that had been her stumbling block. She rose and brushed the leaves and wet mushroom residue from her clothing. She pointed her cellphone light in all directions. Then she received a text on her cellphone.

"IC2. Do UCme2?"

Now Sheila was very afraid. She crouched and carefully aimed her spotlight in decans around the circle of which she was the center. Finding nothing in the woods around her from her crouched position, she rose and did the same thing from a standing position. She found nothing in her line of sight, but she heard the laughter of the teenagers as if a girl were running and a boy were pursuing her through the sough.

Sheila envisioned the satyr pursuing the nymph through the forest. She envisioned the lusty satyr catching the nymph, and having his will with her. She imagined the nymph, who had been ravished, weeping as the satyr left her, laughing because he had had his way with her.

Sheila did not like whoever was tormenting her, so she texted back, "WhoRU?"

"IM in your dreams," the monster texted back. Then it continued, "Do U hear the couple in the woods?"

"Y," she texted. "So what?"

"That's the sound of US."

"U creep! Stay away from me or I'll call the police!"

Getting no response to her threat, Sheila stepped back on the path and quickly made her way home, careful not to trip on any of the other roots on the ground.

The listeners remained spellbound by the story. The girls and boys huddled together and watched the fire. Kathy, Ann, and Diane were wholly engrossed in the plight of the heroine of the story wondering how it would end. Everyone was keenly aware of the night sounds in the forest. The fire was the only light. Paul stirred it with a stick, and the embers glowed with what he thought was a sinister light. Charles pressed on with his story as Herbert rubbed his hands together—for warmth, perhaps—as his breath was white against the darkness.

Charles paused and looked at his listeners one by one to gauge their reactions. He could see Kathy, Ann, and Diane were waiting anxiously for the next part of his tale. Each of them thought she might be the Sheila of the tale. Herbert and Paul looked at Charles sidewise with concern in their eyes. He knew they thought this story might end badly. What would that do for their night's fun? Charles nodded. Then he went on.

That night, Sheila received an email from a person with the handle, "Satyr4U." Its title was, "Waiting for You," and its text was, "ICU now!" Sheila shut down her machine and drew the shades to her room. She had an exam the next day, so she focused hard on her class materials. When she went to bed, she pulled her covers over her head as protection from the torment that she tried to ignore.

She finally slept and dreamt of being pursued through a forest of mushrooms by an evil figure with horns and goat feet. When she looked down, she saw that she was fixed to the ground. Her legs had become fused and were covered with bark. She was turning into a tree in the middle of the mushrooms!

The monster that sought her came and was perplexed that she had disappeared. Hearing the laughter of another nymph, it went off in pursuit of the girl. Sheila awakened in a cold sweat, and badly needed to go to the bathroom. This whole thing was getting out of hand.

The pressures at school were one thing—and she could deal with that. The pressures from this obsessed monster that she had never seen were another thing entirely. She wanted to get to the bottom of the mystery, but she knew in her heart that the only way she could do that was in the woods. She felt her violent temper would protect her from any threat if only she could face it.

The next morning at the family's breakfast, Sheila mentioned the texts she had received after she fell in the woods. Her mother was concerned. Her father wanted to call the police immediately. Sheila said that she could handle the situation. After all, she always carried her cellphone. Who would try anything when he knew all she had to do was dial 911 to bring the police?

Her father was not impressed with this argument, but he knew his daughter's desire for independence, so he backed down. He didn't tell his daughter, but he would go into the forest to see what might be threatening her. He would take care of the villain if he lurked there, and if he did not, he would have the satisfaction of knowing that the monster was a figment of his daughter's imagination.

So the next night, when Sheila came through the woods later than ever before, she heard a great rustling, and she saw a flashlight aiming every which way as if searching. A deer bounded across the path in front of the girl, and she saw red eyes off the path to either side ahead of her. Tonight there were no sounds of boys and girls frolicking in the darkness. There were no insinuating text messages. She had no trouble navigating the path to make her way finally to her back door. Out of the woods behind her came her father, with his flashlight still on.

"Oh, Dad. It was you. What were you doing in the woods at this hour?"

"I was looking for mushrooms. I found nothing, though I looked everywhere. Maybe I'll try again during daylight hours."

"Dad, thank you for trying to protect me, but I can fend for myself. Did you know you scared a deer? And I saw red eyes in the woods along the path."

Charles saw the girls' relief at the appearance of Sheila's father. He modulated his voice to be reassuring as he continued. Paul and Herbert were waiting for the next twist in the story.

"Those would be rabbits or foxes, or both. When you shine your light in their eyes, they reflect red. Anyway, I didn't find any monsters out there."

"And I didn't get any text messages either. We should both calm down. I have work to do, and Mom will be worried about you. I won't tell her a thing. Just let me do my work and live my life. I'll be all right. I promise."

"Okay, Princess. Keep an eye open for ogres and monsters in the meantime."

"Hahaha. The only monster in the woods tonight was my father."

In her inbox, Sheila had another email from Satyr4U. This one read, "So close!"

Sheila replied, "So what?"

"Tomorrow night I'll CU."

"Not a chance, U creep!"

Sheila closed her computer and returned to her books. When she had finished studying, she decided that she might just let her father play a role in her life after all. At breakfast, she asked her dad to meet her halfway down the path that night at nine o'clock. That way, she thought, the would-be assailant would not be alarmed by her father's thrashing through the woods with his flashlight. Instead, he would be surprised by her father and perhaps caught while he was prying into her life.

That night, Sheila was confident finding her way down the path, because her father was going to be waiting for her halfway home. She had not figured on hearing a girl screaming in the woods and fleeing someone who was calling for her to stop and listen to him. The noise was a story in itself because it told of a struggle and flight, a sudden silence, and then thrashing in the woods.

Ahead of her, Sheila saw a light depart from the path and strike out in the direction of the noises. She guessed her father had decided to become the rescuer. Then everything went silent. Sheila, who had stopped to listen to the drama that was being performed in the woods to her left, struggled to hear what was happening now. She heard nothing. She aimed her light off to the left side of the path.

Then she felt a touch on her shoulder and the hot breath of someone right behind her in the dark. She dropped right to the ground and kicked behind her. She rolled on her back and pointed her cellphone light upwards and all around. No one was there.

As she got to her knees and stood up, she realized that she was now covered with dead leaves and moss and squashed mushrooms. She brushed herself off, did a three-sixty turn with her light and then proceeded along the path toward her house.

Halfway down the path was her father, patiently waiting for her as he had promised to do. She hugged him, and as he hugged her back, he asked what had kept her. She said she heard terrible things in the woods and then a more terrible silence. Her father asked whether they shouldn't investigate. She said perhaps not because she had a lot of work to do and it was late. She thanked her dad for coming to help, but she really did not need his assistance after all.

The next morning, law officers were searching the woods for a missing girl who had not been at home all night. They eventually found her unclothed body off the path in the woods. She had been savagely raped and then murdered. The area where the body was found was surrounded by a yellow police crime line tape. The homicide detectives went house to house in the neighborhoods around the woods to ask what anyone might have seen or heard the night before.

When they came to the Connaught residence, Mrs. Connaught took the officers' cards and told them she would ask her daughter to be in touch if she knew anything that might help the authorities in their investigation. She texted her daughter about the current events surrounding the murder and told her that she had the officers' cards in case Sheila had information that could help them.

Sheila had exams all day, so she had turned off her cellphone and placed it in a holding box. The school had strict rules about students not bringing anything to an exam room that could compromise the integrity of the exam. Therefore, it was very late in the afternoon when Sheila received the news about the murder.

She went pale and texted her mother that she had heard the whole thing while she was walking home on the path. She texted that she would write down everything she had heard and send the account as an email attachment to the officers.

Meanwhile, she texted, she would be home late again that night. She mentioned that she would be asking the captain of the football team whether this one time he could accompany her from the bus stop to her back door. After all, he was going to take her to the Halloween Ball.

Sheila's float was coming together nicely, but she had to attend to a number of details herself, and that put her off her intended schedule. As a result, she did not meet the captain of the football team as she had intended to do. She made her way home alone as she always had before.

The crime had been accomplished, she thought, so lightning would not strike twice. Besides she was excited because tomorrow was Halloween and the Halloween Parade. The Homecoming football game and the Halloween Ball would all occur as the climax of the fall season. She would ride on her float. She would preside as Homecoming Queen over the game, and she would go to the Halloween Ball with the captain of the football team. She imagined what a grand day it would be if the team won the game!

So it was in a spirit of exultation and exuberance that the beautiful, young Sheila Connaught made her way down the path through the woods toward her home. Her light shined on the path, and the darkness broke before her and then closed in behind her like a shroud. Sheila heard the snapping of twigs and branches in the woods, but she thought the deer might be wandering as it had previously. Her ears pricked up when she heard what she thought was urgent whispering.

"How can it be you?"

"Who's that? Stop where you are."

"You know who this is. I've been waiting for you."

"Waiting for me?"

"Yes, waiting for you. I'm the satyr that's been texting and emailing you. I thought that was you last night. But it wasn't, was it?"

"Stay away from me! I'm dialing 911 right now."

"Too late, Sheila. Much too late."

Charles could see Diane's teeth were chattering from fear. Her nails dug into his arm. Ann and Kathy were snuggling close to their companions. This story was going places they had not bargained for. They wanted a happy conclusion, but the story was heading on a tragic curve. How would it end?

The import of the monster's words sank in as Sheila aimed her cellphone spotlight to one side and another. She felt a breath on her cheek, but it was only a breeze. She thought she felt a hand on her thigh, but her hand struck empty air as she tried to push the hand aside. Sheila realized that she was in the presence of the monster that had murdered the poor girl whose body had been found raped and naked in the woods. She had been the intended victim.

Now, she thought, she would be the murder's second victim if she could not think fast. She texted with both hands, "Help. Path. Now. Murder!" and sent the message to her parents. Then she screamed at the top of her lungs, "Murder! Murder!" A huge body collided with her, and the two fell among the sough at the side of the path. Sheila's cellphone flew from her hand. It landed face down so its spotlight faced upwards.

Sheila felt hands groping her, and a shaven male face trying to kiss her on the mouth. She struggled, and the man's fist came out of nowhere. She was screaming and scratching, kicking and trying to roll free. The monster was too large for her to prevail. She continued to scream as she had heard the last victim scream, and she decided that screaming was the only remedy if it could only be heard.

The murderer's hand ripped off her panties, and his hand groped down there as she writhed and continued to scream. The monster arched his back above her and in the outline of his face, Sheila saw the football hero and her date for the Halloween Ball looming over her and ready to violate her and then murder her.

Sheila screamed one more time and pulled her face aside to avoid the monster's fist, which hit the ground beside her head with such force and noise she could not believe the wooden sound came from the same source. The monster crumpled upon her with its tremendous weight, and she thought her body would be violated, and then her life would end.

Those things did not happen. The monster somehow rose up and rolled aside on its back. Another figure appeared and shone a flashlight's beam at the body of the high school football hero. Sheila could not believe what was happening. She was now free. She rolled over and pulled her legs up so she was on her knees, and when she tried to stand up, she was grasped by large hands that reached around her and held her in a bear hug while she trembled and shook violently. She heard her father's voice.

"There, there, princess. It's all right now. Everything is all right. You're safe. The police are on the way. The monster is over there in the leaves. He'll not be harming anyone tonight or anymore. Don't worry, sweet. You were right, after all. He was waiting for you all the time."

"You were right, Charles, that is a very chilling story. I felt the goose bumps on my arms from the start."

"I did too, Ann," remarked Diane.

"It's every girl's worst nightmare come true," said Kathy.

"Except Sheila the female heroine in the story was not killed," Herbert interjected. Ann punched him in the arm.

"The heroine does not have to be killed for the story to have its effect," said Charles.

"Okay. I think we have time for one more story tonight." Paul was always the organizer, and everyone expected him to tell a story. Instead, Kathy wanted to tell a story.

"After that last story, I think it's time to change the tone a little and get off Halloween. My story is true. It really did happen. I'll tell it if you don't laugh at me."

"We won't laugh at you, Kathy. We may laugh at your story, though."

"Herb, stop that. We promise we won't laugh," said Ann. She looked around at the others, and they agreed, the boys reluctantly. This is the story that Kathy told:

If You Don't Brush

Billy said that we shouldn't be afraid of the hunchbacked old crone who roamed through the neighborhood at odd hours leaning on her cane, but I was not so sure. Every time I saw her, I was reminded of the Grimm brothers' tale of Hansel and Gretel.

I did not want Billy to be Hansel, and I certainly did not want to be Gretel. Billy would not listen to me. Instead, he waited until the old woman slowly walked along the path leading into the public park late Friday afternoon, and he went right up to her to say hello. I went right after him. I had filled my pockets so we could leave a trail behind us. Hansel and Gretel had used bread crumbs that the birds ate, so I was making an innovation that might help.

Billy's greeting seemed to make the crone delighted. She screwed her face into what might have been a radiant smile if her teeth were not so bad. She was missing her top front teeth, and her tongue was visible working in her mouth as she spoke. She said that it was a beautiful day for a walk in the park. Would we join her?

Billy asked her what her name was, and she said it was Marianne Smith. She asked for our names, and Billy told her that we were Billy and Sandy. At this, I poked Billy in the back, but he did not regard me. The woman asked if we could wait a moment while she found her teeth. She then fished into her dress pocket and came out with artificial teeth that she fitted into her mouth. She said that she could speak better with the teeth in than out, and now when she smiled, she did look radiant. I began to relax.

Marianne began telling us the tale of how she had lost her teeth. She said that her family always had bad teeth, and everyone ended with some sort of bridge or inlay of false ones in old age. She said that when she looked in the mirror in the morning before she put her teeth in, she thought she looked like a wicked witch. Did we think that she looked like a wicked witch? She wanted to know.

Billy fearlessly told her that we were afraid to talk with her because of how she looked. She nodded sagely, and she told us that she had the misfortune of losing all her children to accidents and wars. She was alone now, living in a house one street over from the park. She hoped she would not frighten people, but she knew what they thought.

She asked whether we brushed our teeth every day. When we hesitated and looked guilty, she pulled out her false teeth. With a laugh, she pointed to her mouth and said, "This is what you will get for not brushing!" We both shuddered and ran. We remember that meeting to this day.

"Is that the end of your story?"

"Yes, I'm done."

"And the story is true?"

"Indeed it is true."

"Prove it."

"Come on, Herb, she doesn't have to prove that her story's true."

"But I can prove it."

"So prove it so we can all go home. I'm exhausted," Ann said with finality.

"Well, Herb, why don't you ask the old woman herself because she's standing right behind you?"

"So here you are, children. I thought you might be back here in the woods," the crone said, standing behind Herb and supporting herself with her cane.

"Grandma, you found us. I was just telling them a story how you're always scaring little children by removing your dentures and telling them to brush their teeth. Do you want to join our storytelling?"

"No, dear, but I will take out my dentures and show everyone what happens when you don't brush. I'm taking them out now. There! See?"

In the last glow of the fire, Kathy's Grandma's wrinkled face and hooked nose were the perfect illustration of the story everyone had just heard. The old woman cackled very convincingly before she put her teeth back into her mouth. She smiled, pleased with herself.

Paul said, "I think I hear a chainsaw starting, so it must be time to go. I'll see you all in school."

The others got to their feet in a hurry and moved out in all directions toward their separate homes. Finally, only Kathy and her Grandma remained at the fire site. Kathy carefully covered the fire over with snow using a dibble she had brought for the purpose. Then she took her Grandma's arm and walked carefully along the snowy path out of the woods toward their home.

"It was snowy, wet and stormy, but did you manage to have fun this year?"

"Yes, Grandma. And do you know the best thing that happened?"

"No dear. Tell me."

"You. You appeared at just the right time."

"When I was your age, I liked to tell scary stories with my friends on Halloween, too. We did it come rain, or sleet, or snow. I'm glad you like to do that, too. One day you might have teeth like mine to end the games of your granddaughter."

"Grandma, I brush my teeth. You know that."

"So did I, Kathy dear. So did I. Hahaha."

"Oh, Grandma. Please stop kidding me. I'm tired from all the telling and listening, and I need to get to sleep."

As the two reached the edge of the woods, a great rustling sound came from the tree just above the path. It was the sound of the wings of a large barn owl unwinding and breaking through the obstructions to the open sky. It was, Kathy thought as a chill ran down her spine, the perfect ending to the perfect Halloween night.

Ridge Riders

My name is Angel Day. That is not a joke. Dad's family name was Day. Mom always wanted a little angel. So go figure: I use a lot of pseudonyms. For a while, I ran with the handle RidgeRider, until the deaths and disappearances of all my friends and fellow motorcyclists began.

As I look back on all the bad luck and mayhem, I probably should have guessed early on that something supernatural was affecting events around me. In the press of events, as I struggled to survive, I did not have a clue. I just kept playing my video games and tuning out of the cruel, external world.

The more I got involved, particularly in role-playing games, the less aware I was of what the games were doing to me. After a while, I became the games, and everything changed. The death of my friend Rudy brought me back from the brink. I shudder to recall the midnight ride when I found him.

Rudy, like the rest of us, was a free spirit caught in a world strangling his soul. He would play video games all night, except when he climbed on his Hog for his midnight ride along the high ridge where the power pylons run in a series. He set the trend. We imitated his macho style.

The police left us alone as long as we stayed off the main roads. No one rode the ridge except the fearless. Rudy knew no fear. For a while, I was like him. We would ride alone or together in the moonlight along the ridge, laughing and gunning our cycles, sometimes doing wheelies skirting the edge of the cliff that led to the valley. Death was a risible fiction: we were going to live forever just like in our games.

One night, I found Rudy near his bike on its side, its front wheel still spinning. He sat there like a zombie in the moonlight, a stupid grin on his face and smoke rising from his ears. I kid you not—smoke! I tried poking him to get a reaction, but he just sat there, silent and weird. I checked his pulse and found none. I panicked. I broke all our sacred rules and dialed 911.

I waited until the rescue team was visible along the ridge. Then I rode in the opposite direction. The rest is history. Rudy was found dead of an apparent cardiac arrest. His parents wasted no time to bury him along with their guilt and shame. No one knew I called 911 that night. I put a basket of bright plastic flowers on the ridge where I found Rudy. He would have smirked and shrugged at the gesture if he were still alive. I missed him.

I would have thought Rudy's death an isolated, freak event, but two weeks later, I was riding the ridge again, and came to the place where I put the basket. There, next to the basket, was Abby's body sitting in the same way as Rudy's had been. Abby had smoke coming out of her ears and no pulse. She felt cold to the touch. I saw her bike on its side by the base of the nearest pylon. My hair stood on end. I looked around frantically using the light from my cellphone. No one else was in sight, but it was dark.

I called 911 and waited for the rescue team to come into view. I escaped in the opposite direction. As with Rudy, the coroner judged that Abby had died of a coronary attack. Hers was the second freak attack at the same place at roughly the same time of night. The police began looking for the person who placed the 911 call and asking questions. They never discovered me in their search.

On the Net, the other ridge riders spread rumors in our chat room about the strange, spooky deaths of Rudy and Abby. Some warned of riding the ridge at all. Sammy texted that the goat killer murderer might be responsible. Anita texted that a vengeful ghost haunted the ridge where the two had been killed.

Arnold, a macho man, texted that he was not afraid of ghosts, and the goat killer was not known to have struck individuals: it killed only couples. He bragged that he would ride the ridge as he had always done. His body was the third I found in the same place as the others. Again, he was sitting with smoke coming from his ears. I was in a quandary because of the police's interest in the 911 caller on the two former occasions. This time, I did not call 911. Instead, I rode my bike home and waited.

The next day at noon, a construction crew found Arnold's body where I saw it the prior night. Three teens dying of cardiac arrest at midnight in the space of five weeks was deemed worthy of a massive investigation. Murder was suspected. As a consequence, all the known friends and associates of the deceased were interviewed by Inspector Dermat, of Police Homicide. The police had no idea about our being gamers together, or about our using the chat room to share our nocturnal activities.

Dermat interviewed Sammy, but he did not give up our secret. In our secret chat room, Sammy texted the policeman asked about the 911 caller and the motive for murder any of the victims' friends had. Sammy said he knew nothing about either matter. Anita texted she had not been questioned but knew nothing. She heard the police were patrolling the ridge.

I resolved not to ride the ridge for a while. I could not imagine what had killed the three bikers, but I was more afraid of encountering the police, than coming face to face with the killer.

Meanwhile, the entire city was buzzing with theories about the mystery of the ridge rider killings. I followed the features written by Sheila Cranberry, an investigative journalist. From her articles, I gathered the investigation was going nowhere. Forensic evidence showed tracks of many motorcycles along the ridge. None of the townspeople knew anything of substance regarding the killings. Dermat's investigation was going nowhere.

Cranberry dug into the data to discover Anita's being a classmate of two of the victims, Rudy and Abby. The investigative reporter elicited information about the victims' love of riding the ridge at midnight for fun. She wrote nothing about our online association and nothing about me. In her third article, she began to ask rhetorical questions about the methods of the murders. She broached the subject of paranormal causes. The paper did not publish her articles afterward. It was as though she had touched a live wire and been forced to go silent.

Because of the ongoing official investigation, I retreated into my shell and just gamed. While I played, I had vivid recurring images of the deceased bodies sitting on the ridge with smoke coming out of their ears. I wondered what would cause the smoke. I searched the Net for answers.

I read an obscure piece about a woman showing up in a hospital in Chicago breathing smoke that turned out to be produced by a toxic mix of chemicals she had ingested in a suicide attempt. Each of the three victims had experienced hardships. I could imagine any of us committing suicide. I could not imagine us entering into a suicide pact. Since nothing in the public record indicated the presence of toxic chemicals in the victims' bodies, I thought suicide should be ruled out.

I posited the three might have died of fright. I conjured images scary enough to stop their hearts. Yet their postures when I found them did not show signs of being discomfited. In fact, they appeared to be at peace. They were all seated on the ground. Their eyes were wide open. I kept coming back to the fact of the smoke rising from their ears. Perhaps, I thought, some supernatural agent was able to stop hearts from beating instantly and to make brains boil.

After another three weeks, the police homicide investigation was terminating in a cold case. Police patrols of the ridge diminished. I began to ride the ridge again. I felt cold and lonely as I motored along the ridge. I was alert to whatever danger lurked at midnight. I often stopped in the place where my three associates had died. I looked in all directions and listened carefully for any sound that might lead to an answer.

One midnight, Sammy came from the opposite direction. We met near the base of the pylon where the others had died. Three small baskets of flowers now marked the places where their bodies had been found. In the darkness, we decided to dismount and sit for a while to talk. We talked about Rudy, Abby, and Arnold.

While we discussed the strange deaths, we heard snapping, popping sounds. We looked all around but saw nothing capable of making the sounds. The night air was cool because of a slight breeze. My spine tingled. Disconcerted, Sammy said we should be riding now. We left the spot, and I discounted what I had heard.

Sammy returned to the pylon the next night. I was not there because I got lost in a game. I know he was at the pylon because the day afterward, construction workers found his dead body below the pylon. This fourth death made everyone in the community think a serial killer was rampaging in the area.

In the chat room, Anita texted Sammy told her he wanted to investigate sounds he heard near the pylon on the ridge. That made sense to me. I did not respond to Anita's text. I wondered whether Sammy's ears had issued smoke as the other three victims' ears had done. I knew that Anita was curious because she texted something about needing to know the truth. I was afraid for her, but I did not dissuade her from riding the ridge.

A policeman dispatched to watch the ridge, apprehended Anita and took her to the police station for questioning. She was arrested for murder, but because she was a minor, her name was not used in the press. From her, the police learned about our secret chat room. They learned our chat room names. They learned about ridge riding. They learned my handle RidgeRider.

I immediately changed my handle, and RidgeRider disappeared from the Net forever. I stopped visiting the chat room. I thought the police had no way to make a murder conviction stick. Anita could never have killed her friends. I realized, though, that the police would discontinue their surveillance of the ridge because they had a prime suspect. I was free for a while to investigate on my own.

With trepidation, I pulled on my slickers and rode my Hog up the ridge in a light drizzle. Fog rose from the valley. I stopped by the pylon and surveyed the four baskets representing the four victims under it. The air was wet and still. I heard a slight crackle. Then I heard a hiss and pop. I looked around. I looked down into the valley. I saw no one in any direction.

I noticed an acrid smell. A faint blue light appeared in flashes. I looked for the source. My eyes ran up the pylon to where the power lines ran through the metal skeleton that held them. I was mesmerized by the glow of the blue light. It was cool and alluring when it shone. It was a will o' the wisp. I watched the place where the light sparked in the sleeve for the power line.

I had my hand on the metal frame and was about to ascend when I felt a hand on my shoulder. I almost died of fright. My hair stood on end. I breathed in consciously. The hand on my shoulder was palpable. The figure behind me was chortling. I was afraid to turn around.

"I don't think you want to make the same mistake your friends did, do you?"

"Don't touch me. Get away."

"You've nothing to fear from me."

"Stand back. Let me look at you with my cellphone light."

"As you wish," the figure said, as he took his hand off my shoulder and stepped back.

I pulled out my cellphone and tapped on its light. There stood a homeless man I had often seen in town collecting bottles and cans. His beard and hair were streaming with water. He held a plastic bag with his collection of gleanings. His teeth were rotten and visible in his smile.

"You're the homeless man who's always collecting things."

"You are most observant. Let me guess. You are the one who placed the four baskets of flowers for the dear departed."

"How do you know that?"

"I watched you do it. I am not noticed much. I watch, though, and I know things."

"What do you know about my friends?"

"I know four of them are dead, and one is in jail, fighting for her life."

"Why didn't you tell the police about me?"

"No one asked me about you or anything else for that matter," the man said, as he dropped his bag on the ground. "I've watched you ride the ridge as I did with a bicycle many years ago. I rode here before the pylons were laid and before the power lines were strung."

"Did you see what killed my friends?"

"What killed your friends is very difficult to see, but when you see it, it comes in a flash and suddenly is gone."

"So what is it that killed my friends? Please tell me."

"You've seen as much of it as you can without suffering the same fate as they. You've had your hand on the metal skeleton that could kill you."

"Are you trying to tell me that this metal scaffold is the murderer?"

"It's not quite that simple, but the easy answer is yes, this metal tower killed all four."

"How can that be?" I asked him, intrigued by his nonchalance.

"The power that runs through those lines above us is so potent that if you touched a wire, you would instantly be fried and your blood and brains boiled."

"And my ears would exude smoke?"

"Most likely, yes. The current that would run through your body would be like a stroke of lightning. Some have survived a direct hit from lightning, but most have perished."

"So my friends climbed up this frame and touched the power line?"

"Near enough, they did. But the power in those lines is so great that they did not have to get all the way up to the lines themselves."

"How far up would they have to go?"

"The second horizontal beam or a little higher would be enough to cause electrocution. It would be the same as if you stuck a fork in your electrical outlet at home. Only here there's no fuse or circuit breaker." He laughed.

"How can you laugh about this?"

"Electricity has been around a long time now. The principles are well known. Why people don't treat it with respect, I just don't know."

"Why did my friends climb this tower?"

"They climbed it for the same reason you were going to climb it. They were curious about the light from the blue electric sparks. They thought they could see the blue light better if they got closer to it. Indeed, it coursed right through them, one by one. Did you think, perhaps, evil witches fried them with their magic wands?"

"I had no idea what killed them. The papers said they died of cardiac arrest."

"If I were a coroner, I would say cardiac arrest. Electric shock will stop the heart dead."

"Why haven't you been to the police to tell them this?"

"Look at me. Do you think the police would believe me if I told them such a thing?" He smiled ruefully, and I knew he was right.

"I can't go to the police either, but for a different reason."

"You don't want to be on their radar, so to speak?"

"That's right. So tell me, what do you think I should do with this information?"

"Let it save your life. There, on the pylon, is a sign that says Danger and a lot of other things about this scaffold. You never read the sign. Your friends didn't read it either. So here we are. Are you any wiser for my having deterred you from climbing to see the blue flame?"

I looked up and saw a beautiful blue arc of electricity as if it were responding to what the homeless man just told me.

"My friend Anita is in jail on charges of murder simply because the police found her up here."

"They'll never convict her of murder with what they have. She'll be held for a while and freed sooner than you think."

"Tell me why you came here tonight in the rain."

"Some nights I cannot sleep, so I do what I did when I was a boy. I walk the ridge now because I'm unsteady on a bike at my age. Rain or shine—the weather doesn't matter to me now. I'm not afraid of getting wet. I'm not afraid of the blue fire anymore. Why don't you get back on your bike and ride away? I'm going to wait here and watch for a while."

"I don't know your name. I owe you thanks."

"You don't need to know my name any more than I need to know yours, angel. You owe me nothing. This scaffold wanted a death tonight. If there's something owed, it's the scaffold." He laughed and shook his head. He had a crazed look.

I left the homeless man gazing upwards, waiting for the blue fire to arc again. I revved up my Hog and rode the ridge for a while and returned to the valley.

Two days later, I read in the newspaper the investigative reporter's account of construction workers finding the body of an old, homeless man under the power lines where the bikers' bodies had been discovered. In the same issue of the paper, I read the news of the release from custody of my friend Anita. The police reopened their murder investigation because, they said, the murderer had not been found after all.

I returned to my gaming somewhat sobered by my latest experience on the ridge. The homeless man had saved my life. He had climbed the metal frame and felt the final fire. The frame had taken him instead of me. I wondered whether he was conscious of his sacrifice.

Perhaps, I thought, there was something in what he said about the frame being owed a life that night. I shivered when I thought how close I had come to death by electrocution. Yet, when I think of the indescribable beauty of that blue arcing electric fire, I envision ridge riding toward that flame not just for a night or a moment, but for eternity.

The Haunted Scriptorium

I arrived at the monastery right on time, as was attested by the hollow ringing of the bells in the carillon. The unearthly quiet, having been broken like a spell, the fathers and brothers were now everywhere evident, crisscrossing the greensward at the center of the monastic buildings.

Some were proceeding to the refectory. Others were strolling to the library. Workers were coming from the fields. Workmen were putting up ladders that could be climbed for pointing brickwork and old stone. Brothers carrying mops and pails were rushing to the dormitory to be sure the floors were cleaned before evening prayers.

Out by the graveyard, I noticed a burial taking place with a small group of religious people officiating over a very private interment that I might have missed if I had focused on the routine scurrying. Seeing that the head monk was one of the concelebrants at the graveside, I wandered back to stand beside him reverently until his work had been completed. He had invited me this afternoon, and I needed to know from him how we were going to proceed.

The burial service continued in Latin. A brother swung a thurible with its fumes of incense spreading like a shroud over the open grave. Three monks in a line maintained an attitude of devout prayer, and their eyes remained fixed on the grave as if it were an icon.

Since we religious are, by our own volition, among the dead already, I supposed that they saw the grave as I did. For us monks, it was our right habitation and goal. The grave was the gateway for the soul, as much a passage as the frail, once-human, decomposing body in the small black box with the golden handles that was ready to be lowered on signal.

When the ritual had been completed, and each celebrant had taken the dibble and scattered a few token pieces of earth on the coffin, the monks gently lowered the coffin into the grave on the suspender straps until it hit bottom. Then, they signaled the diggers to fill the grave with the same earth that had been excavated from it. The lead monk turned to acknowledge me and motioned that we should walk together for a few minutes and talk.

"I'm glad you've come, Brother William, for burying the result of a problem does not bury the source of the problem. It happened after vespers yesterday in the scriptorium of the library. We found Brother Anthony, may God rest his soul, naked as the day he was born, sitting by the lectern laughing. He was bleeding profusely from his nether parts and had been doing so for such a long time that the floor under his chair was a pool of blood."

I had expected a horrific account, but nothing like what the monk recounted. Had Brother Anthony been possessed in some way? Why else would he have been found laughing? I instinctively looked behind us to see the others of the community grouped in twos and threes, darkly muttering among each other. I turned back to the monk and focused on the details of the scene he had imparted to me. He continued his exposition when he thought I had digested his first words.

"In his right hand, like a scepter, he wielded an old kitchen knife. In his left hand, like a little ball of wax, he held his vital parts, which he had severed from himself with the knife. On the lectern was a single page from a manuscript, but the text was impossible to discern because it was covered with the monk's blood. By the time I had been summoned, he had lost so much blood it was a miracle that he could still sit and hold himself upright. When I appeared before him, he got a wild look in his eyes, raised his knife and plunged it into his heart. Brother Simon tried to stop him from taking that irrevocable action, and he was cut badly in the hand. Brother Simon is in the infirmary now, and I'm told he'll recover physically. I'm not at all sure any of us will recover mentally."

"To what do you attribute the unfortunate accident? Surely we have had suicides before."

"We've now had four such suicides in the same place, by the same method, in the last four weeks. We've kept this quiet, but the whole monastery is whispering about it now. The talk is of a curse or a ghost, or both in the scriptorium. Whatever it is, it lures young men to the place in the middle of the night and influences them to emasculate themselves and then take their own lives."

The number of suicides in a brief period was unprecedented, I thought. Indeed, an epidemic was underway. I well understood the monk's concern. Not only were the victims unfortunate if not damned, but the institution was also in jeopardy. How could His Holiness, the Pope, countenance keeping such an apparently diabolical place open? I was already envisioning a team of exorcists descending on the monastery. For a moment, I saw the future ruin of what today looked innocent enough on the exterior. The green grass, the blue sky with puffy white clouds were replaced in my imagination by a lightning riddled mass of blood red sheets pouring rain upon half an arch and a full graveyard.

"I'm afraid that Brother Anthony will not be the last to suffer. I've made an exception to the rule for the burial of suicides to inter these religious in our graveyard. I suppose I should inform my superiors of my actions in this regard, but that is my affair. The reason I've summoned you is to discover what is going on and to stop it as soon as possible. Although, the activity of the monastery yard masks a deep unrest and suspicion that ours is no longer a holy place of God, but a sanctum of the Devil."

"Can you tell me if there is any common thread among the victims that would suggest that they might have acted in collusion?"

"I've thought of that possibility, but the four brothers were not in a claque or members of a cabal. They slept in separate quarters, worked in different areas and never associated in private, except in prayer. They all sang in the choir—beautifully, I might add, but they had no connection to each other before they went into orders, and their only firm link is the order of their departure from the earth."

Though nervous and unkempt, the monk was not an unintelligent observer, and his thoughts were parallel to my own initial suspicions. In religious houses, the relationships of people are well known. I believed the monk when he said the brothers were not involved in a suicide pact together. The monk was observing me closely while I thought about his conjectures. As if reading my mind, he continued with his summation, which led, inexorably back to me.

"I've wracked my brain and prayed to find answers, but I've found none. That is why you're here. You have a reputation for investigating certain impingements on the holiest of places. I entrust this task to you. You'll have your own room and freedom of access to all areas of the monastery for as long as you stay and work on this matter. I only ask that you use the utmost discretion in your investigation. I fear that if the wrong message were sent, my flock would flee in all directions."

"Do you believe that no word of what has happened has reached outside the monastery?"

"I have no reason to believe that. No one has been permitted to take leave for the last four weeks. Any contact with outsiders has been accomplished by my people in pairs. Everyone knows that we must strive to solve our problem by ourselves."

"That way, you avoid for a while the public shame and open notoriety."

"Yes, but private guilt and festering fears may be more dangerous in the long run."

"Will you appoint an insider to help me with my investigation? That would make things easier, and it would focus my questions and my approach."

"Brother John, our librarian, is standing by to be your confidant and second. His discretion is unquestioned. He is in charge of both the library and the scriptorium. You may trust him implicitly."

"And what have you told the others about the reason for my being here?"

"You are here to do research on the history of the scriptorium for a monograph to be published by the Vatican. The recent mishaps are a very minor part of that story."

"Do you mean to imply that there have been other deaths at the scriptorium?"

"From time to time, yes, there have been other incidents."

"And do you have a list of those, with the circumstances of each?"

"Brother John has everything you need. When would you like to begin work?"

"I will start right away after you give me a letter authorizing me to make whatever contacts I choose in the performance of my duties."

"I have your letter of authorization right here. Take it. You may, of course, dine with us in the refectory and pray with us in the chapel at the canonical hours. We welcome you to participate however you like in the life of our monastery."

"Let's hope I won't be participating as Brother Anthony did last evening. Right now, I'll beg your leave and proceed to the library to see Brother John."

In the library, I found Brother John was reviewing the replacement of the volumes that had recently been drawn for reading at the oak tables that comprised the reading room. He told me that too often monks had returned the books improperly, so he had instituted a new rule that only he would restore all volumes to their proper places. That way no book would be lost by misplacement.

I asked him whether we could talk somewhere privately, and he led me into a small conference room in back of the head table at the front of the room. When he closed the door behind us, I knew it was sound proof. We could, therefore, talk candidly.

"What can you tell me about the recent death of Brother Anthony?"

"Yesterday morning, I opened the library at six o'clock, as I always do. I then put my things in order and went to open the scriptorium. The door was still locked, but when I opened it I saw Brother Anthony sitting at the lectern laughing with that knife and his severed genitals. I asked him what he was doing, and he only smiled and held up his two hands."

This account accorded with the monk's, but the monk might have been parroting what this first observer had reported. He continued describing the horrendous scene in a matter-of-fact manner.

"Blood was everywhere, and I might have tried to help the man, except that I would have contaminated the scene. Instead, I called for help. Brother Anthony passed out and was taken to the infirmary. He may have died in the scriptorium. He may alternatively have died at the infirmary. I made a careful record of what I found in the scriptorium after his body had been taken away. I'll show you what I wrote in due course."

"I'm told that Brother Anthony is not the first person you've found in the same attitude and that all the others died in the same way as he did."

"Yes. Four have died in four weeks. Then, of course, there are others. Many others. I made a list that I'll share with you. Our records indicate that every decade, we have a spate of incidents exactly like Brother Anthony's. Looking back to the beginning of the Sixteenth Century, this has been so."

I was now fully engaged by the longevity of the problem. I began to think I might be able to eliminate all living suspects and focus entirely on enduring forces as the root cause of everything that had happened in the scriptorium.

"Go on."

"No human agency has ever been associated with what happened in the scriptorium. No common thread connects the victims of these horrible crimes. Always the deaths have come in fours. Always after the fourth death, someone like you has been called to help. Nothing has ever been discovered to unravel the mystery. I'm glad you're here to help us. I want to give you every chance of success, but I don't know how I can be of any help to you."

"Please give me copies of all your records of these suicides. Judging from what you've just said, I'd guess the number of deaths would approach four times the number of decades the monastery has been active and in service."

"If you have copies of records written by the investigators, I'd like to have those as well."

"You'll have copies of all the documents that exist. I'll also give you a tour of the library and the scriptorium right now if you like."

I found the library the same as that at any other monastery of the order. The scriptorium, which had not been used in generations, was also very much like other scriptoria I have surveyed, except for the chalk lines that showed the extent of the blood that had flowed out of Brother Anthony's body onto the floor beneath the lectern.

The librarian had cleaned up the area, so it was difficult for me to imagine what he had found yesterday morning. When I had seen everything that was immediately apprehensible, I asked to see any secret compartments, trapdoors, alcoves and trick accommodations. Brother John told me that, as far as he knew, there were none such.

"You said that you found the door to the scriptorium locked from the outside yesterday morning?"

"Correct. I had to get the iron key on my large ring to unlock the door."

"And you locked the door the night prior, after assuring that no one had been locked inside?"

"I followed the written procedures to the letter, just as I had done the previous three times. In each case, I was caught totally by surprise as I entered the scriptorium. On the first table under the lectern, the victims had placed their neatly folded outer garments, and then over those, their undergarments. The knife must have been concealed under their outer garments. Did they tell you that the knife used was the same knife for all four men?"

"No. That information is new to me. Where can I find that knife?"

"Brother Carlo in the refectory can show it to you. Let's walk over there and find him. It is my supper time anyway." Brother John then locked the scriptorium and the library and led me to the refectory.

Brother Carlo, who broke off temporarily from his mealtime tasks, laid the knife in my hands as if it were a poisonous viper. He was visibly afraid of handling the weapon that had taken four lives in quick succession. I was impressed with the brother's fear, and I felt special warmth in the handle of the knife as if it were alive. I asked whether I could take the knife with me, and the brother seemed relieved that I had asked to do so. Brother John remained at the refectory, while I returned with the librarian's master ring and keys to the scriptorium.

The sun was descending, and its light was falling in the scriptorium, so I lighted a candle there and sat down at the first table to contemplate the facts I had learned. I examined the knife in the candlelight and the scriptorium door's key as well. Both were warm to my touch. I listened intently and opened my mind to associations; however, the silence in the scriptorium was preternatural but engaging. It seemed to bespeak a spirit of great emptiness, loneliness, and mystery.

I took the scriptorium key in my left hand and raised the knife slowly in my right hand. Their heat increased, and I felt a cloying in my right hand as if the knife were trying to fuse itself with my hand. Simultaneously, I felt the key shift its balance and caused my left hand to migrate in the direction of the scriptorium door. I had to make a great effort to release both hands at once.

The key with the ring and the knife clattered on the table, but they would not lie still. The key and knife aligned themselves with a vanishing point in the corner of the room. I took the candle in my right hand and moved to the corner, where the two lines converged.

As I moved, the candle guttered against the candle's wick. A breeze, emanating from the corner of the scriptorium, was affecting the flame. I searched the corner with the candle to determine where the breeze came from. A small fracture line, no larger than the width of a fingernail, seemed to be the source. I returned to the table and lifted the knife to prise around the area where the breeze blew through the plaster wall. The knife seemed to wield itself as it found a way into the fissure. It twisted this way and that, until I saw the plaster surface drop in chunks and powder, revealing a keyhole.

The knife worked around the keyhole until it was entirely free from the plaster case in which it had been set. I went back to the table and retrieved the key ring. The scriptorium key I had used to enter this room was not the key that fit the lock in the wall. Instead, it was a smaller key, so encrusted with rust, that I did not think it could possibly work a lock. Once I had inserted that key, the lock turned as if by its own accord. I heard a snap, and the floor beneath me fell through.

I fell with the floor onto a flat surface of stone four feet beneath the scriptorium's floor. Fortunately, I had not been harmed by the fall. Reaching up to fetch the candle, I saw that the floor through which I had fallen, was apparently a trapdoor. In the area around me, below the upper floor, were large openings that contained twelve ancient coffins. My candle threatened to blow out on account of the breeze, which had intensified because of the wider aperture I had created.

I ran the candle along all sides of the opening to understand where the breeze came through, and it seemed to come through cracks in the stone floor itself, which must, I deduced, cover another enclosure below it. In a moment of inspiration, I took the knife by the handle and waved it along the area where the coffins lay. It gravitated like iron to a magnet that was a single coffin with the label: "Fra. Angelico." If I had not pulled back with considerable force, the knife would have stuck fast to that coffin. I believed I now had enough information to push my investigation along new lines.

I examined the trapdoor mechanism for the latch that held the false floor in place and discovered a rope that allowed a person on the level above to raise the trap door and, simultaneously, to use the key to fasten it in place. After a number of futile attempts, I managed to pull the trapdoor into place from the scriptorium floor. I then pulled the key from the formerly hidden lock.

The flooring now having been restored, I returned to the table and contemplated the tokens and the mechanical sequence I had followed to find the secret crypt. I knew I had to get to the monk who had summoned me to give him my new intelligence, but I found that the scriptorium door was now locked from the outside, and I could not use any of the keys to open the door.

My candle blew out, leaving me in total darkness. I sensed that the breeze was increasing in both force and temperature. It was becoming extremely hot in the room. I sweated profusely and was inclined to remove my cassock when I realized that each monk who had emasculated himself had removed his clothing before doing the deed that ultimately ended his life. I laughed out loud when I made the connection, and I realized that my laughter was probably very much like the laughter that the Brother Anthony had exhibited when he had been found.

I carefully set my candle down and groped for the knife, which I held in my right hand away from my body, and with my left hand, I groped at my vitals to assure that they were still attached to my body. I was relieved to find my genitalia intact, but my right hand felt a violent force, and I had to drop and roll to avoid the knife from sweeping the area where my vitals had been only a second before.

There was no human agency working against me: of that I was sure. The powers that were trying to undermine my confidence were the hot breeze, which now burned like a black flame, and the hot knife, which wanted to melt my hand while guiding it home to emasculate me. As I rolled in contention with the breeze and the knife, I heard the key ring with the keys fall with a clatter on the floor and slide toward me. With my left hand, I struggled to find the keys, and when I did find the ring, I rolled toward the corner, where I had uncovered the hidden keyhole.

There was no reason for me to repeat the ritual of the key and the trapdoors, except that I had no alternative. As I fell through the trapdoor onto the floor below the scriptorium, I lost control of the knife and heard it strike home against metal. I ran my hand across the area where the magnetic coffin lay, and I discovered that the knife had stuck to it. Try as I might, I could not free the knife from the coffin, but I reasoned that now I was not at risk to be self-emasculated. I also sensed that the violent heat of the breeze had abated. Instead, the breeze now blew cool, and it was becoming uncomfortably cold. I felt a chill because of my sweat-drenched cassock, but I resisted removing it.

I resolved to lie on the floor below me and wait. The music of the breeze through the stone floor below me lulled me and finally put me to sleep. There, I must have lain until morning, when Brother John, the librarian, found and awakened me. My patron came and expounded on the cruel story of Brother Angelico, the first librarian and master of the scriptorium archives, and owner of the knife that now clung to his coffin.

The Guru's Ghosts

The old man looked up at the stream of light coming through the narrow window near the top of his cell. He followed the light downwards, to where the motes danced, and finally to the earthen floor where his robe and staff lay.

What roused him was a footstep at the end of the long corridor, through which he had been dragged by two rough guards. He thought one of those guards might be coming back for him because today he was to be brought before the magistrate. He was not in the least worried about that, but he was worried to be away from his inner circle. They counted on him, and he liked to exert his presence in their behalf.

The guru had a presence that made most men pay close attention to what he did and said. His snowy hair sprang out all over his head like an aureole, and sprouted around gay eyes and a perpetual smile. Seraphic would be the right word in another theological sphere. Perhaps the word holy was right under the circumstances.

The footsteps continued down the corridor, and as the person neared, the guru raised his right hand in the ancient form of greeting, the index finger touching the thumb and the other three fingers spread a little and curled slightly. Then, in the shaft of light, stood Butu the boy.

"Old man, I came to warn you. Another man has died horribly. He was the man who claimed that you murdered a man in your youth. His wife and daughters found him at the table in their house, sitting in a chair with his hand on his chest. They claimed you killed this man to prevent his speaking against you in the court. I heard everything. One of the officers asked her how a man in jail could have done this thing. The wife only wailed and keened, rocking back and forth as she sat on the floor. She watched them take her husband's corpse away so it could be burned. The officer was angry that another witness had died. What should we do?"

"Rejoice in life, my son. Only the dead know no fear. I hear footsteps coming. Stand aside and listen carefully and learn."

The guards came up behind the boy and shoved him aside. They gestured to the guru to put on his gown and come with them. They unlocked the cell and stood back while the prisoner stepped out, a short man and rail thin, between two burly strong men.

Then, in procession, the old man with his staff, the two guards on each side, and the boy behind them, paced down the corridor and up the stairs at the end of it. When they breached the jail door and entered the street, a throng awaited them, women in saris and men holding garlands of flowers. Smoke rose from incense burning. Musicians played, and people held their hands pressed together as if their prayers had been answered. The guru blinked and waved and nodded.

A newspaper photographer snapped a picture that was destined to be front-page news throughout the country that evening. The national news team covered the slow procession through the crowd a short distance to the courthouse steps, where a reporter was waiting.

"Holy one, a moment, please. What do you have to say about the star witness against you, who was killed last night?

Did you have anything to do with that killing? And what about the other five who have suddenly died?"

The old man blinked and focused on the camera, not the reporter. He smiled radiantly and said, "I am responsible for all of it." And he raised his hand as if to indicate his followers crowding all around him.

"Excuse me, old man; are you saying that you killed all six witnesses against you?"

The guards could wait no longer but roughly edged the guru past the reporter before he could answer the question. The boy had trouble threading through the crowd that closed behind the guru as he entered the court building and proceeded to the waiting room where the public defender was waiting. There, the guards left the guru and the public defender alone together, while the boy stood outside patiently.

"I suppose you've heard that there is no longer a case against you because the last of the witnesses has died, some say of fright. While you were in your cell one man died by garroting, one woman by a knife, one young man by the bite of a cobra, another by a pistol shot, and the last woman but one by drowning. You could not have murdered these people, but the judge will want to know whether you are responsible."

"I am responsible for everything. Where is your faith?" The defender at first looked ashamed. Then he brightened up.

He ventured, "I don't think the magistrate can keep you in jail any longer because no case can be brought without living witnesses. So you will be set free."

"How can they free a man who already is free?" The guru spoke with a disembodied voice, as if in a trance, his inward look complacent and resolved at the same time. His defender, however, was becoming alarmed. He decided to tell the guru what was likely to happen next.

"The authorities will not want to let things go. They will want to find some way to link you to the deaths of the six witnesses. I would not be doing my job as your defender if I did not advise you to confess to nothing where no proofs can be brought forward. You are the only one who stood to benefit by the deaths of these people, so you alone had the motive to kill them. For today, please let me speak on your behalf so you can walk away from the court and the jail."

"I'll let you speak, but not for me. I want to be with my people because they need me. Say what you have to say so I can be with them. While I wait, I'd like to have the boy sit with me. Please let him enter and sit on the floor beside me."

Seven hours later, after a tense ten-minute hearing, the guru was free to go as he pleased. The reporter who had questioned him that morning, waited all day to pursue his line of questioning. The old man looked the reporter in the eyes, with a look of such reproach that the reporter fell speechless.

The old man passed in front of the reporter and was swallowed up by the crowd of his followers. They ushered him to a late afternoon feast that had been prepared by the village women. While everyone else ate and drank, celebrating their holy man's release, the guru sat cross-legged on a saffron cloth, the boy beside him, and taught about freedom.

The reporter chose to interview one of the guru's long-time followers while the old man taught.

"Can you tell me anything about the guru's past?"

"What do you want to know that is not already well known by everyone?"

"They say he used to sell threads in the marketplace, and that he killed a man, and that he swindled a lot of people before he became a holy man."

"Since you know these things, why are we talking?"

"Did your guru have anything to do with the deaths of the six witnesses against him?"

"What do you think?"

"I think he had much to gain from their deaths. I also think that it was more than coincidence that all the witnesses died while he was in jail."

"Again what do you want me to tell you?"

"How did the six witnesses die?"

"Earlier, when you broadcast the facts of the six cases, you said that the last man died of fright, one man died by garroting, one woman by a knife, one young man by the bite of a cobra, another by a pistol shot, and the last woman but one by drowning." This handlist of deaths was recounted with increasing alarm. The reporter shook his head. The critical question remained, so he asked it directly.

"Yes, but who did all these killings?"

"Perhaps no man or woman did these things."

"Are you suggesting that some spirit killed these people? Then let me ask whether it is true that the guru's ashram practiced black magic?"

"The guru is a most holy man. He is revered as a man of peace. Just look at how his people adore him there where he is teaching. They hang on every word. They believe in him."

"Such holy men have power, don't you agree?"

"I do agree. Now I have to see to the old man's needs. Please excuse me."

The reporter shook his head and looked around. At his side he felt a presence, and there stood the boy looking up at him expectantly.

"You are the guru's boy. Is that right? Well, then, what do you have to say about what has happened here today?"

"Only the dead have no fear." The young boy spoke with the wisdom of a sage.

"Yes, I've heard him say those very words. Do you know what he means by them?"

"The living fear. The dead do not fear. Nothing is said about the need to fear."

The reporter was entranced by the boy's calm lucidity. The boy seemed impervious to normal human emotions. He did not seem to be capable of the fear he spoke of. Intrigued, the reporter asked him, "What do people fear?"

"They fear dying."

"Did the six witnesses who died fear that they would be killed before they died?"

"Believe it."

"So, boy, who or what killed all those people?"

"The guru takes everything upon himself. Yet he was in a jail cell all the time that these people met their ends."

"Do you know anyone who can tell me how all that happened connects?"

"My mother may be able to help you. She is the woman in the blue sari at the second table with the food. She is looking our way. Please wave. Perhaps she'll talk with you."

The reporter saw the woman waving back at him and was so struck by her beauty that he did not see the boy vanish. The reporter looked around, and the boy was gone. He then walked over to the woman's table and asked whether he could ask her a few questions.

"Your boy is very intelligent."

"One day he'll be a guru like the old man, perhaps. He is the guru's disciple."

"How do you account for all the deaths of witnesses against the old man?"

"Liars come to evil ends. Do you agree?"

"I know many liars who have not yet met their ends. Politicians are among those."

"Yes, but those who bear false witness may be in a special class of liars."

"Can you tell me about the lies they were planning to tell?"

"For one thing, some of them were scheming to lie about the old man's having had sex with very young women who came to learn from him. Two of the women were said to have become pregnant, but they died before giving birth. Three others' parents were going to bring court proceedings against the guru because their virgin daughters had been defiled by him. All the parents and their daughters died mysteriously." She spoke with disdain about the common rumors and false accusations. When she said the word "mysteriously," she grasped the reporter's sleeve for emphasis.

He pulled back his sleeve and asked the question that might shed light on the mysteries. "Don't you find it strange that all the people who were going to incite proceedings against the man died suddenly?"

"Holy matters are a mystery to men and women. I knew that one of the girls who accused the guru had been defiled by her young cousin. He was afraid of being discovered as the culprit because then he would have had to marry the girl. He had the idea that the girl should falsely accuse the guru of having ravished her. She died of a guilty conscience, I think. Of course, the cousin also died of a lingering fever after he was bitten by a rat. Village life can be complicated; don't you think?"

"Garroting is not easily explained as an accident."

"You mean, the man whose head was found severed from his body. A great mess that was. The man was a Thugee thief and, it's believed, a murderer as well. When young unmarried girls needed to get rid of an unwanted pregnancy or newborn, this man took care of the details. Some witness he would have been, if only the magistrate knew the real facts."

"You seem to have an explanation for at least a few of the murders. How do you account for six murders happening in a very short time—the time when the guru was in jail?" The reporter wanted answers that would satisfy his readers. He needed cold facts or at least solid conjectures. He refused to print mumbo jumbo and suppositions. While he waited for her answer, he noticed a snake charmer had started playing a flute over a basket. A hooded cobra appeared to dance to the music, but It was only following the flute's end as a target for a strike.

"Young man, sit down for a while and eat something— perhaps some tandoori chicken. Night is coming and possibly it will rain. I don't mind it's getting dark and wet. If you want to know the truth, I'll tell you. Why are you suddenly shivering?"

"I felt a cool breeze at my neck just now."

"I'll light a candle while we talk. The cold is coming. Perhaps it means something more than the nightfall."

"I'm not at all superstitious."

"That is good for you, but it may not be good for your story."

"I don't follow you."

"Once, long ago, the guru who is sitting over there, was a boy just like my boy, and he studied with a powerful guru who was the wise man in this region. It is a very ancient tradition to pass the wisdom down through the generations to the young men who have the gift of seeing. I did not know my son had the gift until I looked for the reasons why the guru chose him."

The guru sat with his legs crossed looking inward as holy men are used to doing. The boy sat patiently watching his mentor, memorizing his posture and attitude.

"Gradually, I came to understand the gift my son was born with. The gift is like a spirit, and it is both a blessing and a curse. Once my boy was recognized by the guru, he changed and from that time, he was no longer my son. He was the guru's heir apparent. I knew better than to stand in the way of those two men. Women know little about the bonds of man to man, but I had seen the signs before. Resistance is not only futile; it is fatal."

"You were going to tell me about the spirit."

"As I was saying, the wisdom that is passed has a power of its own. This power is not only the power of ideas but also the power of life and death. The wielder of this power often does not know its effects until they have become manifest. That black thing that sits on your shoulder now is an example. Don't move. It is only curious. Look at the candle's flame, and it will go away."

"What black thing do you see?"

"I see the black care you're always bringing with you. Will I get a story? Will I be able to file the story on time? Will it make me famous? Can I check my facts? Is the story true essentially? This care hides the truth from you. It is the thing that kills."

"And did you really see this thing or did you just want to scare me? You certainly scared me."

"You judge. Anyway, look how my son is now sitting near the guru, hanging on every word. He is like a shadow in the guru's shade. The torches have been lit, and the guru's hair is red and golden in the light. See what a holy man he is. Your cameras can make much of him in this light."

"So what you're suggesting is that all these people who died had their own private stories that led inexorably to their deaths, perhaps influenced by guilt about their preparing to lie about the guru's past."

"Not everything that has been said about the old man is a lie."

"So he was a thread dealer?"

"Yes, so I am told. It was a very hard life at the bottom caste. He was untouchable, never destined to rise. At that level you meet evil and strange people. You live on the edge, and you struggle to survive. Imagine selling the means of tying together materials, without having the needles or materials to make the thread useful. That is like the spirit that binds my story together, and ties my boy's life to the guru's."

"What happened to your boy's father?"

"Everyone knows that the boy is a bastard son. I was raped just after I was married, and I lied to my husband and told him the child within me was his. When the child was born, my husband knew at once the boy was not his, but I could not tell him who had fathered my child."

The reporter nodded. He understood the predicaments of the husband and the wife. The woman felt impelled to continue her story.

"For shame, my husband left the village and went far away. I never heard from him again. My husband's family suspected what had happened, but to save face in the village, they gave me a dwelling and an income, which continues today. They don't communicate with us, except at the Festival of Lights. So I have had time to dwell on things that ordinary married women do not have the luxury or inclination to explore."

"I'm afraid I deflected you from answering my question."

"If you'll be patient, you will discover that what I have told you connects to the story and the answer you desire. You see, the man who raped me was the old man sitting over there. He won't admit it, and I won't accuse him in a court of law because he did not know what he was doing at the time. The guru and my son communicate so well in part because they are father and son. But they are more than that. Because the guru was married to my mother, they are grandfather and grandson, too. Does that appall you?"

"It does, but I've heard stranger tales than yours." He seemed imperturbable, but his calm demeanor showed why he was the perfect listener.

"Well, let me continue because there is more.

"My husband was from a warrior caste, and my family was from a business caste. My husband was betrothed to me in an arranged marriage after he raped me and paid my family a large compensatory dowry. He is a scion of the great Hinduja brothers, who sell their weapons in the major capitals of the world. His caste is known for taking whatever they want by force."

He said, "I know all about the Hindujas. Their wealth and power awe monarchs."

"My caste is known for liking money, and we pray to Lakshmi. I know by your style that you are a Brahmin so you will understand these things. You will know that my husband and I were never meant to remain together. It is enough for me that I have the money I need to live on comfortably. The villagers ask no questions, as long as you have enough money. They can gossip, but they dare not make accusations in court. They don't know what will happen to them if they do so."

"So now are you saying that the village enforces its own rules? Does that mean that the six witnesses were killed by the villagers?"

"For a Brahmin, you jump to conclusions in a hurry. Have some more food. I can see in your eyes that you are anxious for me to come to a point. Unfortunately, I have to weave my story the way I do so you will finally understand. I can't just state in a paragraph, everything I mean to say, and then elaborate in lesser and lesser paragraphs for an editor to trim wherever he will. Be patient. Your caste has all the time in the world before Nirvana. Some things, though, you must learn from those in lower castes, who remain stuck in their places for many thousands of generations, with no hope of rising."

"You have said that the guru sitting over there next to your son began life as an untouchable. How did he rise to become the holy man he is? Surely such a rise in a single lifetime is unprecedented."

"The old caste system that gives you and your caste such prestige, is breaking down in the new age of media. Catch the eye of the news reporters like yourself, and anyone can become anything. Not the reality, but the story matters. The guru looks, talks and acts like a holy man. His holiness may be contested but not impeached. Forces beyond him control how his image is maintained. He learns quickly that he does not orchestrate history. History orchestrates him.

"It has often been maintained that the holy man slept with many women who studied with him in his ashram. This is not only true, but inevitable. When he began teaching, he taught untouchables whose rapport he gained by any means, including sexual. His endowments became legendary, and the women who birthed his children seemed to live charmed lives, as long as they never told who was the father of their children. If he sired one child, he sired ten thousand."

She paused and poured tea. She laid a bowl of sweet cherries on the table next to a plate of sliced limes and another plate of dates and figs. When she was satisfied with the setting, she continued her exposition.

"It has been said that the Western Emperor Charlemagne's blood runs in the veins of eighty percent of Europeans. Well, the guru's DNA is tangled in the blood of countless untouchable babies, all of which carry his uncanny intelligence and character. When his message was heard by women of my own caste and the warrior caste, they came to study with the holy man, not caring whether he was of a lower caste than they. It became a badge of honor to have the guru untie their virginal knot, and set them free from the illusions of maidenhood."

"So, now you are telling me that the accusers were right about his being a seducer of women at his ashram?"

"I am telling a story. Please let me finish it. So, the thread dealer began to deal in materials and needles as well. He was given gifts by his many concubines, who never hoped to marry him because a holy man does not marry. They were naturally delighted to learn of their own sexuality through him, and to know that they were not aberrant in their human desires and feelings. He taught the Kama Sutra in ways they had never imagined. They were grateful to the man for his energy and probity, his wisdom and gentleness. He became the exemplar for the husbands they would one day have, perhaps. Where was the vantage for a lawsuit in all of this?

"In my own case, love of money led me to a brothel, where I entertained all sorts of men of all castes, since sexuality never did know about levels of society. I worked in a brothel for money because that was what my family understood. I only began working there after I had been raped by my handsome, warrior future husband."

The reporter interjected, "But you were still owned by the brothel, weren't you?" He ate a slice of lime and took two cherries. She fetched and placed a bowl of fennel seeds on the table. She ate two seeds as she considered how to pick up her train of thought.

"His family was induced to buy me out of my brothel, when my family decided there was more money to be made in that than in my meager earnings on my back. So, they did the calculations and extrapolated from my then age of twelve, until my end of useful life as a prostitute of thirty-five at fifteen customers a day, seven days a week, with factors for inflation and currency depreciation. My betrothal was a business transaction that had one fixed fee, plus marriage gifts in envelopes of cash. Yes, I was beautiful then, so my parents were able to drive a hard bargain."

"You are beautiful now, and from your boy's age, I would guess you are not more than twenty years old."

"Thank you, and near enough. So, now I see the shadow increases, like a stole about your neck. You have black cares of a different kind than you did when you first sat down. You are thinking what it would be like to sleep with me. Know that I am very expensive, but I have more to tell before we get to that. When I am finished, we'll bargain. See how my son dozes while the guru drones on. A dozen women in saris listen as he teaches now. I know them all. They have all been to bed with him, and five have borne his children. They are like an extended harem, and he knows each one as if she were his daughter."

"How does the killing fit in? I'm feeling a chill all of a sudden." In fact, he felt creeped out and trembled involuntarily.

"I expected that you might feel the nearness of the spirit now. It rests its hand on my shoulder, like a cold claw. Power does not exist unless it can do both great good and great harm. The more good it does, the more it must be protected from harm. This has nothing to do with human agency. It is a conservation of goodness and evil in the universe. Until we reach the Nirvana state, where all our striving does not matter, we are struggling, as you and I are now, against forces we cannot possibly fathom. Love matters now and hate. Consider the loss when we break through the human dimension entirely! Well, the guru is close to doing just that. See how his hair now seems a labyrinth of fireworks, as he smiles and gesticulates and eyes each of his students? See how my son studies his every movement and gesture? His mind is recording every word."

"Your eyes in the candle's flame are flashing now, and your smile is so gentle. I long to taste your lips." He was smitten by her beauty and the ineffable sadness of her story. He felt a strong impulse to take her in his arms. The table between them was an obstacle he could do without. The boy regarded them from the corner with something like amusement in his eyes.

"Have some more drink. Eat. We are about to turn into the end of the story when all is revealed."

"Tell on! I am ravished."

"So, the guru built a reputation far beyond our village. Because of the news reporting, he became first a national figure, and then an international celebrity. He appeared on talk shows in America, and he signed contracts for the use of his image and his writings. He became a plaything of the international myth makers, even a cartoon figure on a children's program. The untouchable Indian thread dealer became an icon, with moneyed interests to protect him and their investments. His life became scripted. He accepted his inevitable notoriety because it meant that, miraculous as it may seem, he was going to achieve Nirvana."

"So he never changed his ways."

"No. He never changed his ways. He is the same man now that he has become an international figure, as he was while he scoured dumps for pieces of string that he tied together and wound on growing balls. He sometimes had fifteen women in a day in his ashrams. They loved him for the attention he lavished on them. They basked in the light he gave them because he made them feel fulfilled."

"And the interests now protect him?"

"Yes, they do."

"And you have now given me the keys to his secrets."

"Yes, and no. How do you feel? You look a little queasy."

"Because I know the truth, where does that leave me?"

"If you divulge one word of what I have imparted in confidence to you today, you will perish just as the many others who came forward to denounce him. And, of course, you know that I am of the business caste. I have my financial interest in him too. He is my father and my grandfather and the father of my child. Can any of this be proven? You have my words to report, but where is the evidence? If you have it or if you could be perceived to have it, you would end up like all the others. You know that in your soul."

The reporter looked over to see that the guru was now looking directly at him, and so was the boy. In fact, all the women who had been obsequiously fawning over the guru, were now glaring at him across the distance between his table and the saffron material on which the guru sat.

"So where does this leave us?" The reporter felt uneasy now, and he wished he had decided not to interview this intriguing woman, the mother of the child who sat by the guru.

"It's time for us to bargain for my body. I saw from the moment you looked at me that you wanted me and that feeling has grown as we have talked. You know my inmost secrets, so intimacy now must follow as day follows night. You want me. I am available. Now, what do you say to one crore for the rest of the night?"

"One crore? You must be joking! Half a crore, perhaps. In cryptocurrency. I have a wallet on my person with that amount."

"Oops. If I were to decide to eliminate you, I could have that much immediately with no need for the niceties."

"So now it is blackmail."

"Call it whatever you will. One crore, half of which you carry with you. The rest will be paid in gold."

"I hope this night will be worth the expense."

Money was often the final arbiter of news in India. Yet sexuality also added charm and sometimes wit. This woman's charms were legendary, and her beauty promised much. He wondered whether they would be sufficient recompense. She seemed to read his mind.

"I assure you, I will make it worth your while. And I can also assure you that if you should fail to pay me, your black hair will tighten around your neck until you achieve the next state for your soul, whatever that might be."

"You drive a hard bargain. I grant that you are beautiful. In fact, at the moment, I think you are the most beautiful woman I have ever seen. Have you drugged my food and drink?"

"That is an unfair question, Brahmin. Look at the guru, who seems to have been transported into ecstasy. His soul has left his body."

"The boy is looking for the signs of life. The guru may have died."

"So, perhaps your reward for our evening's conversation is right in front of you. If you hurry, you can record the final moments of the famous guru's life. You can spread that story throughout the world, and picture the boy who will take up the mantle and become the guru's heir."

"I take the challenge, and will record the guru's demise with all attendant fanfare if you will lower the price of your body from one crore to one-half crore, the amount that I carry in my Bitcoin wallet."

"You have won the contest. Record the demise now. My friends are ready to serve as mourners on camera. My boy will hold the guru's hand as he passes. When you have completed with your camera work and story and have given me the wallet, then we'll have an adventure beyond your wildest dreams."

The Wakening

Beri Manning walked through Park Cemetery in the early morning. The cedar lined path through the gravestones was a shortcut, allowing her a few moments of private meditation. She was in a dark mood since her boyfriend, Charles, had broken up with her yesterday afternoon and her period began last night. She did not know whether to laugh or cry. The boy was a jerk, but he had been her jerk. His wanting to break up was a surprise. Now she was free but felt hurt.

Beri stopped to consider her conflicted feelings. Unconsciously, her eyes fell on the shadow of the familiar Egyptian obelisk. She was drawn by curiosity to the ancient sundial. It needed a good cleaning. Its base was tangled with the clinging ivy that covered the whole side of the cemetery. Its hieroglyphs were caked with moss and lichen. At its summit, was a metal pyramid, corroded black with age.

Before her father died, he told Beri about the engineering feat that brought the stone needle to town and raised it here. Erecting an overtly pagan monument in a Christian cemetery had initially caused protests. Beri could not imagine why.

Beri ran her fingers over the priest figure, holding the ankh by the loop on top. She thought of her great-great-grandfather, the man her father said was behind the raising of the monument. He was buried under a headstone that the ivy also covered in their family plot. A letter in his hand described the contents of a time capsule that was buried beneath the obelisk. It also alluded to the stone's sidereal powers.

Beri remembered her great uncle's tale about the obelisk's serving as a navigational beacon. A shiver ran down her spine when she recalled his disappearance in broad daylight, right where she was standing now. Her great aunt was standing beside him when it happened. She loosed his hand, and he was gone. Beri felt her eyes welling with tears. She wept uncontrollably and wiped her eyes with her hands.

Beri wiped her wet hands over the obelisk figure with the anhk. The stone felt cold at first. Then it began warming as she rubbed it. She continued to rub the stone's surface. It softened. Her hand pushed through the granite and touched a rounded handle. She grasped it. She felt a strong electric shock, but could not let go of the handle. Darkness surrounded her. Afraid now, but energized by the electricity, she felt along the handle to discover it was an ankh. Her free hand spread out and searched her surroundings. She was inside the obelisk, able to breathe but not to become free. She heard voices.

"Amenra will deliver you to the stars," said a deep voice.

"Wish anything you like," said a voice like her father's.

"Who are you?" Beri asked the voice.

"I am your translation to the stars," the voice answered. "Just hold the ankh and think."

Beri imagined she was on a planet revolving around the farthest star from Earth. She found herself immersed to the waist in a warm, blue liquid under the light of that distant sun. She raised the golden ankh in her hand.

"I wonder whether my great uncle is here."

The image of her great uncle materialized beside her, smiling with an ankh in his hand. "You thought of me, so I came. What do you want?"

"I want to go back outside the obelisk in the park cemetery."

He laughed. "Why would you want to do that?"

"I just want to try it."

"Whenever you want to go there, just release your grip on your ankh. When you do that, you'll never be able to return here, even in death. The ankh is a one-time gift."

"So as long as I hold the ankh, I'll be immortal?"

"Yes, and you'll be able to go anywhere in the universe you desire."

"Is that why you disappeared and never returned?"

"I was afraid to let it go."

Beri released her ankh, and it fell into the darkness. She thought she heard it land before she fell back into the ivy under the obdurate stone. She rose uninjured and continued walking to school, wondering whether she had blacked out. She had her doubts. Across her palm, ran a wide red line as if she had been holding something hot.

Comes the Silence

Before the end, I had a recurring dream. Invariably, it variably ran like this:

It's Friday morning. My last surviving sibling, Simon, and I with our guns drawn walk quickly through a gray land in thick gray fog. A giant follows us shouting loud. Others answer in a rising din.

To run is vain. Hiding and waiting cannot work for us. I turn and aim. I shoot a giant's foot. That slows, not stops him.

Simon turns and runs slightly to his right, firing two rounds, I think wild. I run orthogonal, low and fast. I shoot the giant in the throat. His writhing in anguish is my joy. A giant is down and dying amidst ruins.

Simon is slowing now, sobbing and afraid. I catch and hug him hard. "It's all right," I whisper. "Go on and cry. This is only our first combat of the day."

I tie a long line to him so we'll not lose each other in the fog. As we move again, the line plays out between us. We range wide and make our way among gray ruins and tangled wires.

Drums begin now. The giants' catcalls echo. Suddenly the line goes taut.

I hear clear sounds of giants growling near. I tug the line for Simon to come back toward me. When I think the line has run its limit, it ranges far too wide. It strains. The line's end runs out, lashing through my hand.

I run in the direction Simon is sure to be.

Thunder resounds through the leaden sky. I kneel and grope among broken stones, as the sounds of drums and giants' shouting rise.

My hand finds Simon spread out on the ground, dismembered: giants' work. Screams are no remedy. I hide among the stones, waiting.

The giants come. The thunder sounds again. The giants roar. Then, comes the silence of the feast.

That was my recurring dream. Each time I awakened from that horrifying dream in a cold sweat, my mind teeming with a hundred unanswerable questions. The three biggest questions lingered: Who might the giants be? Who was the Simon in my dream? What caused the blasted urban landscape through which we had tried to pass?

My life, not analysis, answered my questions as I watched my dream come to life in American cities after the Great Election. The trouble started long before Election Day. In fact, the writing was on the wall by late September, when the students went out on strike. Activation of concentration camps through Executive Orders caused protests not seen since 1968.

Police were overwhelmed, so governors called in the National Guard. The Federal Government put the military on a war footing within the United States. Rumors circulated about midnight raids, detention and interrogation of protest leaders, and three simultaneous, wanton massacres of students in Berkeley, Madison, and Cambridge.

When investigative reporters printed leaked information about the undesirables who had been targeted for the camps, their incendiary reports were suppressed. In defiance, they uniformly published their reports on the Internet and drew attention to them by Facebook, Twitter, and other social media. Taken away in the middle of the night as prisoners, the reporters had no due process. They were never informed of their rights. They were told they could not retain legal counsel. Leadership focused only on public order. The reign of terror then began, though the elections had not yet happened.

Military and police oppression led to a general uprising across major cities and towns across the country. Mobs freed prisoners from prisons and jails. Angry people in Anonymous masks carried burning effigies of public figures. By torchlight and candlelight, ordinary people paraded through the streets.

Organizers held vigils and teach-ins. All those who had gained much during the last eight years of "misrule" scurried into hiding out of fear for their lives, particularly people of color and the LGBT community. Bolder citizens looted stores, broke glass windows and set buildings afire. They faced withering volleys from vigilantes with hunting rifles.

By the fatal Election Day, the people felt the need to stop the violence. Aged voters turned out to vote en masse, prepared to pull the levers for Law and Order candidates. These voters far outnumbered the newly dead, whose credentials were used by posers and illegal aliens bussed to polls where identification was not required.

The winning party won in a landslide, granting a mandate unknown in American politics. Over seventy senators guaranteed an override of any Presidential veto, and 400 Congresspersons guaranteed the passage of any right-wing agenda. More pertinent, Congress would not override the Presidential use of Executive Orders to rule by decree. Together the Presidency and Congress could gang up against the Judiciary, whose numbers decreased by four Supreme Court Justices.

Not coincidentally, those died in the violence when the election returns showed a clear victory for the right. Since all fifty governors were from the winning party, and a vast majority of mayors were also from that party, the tendrils of what we later called "The Octopus," extended down to the states and the cities. As power choked the country, Homeland Security forces strengthened the borders. There was no escaping the wrath that was to come.

The names of future victims were already in databases. All the mechanics of enforcement were greased for the day after Inauguration Day. As the people who voted for the losing parties rose up in revolt, the authorities clamped down Marshall Law with curfews across the nation. Shoot-to-kill orders against protesters were taken by vigilantes as hunting permits to settle longstanding scores. Ammunition formerly bought by the opposition party to keep it out of the hands of citizens was now issued to Homeland Security forces to maintain strict control.

The definitive Homeland Security databases were put to use, sorting the people as always, but now with the aim to root out and destroy the opposite party's apparatus and to silence dissenters. Print newspapers were commandeered to print the new government's propaganda. Online reporting and social media were allowed to continue to run free, so dissension could be tracked by special teams of trolls, and dealt with summarily by force of arms.

In the run up to Groundhog Day, the concentration camps filled to capacity. Overflow prisoners were sent to football stadiums as holding areas.

The President addressed the nation on February 1 proclaiming that the immediate evil of public misrule had ended. He announced that, for expediency and in view of a clear and present danger, he would rule by decree in anticipation of later Congressional actions. Supporters of his party cheered him on, while provocateurs stirred up the opposition.

The military and police moved in strength to kill or arrest all troublemakers. Because the prisons and jails were already filled to capacity, the President annexed Cuba by Executive Order and shipped excess Islamist prisoners to that island as a temporary measure. So, instead of ridding Cuba of Guantanamo Bay as a holding pen, this administration made the whole island a prison.

Those who were sent to Cuba were the lucky ones. At first, the people were glad to be able to walk the streets without fear of being shot in a crossfire. By spring, they began to realize the horror of their electoral decision. The "usual suspects" were, by then imprisoned or killed. Special categories of people were targeted in new lists of victims. These lists, updated daily, included anyone known to have linked to those already identified as favoring liberal views. Since a great many so-called conservatives had relatives and friends who were not so inclined, fear spread among the rank and file conservatives about their known associates.

As in Nazi Germany, the apparatus of a counter-intelligence state settled over the land like an iron maiden. Children informed on their parents. Sisters informed on their brothers. Grandparents informed on each other. Husbands informed on their wives and vice versa.

The lists of undesirables grew very long. The President created a Czar for Domestic Order to coordinate activities across governmental departments and cut through red tape. The Czar was familiar due to the electoral process. He was depicted as the monster in the film Aliens, a likeness that stuck in the public imagination.

I noticed that all opposition parties had been targeted for exclusion or extermination. Communists, Libertarians, and Democrats alike were blacklisted from work. Independents came next because they never could be trusted. In the end, only people who were registered Republicans could hold a job or drive a car.

The dream of national healthcare became a sinecure for the winning party. All others had to fend for themselves. Entrenched Public Health Service officers were swapped out with idle Republicans with no other means of support. They wore their uniforms proudly and took over the dispensing of medicines in the national stockpile. Their objective was to turn their industry into a profitable enterprise. As a result, prices for medicines quadrupled in six months.

As for border controls, security was never as good as now. Before August of the first year of conservative rule, a twenty-foot wall was begun along the southern border. Where it was originally designed to keep migrants out, its use gravitated toward keeping American citizens inside. Illegal aliens were not deported anymore. They were branded as outlaws and hunted down like animals.

A cost-benefit analysis was conducted approving euthanasia of all illegals, with cremation instead of ordinary burial. Crematoriums worked twenty-four hours a day, and mobile units on the Russian model roamed the country taking care of bodies of suicides and summary executions.

Nothing in the country was cost-free anymore. Libraries, museums, parks and monuments had huge fees. The government sold tickets to every conceivable event. Parades were no exception. The Fourth of July celebration of 2017 was deemed the most profitable single event of the year.

Uniformed officers marched proudly through the cities of America, no longer applauded because the people feared them. In several cities, the parades turned violent. The uniformed marchers carried weapons loaded with live ammunition. They opened fire on the protesters. Fortunately, ambulances and mobile cremation units were standing by to clean up the mess.

I was blissfully ignorant of most of the atrocities until the authorities came for my parents. As the eldest child, I was left to keep the family together until my parents returned. Gregor, my brother, helped me until the authorities came for him. Then, I was alone with the four others. When I asked the authorities when my family members were going to be released from custody, they gave me no satisfactory answers.

They called me a troublemaker for asking impertinent questions. They put my name on a list. I realized that I had to find a way to get my four siblings to safety. Since each state had imposed border controls to confine people of color and Islamists, crossing from one state to another was difficult. I connected with a friend to an underground network of unlabeled citizens, loosely governed by people known as The Group.

Under the care of the network, we managed to reach the state of Maine and ended at a log cabin style resort on a lake across from Canada. In the early morning of the day after our arrival, I awakened to discover my siblings telling an obvious informer what we had managed to do to get clear. I did not wait for the repercussions of this betrayal. Instead, I climbed into a rowboat and rowed to the Canadian shore alone. I knew the Canadians had directives to return American migrants, but I decided to take my chances. I evaded the guards with dogs. I hitchhiked my way to Halifax, Nova Scotia.

At a small restaurant, I witnessed a televised message the American government was sending to the world. Order was the theme: The United States had been saved from certain ruin by degenerate and corrupt political forces for more than twenty years. Draconian measures had been necessary to right the balance of power. The legislation of a generation of lawmakers was now being overturned by daily decrees. Not satisfied with the response times of a sometimes recalcitrant and ungrateful Congress, the President had vacated Congress and made Martial Law the norm.

As I watched the propaganda with disgust and sadness, I was noticed by two members of the American Government in exile. They moved right in when they saw me crying silently.

"We know just how you feel," the woman said. "It's all so sad. The question is, what is to be done?"

Her male companion chimed right in, "Come with us and we'll help you find a way to right the wrongs. We have powerful friends who can help us."

I answered, "I have just escaped from a nightmare. Do you want to subject me to new horrors? No thanks. I just want to be free."

They both laughed indulgently as if to a child.

"Come dear," she said, "you must be joking."

I stood up from the table and bolted from the restaurant. I thought I heard them laughing at me as if I were the fool. I made my way to the harbor. I thought I would find transportation anywhere in the world from there.

In fact, the harbor was cooperating with the American intelligence agencies. Everyone's papers were checked against the databases. I would have to be careful about stowing away. As it turned out, a small, rogue craft was making its way to Cuba. It needed a crew member to replace one taken by the American authorities. No questions were asked, so I shipped aboard.

The voyage was long, and we sometimes fished along the way. I got to know the captain, a pirate whose knowledge of the coastal regions was profound. Twice we were boarded by U.S. Coast Guard personnel, who searched the boat from focsle to stern. Fortunately, they did not search the special underwater compartment where I lay hidden. We sailed into Havana Bay, and the captain told me the rules for the island, which was now totally comprised of prisoners.

He laughed when he said I'd be most welcome. My problem would be ever getting off the island again. He bid me farewell and good luck. I jumped to the pier as the fog rolled in and covered the bay. Two beggars found me quickly and stripped me of everything I valued. When they saw I had nothing left, they took me to their lair and fed me like an equal.

"What news do you bring from the mainland?"

"America is a nightmare. That's why I came here."

The woman laughed and held her sides. "We know that story well enough."

"The trouble is," her consort said, "here it is no different. Stay with us tonight. Tomorrow you'll see what I mean."

That night I could not sleep. I tossed and turned. My host and hostess must have thought I was asleep. They whispered, but I heard them.

"What do you think she'll bring on the street?"

"The question is, how shall we sell her?"

"Let's try to sell her as a prostitute. If that fails, we'll sell her as food."

I heard the determination in their voices. When they went to sleep, I found a sturdy knife. I killed them both, the man and then the woman. She fought back, but I overcame her. Now, I had a hideout earned by blood. I had provisions to last a few days. I thought I had time to consider and plan for my future.

The next morning, I wrapped the two dead bodies in their bedding and ventured into Havana. I wore the clothes of my dead male host. I pushed my hair up under his hat. For effect, I smoked a fat cigar. On the streets, walked people in colorful clothing, but they all had eyes searching for an advantage. This was an island of thieves and worse. I was glad I carried the knife.

Down an alley, I saw two men forcing themselves on a young girl. She was struggling against them. One was holding her down while the other, with his pants down, was preparing to mount her from behind. I had no trouble slashing his throat.

When the other let go of the girl, I plunged my wet knife into his neck. The knife sank to its hilt. The girl was weeping uncontrollably. She was afraid I meant to do her harm. I had some trouble reassuring her, so good was my disguise as a man. Finally, I slapped her hard and told her to follow me if she wanted to remain alive.

We made our way like a couple back to my hideout. There, I revealed to the girl that I was a woman. I showed her the two thieves and traffickers I had killed. I suggested we should steal a boat that night and sail for Haiti. In the meantime, I advised her to rest while I scouted the harbor to find a suitable boat.

I returned that evening, after finding the boat. I told the girl to eat and gather food for our voyage. She trusted me enough by then to tell me her name. She was called Simone.

The fog socked in the harbor when we left the hideout. Still, we had no trouble finding the boat and taking the lines off the bollards. I had learned much about sailing while coming from Halifax. I told Simone what to do, and she complied.

We cleared the harbor and made our way silently to sea, past the U.S. Coast Guard cutters that patrolled the area. I guessed right that the patrols would be looking for boats going north, not south.

We reached Haiti in three days and put ashore at Port au Prince. There, we learned that the Americans had just begun gassing all people on Cuba to clear the way for new profitable investment opportunities.

Clearly, the giants were at work.

Night of the Sailor Moon

The moon was full, and the air so crisp and clear, you could make out the Sea of Tranquility. Here, at the desert site, a crowd of twenty-odd stalwart believers in alien visitations gathered after Independence Day as we always have done for the kickoff of our annual week-long camp and vigil.

Two newcomers had joined us: a retired Air Force lieutenant colonel, and a wild-eyed female investigative reporter, who specialized in UFOs. Everyone was sharing stories by firelight, while the obelisk stood like a silent sentinel pointing to the stars.

Whose idea the obelisk had been, no one here knew. It was erected just as mysteriously as the events of July 7, 1947, were covered up. On each of its four sides, were inscribed pictures of the two crashes, the recovery, the bodies, and the cover up. A bronze dedication plaque alluded to interred relics of the crash, including tiny bodies. I viewed this as a continuation of the cover-up.

Strangely, the lieutenant colonel agreed with me. An odd fellow, he had written the final official report on UFOs for the Air Force. He laughed at the impossibility of pleasing a naïve and incredulous public. The investigative reporter made his point by chiding him for his complicity in the cover-up.

"The people have a right to know the truth," she screeched. The lieutenant colonel shook his head and as a peace offering tendered her a drink from his flask, which she accepted.

We regulars had begun drinking, too, when a black Infiniti SUV drove up. Two men with crew cuts climbed out and unloaded their scoped rifles, a tent and sleeping blankets. They appeared to be military, perhaps Special Forces.

One pitched their tent, while the other wandered through the assemblage, introducing himself and his associate as alien hunters. He expected aliens to be attracted by the obelisk. He wanted to kill them if they dared to come. The reporter zeroed in on them and began an interview. They appeared to like the attention of the press. The rest of us kept at a respectful distance and ignored them.

The lieutenant colonel told me, "I think those men are frauds."

"Have a few more drinks and reconsider," I advised. "Your name is Clark. I read your book about UFOs. Tell me, with all the misinformation out there already, why did the Air Force consider it necessary to print more of it?"

"Why are you here for this vigil?"

"I'm here because lightning struck twice in this location. I wasn't here to see it either time. Maybe it will strike again. I want to be here for it."

"That's what the Air Force thought, too. My general dreamed up the idea for this obelisk. I found the money in a black ops slush fund to excavate, transport, engrave and mount it here. I consider it my finest work." I could tell he was very proud of his achievement. "It's the only monument of its kind."

"Obelisks have historically been erected to celebrate the intersection of the divine and human. Egypt is full of them."

"The difference is, events on this obelisk actually happened. The proof lies under the long pole."

"Is the Air Force's purpose only to document the events of 1947?"

"Not hardly. If you look closely at the inscribed pictures, you'll discover many events never reported in the open press."

"Such as what?"

"Alien-human hybrids. Alien technology. Star maps. That kind of thing."

"How old would hybrids be today?"

"In earth terms a maximum of 70. At the top of the monument is a titanium cap, laced with rare earth elements in the same proportion as our assayers found in UFO remains."

"You're suggesting the obelisk is at least a beacon. Is it possibly also a weapon?"

"You're saying those things, not I. Theoretically, aliens could find this place on account of the obelisk. As for the weapons idea, I'm not sure anyone knows how to kill an alien."

They spoke in whispers so as not to be overheard. Around the site, were hundreds if not thousands of devotees of the Unidentified Flying Objects. They made small fires and told stories in small groups. They all professed to believe in the advent of aliens.

They would not have come the great distances for this special day if they did not. Most, however, would not know an alien if it looked them in the eye or bit them in the foot. They were here on a lark tinged with a mystery. Who knows but an alien might actually appear tonight? That seemed unlikely. Danger was remote. The fun continued oblivious of the reality.

"Those two alien hunters presume to kill them."

He laughed. "They're frauds. Who knows? They may even be hybrids."

"How can you tell a hybrid?"

"We have special sensors."

"So the obelisk could also be a special sensor?"

"The answer to that question is probably highly classified." The lieutenant colonel became serious.

"What would be classified?" the investigative reporter interjected. "Those so-called alien hunters certainly know how to spin a yarn. I can't use anything they told me. So, will you answer my question?"

"Ingrid, we were just talking about the technical purpose of the obelisk. If there were any such purpose, it would be highly classified."

"That's no fun. I'll have to put in a Freedom of Information Act request for the data."

"And you'll get bupkis. Why don't you focus on what you can print?"

"What do you suggest?"

"You could find and print the meaning of the inscriptions on the obelisk, for one thing."

"Will you give me a hint about why that might be interesting to my readers?"

"Since the obelisk is a historical artifact, sanctioned and registered by the government, its information is now public. While anyone can see it, a special intellect must still interpret it."

"So it's more of your propaganda, Colonel? And you want me to spread your story in the press. Well, I'm not going to be your pigeon."

I mumbled, "The best place to hide something is in plain view."

"What did you say?" Ingrid asked.

"The colonel was just telling me that the inscriptions on that monument tell things that were never published. It contains an open account of presumably classified matters, like the existence of alien-human hybrids."

Ingrid was not convinced. She accepted another drink from the colonel's flask.

"Am I hallucinating, or are you two related?"

"Ingrid is my daughter. Ingrid Clark, this is ... I'm sorry, but I didn't catch your name."

"Call me Max. Hi, Ingrid. Why did you decide to become a reporter? You might have followed in your father's footsteps at Air Force Office of Special Investigations."

"Max, I hate subterfuge and lying. Dad knows how I feel."

"All too well. Anyway, you two talk. Keep my flask. I'm going to walk around the obelisk and take a look at a few details with my cellphone light." He wasted no time walking to the obelisk and swiping on his light.

"Your father knows a lot more than he's telling."

"Always. Security is a religion for him."

"I don't suppose he ever talked about how he'd identify an alien or a hybrid?"

"He never gave me the specifics, only that he'd know one when he saw one."

"I suspect you're as obsessed about UFOs as he is."

"Probably so, only I can investigate things he could not, because of his Top Secret clearance."

"Ingrid, in all your investigations, did you ever meet an alien or talk with anyone credible about UFOs?"

"Aside from Dad, you mean? Well, no. I keep hoping for a break."

"Your father just gave you the break of all time: the obelisk. It's the key to everything he can't say publicly."

"Perhaps, but it's his statement, not mine."

In the distance was the area devoted to the motorcycle clans. They had built a bonfire from superannuated cycles and gasoline. They danced in the firelight like men and women possessed. The dancers' shadows extended across the desert floor, some even touching the obdurate obelisk like a dark thought in the night.

"Still, the obelisk needs interpretation. It stands alone and mute, without someone explaining what it means."

"I'm thinking about it."

Two shots were fired to the rear of the obelisk. Everyone ran to see what happened. On the ground was the colonel. Crouched on either side of his lifeless body, were the alien hunters.

"He looked like an alien to me. What do you think?"

"He looked just like the figure on the obelisk. He seemed to transform when he looked at it. Didn't you see him change his shape?"

"He did. There was no question about it. I'll call the troops."

I walked over and felt the body for a pulse. There was none. I stood up and found Ingrid by my side. Tears were streaming down her face. I handed her a tissue.

"Damn alien hunters! Ignoramuses!" I tried to comfort her, but she was inconsolable.

A Special Forces team arrived and carried the lieutenant colonel's body away, after taking pictures and obtaining statements from the alien hunters. None of the other watchers had seen a thing. The SF team and the alien hunters drove into the night. Ingrid remained at the obelisk. We shared the liquor from her father's flask.

"You don't think your father was an alien do you?"

"He was no alien. They killed him because he told."

"What do you mean?"

"The obelisk was his way of saying what he swore never to reveal. That's the nature of the black world Dad inhabited."

"So this whole thing tonight was a planned execution?"

"Near enough, yes. Dad told me he was in danger. Those alien hunters were beady-eyed killers. Black operators, that's what they were. I've seen many like them before." She took a long draft from the flask. "Now he's gone."

I sympathized with her. As a hybrid, though, I felt relief too, since my secret was now safe at last.

The Crypt Back of the Asylum

The old gabled asylum with blackened windows always frightened me because people went in there, but never came out. Bats lived in the attic and flew out and in all night. Giant brown rats played up and down the stairs and in the basement.

During storms, you would hear thunder shake the walls and water running inside the mildewed walls. Lightning flashes would highlight the Asylum's façade, which looked like the hideous sewn face of a Frankenstein coming back for revenge. In its right eye, which from the street was the second-floor left window, I once saw the bluish image of a ghost rocking in a chair, staring at a television and quietly screaming.

By day, things did not look very bad in the fog and evening light from the outside, though moss covered the roof shingles and external woodwork. The building sagged with rotting wood, so when I walked in through it, I felt sure that each next step would pitch me forward through the flooring, or bring the ceiling down upon my head.

The cold stench of rot and decay made breathing hard, and when an icy hand groped me, I wheeled around, shook involuntarily and felt the goose bumps form. A gaunt, bearded male figure with hollows for eyes took a step backward and asked respectfully whether he might help me. I summoned my courage and said that, indeed, he could.

The flaxen-headed man nodded and took me for a Cook's tour of what he called his humble abode. He advised that I should watch my step as we entered a living room that had gone lopsided and sloped dangerously to the left. He warned that I might feel queasy.

An old-fashioned broom stood upright on its bristles in the middle of the room. An unconnected faucet hovered and poured water continuously into a bucket that never overflowed. A leaden sphere rolled in a narrow channel a few feet off the floor around and around the room. As if it had a mind of its own, the sphere never stopped rolling. When I tried to get my bearings, cobwebs that hung from the ceiling caught in my hair. I lifted my arms and discovered that cobwebs were all over my clothing like a shroud of cerecloth.

My guide smiled archly and asked me whether I was afraid of anything. I said boldly that I was certainly not afraid. In that case, he said, he would show me something very special that he had never shown to any living soul.

He led me out back into the Asylum graveyard, a jumble of headstones now overgrown with brambles and prickly berry bushes. A thin path led through the graveyard to a little stone house, which my guide called the Asylum crypt. This was, he said, where the undead were interred. He said I probably knew that no one who entered the Asylum ever was known to exit it again. Well, all of those who entered were interred in this crypt.

I noticed that the figure now had a scythe in one hand and a spade in the other. He had donned a black cassock with a hood like an ancient monk. His face was becoming very lean, and the outlines of his bones seemed to protrude from his skull. His grin was all jaws and teeth.

It was getting very dark now, and my guide drew an iron key from the rope that hung from his waist. He opened the stone door to the crypt and asked whether I wanted to see what lay inside. I said that I had come this far, and I did intend to see what he could show me. He struck a Swan Vesta, lighted a pitch torch that hung from a ring by the door to the crypt and pushed open the stone door. With the torch held before us, he led me inside the cold, dank chamber.

A large brown rat stopped gnawing on a rag-wrapped bone and scampered off. Four or five eastern worm snakes wiggled across the floor and squeezed themselves down into niches in the crypt's floor. Spiders crawled up my legs and arms, and the cobwebs in the crypt compounded those from the house that I still wore.

At the end of the passage through the crypt, was a throne of ebony. There, the figure settled, still holding the torch, and he began to declaim. His voice started even and rich, but as he spoke, its pitch heightened and his articulation became slurred into a scream. His message was one of horror, in that black and otherwise empty space, but he was heard.

From every corner of the crypt, and from the wet and slimy floor, ghost figures rose to join the figure in his screams. I found myself screaming also. The noise was deafening, and the crypt became a music box made of stone within the graveyard. The shades from all those graves entered the crypt, an impossible gathering because they numbered in the thousands. Then the enthroned figure raised his skeleton's hands with the scythe and spade-like scepters, and we fell silent.

The bats began to flutter into the crypt, their leather wings beating like a million hearts. They flew against my face and, like a putrid wind whirled through the assembly. The figure rose and introduced me to his shades. I curtsied. Then, he gestured for me to assume what he termed my rightful place beside him on the throne.

At that moment, three things happened, but I am still not sure of the order of their occurrence. First, I heard a cock's crow. Second, the torch went out. Finally, a shaft of sunlight entered the still open door of the crypt. As if awakening, I blinked three times. Gone were the bats and the shades and the figure. On the throne were the scythe and the spade. I shuddered and ascended my throne.

Time's Teeth Grind Slowly

Grip bones the glass, sharp scythes slowly swing,
Laughter so faint we hear the deep silence.
Bultures to carrion feasts always wing,
Souls tipped off ladders for twitching suspense.

Slaughter continues. All bills shall be paid.
Full carts for crying the young and old.
For richer or poorer, the man tops the maid,
The hard field won by the gin in the cold.

Blood runs in rivers, all lives to the slough.
Sands in the glass run this way and that.
Dust in the air falls to dust for the plough.
Turn the glass over and rat race the rat.

Time's teeth grind slowly: we all chew on death,
Smoke coats our mirrors until our last breath.

The Plasmoid

Barbara Fontaine, newly appointed Professor of Plasma Biophysics at the University of Practical Physics in Brasilia, was the first member of the human species to detect and communicate with a plasmoid, the first identified inhabitant of the realm of plasma.

There was no mistake: the plasmoid was not a creature that could live in traditional solids, liquids or gasses. The plasmoid lived exclusively in plasma. That was where Professor Fontaine had found it, and so far, she could not discover a way to allow it access to the realms inhabited by humans.

When the Professor and the plasmoid met, the plasmoid did not have a name. In fact, the plasmoid did not have the concept of a name, and it knew nothing at all about humans. Barbara classified the being as a plasmoid, and she postulated that a plasmoid had some form of consciousness as a boundary condition of existence.

She tentatively named her specific plasmoid Salamander. She decided on this name because medieval myth had postulated that the salamander was the denizen of the realm of fire. It was the only creature identified with that realm in the old taxonomies. Denizens of the other three earthly realms—earth, air, and water—were well known in medieval times, as are the denizens of solids, gasses and liquids in our time.

In any case, Dr. Barbara Fontaine felt that she was on her way to academic stardom, because she had isolated Salamander, and discovered a way to communicate with it. Salamander came to know its name, the identity of its isolator, and the nature of humans, who were apparently incapable of living in plasma.

The more the Professor communicated with Salamander, the more Salamander learned about her. The pair developed a symbiotic relationship that, inevitably, became love in human terms and something like love in plasmoid terms as well. The Professor thought that the name she had given the plasmoid might itself offer a key to the being's future.

A Salamander could change color. Why could not a plasmoid change habitats? The more she shared this idea with Salamander, the more Salamander thought about how the Professor might change habitats and join it in the fluid, dynamic, mystical realm of plasma. The Professor had not considered the possibility of a role reversal between Salamander and herself. She felt that a scientist should remain in control, and her specimen should remain her subordinate.

For a long while, Professor Fontaine kept her work with the plasmoid secret. She let no other professor into her lab, and she kept her interns in the dark about her discoveries and experiments. She conducted her communications with Salamander in a setting something very like a séance. Anyone overhearing them would have thought that the Professor was talking to herself.

Salamander had learned from the Professor her human language. Its speech was, naturally, modeled on that of the Professor, down to her intonation and pitch. In a sense, Professor Fontaine and Salamander became doubles and the

Professor discussing things with Salamander was actually the same as the Professor talking to herself.

In her private moments, Professor Fontaine wondered whether she had gone insane. Did the plasmoid exist outside her own brain, or not? She determined that the plasmoid must be real when it began its first attempts to lure her into its infernal, superheated realm of plasma. She knew that she should not enter that realm, but Salamander was increasingly insistent that the Professor could change the state of her surroundings and join him and the plasmoids.

Very late one night, as an indication to the Professor of the possibilities, Salamander dared to make the transition from the realm of plasma to the realm of solids, liquids, and gasses. The moment of the transition revealed Salamander as the image of the Professor in every detail. Salamander was female from head to toe, including the pubic area, breasts, and hair. Professor Fontaine was shaken to her bones to find her double standing right before her.

The creature had every characteristic of its model down to the part in the hair, the mole on the right cheek, and the tiny scar of an old wound on the index finger. There was one problem: the Professor had thought of the plasmoid as a male, not a female figure. Now, she was frightened of what her love for the plasmoid might mean. She had a genuine gender identity crisis.

She gently informed Salamander curtly that she had expected it would be male. The plasmoid simply shrugged and asked her to describe what a male would look like. As she spoke, Salamander changed shape to conform to her description of what a male should look like, how it should feel, and how it should relate to her. Now, the Professor was shocked again to watch Salamander transform into what appeared to be her fraternal twin standing before her.

The figure was male, but it was the image of her, with male breasts and body parts, including a tremendous penis, male musculature, and male facial and pubic hair. Because Salamander was the male projection of her own psyche—or perhaps, as she began to suspect, the inner maleness of her— the Professor was startled into a sense of her own completeness and fell instantly in love with Salamander in a different way than she had fallen for it before.

Sensing her change and being acutely empathetic, Salamander was startled by the Professor's sense of discontinuity, and it fell instantly in love with her all over again also. The lovers waited no longer but flew into each others' arms, and by touching each other all over, they confirmed that they were both real, both warm and both alive.

Learning continued, and the more Salamander learned what the Professor wanted of it, the more it changed to conform, to suit her every wish, and the Professor struggled to do the same. Salamander had no inhibitions or pretensions like the human males whose pretensions and machismo the Professor knew and loathed.

In contrast to those males, Salamander was not intimidated by her intelligence or repelled by her vulnerability. It never shied away from her need for self-expression and communication but remained attentive and solicitous—not obsequious or fawning.

The Professor having what she wanted, but never having dared to dream of, she forgot—for the time being—that the plasmoid was from its own, separate realm where she could never go, or so she thought at this stage in their relationship.

In the natural course of their strange, but evolving relationship, Salamander finally mated with Barbara, whose biological desires were attuned in ways she never conceived of before knowing Salamander. All that the Professor needed to do was to think of what might improve their sexual encounters, and Salamander made it so without being explicitly told to do so.

The plasmoid never insinuated and never complained. He was the perfect lover, always changing because her biology was always changing. Barbara Fontaine had never conceived that her dreams of ecstasy could be instantly gratified whenever she liked. She also could have sex whenever she wanted, however she wanted, and for as long as she wanted it. Where pills had given males stamina for as much as four hours with medical safety, Salamander could continue laving for up to twelve consecutive hours, and leave the Professor exhilarated and exhausted and ready to begin again. And Salamander was the same way, too.

The Professor, who had cloistered herself in her professional live, was reconfirmed as a full-blooded woman, and as a human with wants and fears, but she began, quite unconsciously, to think like a plasmoid. What if other humans could understand and accept the gentle, adaptive ways of this creature, her beloved Salamander? Would she herself be able to accept everything that being a plasmoid implied?

Soon enough, she thought, she was going to be put to the test. For now, she delighted in a relationship that fulfilled her in every possible way and made her proud to be a woman and—alive. Her growing love made her increasingly sympathetic to Salamander, and she learned from Salamander the power of plasmoid empathy.

She might not become a plasmoid, she reasoned, but she could become an empath. Without understanding what was happening to her, the Professor began to change. Her psyche went through the whirling blender of her mate's needs, and she recomposed herself as she discovered every nuance of his desires, which were insatiable and all-encompassing.

Salamander did not make any demands; instead, he merely took the Professors to levels beyond her imagining, and then surmounted those patterns of ecstasy and joy by taking her to other levels of orgasmic engagement, like receding mountains rising before them in a mist.

Salamander was well aware of her need to surpass each former achievement, and he took her slowly to each new plateau, checking carefully so he did not overtax her, or take her even a small step beyond her capacity.

He had an uncanny understanding of the woman's physical limits, but he did not seem to her to have any physical limits of his own. So, she went forward, confident that her mate would be able to withstand additional pressures from her indefinitely. She began testing Salamander by increasing her demands on him, and he worked very hard to lead her onward, to discover dimensions of herself that she had never revealed to others, or had never acknowledged to herself.

In strange, complementary ways, Salamander slowly became the guide, and the Professor followed him. In their discussions of what was happening to each of them, Salamander called this curiosity "circumplex," whereby opposites conjoin to resolve their apparent dichotomies. Salamander had no problem articulating effects in psychosexual terms. Proving to her that he could take her to any heights she dared to climb to, the woman became a melting puddle of emotions in his strong and tender arms.

Tentatively, Salamander began to talk about their future. This was at first shocking to the Professor, because it broached the theme of independence, and opened a whole new world of co-dependence. Salamander began talking about their child and their child's future. Salamander told the Professor that she might not be able to make the transition to plasma, but their child might do so. His arguments were most persuasive, and his lavings helped her to come to his point of view.

Salamander said it knew of no plasmoid that could do what humans—specifically what the Professor—could do. Salamander opined that their progeny might inhabit plasmas and, via plasmas, as a kind of universal trapdoor, inhabit all other states throughout the universe just, as Salamander himself had done, because of what the Professor had taught it.

One day, Salamander said, their plasmoid-human forms would colonize the universe, and provide a new era of peace and understanding. This would have been considered absurd or wildly improbable in the first days of their acquaintance, but now the Professor was not sure. She wrote in her journal that Salamander had a vision of a union between humans and plasmoids that would revolutionize what both species meant at the root.

The more Salamander rhapsodized about his vision of a benevolent future, the more Barbara Fontaine, the woman and the Professor, felt the constructive pull of Salamander's logic. She felt Salamander's compulsion as a powerful personality in her life, a force unlike any other besides her powerful father, whose features Salamander had begun to acquire through her descriptions of him.

One night, the Professor woke in a cold sweat beside Salamander, because she felt a new change coming over her, and she felt a little nauseous and sick. Totally naked, she quietly and unsteadily rose from their shared bed and walked before her long mirror, which reached from floor to ceiling.

There, in the mirror, she saw a figure that changed before her eyes from her bare, human form, lovely in the light from the bath, to a fluid, dynamic molten orange mass, barely confined within the outlines of a human form, but threatening to burst out and scatter her corporeality throughout the room.

The Professor tried to get a grip on herself. She was very good at analysis, and she surmised that on that night while coupling with Salamander, she had conceived the plasmoid's child. Her change, she intuited, was due to her pregnancy. As if in confirmation of this surmise, she felt flashes of hot and cold, and before the mirror, she saw her form change back into the human form that she had known from childhood.

Behind her, she saw that Salamander now stood, smiling, taking her gently from behind with both its arms and then turning her for a very human kiss, which she accepted, weeping as she threw herself into its arms.

Her womb, she felt, was on fire, and the newly-conceived child within her was informing her that it was now in charge of her destiny. Still, she felt she needed to join again with Salamander to reconfirm their bond, and she felt moist and receptive.

He understood her need without her saying anything, and he lifted her and placed her on the bed and spent some time preparing her before he entered her and made her whole again with his presence inside her, laving until first light, and then continuing through the morning. When they had finished, she was desirous to continue but sore from her exertions.

Salamander told her that he would continue, but he feared she would be harmed, and so they broke free from their cloying embrace and slept, or at least she slept, and he watched over her like a guardian.

The Professor knew that announcing her discovery to the public now would be a tragic mistake. She no longer looked forward to accolades and honorary degrees from academia for her work with plasma and plasmoids. She decided she would not subject her mate Salamander or their child in her womb to the humiliation of intrusion by the press, and of an investigation by the police and jealous academics. She decided that she must concoct a story to account for her child and that after the birth of her child, her unnatural husband Salamander must return to the realm of plasma to wait for their child to come of age.

The Professor was only dimly aware that these thoughts were not hers alone, and that the plasmoids, father and child, were working on her thought processes and decision-making capabilities. Her mind was full of doubts and fears for Salamander, herself and their child. The more she thought about her situation, the more she became determined to know what this strange bond between her and the plasmoid meant.

She became convinced that her initial encounter with the plasmoid had been at least as much the result of the plasmoid's desire to communicate with a human as of her desire as a human to communicate with a plasmoid. Whenever she got close to the idea that the plasmoid had come for her, though, she was deflected from the idea by sharp pangs from her womb. Her child was using an investigating finger and toe against the inside wall of her womb to tell her not to proceed with that line of logic, or so it seemed to her at the time.

Professor Barbara Fontaine gave birth to a ten-pound baby boy on the second of October that year. The birth occurred not in a hospital with hosts of doctors, nurses, and a midwife, but on the floor of her own laboratory, without anyone involved but her. Although her mate Salamander was present, she delivered her hybrid child all by herself. In the intense pain of labor, she had breathed like the manuals suggested, and finally pushed out the child, and then the placenta.

She raised the child and spanked it firmly, and it cried for life while she cried for joy. Afterward, the woman cut and tied the child's umbilical cord. She offered the child her breasts, which overflowed with milk, and the child drank greedily, reducing the pain she felt from her overflowing well of food for it.

How beautiful her child seemed while it fed, and it changed color as it fed, and seemed to smile. When her child had finished eating, it fell asleep on her breasts where the milk still exuded and smelled sweet and rich. Barbara wept because her child was beautiful and hers. Then, exhausted from her exertions, the woman slept. All through her ordeal, she had not thought of Salamander's role as the father of her child, or of the implications of the hybrid nature of their child.

The mother and child were clearly progressing well and sleeping fast, and Salamander had watched the whole proceeding with close attention to all its details. Salamander knew he was the proud father of the first hybrid of a plasmoid and a human. Now that he had witnessed birth from a human perspective, he was convinced that his conditioning the woman allowed her to rise to the occasion, and work through the tremendous pain that forcing the child through her birth canal had meant.

He was quietly appreciative of the woman's stamina, and her grace under pressure on behalf of his progeny. She would be a fitting queen in the wider scheme of things, and this triumph would lead to others and greater heights than she had yet witnessed with him.

As Salamander watched their child sleeping peacefully on its mother's breast, he saw it change from its human form to its plasmoid form and back again, and then from its male form to a female form and back again. Salamander understood the signs well enough. The child was hermaphroditic and a changeling too.

When it was time, it thought, this special child would accompany Salamander to the realm of plasma where Salamander was King. Here on Earth, the child would be nurtured by Salamander's wife and Queen. When all were ready, and their family had passed all the tests that Salamander and Barbara could devise, then the execution of the King's great plan of universal conquest would begin.

The Montage

Grandfather was a spectral figure, always puttering around, mumbling incoherently to himself and shaking his head as if in a palsy of violent disagreement. He smelled old. His skin was wrinkled all over. The cold touch of his bony hand sent shivers up my spine.

Glitter came into his eyes when he talked of the hereafter. Grandmother told me to watch after him closely and to care for him after she passed. She made me promise—cross my heart and hope to die. Then Grandmother passed when she was eighty years old. Grandfather and I buried her in the family plot in the backyard.

Until Grandfather passed, I did watch over him. I could do that since my husband had been killed in the Islamic wars, and I had no children. I saw to it that Grandfather had his meals. I cleaned up after him. I helped him up and down the wooden basement stairs to his little cave of a room where I was never to follow him. He never said a word of thanks to me, but I had a promise to keep, and I keep my promises.

When at last Grandfather passed on his 100th birthday, he left quietly in his sleep with a faint smile. He squeezed my hand gently just before he took his last breath. After I laid Grandfather in the ground beside Grandmother in our family plot out back, I was finally alone in their old house, which was my house now, though everywhere I looked, were the relics and memories of my grandparents.

I got right to work tidying the place up. I was starting life anew after the slow decay and death, or so it seemed at the time. As I scrubbed, mopped, scoured, and polished, room by room, the old house came back to life. Then, I scraped, sanded, and painted everything upstairs. Having pulled out all the old, stained carpeting and sanded the floors, I had new machine carpet installed. The stench of age and mildew began to subside, and the fresh smells of turpentine, paint, Lysol and scents from sachets filled the house as they had not done for fifty-odd years.

As for the yard, the teenage boys down the street helped cart away the leafy debris and odd windfall. When the yard had been cleared and mowed, the graves freshened with new fall flowers, and the cords of wood stacked for the late autumn fires, it was time to do what I had dreaded.

Tomorrow I would clean the cellar, including Grandfather's cold basement room. Thinking of that chore gave me the chills. I literally shook with fear of the prospect and had a nightmarish vision of Grandfather going down the rickety basement stairs and hesitating before he pushed open the door and closed it after him. I thought I heard him mumbling in the dark as if he were alive.

I took my cleaning materials and tools to the basement and began at the farthest point from my main objective. My sweeping filled the dank, dark basement with motes of dust. I hauled upstairs old curtain rods, two-by-four studs, old crockery and dishware, cardboard boxes of clothing and knickknacks of all kinds.

As the basement opened up, I thought I heard scratching and coughing from within the little room. I shuddered and took the last loads up the stairs to the first-floor utility room, where the boys would pick them up the next morning.

For some reason, I went out the back door to visit the family grave plot. The iron fence and gate, and the graves were just as I had left them. Grandfather and Grandmother were at rest where I had buried them, or so I thought. My own plot lay beside theirs, waiting for me patiently.

I could wait no longer, so I went right down the stairs to the cold basement room and pushed open the door. Dust rose. The smell of decay, mildew, rot and age was palpable. A small, worn table stood against the earthen wall opposite the door. At the table, were three old wooden chairs. On the table, was a service with three tea cups and saucers. On the floor, I found jars filled with tiny nails and screws. I found a small box labeled, "string too small to reuse." It contained bits of string and tiny fluffs of yarn.

The years had been difficult. Frugality was ingrained by hardship. On the floor, were stacks of newspapers and boxes with mementos gathered by Grandfather over many years. Labeled was the little stocking hat that Grandfather had worn in the cradle.

There was also a thick holographic manuscript, written in Grandfather's familiar hand. Its title was, "Ghosts I Have Regaled." I resolved to clear the room the next morning with the help of the boys who were coming to take away the debris in the utility room.

Exhausted, I climbed up to dinner and to bed, but in bed, I could not sleep. The cold wind blew around the rafters with soughs and sighs. The shutters battered. Grandmother's stuffed animal with the button eyes sat on my trousseau and glared at me until I turned on my bed light.

Then I heard the door slam in the basement. I had to investigate that sound, or I would never sleep. I pulled on my bathrobe and slippers and carried my flashlight down the basement stairs to the door behind which lay Grandfather's cold basement room. I heard behind the door sounds of clattering china and animated, but whispered conversation.

My torch failed. A cold draft whipped around me, and the door simultaneously burst inward with a bang. In total darkness, I forced my eyes to use averted vision. I discerned three human shapes outlined in dim blue neon light in a montage: Grandfather and Grandmother at tea with a third figure who beckoned me as from a mirror darkly.

Viridian Hunger

You flee from me, yet you cannot
Ever defeat our master Death.
His scythe is our common comfort.
You protest, my love, that you cannot
Love me? That you would flee?
How can you say you do not love me?
We are now bound to our dying days.
One touch, and we are wed, we two.
You look for something human, food?
And I look for human hosts as food.
My love is indiscriminate and pure.
I will have all of you, or none.
Besides, you must consider how I grow.
I fester, eat and swell, and make heat.
Your fever tells me that you love.
No love you will ever know is more
Complete or perfect. I am entirely yours.
I am so bound to you I exude in sweat
And when your blood boils, I vent.
You eat where I lurk and I find you
Wanting, while I hungering do
For you what you would do—if you knew
That midnight adventures are no better
Than my invasion of your primordial guts.

My invisible teeth tear at your cells.
Insatiable, I become sated one by one.
Your immune systems are woefully weak.
Your habits are deplorable except
You let me in so easily, and I die happy
In my feast on you, which lasts until we die.
Your defenses are totally without effect.
I am the virus that will with my millions
Of brothers will invade and kill, and then
Jump to your loved ones and your best
Defenders who know nothing of me.
They have no defense against me.
I eat and multiply. You stand and wait.
You cannot find me, and I love to hide.
Ease of entry. Ease of passage. My treat.
Heated body, yours, my best advantage.
So easy is it to get the food I need.
And you, the food, are so easy, so easy.
Viridian rapture, hear it now? The sound
Of wracking pain and headache
Of wailing, primordial wailing
Of waiting, perspiring, raving.
You know—or will know—my signs. I am
Viridian love, whose crypt lies in your bones.

The Man with the Trunk Stones

They looked like tombstones to me, those large slabs that Jim and his friend were loading into the trunk of Jim's black Chevrolet. His friend had rigged a slide and tied ropes around the slabs to haul them in. The back wheels felt the load. I thought the weight would crush the shocks.

Jim was pleased when he had finished. He rolled his pack of cigarettes down from his T-shirt sleeve to have his smoke. When I asked Jim why he had heaved all that weight into his trunk, Jim gave me one of his superior looks, winked, and nodded. When I looked around, Jim's friend had disappeared.

The next morning, we all learned that the Portsmouth drag way had been the scene of a fatal accident. Jim's car had been totaled just after midnight. Jim had been killed instantly when his car had spun out of control and rolled over. Jim's body was now at the morgue. I wanted to tell Jim's friend the situation, but I did not know where to look for him. I would recognize him anywhere: He was a cadaverous man with a limp and a disfigured face.

When the police came to ask Jim's family questions, one officer noticed me and asked me whether I knew Jim. I said that I did. He then asked whether I knew about Jim's drag racing. I said that I did not. I said that I had seen Jim and another man loading heavy slabs into the back of Jim's Chevy yesterday afternoon.

The officer told me that the slabs were tombstones stolen from the local cemetery. He said that stealing the stones was sacrilege. He also said that no one knew the whereabouts of the man who had helped Jim load the stones into the trunk of his car.

When I gave the officer my description of Jim's friend, he got a faraway look in his eye as if he recognized the man from his own experience, probably many years ago. I asked the officer whether he knew the man I had described. He gave me a superior look, winked, and nodded. He said that I was lucky to have survived meeting Jim's friend. He asked whether I was sure Jim's friend had a limp. I said I was sure.

The officer wanted me to think through what I said about Jim's friend simply disappearing. I said that he was there until Jim lighted his cigarette. Then Jim's friend vanished. I remembered the smell of sulfur from the match that Jim had struck. I remembered watching Jim take a long drag on his lighted cigarette. Jim had held the tobacco smoke deep in his lungs. He had gotten a faraway look in his eyes. Then Jim had exhaled, slowly.

"Those cigarettes will kill you, son," the officer said, sternly. I reflected to myself that Jim had not died from smoking his cigarettes. In fact, that last smoke Jim took, remains impressed in my memory as the happiest I had ever seen him.

The Worm Snakes

Life was slow and death quick then, and with all the boggy land it took a long time to reach anywhere. Doc Johnston, who was summoned to cure me, took much too long to get to our little farm, and I died of wasting consumption while he was on the way.

When he arrived, the Doc proclaimed I had passed, and then they buried me right here on this hillock, where redolent honeysuckle blooms, gold and white, would most likely grow.

Later, they buried Mom there in the grave between mine and Grandpa's. Mom had tried hard to keep me alive, and she always said how hard it was for her to go on living without a man around the farm, and then the war came, but not for me. One body buried here in an unmarked, shallow grave was a victim of that war. Another buried surreptitiously was a victim of murder foul, with the murderer never found. Neither of those was family.

My brother paid for these headstones that have cracked, sunk and twisted, and footstones, else you'd have never found us. The way those two willows grew up and heaved the ground with their thick, wandering roots and the way tangled, flowery greenery covered everything always, it seems nature conspired to keep us a secret and failed.

Birds nested and rabbits, black voles, and mice, burrowed here and there for generations, and eastern worm snakes snapped like small flesh whips their way into my coffin to eat their fill and curl about my bones. Alive, I feared worm snakes, but now our intimacy comforts me as I encompass those who compass me.

You came to clear our graveyard and wash our gravestones: for that, I thank you kindly. You've cleaned many other such; I know this from the gentle way you cleared the leafy foliage and washed each stone with bristling brushes and let flesh-colored worm snakes be when they dove for cover through cracks in cover stones placed to keep coffins with bodies down where they belong in this sodden, hallowed soil.

You fought through thick blackberry, gorse and honeysuckle vines down to layers of wet papery sough and rank, mildewed compost, and I saw you press and pull with both your hands and brush back your hair from your brow with soil-black wrists and sweat all over in sunshine, toiling like a happy plowman.

When you came with crook and staff, I thought at first you were the thing whose scythe reached for me when I was sick and brought Mom here later as well. But you didn't smile the way the other did, and you didn't bear an hourglass with its sand run through, wear a hood, limp or smell like sulfur. Even so, I didn't cotton to your disturbing us until your rays of light pierced through the hollow, right to where my rags, and bones and all those worm snakes lay dazzled and wriggling as if today I was reborn and stand anew.

Unholy Names

This day, no church bells ring, eve before light
Songs begin unsinging, witches turning,
Eeking, gasp and cry soulless prayers of night.
Black fires run along the marrow burning.

Unhallowed graves yawn wide without stirring,
Waiting for fleshy bones red worms to eat
The lad who dallied and his maid's crimped ring
Mocking the time, their wasted game complete.

Across the moon's pocked face hags still fly high,
Dip, rise, gyre, laugh and brave it till the dawn.
Black cats arch their backs then spring and lie
Expectant while the scythe is backward drawn.

This one day names come empty at the call,
Unholy children lost before they fall.

Rotten Timbers

I drove to Mordant Acres Estates at nine o'clock that gloomy, drizzly morning. Thick mist was rising in the woods, and the black storm clouds were so thick, you could not tell whether the sun had risen at all.

My car navigation system failed just before I entered the massive housing project, so I had to resort to my flashlight to read the addresses on the mailboxes. I saw that within the gated complex, the great majority of homes were so-called "McMansions" built for the new rich, but they were all empty now because of the economy and the blood-curdling rumors spread in the newspapers and online.

I wove from one empty house to another, all well off the road with long drives, their bodies ensconced in thick woods with perhaps a dormer window showing through the trees. The Elder Home, I had been told, was on Sleepy Hollow Road, near the intersection with Rose Road.

It was not one of the new mansions. It was well over a hundred years old and lay in a depression. The natural underground springs and the surface water runs kept the place drenched. It was not supposed to be occupied. Yet the caller wanted me to do an estimate for repairs. The job was urgent because the property was up for sale, and the owners were aiming to close.

The buyer wanted me to take a look and give an independent opinion. She must have used the old phone book because she reached my land line, not my cell. She was supposed to meet me at the end of the drive by the mailbox, and there she was standing, soaking wet in the rain by the box with number 666 and the sign that read, "For Sale By Owner." The woman seemed to enjoy the wet weather and licked the moisture as it streamed down her pallid face.

"Hello, Milo. It's been a very long time, and you probably don't remember. Anyhow, my name is Uldra Grimmstead Elder. I'm glad you came—and right on time. That's the place down the drive there. Watch the bump as you drive in and the stream before the porch. Here's the key. Take it. I'll just wait here. You know what to look for in the cellar and the attic. You just take a look and give me the key when you come out again."

"Look, it's raining. Why don't you hop in and we'll drive down together? I won't be bothered by your being in the house while I work. I don't want to leave you out here in the cold and wet. It might take me a while."

"Don't worry about me. I like the rain. It's no problem to stand up for a while after all the time I spend lying down. You can do the job by yourself, can't you? 'Course you can. Hahaha. 'Course you can."

With her arthritic fingers, she handed me a very large zinc key that was supposed to open the front door. It looked like a key to a family crypt I had once evaluated, and I shivered to recall the details of that spooky visit. At the moment that I grasped the key, lightning shot through the sky in a triple fork, followed immediately by a deafening crash of thunder.

The woman laughed again, and held onto the key a little longer than I expected, as if to keep us joined while the lightning continued and the thunder cascaded. When she released the cold, metallic key, I felt its weight and looked in the woman's eyes. Her eyes were entirely milk white, like the marble in a classic sculpture, and I knew that she was blind, and I had a flash of memory in my youth of those same eyes upon me looking without seeing.

As I drove down the winding drive, I saw her in the rearview mirror, waving her hands as the lightning struck, as if she were the conductress for a mighty symphony. Ahead, I saw the house emerge from the woods, with ravens rising all around it, and then falling back on their black wings to the boughs and branches that surrounded it.

The woods around the house were a mix of ancient, gnarled trees, and new growth. The line of larches that blocked the view of the front porch from the drive was overgrown, so they crowded the dormers. Four enormous dead trees extended their crooked, bare boughs over the roof, which I could see needed extensive repair. As the lightning continued striking, the dead trees looked like hulking giants with arms and fingers reaching for the house, menacingly.

My job, I thought, was simple, but to do it, I had to get from the drive to the building. That was not going to be easy, because the stream of water that ran into the hollow where the house stood, was continuous and, as Uldra said, cut across the walk that led from the end of the drive to the porch.

I did not have to use my flashlight to make it to the porch because the lightning was almost continuous now. One lightning strike hit so near, I thought it must have been guided to the ground by one of the lightning rods on top of the highest gable of the house.

I thought of Martin Luther, who had been struck by lightning and by grace, survived, and I wondered how close the latest shaft had come to me, and by what chance or grace I had not become its victim. I stepped into the stream, and my foot dropped in, and I sank up to my knee.

I forged forth and found the bottom with my other foot, and then I slogged through the torrent to the other side where the steps to the porch beckoned. By the time I reached the porch, I was soaked almost to the waist, and my work shoes were sloshing and squeaking with the water.

As I stepped up onto the porch, I felt the wood giving way below me. I did not have to stick my probe into the porch to determine that it would all have to be replaced. I walked very carefully across the rotten wooden porch for fear of falling through. That was only the beginning of the rot and mildew that must be general.

The door itself was not fastened, but a great chain with an ancient lock barred the way with links joined to the jambs on either side by iron rings that had been set in the jambs many years ago. I fitted the zinc key into the lock and, with effort, turned the key and opened the lock. I dropped the chain and the lock with the key on the porch and pushed the rotten door open carefully, lest it fall off against my hand.

I turned on my flashlight to enter the dark cavern that was the main vestibule. As I walked through the room, beaming my flashlight to show the way, I heard scuffling on the second floor and on the stairs, and I thought I heard the dim caw of the ravens that guarded the outside, though not religiously. I then heard the house groan, as if it were trying to communicate a warning or to tell me of some great pain it was enduring. I wondered whether the building was going to collapse on me, and had signaled a warning of that very event, but that is a risk of my job, and why I get paid well for what I do.

I mused that I was inspecting the interior of a giant music box of a house that moaned and whistled while I worked. I heard water running as if the roof had dripping holes and a runlet collecting the rainwater was cascading through the house to the basement, which was my first destination, as it was for the water of that raining morning.

I managed to get to the basement door to the right at the end of the great hall that divided the house in two. I pushed the door open and step by step, descended. The stairwell held, and I saw at the bottom ~~was~~ a pool with water running into it from many conduits. I could see the flows from the flashlight, but I could not know their origins.

My flashlight showed thick cobwebs hanging from the ceiling of the basement area, and huge black spiders creeping away from the light. Some cobwebs brushed against my face and hair as I moved, and I hoped the spiders had abandoned those.

In the black water of the basement, my flashlight illuminated two large black rats swim away into a corner, where they dived and disappeared under the oily water. I stuck my prod at the beams under the floor above, and the prod sank in easily to the hilt. The floor was being carried by damp, rotten wood, but the rats did not care any more than I did.

I went to the bottom of the basement stairs, and I stepped onto the basement floor through the black water that gathered there. I mused that rain water was pouring into the basement, but as fast as it poured, some force pulled the effluent from the basement. I found the floor steady and ankle deep, while I explored the enormous space under the joists and struts that held the house up.

A bat dropped from the ceiling and scurried about to find some way of escape, and I heard the noise of rats and their children chirruping about my presence. I knew that my mission was not their concern, and my flashlight found the large bulbous cocoon-like entities that hung from the ceiling of the basement foundations. The spiders had made good work of whatever they had surrounded by their handiwork.

I was glad that I was not among their collection. I could not understand how the spiders had suspended corpses of human size, so they remained above the black surface of the flood, yet were so enclosed that they could be ready, decomposing, to feed several generations of spiders. I had no time for biological investigations, so I concluded my investigation of the basement with the record of twelve human-sized web constructions that were better acclimated to the weather and circumstances than the house itself.

I turned and rose through the stairwell, to the first floor, and ascended to the second floor. I reckoned that the first floor was all for show, as it always was in these cases, and I was right. On the second floor, I found the containers that humans would have named coffins, all safe from the elements, though the floor underneath them was strained to the breaking point.

As the lightning flashed through the windows, the larches played a tune against the still intact window panes. I counted three dozen coffins ranged in the room, and I figured that additional I-beams must be installed to carry them. A bat flew through the space, and three others gathered on my shoulder as if to relay a message to me about the future. I did not care. I knew that the coffins were a configuration. I only hoped that I might not soon be numbered among the undead that were interred there.

So I moved from the second floor, which was a mortician's delight, to the third floor, where more coffins lined the rooms, all closed, but waiting for some external impulse to open and release what was within them. I knew better than open those wooden mouths that ingested the dead and rotting human flesh. I counted the coffins and moved to the attic floor above them. In the attic floor, I found along the ceiling, more bats than I had ever seen before. They released their excreta as I flashed my light on them, and they bustled about and flew around me since I had interrupted their slumber. They had clearly only just returned from their nocturnal searching.

Now that they had returned, they were disgruntled about my light and my presence. I illuminated females with their brood, showing their fangs in warning. All this, I recorded in my memory as part of my deliverable. I saw the runlets of the roof water that fed the basement pool. I heard the ravens and crows cawing their annoyance at my presence inside their preserve. I thought I heard the protestations of the house itself, which seemed to moan and rock as I stepped through my motions.

Finally, I knew I had enough to provide my report. I tripped, though, and found myself on the floor of the attic, covered by spiders and attacked by the bats that ate them. I stood as tall as I could, given my size and the height of the ceiling. I went back down from the attic to the third floor, and then the second and the first, where I found the largest rats running that I had ever seen. They looked at me and then scuttled down the stairs to the basement. I thought for a few minutes while the lightning flashed and the thunder roared. Had I missed anything? Then, I felt a hand upon my shoulder, and I started and turned.

There, in my flashlight's beam, stood an old man in a cape with a scythe over his shoulder. He had an inordinate smile, and his crooked finger beckoned as if he were trying to lure me to look at something I had overlooked before. I followed him to the fireplace that ran straight up through the decrepit mansion. He had no trouble crawling up the flue, and I followed him because I thought I had no choice. Up through the enormous chimney complex I rose, scattering flying squirrels and bats and spiders. We reached the roof and crawled out above the house to walk the slate roof itself.

The black figure in the flashing of the lightning kept his black robes flowing and indicated what he wanted to show me by gesturing with his scythe. I saw the way the water flowed from the roof and ended in the basement. He then, without effort, jumped to a giant conifer to the rear of the building and clambered down. I followed him so we stood in the overgrown backyard of the mansion. With a curled finger, the strangely familiar figure beckoned me to follow him.

We walked through brambles to a clearing in the woods, where an iron fence separated the former living from the dead. An old cemetery was there, illuminated by lightning flashes and adorned by gravestones and crypts and mausoleums. The hooded figure gestured with his scythe to an open grave as if to invite me to try it on for size. I shook my head. I was not ready for that kind of play. I noticed that the last names of most headstones were Elder. I said, "I have enough, and I must be going now."

The figure did not deter me as I made my way back through the woods to the house, and then around the outside of the house to the front porch. There, by the lightning, I traversed the running stream, which ran at the same level as when I entered. I made it to my vehicle and looked back one more time.

Above the house in the lightning, I saw the ravens rise and fall. I heard the water streaming all around the place. I fancied that I heard the house itself moaning intermittently as the storm ranged above it. I then decided I had to go back again across the water to place the chains across the door and retrieve the key from the ancient lock. Why had I been so hasty as to leave this undone?

I forded the stream for the third time that morning, and when I reached the porch, I rejoined the chain and locked the lock and retrieved the zinc key. The house was as I had first encountered it. Then, I forded the stream for the fourth and final time that day, and then, dripping wet, I waited to get into my vehicle while the water streamed from my clothes. I listened to the symphony that the house and nature played, and I swatted several spiders that crawled over my clothes and skin. When I thought the time was right, I backed out the drive to the place where the mailbox and the realtor's sign, and my client stood.

She was smiling when I arrived as if she had accompanied me and now was waiting for what I thought of the adventure we had experienced together. I gave her the zinc key, and I told her everything that I had seen during my visit. She did not interrupt me but nodded while I recounted my experience. While she listened, a raven flew to her and perched on her shoulder. As I talked, the bird accepted something that she fed the bird. Every time she fed the raven, it cawed after it swallowed the morsel, and in unison, the raven's cohorts rose from the branches around the house and descended again.

"You have done well, my son. I am satisfied with your inspection. Do you have any recommendations for me?"

"It seems to me that you'll need some steel reinforcements of the floors in which you have the coffins. I don't think you'll need to worry about the water's flow because the drainage is sufficient to handle all runoff."

"Anything else?"

"You might want to install feeders for the ravens and the bats around the grounds. You heard the ravens while you fed the raven on your shoulder. They're hungry. As for the bats, their food is well established. If you can allow the rumors to subside somewhat, you'll find that the food will come for them."

"Young man, how will I ever repay you?"

"There is no need for repayment above what we agreed to in our contract, Uldra."

The woman drew forth a pouch with twelve gold coins and handed it to me. I counted them for form because I knew she would not cheat me.

"So you saw my friend with the scythe and survived the encounter?"

"Yes, I saw him and survived. It was unexpected."

"As it always is, my son."

"So now I must be going."

"Yes, and be safe. You never know these days what might happen."

I saw that her hair was streaming with water, and her tongue occasionally licked her lips. She was quite comely if you ignored the white of her eyes. I started my vehicle and began to drive off, when through the rearview mirror, I saw the man with the scythe come up behind her and gently take her by the waist. They looked like an old American painting of a farmer and his wife, though much transformed. I kept right on driving out the way I had come in, and as I drove, the black clouds dispersed, and the shafts of sunlight streamed through. The storm was over.

I stopped by the exit to the main thoroughfare, where I had to decide whether to go right or left. It was not yet noon, and I took a coin and flipped it. I had business in both directions, but no fixed time for any of it. I felt lucky today, and when the coin showed heads, I turned to the right. My clothing was soaking wet from the belt down. I hoped I had swatted the spiders.

The next house on my list was a prime, just-built estate with no vestiges of age or decrepitude. I certainly did not want to bring those degrading elements with me for the inspection. I looked in the back of my vehicle and saw that my own scythe was still intact and ready for use. You just never know these days when that might come in handy.

I figured I had missed the lightning barely and the man with the scythe also. I pulled out on the highway and came up to speed. I felt the pouch with the twelve gold coins. I was then reassured that it was going to be a great, sunny day after all.

The Visitor

It was a cloudless, mild spring day in the Massachusetts countryside. Fruit trees were in full flower and the dark, brooding woods shot through with light green leaves. The graveyard, in contrast to the chaos of the surrounding misty, cluttered woods, was a maze of orderly respect.

Graves were arranged in neat lines, some with particolored pots of flowers and small flags that waved in the early morning sunshine. There were mausoleums and crypts, scattered among the orderly plots, some with imposing iron fences adorned with ornately spiked tops.

Rachel Vogelgesang, second lieutenant, U.S. Air Force, was the Honor Guard officer in charge of this particular funeral. She was a perfectionist with a reputation for meticulous planning. It had taken two hours to prepare for the departure, and over two hours for the Honor Guard to drive out from the base. For her, the reputation of the Air Force and the U.S. military was at stake at every burial they served. At the special request of the decedent's father, she had arranged an over-flight before Taps and the twenty-one-gun salute.

She parked the van in the cemetery grounds at a respectful distance from the newly opened grave. The Honor Guard personnel climbed out and formed up with the presentation flag, immaculately polished rifles, and the electronic silver trumpet.

Rachel reported their arrival to the Rev. Hiram Couch. The Reverend, a circumspect and spectral figure, pointed out the bereaved mother, who would be receiving the honorary flag.

"It might be best for the Honor Guard to stand alongside the open grave, opposite from the family and guests," he suggested.

"Yes Sir," Rachel agreed. "I only hope the impending rain holds off until we're done."

She returned to her troops and called them to attention. The Honor Guard, with Rachel in the lead, took their place, while the small assembly of mourners stopped milling around and sat around the bereaved mother and father. A beautiful young woman, dressed in black and sitting next to the deceased's mother, wept inconsolably, but no one except Rachel paid any attention to her. She was the only civilian present, outwardly affected by the sense of loss.

Rachel gave a discreet nod to signal they were ready, and the Reverend began the service. It proceeded with reverence and without a word misspoken. The Reverend did an admirable job of the eulogy, with the traditional theme of "In an instant, we shall all be changed."

Symbolically, clouds began to gather during the service and the bright spring morning turned dark and ominous. There was no rain predicted, but in New England, anything can happen with the weather within the space of a few hours. Rachel scanned the skies for rain and spied a hawk circling overhead.

After the Reverend's address, the Honor Guard waited for almost five minutes, listening for the sound of overflying aircraft, but heard only the birds singing. The rapidly massing clouds made it impossible for anyone to see an aircraft, even if it flew directly overhead. Finally, Rachel thought she heard the distant rumble of engines, but she could not be sure—it may have been thunder. However, it was enough for her to raise her silver trumpet and a beautiful rendition of Taps crowned the service. She lowered the horn and ordered the Honor Guard to present arms. Three volleys of the Guard's seven rifles rang across the cemetery.

In the silence that followed, one female member of the Honor Guard picked up three of the spent shells and handed them to the Lieutenant with a salute. Two other airmen carefully unfolded, then refolded the presentation flag. One presented it to Rachel, who carefully tucked the three spent shells into the body of the flag.

She went forward to the bereaved mother and presented the flag, "with thanks from a grateful nation." As the mother accepted it, Rachel noticed she was close to tears, but she didn't cry. She was from a military family and was determined not to cry at her son's funeral, unlike the young woman sitting next to her. She continued to weep uncontrollably, tears streaming down her cheeks. Rachel stepped back, stood to attention and saluted the flag she'd presented. She then rejoined the Honor Guard and marched them back to their parked van, where she ordered them to stand at ease. They waited silently for the guests to depart.

While the civilians slowly dispersed, the young woman approached Rachel and thanked her and her people for their presence. She said she'd never attended a memorial service quite so respectful and added that Rachel played Taps so beautifully, she would never forget the experience and believed the decedent would have been very proud.

She went on to explain. They had decided to marry after his third tour in Iraq. If only he'd quit after his second tour, she moaned, things would have been different, although she understood that he did not want to let down his buddies. He was a true patriot, just as the Rev. Couch had said, killed by an Improvised Explosive Device, with only one more week to serve.

The young woman lifted her kerchief to her nose and said it all seemed so unfair. If they'd married after his second tour, she, not the man's mother, would have received the honorary flag with the three cartridge shells. Now, she had nothing left, but a few pictures and her memories. She wiped her tears away with her black-gloved hand as she walked away alone, her head bowed. A few drops of rain had begun to fall, but the woman hadn't noticed, she was too caught up in her despondency.

Rachel ordered her troops to prepare to depart while she sought out the Reverend to let him know how proud they were to have helped. She would doubtless see him again at another funeral, so many young airmen, sailors, soldiers and marines had fallen. Then too, so many older military veterans were being buried now, the Honor Guard's schedule was full.

She mentioned the woman's compliments to the Reverend and her trumpet playing in particular. She shook her head at the thought since she only held the electronic silver trumpet, the instrument played itself. The music it played so sweetly came from a recording but, she supposed, what mattered most was the effect.

"Pity the overflight didn't go as planned," the Reverend observed, "but I appreciated you taking the initiative when you heard what might have been an aircraft. But I think it was thunder." As if to punctuate this, more thunder rolled across the sky, and the rain fell harder. He pointed to the roof of a crypt, where a giant red-tailed hawk perched, surveying the ground for mice or voles. "They are an ancient symbol of war, you know. They always come for a military funeral."

Rachel and the Reverend mused on their observations for a few moments, lost in their separate thoughts. The hawk watched them, moving its head from side to side. Then, the Reverend shook Rachel's hand.

"I won't forget this sad day, or your service," he told her. She nodded, smiled faintly and went to the van ready to drive back to base. The Honor Guard had two funerals the next day. She felt her electronic silver trumpet was a chanticleers singing all over New England in a springtime of fresh graves and final regards.

As she prepared to drive out of the graveyard, Rachael observed the young woman watching as the gravediggers covered her fiancée's coffin with earth. The Rev. Couch stood solemnly beside her for a moment then, taking her hand, he led her to the crypt on which the hawk still perched.

He unlocked the gate surrounding the crypt then, using a large key hung from his waist by a tether, he unlocked the door to the crypt. With some effort, he pushed open the door and motioned for the woman to enter. The woman turned and, for one last time, looked at the grave of her beloved, before disappearing into the crypt. The Reverend pushed the door shut again, locking it with his key.

Shocked, Rachel opened her door and ran through the pouring rain in pursuit of the Reverend. The hawk flew down from the low roof to perch upon his arm as he set off toward the woods. The thunder crashed, and rain lashed down so hard, even the gravediggers had taken shelter in their truck. A fine mist rolled across the graveyard as she shouted after the minister.

"Why did you lock her in the crypt?"

"She's dead!" He shouted back, struggling to make himself heard above the rain. "She committed suicide when she learned of his death. That was her family crypt and her final resting place."

He went on to explain that while praying the previous evening she had come to him as a vision, asking to be present at her beloved's funeral. He thought it was the least he could do and agreed. The woman Rachel had spoken to was a ghost; she should feel privileged to have shared the experience. With that, he turned and walked into the woods, the hawk still perched on his arm.

Rachel returned to the van and drove out of the cemetery. She'd heard rumors about Reverend Couch's odd behavior at funerals but never witnessed the associations he brought with him. She thought about asking her comrades about what she'd witnessed but realized they'd fallen asleep. No one else witnessed the mysterious actions of the Reverend and the woman near the crypt, and she was sure she'd not dreamt it. So what could she tell her troops?

She decided she would tell them nothing as there was nothing she could say that would be believed.

Red Rictus

It was a dark and stormy night, and the bats dropped, one by one, from the attic ceiling, before swarming out into the elements to feast. I heard them beat their leathery wings up there. It was time for me to rise with the others.

We had much to do before midnight when the great change would come, and all the saints would be ranged against us. I shook my head and sat bolt upright. I felt weak, and I salivated. Around the room, others were sitting up in their coffins for our shared purpose, finding food. Like the bats in the attic, we on the second floor climbed out of our coffins and made our way down the rickety stairs to the first floor. There, we went out the double doors into the darkness, each taking a separate path. We were unaffected by the heavy rain and unfrightened by the forks of lightning that tore through the clouds and showed us the way to our prey.

Stalwart parents and children were making their ways with umbrellas to visit those rare dwellings that still displayed a porch light or a candle in the window. There, the kind people would dispense treats. They were our lures. We did not have to go far for food: the food would come to us.

As for our being recognized for what we were, we would be considered dressed for the occasion. Our antics would not be noticed in the general melee. I looked for a pair of parents, with at least two children. I planned to separate the one, most likely to provide a good meal from the other. He or she would not be missed—what I had in mind would not take long. After all, I had no intention of killing anyone.

I saw just what I needed waddling down the muddy path to a farmhouse. A man and woman under separate umbrellas were herding a group of six children toward the door with the light over it. I struck swiftly, taking the obese woman aside and nicking her neck so the blood flowed. I lapped it with my tongue as fast as it spurted out. I held her nose and mouth so she could not cry out. Instead, she passed out and fell to the ground, her umbrella remaining open to shield her and me from everyone else's view.

I fed and felt the drops of rain on my head and back. When I had finished, I licked the woman's wound so it closed. Then, I awakened her with a smelling salt that I carried. I raised her gently to her feet and gave her the umbrella. She seemed dazed, but she mumbled her gratitude as she plodded forward to find her husband and the children. They had gone to the next farmhouse down the road. She would have no trouble finding them if she kept on the path.

I had time now to enjoy the night. Sated from my blood feast, I listened for the sounds of this special night. I heard distant laughter as well as false screams and shrieks of children dressed as clowns and witches. I could tell the difference between the children and the real witches of the evening, whose jagged paths I could discern in the lightning's flashing. They waved one hand while the other held the ragged brooms.

They reveled in their powers. Like me, they had around another hour before they had to retreat. I joined the laughter when I saw one of my fellow vampires chasing a cow that had escaped from a nearby pasture. The animal loped along with the vampire jumping toward it and trying to latch on so it could drink the blood spilling from the slight incision that its teeth had made. From all outward appearance, he seemed to be chasing the animal back whence it came. If I had not been lucky with my prey, I might be tempted to help hold the animal while the vampire fed on it.

I must have smelled of my own conquest because another vampire decided to feast on me. I turned and bared my teeth. She smiled in return with something like a curtsy. Then she rushed after the cow. Two could feed on one cow at the same time. In her wake, ran a gaunt figure with what at first I thought was a rake. I was wrong. In a flash of lightning, I saw that the man was carrying a long, sharpened stake.

I stuck out my foot, and the man fell to the mushy ground and let his spear fly. I picked it up and examined it as best I could in the dark. It was well sharpened at one end. I guessed that the wood was from an oak or rowan tree. This stake was a vampire killer. I walked away, keeping the stake at my side so the man could not see that I had it with me. Frantically, he groped the ground for his weapon. The female vampire found him there and rode upon his back. She then began to feast on the man she rode. It was a touching sight. The man was so terrified, he seemed to have turned to stone. He was being eaten by the very prey he had been stalking.

It was getting late now, and I sensed a general movement of the vampires toward our home. The ordinary humans were deciding to return to their homes also. So, red feasting and the trick-or-treating was done for this Halloween night. I walked fast, and then I began to run as my comrades raced to get back into our house and into our coffins before the midnight chimes rang out. I heard a rustling behind me and looked back to see a hooded figure raising a scythe as if to reap. I turned and forced my spear into the figure. Death smiled in recognition as its scythe sliced.

E. W. Farnsworth

E. W. Farnsworth is a consultant to law enforcement, military and intelligence agencies. He lives and writes in Arizona, USA. Farnsworth's collection of crime stories, *John Fulghum Mysteries*, and his romance/thriller, *Engaging Rachel*, were published by Zimbell House Publishing LLC in 2015. *John Fulghum Mysteries, Volume 2, The Pirate Tales* and *Baro Xaimos: A Novel of the Gypsy Holocaust* were published by Zimbell House in 2016. His collection of Arizona western tales, *Desert Sun, Red Blood*, was published by Pro Se Productions in 2015. Farnsworth's spy stories, Secret *Adventures of Agents Salamander and Crow*, will be published as serial Single Shots from Pro Se Productions in 2016. *Bitcoin Fandango*, Farnsworth's picaresque novel about global intrigue in cryptocurrency enforcement appeared from Greenman Arizona Press in 2015. *DarkFire at the Edge of Time*, Farnsworth's collection of twenty-five science fiction stories, was published by AudioArcadia in England in 2016. In 2016

Zimbell House will publish Farnsworth's collected romance stories as *Among Waterfowl & Other Romance Entertainments*, and in 2017 it will publish two John Fulghum, PI, mystery novels.

One hundred sixty of Farnsworth's short stories were published in numerous anthologies during 2015 and 2016, including many in Zimbell House Publishing LLC, Audio Arcadia, and Horrified Press anthologies. Some of E. W. Farnsworth's sci-fi stories and modern fables are available online from Ether Books and Jotters United in the UK and fictuary.com in the US. Two of his John Fulghum mysteries are scheduled to be online late in 2016 from IndelibleCHAOS in India.

E. W. Farnsworth is now working on an epic poem, *The Voyage of the Spaceship Arcturus,* about the future of humankind when humans, avatars, and artificial intelligences must work together to instantiate a second Eden after the Chaos Wars bring an end to life on Earth.

Further information on the author can be found at the following URLs:

http://www.femalefirst.co.uk/books/e-w-farnsworth-desert-sun-red-blood-899035.html

http://www.zimbellhousepublishing.com/author-spotlight/e-w-farnsworth/

http://cindygrigg.com/2015/09/19/author-e-w-farnsworth-shares-his-inspiration-for-his-short-story-mobile-dusters-as-featured-in-psychopomps-shepherds-of-the-dead/

For continuous updates on the current and forthcoming works of E. W. Farnsworth, please see:

www.ewfarnsworth.com.

Acknowledgements

"The Black Marble Griffon" was first published as a separate story in *Hypnos Magazine* of Radiumtown Press in November 2014. The story won the 1st Prize Award in the *Hypnos* international short story competition for 2014.

"Helen Screaming" was first published as a separate story in *Dragon Tempest Anthology #2* of Dragon Knight Chronicles Press in July 2015. The story won the 1st Prize Award in the Dragon Knight Chronicles international short story competition for 2015. Permission to reprint in this collection was graciously granted by Kathryn Jenkins, Horror Editor, Dragon Knight Chronicles, in an email dated March 25, 2016.

"The Wasps" was first published as a separate story in *Aestas 2014* of Fabula Press in November 2014. The story won the 1st Prize Award in the Aestas 2014 international short story competition. Permission to reprint in this collection was graciously granted by Anirban Ray Choudhury, Editor, Fabula Press, in an email dated March 26, 2016.

The following works were first published as individual stories and poems in the indicated horror anthologies from Zimbell House Publishing, LLC, in the USA in the period 2014-2016. Permission to reprint them in this collection was graciously granted in an email of March 23, 2016, by Evelyn Zimmer, Publisher.

"The Brass Gong," *Curse of the Tomb Seekers*, December 2015

"Camp Fire Stories," *On a Dark and Snowy Night*, March 2016

"End Times Constrictor," sonnet included in "Camp Fire Stories," *On a Dark and Snowy Night*, March 2016, was first published in the Writers Treasury Dragon Knight Chronicles Halloween Contest in November 2015

"The Creature from the Black Stone Reservoir," *Dark Monsters*, January 2016

"Curse of the Ship Burial," *Curse of the Tomb Seekers*, December 2015

"Pandemic from the Grave," *Tales from the Grave*, October 2015

The following works were first published as individual stories in the indicated horror anthologies from Horrified Press in the United Kingdom in the period 2014-2016. Permission to reprint them in this collection was graciously granted in an email of March 24, 2016, by Nathan J.D.L. Rowark, Editor.

"Body Wagon," *Detectives of the Fantastic, Volume 2*, Thirteen O'Clock Press Horrified Press, November 2015

"The Cold Ghost Tentacles," *Loch Shock* Horrified Press, December 2014

"The Crypt Back of the Asylum," *Supernatural* Full Moon Books Horrified Press November 2015

"Montage," *Supernatural* Full Moon Books Horrified Press November 2015

"The Plasmoid," *Oh So Naughty* Full Moon Books Horrified Press January 2016

"Ridge Riders," *Detectives of the Fantastic, Volume 3*, Thirteen O'Clock Press Horrified Press, Not Yet Published March 2016

"The Visitor," *Tales from the Graveyard* Thirteen O'Clock Press Horrified Press March 2016

"The Zombie Tontine," *October's End* Horrified Press, September 2015

"Hornpipes for Mariah," was first published as a separate story in the *Sci-Fi and Fantasy* Anthology of Audio Arcadia

Rickshaw Productions in England in July 2016. Permission to republish it in this collection was graciously granted on March 25, 2016, by Lindsay Fairgrieve, Editor.

"Rictus II," a story included in "Camp Fire Stories," *On a Dark and Snowy Night*, Zimbell House Publishing LLC, March 2016 was first published separately online in 2015 at https://www.edhat.com/site/tidbit.cfm?nid=160966 by EDHAT Santa Barbara. The story received an honorable mention in Edhat's 7th annual Halloween story writing contest.

"Unholy Names," a sonnet included in "Camp Fire Stories," *On a Dark and Snowy Night*, Zimbell House Publishing LLC, March 2016 was first published separately online in October 2015 by Booksie at http://www.booksie.com/horror/novel/everafterdarling/spook y-halloween-poetry-contest-2015/chapter/1 http://www.booksie.com/mystery_and_crime/poetry/wickeng el/unholy-names

"Moonstruck," a sonnet included in "Camp Fire Stories," *On a Dark and Snowy Night*, Zimbell House Publishing LLC, March 2016 was first published separately online in *Massacre Magazine* in the United Kingdom in October 2014.

"The Worm Snakes" was first published in the *JU-LIT-ZINE* by Jotters United in March 2015 at the following URL: http://jottersutd.wix.com/jotters-united#!Other-Places/cm3r/BlankListItem0_i6vyt7rn32_0 . Permission to republish it in this collection was graciously granted on March 28, 2016, by Nick Gerrard, Editor.

Reader's Guide

1. Halloween is a traditional time for horror stories. E. W. Farnsworth's stories often invoke All Hallows Eve or the evening before All Saints Day as a context. Give examples from this volume and discuss the author's strategy for maximizing the horror of the occasion.

2. Many E. W. Farnsworth tales refer to recent discoveries in archaeology and science. Such discoveries often imply that received history contains gross errors that powerful factions want to maintain as truth. What instances from this collection show the dangers of knowing too much of the truth? Do you find those dangers to amplify or diminish the horror factor in the stories concerned?

3. What trappings of traditional horror stories can you find in this collection? Does E. W. Farnsworth use traditional approaches, or does he add new details to enliven and enrich the traditions?

4. In many of the stories in this collection the connections between ancient cultures and modern times are explored with menacing implications. Two such examples are the brass gong and the Egyptian virus. How are such connections fraught with possibilities as well as dire consequences? And why do people in modern times find it difficult to realize the beneficent value of ancient cures?

5. Vampires and zombies are the central focus of at least two stories in this collection. In both cases, conspiracies of various kinds legitimate the legendary figures. Discuss the ingenuity of survival strategies in these stories. How, for example, does the zombie tontine actually function? Why is it unlikely the Haitian zombies will be destroyed?

6. Curses are a mainstay of E. W. Farnsworth's horror fiction. Discuss this idea with reference to "The Guru's Ghosts" and at least one other story in this collection.

7. Academicians are major characters in E. W. Farnsworth's horror stories. They have the time and can obtain the funding to do research on arcane and often forbidden subjects. They also have the intellect and connections to probe beneath the surface and get to the horrible truths that lurk there. Compare and contrast any three such characters.

8. E. W. Farnsworth's stories are literary by allusion and implication. Beowulf, for example, is referenced in "The Creature from the Black Stone Reservoir." How does the author revive literary creatures by bringing them into contact with modern heroes?

9. Many narrators and major characters in E. W. Farnsworth's fiction are female. In some respects, they are more heroic and have deeper feelings than his male characters. Find four stories with female leads and compare and contrast those figures with males in the same or other stories in this collection.

10. Color symbolism abounds in E. W. Farnsworth's horror fiction. Evident symbolic colors are black and red. Using at least four examples, show how colors underscore major themes in these stories.

11. E. W. Farnsworth uses stories within stories to amplify major themes in the overarching stories that contain them. Discuss with particular attention to "Camp Fire Stories."

12. Horror often arises from the discontinuity between the commonplace and the bizarre. Some characters in E. W. Farnsworth stories are forced to deal with situations for

their own survival. Other characters in his works are merely witnesses to the symbols and attributes of hidden evil. Explore this idea of discontinuity with specific examples.

13. Throughout E. W. Farnsworth's stories characters find themselves in small closed spaces like caves, crypts, dark spaces, bars, enclosures in the woods at night, graveyards, graves, mausoleums, and coffins. How do these claustrophobic settings contribute to the intended horrific moods in particular works?

14. E. W. Farnsworth's love of Edgar Allen Poe is evident in these stories and poems. Give three examples of the author's playful allusions and homage to stories or poems of the supreme master of American horror.

15. Which of E. W. Farnsworth's stories is most likely to give you recurring nightmares? Why?

16. Irony is a major feature of E. W. Farnsworth's short stories. Sometimes irony is combined with humor. Sometimes it is an integral part of a tragic design. How is irony used as a major plot element in at least two of the stories in this collection?

17. The Shakespearean sonnet form is often used by E. W. Farnsworth when he wants to draw together three separate but related ideas into a single design. The three quatrains of this sonnet form are each associated with a single idea. The closing couplet contains the integration and resolution of the ideas in the preceding quatrains. Do you think the form is appropriate for horror? If so, why? If not, why not?

A Note from the Publisher

Dear Reader,

Thank you for reading E.W. Farnsworth's collection of short stories, *The Black Marble Griffon & Other Disturbing Tales.*

We feel the best way to show appreciation for an author is by leaving a review. You may do so on our website: www.ZimbellHousePublishing.com, Goodreads.com, Amazon.com, or Kindle.com.

We hope you enjoyed this collection of his short stories.

Other Works by E.W. Farnsworth

John Fulghum Mysteries
John Fulghum Mysteries Vol. II
Engaging Rachel
Pirate Tales
Baro Xaimos: A Novel of the Gypsy Holocaust
Fairy Tales and Other Fanciful Short Stories
Among Water Fowl and Other Entertainments

Coming Soon

The Wiglaff Tales
John Fulghum Mysteries, Vol. III: Blue is for Murder